Caught off balance, Claire bumped into the arm of the sofa. A split second later she was sprawled across Zach's lap.

Nose to nose, they stared at each other. The intensity of his gaze was enough to take most women's breath away. She tried to yank her hand free, but he effortlessly restrained her. She glared at him, her instincts telling her to scramble off his lap, but the angle of her body and his tight grip made it impossible.

"Let go, you jerk."

He let out a low whistle, his breath lifting a strand of her hair. "Jerk? Am I supposed to be insulted? That's about the nicest thing you've ever called me."

"I could say something worse, but I won't lower myself."

"Temper. Temper," he responded, obviously enjoying baiting her.

She wiggled, pulling her arm, trying to twist free. Lurching sideways did no good either. He merely anchored her more firmly to her chest until her breasts were nestled against him. She tried again, squirming in his lap. A slow, sensual grin spread over his face as she struggled, getting nowhere.

"Honey, didn't anybody ever tell you not to move around like that unless you're looking for action?"

Shock arced through like an electric current and she froze, embarrassingly aware of the masculine contours of his body as it pressed against hers. Without thinking, she swung her free arm, intending to slap him. He blocked the blow, manacling her wrist in his large hand.

They stared at each other; the gleam of desire in Zach's deep blue eyes was impossible to miss . . .

THE HIDEAWAY

Meryl Sawyer

Zebra Books
Kensington Publishing Corp.
http://www.zebrabooks.com

ZEBRA BOOKS are published by

Kensington Publishing Corp.
850 Third Avenue
New York, NY 10022

First Printing: November, 1997
10 9 8 7 6 5 4 3

Printed in the United States of America

The best way to love anything is as if it might be lost.

—G. K. Chesterton

Prologue

A hunter's moon hung low over the mountains, its light searching through the pines like a powerful beacon. Swirling gusts of wind ruffled the aspens as two men crouched in the shadows of the trees. Rock and roll blared from the nightclub nearby, the song ending in one long riff from the lead guitar. Above, in the ancient cottonwood, a horned owl hooted once . . . twice.

A cloud slipped over the moon, slowly cloaking the small area behind the nightclub in darkness. When the last ray of light vanished, the men vaulted out of the shadows. The older man eased open the door to the bear's shed even though the rusty hinges could never have been heard above the band now playing a country tune. Looking over his shoulder to the back door of the club, the tall, younger man with a shaggy beard kept watch.

Outside, the June air was cool and laced with the scent of pine, but from the shed came an oppressive odor of moldering straw and dank fur. The bear snuffled, sensing danger as the men tiptoed into the shed. The beast hunkered down on his haunches, instinctively baring teeth that weren't there.

"Grab his chain," commanded the older man.

A second later, the thick chain clinked in the bearded man's powerful hand. The bear stiffened, knowing what the sound meant. It cowered, anticipating a blow to the head. When it didn't come, and the chain again clinked and pulled, the bear took a tentative step forward.

"Come on," the older man urged. "We haven't got much time"

With another jingle of the chain, the bear followed, too terrified to disobey. The older man checked to be certain someone hadn't emerged from one of the adobe bungalows next door to the nightclub—known as The Hideaway. The bungalows were usually rented by the hour. The moon had reappeared, flooding the area with light, but no one had come out of the club or The Hideaway.

"We're outta here," whispered the younger man, tugging the bear along.

They headed toward the pickup truck hidden in the pine trees, the bear lumbering along, too frightened to ignore the rattle of the chain. It took both men to boost the animal into the pickup. They hooked the chain to a special latch, then quickly tied the bear down. With a thumbs-up sign, the other man hopped into the cab.

The bearded man stood behind the truck and checked to make sure the tailgate was locked as the motor kicked into gear. Then he said to the bear, "The worst is over big guy."

Clouds scudded across the moon as the pickup shot into the darkness without turning on its lights. The owl called again, shrill, lonely hoots that seemed to reach the whirlpool of stars overhead. The band began a new tune, and the bearded man paused, listening to his favorite song, "The Devil Went Down to Georgia." The night's work done, he couldn't resist humming along.

> *Fire on the mountain! Run, boy, run!*
> *The devil's in the house of the rising sun.*

One

The wolf was at the door—literally.

Claire Holt unlocked the rear entrance to The Rising Sun gallery and saw the animal peering through the front door. She paused, her nerves responding on an instinctive, primitive level. She adored dogs, but Lobo frightened her.

The dog was a hybrid, part shepherd, part timber wolf. His lush silver-gray coat glistened in the sunlight. He had an aloof, almost regal bearing, worthy of the show ring. Yet his eyes had the sinister, predatory glint of a natural-born killer.

Along with the wolf-dog, came someone even more dangerous—his master. Her gallery was several steps below street level. At this angle, all she could see was the dog—and long-steely muscled legs clad in faded denim.

"It's all right, Lucy," Claire told her own dog.

The golden retriever hadn't spotted Lobo, or she would have hidden. Lucy was frightened of most dogs, especially large dogs capable of killing. She wagged her tail, looking up at Claire as if to ask why they were so late in opening the gallery.

Last night. The words shuddered through Claire with frightening intensity. It was nothing short of a miracle that she was here after what had happened. Her head throbbed, and every inch of her body was sore and achy. For the life of her, she couldn't dredge up a coherent memory about those hours after midnight in The Hideaway.

She was not up to facing Sheriff Zachary Coulter and his wolf-dog, Lobo. Ducking into the storeroom, she tore open a foil packet of coffee, dumped it in the container, and flicked on the coffee maker. After last night, she was going to need a major caffeine boost to keep going. She doubted that she'd slept more than fifteen minutes.

A powerful fist pummeled the front door. A two-legged wolf if there ever was one, Zach Coulter had been the town's bad boy when she'd been growing up. Now he was sporting a badge. Unbelievable.

"I'm coming. I'm coming."

She wiped her moist palms over her denim skirt as she walked toward the gallery's entrance with Lucy limping at her heels. She knew exactly why the sheriff was here, and she was going to be thrilled to say that she had no idea what had happened to Bam Stegner's bear. She unlocked the door and swung it open.

"Good morning, Sheriff."

Zach Coulter had one powerful shoulder braced against the doorjamb, his long, booted legs crossed at the ankles. He was taller up close, but then six-two in a Stetson and sharkskin cowboy boots seemed even taller to someone stretching it to make five-five. This near, he seemed bigger, more powerful than she remembered.

His hat cast a dark shadow across his face, emphasizing his square, uncompromising jawline. He thumbed back the hat and revealed deep blue eyes trimmed with dense lashes the same shade as his gloss-back hair. Those eyes gave him a smoldering sensuality some women found appealing.

Claire thought he was just plain cocky. He didn't wear a badge or carry a gun. Why bother? No one in their right mind would cross a hell-raiser who was even tougher now than he'd been in his youth. Just the sight of him brought back a memory she'd spent years trying to forget, and she had to force herself to look him in the eye.

The intimacy in his gaze startled her. For a moment she recalled too many things she'd spent years striving to forget. The gentle touch of his hand on her cheek. The low, raspy sound of his voice when he whispered in her ear. The promises they'd made under the stars.

She tamped down the unwelcome memories and seared him with her drop-dead glare. Most people backed up or backed off when she did this; not Zach.

"Real late, aren't you?" He sauntered into the gallery, his dog beside him.

Claire reached down to give Lucy a reassuring pat, but amazingly her dog was wagging her tail. Lucy wasn't the least bit intimidated by the animal, that could easily have passed for a real wolf.

"Your sign says you open at eleven," Zach drawled. "It's past noon."

She adjusted the silver and turquoise clasp that secured her long, blond hair at the nape of her neck. Usually it tumbled to her shoulders in waves that defied a brush, but she'd been in too much of a hurry to fool with it. She hadn't bothered with makeup either. Not that she cared what Zach Coulter thought.

"I was running behind this morning. Are you interested in buying a painting or perhaps a bronze?" she said with a straight face, positive the only thing he considered art was a centerfold.

"Nope." He removed the black Stetson and tossed it like a Frisbee. It sailed across the gallery and landed on Wild Horse, her best bronze, as if the statue were a cheap hat rack.

"Just make yourself at home."

The cool air in her gallery developed a thickness, an intensity. The taut silence was underscored by the click-

click, of the dogs' paws on the buffed wood floor as they wandered toward the back alcove, leaving them alone.

Suddenly, the large gallery with its whitewashed walls and cases displaying Southwestern art seemed too small. The sheriff's dominating, masculine presence radiated a certain intimidating ruthlessness. If Zach Coulter hadn't been the law, he would have been running from the law.

"It must have been a hell of a night!" His lips quirked into a knowing smile.

Last night *had* been an unbelievable night. No wonder her eyes were more red than green with dark circles to make them look even worse. She mustered an insolent stare despite a jackhammering headache, another legacy of the previous evening.

"My private life is none of your business."

He reached into the pocket of Levi's that had been washed so many times that they were more gray than blue. How he managed to jam his hand into jeans so tight—let alone get something out of the pocket—was one of life's unexplainable mysteries.

He withdrew a swatch of black silk no larger than an eye patch and dangled it in front of her nose. "Lose something?"

It took a split second to realize those were her panties, and she knew *exactly* where she'd lost them. Oh, Lord, what had happened to her? Why couldn't she remember more?

She opted to brazen it out. "Why on earth would you think they're mine?"

How had Zach Coulter—of all people—gotten them? She had searched frantically, but had been unable to find them. Why hadn't she checked more thoroughly? Zach must have gone to The Hideaway when Bam Stegner reported his bear stolen and looked around, finding the panties. But why would he think they belonged to her?

Zach hooked his thumbs in the waistband of the skimpy

bikinis, stretching them out to full size, and held them up to her silver concho belt. His irreverent grin made her want to smack him. "Your size exactly."

"Is there a point to this?" she asked, reluctant to tell an outright lie and say the panties weren't hers.

Zach's marine-blue eyes swept from the tip of her head down her stone-washed denim dress to the toes of her moccasins in a heartbeat, seeming to see right through to the sexy panties that matched the ones in his hand.

"Last night at The Hideaway—"

"You bitch!" Bam Stegner burst through the door, slamming it so hard a prize-winning basket woven from yucca, bear grass and rare devil's claw crashed from its pedestal to the wooden floor. "Where'n hell is my bear?"

Three hundred pounds of enraged bully with jowls like saddlebags glared at her. Bam's bare chest was partially covered by a red leather vest, but it didn't conceal a gut that slopped over a silver skull-and-crossbones belt buckle. A tattoo of a snake wound up his beefy arm to stick its forked tongue out at her from the top of his naked shoulder.

Bam's jeans and boots were splattered with reddish mud. It was in his gray ponytail, too. Bridging close-set black eyes were scraggly brows flecked with mud probably kicked up from his Harley. He was so furious, his hairy chest heaving with rage, that she was actually glad Zach was beside her.

Bam Stegner owned the Hogs and Heifers nightclub and the adobe bungalows next door known as The Hideaway. Although he didn't look it, he was one of the richest men in Taos. Most of his money came from illegal activities. He'd done time in prison, but these days he was too slick to get caught.

If he hadn't been so evil, Claire would have found him comical. He insisted on wearing enormous silver spurs even though he rode a Harley, not a horse, claiming to be an ex-Hell's Angel. In the winter, when snow piled up in town, he wore a T-shirt under his vest. The rest of the year, he didn't bother with a shirt, relying instead on a collection of leather vests from the seventies.

"What bear?" she asked, justifiably proud of her calm tone. She hated Bam Stegner so much each breath burned in her throat with the urge to tell him off, but she controlled herself.

Bam stomped toward her, the spurs on his boots clinking, his huge fists flexing as if he intended to strangle her. "Don't play dumb with me. When you twitched your tight ass into my club last night, I knew you were up to something. If I don't get Khadafi back, you're gonna to be sorry."

"I don't have your bear. Look around." She waved her hand in the direction of the two dogs at the far end of the gallery. "Go to my place. Check it out."

Bam grabbed her arm, his dirty nails biting into her bare skin. "Look, bitch—"

"Let her go." Zach's voice was low, yet as sharp as a new razor.

Bam released her but still stood menacingly close, his body odor so foul that she wanted to take a bath in lye. She stood her ground, glaring back at him.

"Stegner, leave. Let me handle this," Zach said.

"Arrest her ass. Throw her in jail until she tells where Khadafi is."

"Isn't he over in Iraq where he's supposed to be?" she asked, unable to resist taunting him.

Bam lunged toward her, grunting and huffing. Zach's powerful arm shot out with the deadly swiftness of a rattlesnake and halted Bam mid-stride.

"Get out, Stegner."

The devil himself wouldn't have argued when Zach used that tone of voice. Bam swaggered to the door, his anger echoing through the room with each spur-clanging step that left clods of mud on the polished floor.

"If I don't get Khadafi back, you're gonna pay, bitch."

"Stegner," Zach's voice boomed through the gallery. "Don't threaten her. If anything happens to Claire, I'm coming after you."

Bam slammed the door so hard that only a miracle kept the glass from shattering. Relief hit Claire like a tidal wave, almost knocking her to the floor. She'd known Stegner would be furious about losing his bear, but she had never anticipated he would try to attack her in broad daylight. She knew she should be grateful to Zach, but her pride—and the past—kept her silent.

"You're brain dead." Zach cupped her chin with his hand. "Why did you provoke Stegner like that? He'll be after you now."

She shrugged, pretending she wasn't concerned, but it was difficult because his strong fingers were distracting her. "I've got a gun here, and another at home."

"Leave Stegner to me," Zach said, his thumb making a slow sweep across her lower lip and back again. He took his thumb off her lip but didn't move his hand. It still cradled her chin, his powerful hand tilting her head upward so she had no choice but to look at him.

The suggestive gesture and the sensuality in his blue eyes kicked up her pulse a notch. It wasn't hard to understand why he'd earned a reputation as the town stud. Women threw themselves at Zach Coulter. Well, she wasn't that stupid. She'd learned her lesson years ago.

She batted his hand away. "You're going to take care of Bam Stegner the way you took care of Khadafi?"

If looks could have killed, she'd be pushing up daisies. "Keeping a pet bear is not against the law."

"Khadafi wasn't a 'pet' and you know it." Her voice kept rising with every word despite her best efforts to temper it. "Bam named him Khadafi so men would think they were macho and patriotic when he staged fights with the bear. What kind of man gets a thrill out of having his picture taken beating up a defenseless, half-starved bear? Bam had the bear's teeth and claws pulled out, so he couldn't fight back. Now, I ask you, is that fair?"

"I saw the pictures you showed around town, but I couldn't catch Stegner actually staging a bear baiting. Even if I had, it isn't illegal in this state."

"You should have arrested Bam on animal cruelty charges. That shed was an abomination and the bear wasn't fed properly."

"You know I tried. The animal regulation inspector found the facility satisfactory."

"Bam bribed him."

"Probably," Zach conceded, his world-weary expression intensifying, but I couldn't prove it. The bear is personal property. No matter how just the cause—stealing him *is* against the law."

"I did not steal Khadafi," she said with total honesty. Search the gallery. Search my home. Search me."

"Now, you're talking," he said, his eyes taking a leisurely tour of her body, starting with her hair and slowly dropping to her lips. His gaze lingered there an uncomfortably long time before detouring to her breasts. Then his attention centered on the deep V of the shawl-collared denim dress edged with scarlet whip-stitching.

Most people would have been fascinated by the polished silver sunburst with the turquoise cabochon hanging from her neck on a sterling chain. The dramatic piece matched the smaller earrings she'd worn, hoping to interest customers in other pieces by this artist. But Zach wasn't looking at the jewelry. From his superior height, he was gazing down the shadowy hollow between her breasts.

"This might just require a strip search," he said with a grin that canted to one side in a way some women would have found adorable.

The thought of his large hands on her did ridiculous things to her heart rate, which infuriated her. She resented the familiar way he'd touched her a minute ago. No doubt, he was experiencing a hormonal overload that made him manhandle anything in a skirt. Well, forget this skirt.

"Get your mind out of the gutter. I'm dead serious. I did not steal the bear. l have no idea where it is."

"But you know who did."

Again, she was completely honest. "I have absolutely no idea who stole Bam's bear, but I'm not going to pretend I'm sorry."

He moved closer and she resisted the urge to step back. "I'm not bothering to look for Khadafi. I've got a bigger problem than Stegner's bear. Somebody blew out Duncan Morrell's brains last night at The Hideaway."

Duncan dead? The news hit Claire like a knockout punch. Her breath stalled in her lungs, and for a moment the killer headache vanished. She despised Duncan, but she had never wished him dead. It was impossible to imagine a world without the conniving Duncan Morrell. "He's dead?"

"Yes, and I'm pissed big-time. This is a quiet little place. I don't want a murderer living in my town."

"Who did it?" she asked.

"Stegner claims you murdered Morrell."

"That's ridiculous!" she shot back, but a fission of alarm lanced through her. Duncan was her arch enemy. And she'd been at The Hideaway until dawn. Worse, she didn't remember what had happened.

Zach jammed the panties into his back pocket. "It's logical—even coming from a creep like Stegner. You and Morrell were rivals. He'd stolen your most profitable artist, right?"

"I didn't have a contract with Nevada," she said, aware of the bitterness etching every syllable, but unable to soften her tone. She'd discovered Nevada while she'd been working in a Phoenix gallery, raising money to open The Rising Sun. She'd nurtured his talent only to have Duncan lure him away. "He was free to go to another gallery."

"Didn't you accuse Morrell of selling phony lithographs?"

She couldn't deny it. "Yes, but I wasn't the only one who suspected he was selling counterfeit prints. Other gallery owners had complained. Look, I despised Morrell, but I didn't kill him."

"Okay," Zach said, leaning so close she couldn't miss the trace of citrus aftershave or the challenging glint in his eye. "I believe you, but your panties were found in the bungalow next to where Morrell was killed—along with your wallet."

"My wallet?" She vaguely remembered dropping her purse in that dark room last night. Had her wallet fallen out? The air siphoned from her lungs in a dizzying rush. Her panties *and* her wallet. She couldn't be that unlucky, could she?

Two

"It can't be my wallet." Claire dashed across the gallery to the alcove by the back door where she'd left her purse. She grabbed the hand-tooled leather bag and dumped the contents onto her cluttered desk.

A checkbook, a Daytimer, keys and a few loose coins. No wallet.

She dropped into her chair, groaning. *Last night.* So much of it was a blur. She was positive someone had put something in her drink. Snippets of memories whirled like dervishes through her brain, and she recalled the muffled *thunk* of her purse hitting the bed. Her wallet must have fallen out.

Oh, Lord. What had she gotten herself into this time? The little bit she did recall about the previous evening frightened her. A dark room. A man. A door slamming shut, leaving her in the darkness with a total stranger.

"Do I smell coffee?" Zach asked, interrupting her thoughts.

"Help yourself," she said, grateful for the opportunity to stall. How was she going to explain her wallet being in that room at The Hideaway?

He was back in a minute, handing her a mug of coffee. "It's black. Looks like you could use it."

She took the coffee without meeting his eyes, the aroma making her empty stomach rumble. "My wallet must have been stolen while I was dancing at Hogs and Heifers," she said, deciding the sheriff might believe this explanation.

Zach scooted some papers aside and leaned against her desk, one leg hitching over the burnished wood until he was half-sitting. "Really?" His insolent grin said hell would freeze over before he bought *that* bridge. "How much do you figure they stole?

"I'm not sure how much money was in it."

"We've got mighty thoughtful crooks in these parts. They swiped your wallet but left the credit cards along with ten dollars and twenty seven cents. Then they planted it between the bed and the wall in one of The Hideaway's rooms."

She held her ground, directing her gaze not to leave his so she wouldn't appear to be lying. She hated it when people weren't honest, but there was no way she could discuss what had happened last night with this man.

"May I have my wallet back?" she asked, all innocence, extending her hand. Not only were his jeans tight enough to get him arrested for indecent exposure, his chambray shirt was rolled up at the cuffs, exposing his powerful forearms tanned by hours in the sun. The shirt stretched across massive shoulders and accentuated impressive biceps. It was perfectly obvious he didn't have the wallet on him.

He took a long, slow sip of his coffee before answering, his unsettling eyes peering at her over the rim of the cup. "It's back at the station with the rest of the evidence."

"Evidence?" She shot to her feet. "Now just a minute—"

"No, you wait. There's been a murder in my town. The killer isn't getting away with it. I'll return your wallet—and your panties—when the case is solved."

"But I need my driver's license and—"

"What you need, sweetcakes, is an alibi." The strange look he gave her set off a warning bell. "Do you have one?"

Alarm rippled up her spine erupting in a film of moisture across the back of her neck. She didn't have an alibi, but she mustered a sassy tone. "Why? Am I a suspect? Do I need a lawyer?"

Zach infuriated her by taking his time, having another swig of coffee. "Call an attorney if you want."

"I have nothing to hide. I didn't kill Duncan Morrell."

"Let's start with your alibi. You came to Hogs and Heifers with Seth Ramsey, right?"

Not trusting her voice, she nodded, then took a swallow of the high octane coffee. It jolted her queasy stomach and hurled through her veins, giving her a much-needed boost.

"Why did you go to the club when you were feuding with Stegner over that damn bear?"

"It was Seth Ramsey's idea. He wanted to hear Flash and the Rusty Roots. They're the best band to hit Taos in years. Too bad they were playing at Hogs and Heifers."

Zach's eyes narrowed slightly, emphasizing the tiers of lashes framing his deep blue eyes, but he nodded, apparently buying her explanation. His expression never changed, but she was positive that he suspected she was hiding something. Fine. Let him prove it.

"Did you sleep at Ramsey's place or yours?"

A flash of golden fur caught her eye, and she glanced up to see Lobo and Lucy out in the main part of the gallery. Lucy was circling a display case, the hitch in her gait more pronounced than usual, and Lobo was at her heels. She'd forgotten all about the dogs. Welcoming the distraction, she asked, "Just what is your dog doing?"

"Lobo's following your retriever, his nose up her tail." A mocking grin carved his sensual mouth. "Dogs aren't much different than men. Get a whiff of something they like and—"

"You're disgusting."

"Coming from you, that's a compliment."

She snapped her fingers. "Lucy, over here."

The retriever limped to her side, followed by Lobo. Even though Zach's dog was part wolf, he was superbly trained. Obeying a wave of the hand, Lobo sat at his master's feet, but his eyes were still on Lucy.

"You spent the night at Seth Ramsey's place."

"No. I didn't. I went home and slept—alone." She didn't volunteer that Seth hadn't brought her home, or that she hadn't returned until dawn, hoping the murder would be solved without having to reveal her secrets. "Am I really a suspect?"

"I've got a laundry list of suspects. About five thousand people live here. I figure about half of them wanted Duncan Morrell dead." He balanced his coffee cup on his knee. "Most murders fall into two categories, crimes of passion or crimes of greed."

"In addition to the suspicious print scam, Duncan was involved in shady real estate deals, too," she told him. "Maybe someone was upset about losing money."

His stare drilled into her, and suddenly the back of her neck felt warm as he asked, " 'What do you think goes on at The Hideaway?"

"Aren't those like motel rooms you rent by the hour?"

"Yes. You name it, and Stegner makes sure you can get it at The Hideaway. Drugs. Prostitutes. Kinky sex."

"Of course, you never caught Bam Stegner doing anything illegal." The second her sarcastic comment left her lips, she regretted it. Why did she blurt things out without thinking? A smart woman would not antagonize a man like Zach Coulter.

Zach's eyes were no longer sparkling blue. Now they were bleak gray and as cold as the winter sky, reminding her that his hair-trigger temper was legendary and had been since his youth. He'd defended his alcoholic mother in fistfight after fistfight even when he had to take on older boys or a gang. Some people might tangle with the likes of Bam Stegner, but they did not provoke this man.

"I've busted a few people for minor narcotics violations and arrested a hooker or two out there," he replied, his tone lethally calm. "I just have T-Bone, my deputy, to help me cover the entire county. I'd need to have real good proof that something major was going down at The Hideaway before I call the state police for assistance."

She could have flung Khadafi at him again, reminding Zach how he'd failed to help the abused bear, but she sensed that she was in real trouble here. "So you're saying The Hideaway is infamous for sex and drugs. Duncan's murder was a crime of passion."

For a long moment, he again studied her in that disconcerting way of his. "I don't know yet. Let's start with who you saw at the club last night."

She clearly remembered walking into Hogs and Heifers, her heart beating with the wild pulse of the music, secretly thrilled to know that somehow—some way—Khadafi was going to be stolen. Before midnight.

"Angela Whitmore and her—ah—personal trainer were at the table next to ours."

"Okay. Angie was there with a studmuffin young enough to be her son."

She wanted to defend her best client, but it was difficult. The forty-something woman was wealthy enough to buy the best art available. So what if she had a thing for younger men? Trophy wives abounded. Fair was fair.

"Nevada was there with two women. I didn't know either of them."

"The town stud in action."

Claire ventured a quick peek at the bulge in his jeans. Zach's reputation—and his build—relegated an artist like Nevada to the minor leagues. Personally, she preferred a more sensitive man, but most women would have jumped at the chance to spend one night with Zach Coulter.

"It was dark. The place was jammed. I saw Lowell Hopkins, who runs the gallery across the plaza. There might have been others I knew and didn't see. The only light was the Silver Bullet sign over the bar and the candles on the tables.''

She could have added that after her first drink, she was a little woozy. The second knocked her for a loop. Looking back, she was positive someone who worked for Bam had slipped something into her drink. But she had no intention of telling the sheriff the details unless she had no alternative.

Zach rose to a standing position, an athletic movement that emanated barely restrained power. Lobo shifted to his feet, too, silently rising on all fours, his gaze still locked on Lucy. The retriever wagged her tail, which was unusual considering Lobo's size and fierce expression.

"I may have more questions later," Zach said over his shoulder, heading for the front door.

A thought suddenly hit her as she followed him. "Wait. I . . ."

He suddenly halted, swinging around, and she bumped into him, her breasts pillowing into his chest. For an instant she felt his heart beating against her own. Her pulse thrummed noisily, painfully. The past rose, swift and sure from some hidden well-spring inside her. She lurched away and bumped into a display case.

"You remembered someone else who was there?"

"No, I . . ." She inspected the beaded toe of her moccasin. "Do you have to tell anyone I lost my wallet at The Hideaway? Do you have to mention me at all? I mean, it could be bad for business.''

Zach hooked his thumbs through his belt loops, his silhouette etched starkly against the summer sunlight streaming through the gallery's windows. Unexpectedly, her heart accelerated as she vividly recalled another day—years ago—when he'd stood, facing her, his back to the blazing sun.

Memories stole past the barrier she had kept in place

for so long, and she saw, not the man before her, but a much younger edition. The town bad boy. They were alone by a mountain pool. His back was to the sun, but the shadow cast across his face didn't conceal the heartfelt emotion. Everyone else in town assumed Zach Coulter was as tough and unfeeling as the rugged mountains ringing the town.

But she knew the truth, knew it in her heart and felt it in her soul. He could be hurt just like anyone else. So, she took him into her arms that summer day, a mistake that changed too many lives.

"Tell the truth, princess," he said, his words jarring her back to the present. "You don't want Daddy to know."

"That's part of it," she conceded. "I took a stand against Bam Stegner over the bear, I would rather no one knew—"

"You don't want your father to find out that not only did you go to Hogs and Heifers, you were in The Hideaway. What were you doing there?"

"I never said I was there. I don't know if my wallet was lost or stolen," she hedged. "I would prefer that this doesn't hit the papers. It would be bad for business."

"Why should I help you?" His mouth quirked into a suggestion of a smile. "You wouldn't spit on me, if I were on fire. Would you?"

The bitterness in his tone made her shudder inwardly. She'd come back to town a little over a year ago. Zach Coulter had returned to his hometown a year earlier, but she made dead certain their paths never crossed. She'd thought he hadn't noticed, but obviously, she was wrong.

"I'm sorry, I . . ."

"You treat me like shit, then you want my help."

"I didn't do anything—"

"It's going to cost you."

"I don't have any money. I didn't take a nickel from my father to finance The Rising Sun. You—of all people—must know he would never want my mother's gallery reopened. Another T-shirt shop in this building would have been his choice—and you know it."

A moment of silence stretched between them fraught with memories of the past. And thoughts better left unsaid.

"I worked in Phoenix and saved enough money until I could open this gallery," she added when the silence became unbearable. "I'm barely scraping by. This season will make or break me."

There might have been a grudging hint of approval in his intense blue eyes, but she couldn't be certain. "I wasn't talking about a bribe."

His gaze roved over her with deliberate slowness, tracking the curves of her breasts before dropping to the silver concho belt. The denim dress was smocked with elastic from beneath her breasts to the bottom of her hips. There it flared into soft folds which fell broomstick style to her ankles. Suddenly, the dress seemed to fit much too tight as he inspected the lines of her body.

"There are laws against sexual harassment," she said a little more angrily than she intended, but he infuriated her. Zach Coulter belonged on Mars where there was no sign of intelligent life. Once he might have had a vulnerable side, but time had erased every trace of it.

Zach arched one black eyebrow questioningly, then he grinned. A second later he began to chuckle. Both dogs cocked their heads and stared at him. He moved closer until he was hovering over her, and she could smell the citrus scent of his aftershave. And see the gleam of amusement in his eyes.

"Sexual harassment? Sweetcakes, I just thought you might say hello when we pass on the sidewalk."

Zach grabbed his Stetson off the majestic bronze of Wild Horse, an Apache warrior. He touched one finger to the hat in a mock salute, then strode out of the gallery, Lobo beside him. Claire closed her eyes for a moment, feeling the color flaming her cheeks and seething at how easily he had tricked her.

"Making a fool of yourself is the least of your problems," she muttered. A cold shiver spread through her as she remembered going into the pitch-black room at The Hideaway. Her behavior had been so out-of-character, so reckless. Under normal circumstances, she would never have stayed in a dark room with a strange man.

Her foolishness now had her linked to a brutal murder.

"Awesome! Truly awesome!"

Claire opened her eyes to find Vanessa Trent breezing into the gallery. The actress was staring at Zach Coulter's back as he opened the Bronco's door for Lobo.

"I assume you mean the dog," Claire said. "He's part timber wolf."

"No, I meant the 501s. The man is all wolf. Who is he?"

"That's the sheriff, Zachary Coulter," Claire reluctantly answered.

Vanessa Trent had the potential of being one of her best clients, but the actress was more interested in sex than art. She freely discussed her sexual escapades, even though she and Claire weren't close friends. Claire couldn't help feeling sorry for her. The actress had made her fortune on a top-rated sitcom about aliens who divided their time between a fast-food restaurant in the Bronx and a spaceship orbiting Mars. The show exploited Vanessa's body, ignoring her talent.

The actress had sex appeal in spades. Long black hair and sapphire blue eyes highlighted perfect features. Most women would have insisted Vanessa's breasts were the work of some pricey Beverly Hills surgeon, but Claire doubted it. Vanessa was simply one of those women blessed by nature with striking beauty and a figure to match.

"The sheriff? Really?" Vanessa managed to pry her eyes away from the tail pipe of Zach's Bronco as it disappeared around the corner. "I thought the old guy—"

"Ollie Hammond is the chief of police. He's in charge of crime inside city limits. Zach's the law in the county."

"The law, huh?" Vanessa ran the tip of her tongue over gloss-pink lips shaped like a full Cupid's bow. "The sheriff looks like the type who would be into down-and-dirty sex."

Claire couldn't deny it. Rumors about Zach Coulter were too prevalent to dismiss entirely. *Like father, like son.* An image appeared in her mind, startling in its clarity. She knew exactly what his magnificent body would look like without clothes. And how the angular, yet sensual planes of his face would look when he climaxed.

"I've never slept with a sheriff before," Vanessa mused. "Tell me about him. He isn't married, is he?"

"No," she answered, wondering if his parents' tragic marriage made Zach unwilling to tie the knot. Or was he just content to tom-cat around?

Vanessa's eyes sparkled with wicked delight. "Come on. Details. I want details."

"There's not much to tell," Claire said, but she really meant there was a limited amount she was willing to disclose. "Zach grew up right here in Taos. His father owned the local photography studio, and his mother, well, she had a drinking problem."

"We have a lot in common. My papa got tipsy now and then, too."

Tipsy did not describe the down-and-out drunk Zach's mother became, but Claire didn't elaborate. "Zach ran wild. He got into a lot of trouble . . . especially after his father was killed in an automobile accident."

"Tragic," Vanessa said, but Claire knew it was only a word to the actress. The accident was truly tragic. It changed both their lives forever. It wasn't something she discussed with anyone, least of all a woman interested only in a hot affair.

"The day after Zach graduated from high school, he

disappeared. No one heard a single word from him, and everyone thought he'd landed in jail somewhere."

"What about his mother? Didn't he call her?"

Claire couldn't meet the actress's inquiring gaze. It was a disgrace to the entire town that Melanie Coulter had been buried in a pauper's grave, nothing but a wooden cross, carved by her son, to remind the world that she had once lived and loved. And had borne a son who'd stuck by her right up to the end—the night she'd passed out in an alley and had frozen to death.

Even now, more than a dozen years later, Claire could still remember standing at the bank's door, a twenty-dollar bill clutched in her hand, her father blocking her way. Down the street she saw Zach, his back stiff with pride as the blizzard swirled around the only coat he owned, a thin windbreaker. No one would lend him enough money to properly bury his mother.

"Zach's mother died halfway through his senior year."

There must have been something in her voice or expression that telegraphed the guilt Claire still felt. Twenty dollars wouldn't have been enough to purchase a headstone, but it would have shown Zach that someone cared.

Vanessa gazed at her, openly curious, asking, "Are you involved with him?"

"No, of course not." She did not count the summer long ago when they'd been together every day. Their relationship might have developed into something, but the automobile accident and her father's obsessive behavior put an end to it.

"So how did he become sheriff?" Vanessa asked.

"The elected sheriff died unexpectedly and Zach applied for the job. He hadn't been in prison. He'd gone to the West Coast and joined the San Francisco Police Department. Later he became a homicide detective. We don't get law officers with those credentials. He was appointed to fill the vacant position, but he'll have to run for office next year."

"San Francisco . . . my favorite city. Why would Zach leave such an exciting city for—" Vanessa clapped a hand crowned by coral nails over her mouth. "You know, I love Taos—in small doses. I like doing summer theater while my show's on hiatus, and I like the skiing. But I can't imagine someone like that wolf being happy living here."

Claire agreed, knowing most people in town also wondered about Zach Coulter. Many had been shocked at the bad boy's audacity in returning. Others had openly taken bets on when he would leave, but it was almost three years since his return, and Zach showed no signs of heading back to the city.

Vanessa eyed Claire suspiciously. "Why was the sheriff here?"

"Duncan Morrell was murdered last night."

All the color leached from Vanessa's face, leaving two patches of coral blush across her sculpted cheekbones. "No. I can't believe it." She sagged against the display case and stared out the window at the plaza, slack-jawed. She squeezed her eyes shut, but tears slowly crept over her long, silky black lashes and trembled on their tips before silently cascading down her flawless cheeks.

Vanessa cried silently for a few minutes while Claire struggled with what to say. She despised Duncan but she was sorry he'd been killed. Even so, she couldn't imagine someone like Vanessa, a famous actress, caring so much about a major sleaze like Duncan. Maybe it was just acting; Vanessa tended to be overly dramatic at times.

Finally, Vanessa spoke. "Duncan was just in Los Angeles. I bought a dozen lithographs from him for an investment. He was so alive, so . . ."

Now was not the time to tell Vanessa that Duncan had probably sold her phony prints. Obviously the actress knew

Duncan better than Claire had thought. News of his death had hit her hard.

Claire realized she should feel terrible about someone dying, but all she felt was hollowness and disbelief. Duncan Morrell considered her a rival from the day she reopened the gallery, and he'd promised to ruin her. He'd almost succeeded, and he might still—from the grave. Luring away her best artist, Nevada, had brought her to the brink of bankruptcy. If the gallery didn't have a great season this summer, she would have to close it.

"If only I hadn't missed my plane last night," Vanessa said, dramatically fighting a fresh wave of tears. "I might have seen him, and prevented this. We were planning to spend last night together."

Last night. The words kept echoing through Claire's head. Once they'd had a sensual, erotic ring to them. Now they were truly ominous.

Three

Zach Coulter sped down Kit Carson Road, still smiling. He had Claire Holt right where he wanted her. Okay, not exactly *right* where he wanted her. Beneath him, her wild blond hair spread across his pillow would be perfect. She belonged on her back looking up at him—not looking down her nose at him.

"Claire can be a real bitch," he told Lobo, and the dog sitting beside him cocked his head as if he understood.

Zach hadn't worked so damn hard to make something of himself just to let Claire Holt act like he was white trash. Those days were over, finished. He refused to allow anyone to treat him like shit—least of all her. Things had changed. This time Claire wasn't going to blow him off. This time he had the winning hand. She needed him.

"Claire's in real trouble, but she hasn't figured it out yet," he said, deliberately speaking out loud. Lobo was remarkably well trained, yet the call of the wild still ran in his blood. Talking to him was Zach's way of reminding Lobo that he was man's best friend, not a wild animal. He gave the dog a quick pat, thinking about Claire.

She was a ballsy chick—stubborn and impulsive as hell. Showing up at Hogs and Heifers had been like waving a red flag in front of a bull. Bam Stegner was bound to blame Claire for Khadafi's disappearance. She'd raised a ruckus, showing everyone pictures of Stegner's half-starved bear.

People were outraged, but there wasn't a damn thing that could be done—legally.

Of course, that hadn't stopped Claire.

He rounded the corner on two wheels, remembering the way she'd looked this morning. Blond hair dragged back into a ponytail. Her usually sparkling green eyes weary from lack of sleep. Her sensual mouth alluringly tilted upward at the corners even when she couldn't conceal how pissed she was to have to deal with him.

He checked the rearview mirror and saw a rooster tail of dust appear as he drove onto the gravel road that led to the station. "I'm not going to pamper Claire the way everyone else does. I'll be as crude as I damn please and she can just deal with it."

Lobo cocked his head as if to say: you were pretty rough on her back there.

Zach patted the dog's head. "You're right. I was tough. I learned the hard way that only the strong survive. Let's see if Claire can handle it."

He had his pick of women, and had since he could remember. He'd spent more nights than he cared to recall in different women's beds. But certain women were like a tune, once they were in your head, it was impossible to get rid of them. Something about Claire Holt sang to him.

And always had.

His family had been dirt poor, even though his father tried hard to earn a good living. Zach had envied Claire's fairy tale existence. Her father owned the biggest bank in Taos while her mother ran a prestigious gallery.

Claire had been polite, but she had an attitude that dared anyone not part of her inner circle to approach. Zach had been powerless to resist the challenge. He still couldn't.

"She hasn't changed much since high school," he told Lobo as he turned down the side road leading to the station. "Except physically."

Claire's leggy body had matured, leaving subtle curves in all the right places. She had a waist he could circle with his hands—and high, full breasts. Not wet T-shirt material, for sure, but sexy as hell.

Her unruly hair was still the same dark blond with shifting shades of lighter color and just a hint of red. Her eyes were the same vibrant green flecked with gold—and full of the devil. She had a woman's body now, but he sensed the same recklessness that had allowed him to lure her away from her friends and her parents.

For one memorable summer.

He drove into the station parking lot and pulled into the space marked Sheriff Coulter. Usually, he looked at the sign with pleasure. He'd made something of himself, a feat most people in town would have sworn was impossible. Coming home, assuming a position of importance gave him immense satisfaction, a sense of pride represented by the sign.

But today he barely gave the sign a glance. Instead he jumped out and Lobo leaped out behind him. The small building wasn't much to brag about. The sheriff's station looked like an updated log cabin—exactly what it was. Once it had belonged to the division of the Forest Service responsible for the Kit Carson National Forest.

At the rear of the building was a small booking area that still used an old ink blotter to fingerprint, and an ancient Polaroid for mug shots. His buddies on the police force in San Francisco would have laughed at the antiquated equipment. They would have rolled on the floor if they could have seen the jail. Two cells and a drunk tank with six cots.

"Let them laugh," he said to Lobo.

Zach hated the big city with its endless parade of criminals. In Taos the most men he'd put in jail was after a brawl at The Neon Cactus when the Steelers beat the Cowboys. He'd booked eight of the drunks to keep them from killing themselves while attempting to drive home.

Crime in Taos was rare. Until now. Someone had been brutally murdered. Zach had something to prove to himself, to Claire, to the whole damn town. He was going to catch the son-of-a-bitch who'd killed Duncan Morrell.

"Here, Zach." Mildred, the dispatcher handed him several message slips the second he swung open the thick plank door. "T-Bone's back. He needs to see you."

"Thanks." Zach planted his Stetson beside T-Bone's dusty cowboy hat on the ram's horn hat rack, another legacy of the Forest Service.

He went into his office with Lobo at his heels. Mildred followed, a mug of steaming coffee in her hand. As much as he tried to discourage her, it was impossible to keep the older woman from trying to mother him.

"I dusted the murder scene. The prints are on the way to Santa Fe," T-Bone announced as he same through the door. Instead of his usual gap-toothed smile, his deputy's freckled face was dead serious. "They'll check them against the DMV's print files."

Zach dropped into his chair, weary at the thought of all the work ahead of him. He needed a few hours' sleep, but he wasn't going to get it. "Half the people in Taos are rich folks with homes in other states. They'll have drivers' licenses from out of state."

T-Bone brushed back a hank of red hair. "I hadn't thought of that."

"It's a start, though. We might just catch the bastard."

Zach reminded himself that he'd been sick of the city. This was the price he had to pay. Instead of a crack homicide team, he had a green kid for a deputy. Worse, Taos was too small to have its own lab or forensic team. He had to rely on the State Police facilities in Santa Fe.

There were no cell phones in Taos either, and there weren't any high-tech computers linked to the squad cars.

This was basic police work without the cutting edge of technology that big-city law enforcement officers relied on.

"I want you to go out to Stegner's place. Talk to the bartender and the waitresses. Get a list of people who were there last night," he told T-Bone. "See if you can discover who was in that room with Morrell. This morning I couldn't find anyone who'd even seen him at The Hideaway until he turned up dead. But you might uncover a new lead. Leave Seth Ramsey and Angela Whitmore to me. I've already questioned Claire Holt."

"Right." T-Bone turned to go.

"One other thing. I don't want any leaks. Not one word to anyone—even your wife—about the investigation. Don't mention the wallet we found next door to the crime scene."

T-Bone assured him that he wouldn't discuss the case and left. Zach picked up the phone, asking himself why he bothered to protect Claire Holt. Let her damn father find out that she wasn't a little angel.

Alexander Holt.

The name alone still had the power to make his guts twist. The bastard had done his best to ruin his life. Why? Because Zach Coulter was the spitting image of his father. And because he'd dared to touch the little princess, Claire Holt.

At sixteen, Zach had lost his father in a fiery crash that became the biggest scandal since D. H. Lawrence had hit town. Little more than a kid himself, Zach had been saddled with a mother who loved booze. They'd had no money. Zach was forced to work after school. Every time he managed to land a job, Holt found a way to get him fired.

Zach dialed the coroner's office, thinking of how hard Holt had tried to block his appointment as sheriff. But now he wasn't a young kid. Zach's credentials had been too good for the commission to turn down. Tohono's backing hadn't hurt either.

The balance of power had shifted considerably in the

years Zach had been away. Once, the Native Americans had less say in local politics, but the popularity of the casino they'd built on their land had given them political clout. When Tohono, governor of the Taos pueblo, said he wanted Zach appointed sheriff, people didn't like it, but they'd been forced to accept it.

Zach had at least a dozen good reasons to hate Claire's father, but one stood out in his mind above the rest. His mother. She had a proper headstone now, and fresh flowers on her grave each week, but he'd never forget what a son-of-a-bitch Holt had been. Zach had promised to sweep the bank at night and keep the toilets clean for a year, if Holt would lend him the money to bury his mother. Holt had flat refused.

Claire had stood by, silently watching.

"Doc Reilly," he said when the coroner's office finally answered. He waited, still thinking. He'd get his chance to pay back Alexander Holt. Patience wasn't his long suit, but he was forcing himself to play the waiting game.

"Hey, Doc," he said when Reilly came on the line. "Did you establish a time of death yet?"

"Well, I can't rightly say. It was cold last night and both windows in that room were wide open. Cool air slows down rigor mortis. Morrell could have been dead a lot longer than I first figured."

"What about lividity?" Zach asked, knowing blood flowed to the lowest point after death. Often the amount of blood on the underside of the corpse helped establish time of death.

"That head wound caused severe blood loss. I couldn't get any lividity calculations."

"Come on, Doc. I need some idea of when Morrell was killed."

"Wel-l-l . . . I'd say sometime between midnight and 6:00 A.M."

"Christ! Can't you get any closer than that?"

"No siree."

Zach hung up, asking himself why he gave a damn about Claire Holt's alibi. She hadn't been there for him when he'd needed her. She'd been staring down at her shoes—a habit she still had—when he'd walked out of the bank, not knowing how he could possibly bury his mother.

Okay, that had been years ago. Claire had been a teenager, suffering over her mother's death. She was easily influenced by a father who still managed to dominate the town. He understood, but some small part of him couldn't quite forgive Claire, especially when he'd come back to town a success and she'd snubbed him.

Shortly after Vanessa Trent left the gallery, the part-time assistant came in and Claire went out for lunch. She walked slowly across the centuries-old plaza with Lucy beside her. Brick pathways crisscrossed the square shaded by enormous cottonwoods and flanked on all four sides by adobe buildings. The pueblo-style structures housed galleries, Indian jewelry shops, restaurants, and the T-shirt stores endemic to every tourist mecca.

Centuries ago, the plaza had served as a meeting place for Indians and traders, but now the square catered to visitors flashing Visa cards. As usual craftsmen from the Taos pueblo sat on hand-loomed blankets with silver belts, jewelry or pottery, spread out before them. Huddled around were clusters of tourists, bargaining.

This was the beginning of the tourist season, which was extremely short, lasting from late June to September. The success of Claire's gallery depended on these visitors who were just beginning to filter up from Santa Fe to Taos. She needed them to make enough purchases at The Rising Sun to pull the gallery out of debt.

"Hello, Luz." Claire waved and the young woman

greeted her in Tewa, then returned her attention to the tourists inspecting the silver jewelry she was trying to sell.

Claire took the short cut across the plaza past the Victorian bandstand in the center and sat on a wooden bench under the shade of a stately cottonwood. Lucy settled at her feet, her bum leg stretched out at an awkward angle.

"Are you okay, Lucy?" Claire asked. The dog responded with a wagging tail.

Church bells rang as clear as the midday air that fluttered the leaves on the cottonwoods. The mouth-watering aroma of blue corn tortillas and chiles roasting on a piñon grill drifted over the plaza. Usually Claire would have gone to Tortilla Flats for lunch, but she was too tired.

Her mind returned to the mysterious man at The Hideaway. Who was he? Claire wished she had an answer. Part of her was still thrilled by the experience, but another part of her was deeply troubled.

"Oh, Lucy," she said to her dog in a low voice, "what was I thinking?

She stared at the rugged mountains, the crested butte of Taos Mountain dominating the other majestic peaks. The sky was a sharp blue, and close. Near enough to touch. Its beauty ignited a hum deep in her chest and she almost wanted to sing. Anything to blot out the trouble last night.

She loved early summer in the mountains when the fresh green leaves shimmered on the aspens and the cottonwoods' stately branches were dressed with deeper green. Clusters of yellow daisies bordered the plaza, growing along the walkways. Stands of sweet-smelling lilacs were visible down the street. They had blossomed along that adobe wall when she had come here as a child, clutching her mother's hand. The flowers were as fragrant now as they had been then, she thought, reminded of her mother.

She bent over and stroked Lucy's lame leg, whispering, "I miss my mother so much at this time of year. As soon as warm weather came, we'd have lunch in the plaza and talk."

Lucy licked her hand, sympathy in the retriever's amber eyes. Claire sat up, thinking that here, and only here, she felt her mother's presence. After her death, Amy Holt had been cremated. As if it were yesterday, Claire remembered going into the forest to scatter her mother's ashes.

Her father had opened the tin box, and Claire had been surprised to see it was filled with a fine gray powder. Go ahead, her father had told her. Sprinkle the ashes. With a trembling hand she eased her fingertips into the soft flakes.

How could this talc-like substance possibly be all that was left of her laughing, vibrant mother? The ashes clung to her fingers, and her vision blurred as she remembered so many happy times with her mother. They'd never share another joke. They'd never inspect another piece of pottery to decide if it was good enough for the shop. They'd never spend all day in the kitchen making Christmas dinner. They'd never . . . they'd never . . . they'd never . . .

Those happy times were gone, reduced to nothing more than a tin box full of fine, gray ashes. "I love you, Mama," she said to the handful of gray flakes. "I miss you already. I miss you so much."

Hot, salty tears stung her eyes and spilled down her cheeks. "I should have told you how much I love you. I always thought there would be time to say it. Please, Mama, hear me now. I love you."

She slowly lifted her hand to the bright blue sky doming overhead, and the breeze caught the gray powder. It drifted high in the air, floating out of sight in an aching heartbeat. "Good-bye, Mama, good-bye. You're with God now. He loves you as much as I love you."

The next handful of ashes were no bigger than dust motes, but the fickle breeze was riffling down another mountain ridge, leaving the air around them silent and still. The ashes settled on the leaves and dappled the brown toadstools poking their caps through the dark, loamy soil. "I'll never forget you, Mama, never. I promise, I'll make you proud of me."

At last the box was empty, but a thin layer of gray coated her hand. Claire brought her fingertips to her lips and kissed the talc-like powder, knowing this was the last time she'd ever touch her mother. A little voice inside her head, whispered: "I'll be here in the hills, in the trees, in the flowers, in all the things we love. I'll always be with you, Claire. I'll be watching over you, darling."

Claire kept kissing her own hand, not even trying to hold back the tears. "Mama, I'm—"

Her father hugged her before she could finish. She collapsed in his arms, silently telling her mother how sorry she was. *Mama, I'll never forgive myself for what I did to you.*

All that remained of her mother was high on the mountain slopes, the slopes Claire now saw from the plaza. She whispered to Lucy, "Mother's up there, watching over me."

Gazing at the majestic mountains, she felt her mother's presence, her eternal love. The heartache came, as it always did, upon seeing the mountains in their glory and remembering her mother. With the bittersweet twist in her heart came an inner peace, the knowledge that she was home again, close to her mother.

"Home. Oh, Lucy, it is so good to be home." She'd been determined to leave for college and start her life somewhere else. For more than a decade, she had wandered, searching for . . . something.

One lonely night she finally admitted the truth to herself. Running away did not change the past. Her mother was dead and nothing was going to bring her back. Claire had cried and grieved and cursed herself until she was as dry and brittle as the needles beneath the pines that her

mother had so loved. Only then, when the last tear had
dried, had Claire known what she must do.

Claire returned home, prepared to open her own gallery and was thrilled to discover the building where her
mother's gallery had been was for lease. Reopening the
gallery and using the same name, The Rising Sun, had
caused problems with Claire's father. He liked to pretend
the past never happened even though the town still gos-
siped about Amy Holt leaving her rich, handsome husband
to run away with Jake Coulter.

But Claire had learned something important during her
years away. This village—and its earth-colored buildings
with their flat roofs and rounded corners—was steeped in
history and tradition. The natural beauty and rich heritage
of this special place was in her blood. If she wanted to live
here, she had to deal with her domineering father, who
had never remarried.

And with the demons of the past.

She could blame Zach Coulter for not telling her about
their parents' affair, but she had to admit that she'd handled the situation badly. To this day, she still experienced
an overwhelming sense of guilt when she thought about
her mother's death. Seeing Zach brought back all those
disturbing memories.

"Zach is a Coulter and just being near him upsets me,"
she said under her breath.

Zach's father had shattered her life, ruining their happy
family. Forgetting was out of the question. Zach was a mirror image of his father. Every time she saw him, the pain
of her mother's death returned full force.

Worse, Zach's presence in town made her father even
more irritable. From the moment he'd learned of his wife's
betrayal, Alexander Holt had changed. The light had vanished from his voice, his smile. He'd withdrawn, and time,
instead of healing, seemed to make him more and more

depressed. The father—who had been so loving, so incredibly wonderful when she'd been a child—disappeared.

No, she couldn't forget what the Coulters had done to her family. She had felt sorry for Zach when his mother had died, understanding the pain of losing both parents in such a short period of time. But she couldn't forgive him.

Not only was Zach a clone of his father, he audaciously took up where his father had left off. If a fraction of the rumors were true, he'd slept with half the women in town. Just like his father.

Lucy sat up and nudged her hand, asking to be petted. Claire obliged, stroking the dog's silky fur, saying, "There's no denying it. The Coulter men have a potent appeal."

Zach had inherited his virile attractiveness from his father, and like her mother, Claire responded. She refused to let a physical reaction get the best of her. She wasn't a silly teenager with a crush on the town's bad boy. She was a grown woman who knew better.

Years ago, her mother had been seduced by Jake Coulter's charms, joining the legion of women who had fallen for a man with a wandering eye. A lifetime of hard work in building a gallery and a devoted, happy family had been the price Amy Holt had paid for a tumble in bed with Zach Coulter's father. Incredible stupidity; a mistake Claire did not intend to repeat.

"Claire?"

She hadn't realized she'd closed her eyes until she opened them to find Tohono standing before her. As usual the elderly man's pewter-colored hair was swept back into a sleek bun knotted at the nape of his neck. His broad face was weathered by years on horseback, riding across his beloved reservation. Deep lines furrowed his brow, a mark of his many terms as governor of the Taos pueblo.

She patted the spot on the bench beside her. "I guess you heard the news. Someone stole Khadafi."

Tohono slowly sank onto the bench and crossed one leg over the over. He buffed the pointed silver tip on the cowboy boots that he'd worn for as long as she could remember. The cuff of his shirt skimmed across the gleaming silver. He wore the shirt unbuttoned, revealing a bronzed chest and sterling pendant with a chunk of deep blue turquoise in the center.

"Khadafi's story was on the radio this morning." He withdrew a transistor radio from the pocket of his shirt.

"What did it say?" she asked, knowing Tohono listened only to the voice of the pueblo, KTTP. The Native Americans who lived in the Taos pueblo were a tight-knit community and didn't care about the white man's news. KTTP broadcast news in Tewa, the only language that mattered.

"The radio says San Geronimo called the bear to his side."

Claire knew San Geronimo was the patron saint of the Taos pueblo. His word was sacred to Native Americans.

"San Geronimo says hunters must always pray before killing for food. They need to ask the creature to give its life for the good of the tribe," Tohono told her.

She listened to his solemn voice. Although he was the leader of the Taos pueblo, Tohono was part Navajo, a descendant of the most gifted storytellers, the Talking Water clan. She knew he would weave together their mythology and his political slant to formulate the official position of his people on the disappearance of the bear.

"Even plants have a right to live. That is why my people pray and perform dances of thanks at harvest," he continued. "It is our way of saying we are all equal on this earth. We honor those who help us sustain life. We do not make them suffer needlessly. It is against everything San Geronimo teaches. Is it any surprise the great one called the bear to his side?"

"San Geronimo is very wise," Claire said, realizing this

was Tohono's way of telling her Khadafi was safe without saying where he was or who had taken him.

Maybe Tohono himself didn't know. He was a godfather with as much—if not more—power than any mafia don. He had relinquished his place as governor six months ago to let his eldest son have the title. Even so, he was still the leader of his people. All Tohono had to do was say San Geronimo was unhappy with the way the bear was being treated, and it would be taken care of.

"San Geronimo knew what to do," Claire agreed with a smile, last night temporarily forgotten. The bear was out of his misery, and she was thankful.

Tohono put the radio to his ear for a moment as if he were listening, but she watched him survey the Native Americans selling their wares. His keen eyes were looking for mass-produced goods that weren't handmade at the pueblo. If he caught someone selling a cheap import, trying to pass it off as authentic, the punishment would be sure and swift.

And beyond control of the white man's sluggish legal system.

Apparently finding nothing, his gaze returned to Claire, and he studied her intently. "Be careful, Claire. Your heart is good, but your head is too strong. You should never have gone to The Hideaway last night. Now the coyote comes out of the darkness. Beware the coyote."

Four

Claire heard the telephone ringing, but she kept her eyes on the flickering candles and let the warm water in the tub soothe her. She'd closed the gallery at nine, then had come directly home, expecting to drop into bed and fall asleep. Despite being bone-weary, she had been unable to sleep.

Last night. If only she could remember more about what had happened. It had been a thrilling, erotic experience. Everything was clear—up to a point. Then her memory degenerated into flashes of sensual impressions.

Why had she let the mysterious stranger kiss her even when she realized he hadn't told her his name? It was completely out-of-character for her and the thought terrified her. She usually held herself with a certain reserve, an aloofness that came naturally. Once she thought the distance she automatically put between herself and men was the manifestation of the shyness she tried to conceal by being friendly and outgoing.

But there was an invisible line she wouldn't allow a man to cross. She couldn't say just where that line was exactly, yet she knew it, felt it. It took time and a level of trust had to be established before she made love to a man.

Last night that invisible barrier hadn't been there to protect her.

Once her father had bluntly pointed out that the older

she became, the more she acted like her mother. At the time she'd argued, but now she supposed it was true. Genes or something. She looked exactly like Amy Holt. She realized how much it must hurt her father to look at her and see the wife he'd loved and lost so tragically.

"Am I behaving just like Mother?" Claire wondered out loud.

The thought jarred her and she sank lower into the water until it sloshed against her chin. As if it had happened today, not years ago, she saw her mother in Jake Coulter's arms and heard the horrible sound of the door she'd slammed on them echoing over and over in her heart. The painful memory cast its long, dark shadow over her, and she closed her eyes asking herself the same question she'd asked thousands of times.

Why had her mother succumbed to temptation, throwing away the love of a wonderful man for a fling with the town stud?

Was she any better? Claire wondered. She hadn't stopped kissing the stranger. Was her similarity to her mother more than just a physical resemblance? Well . . . maybe. Claire loved finding talented artists and marketing their work just as her mother had. And Claire felt a special bond with animals—just as her mother had.

In the bedroom adjacent to the luxurious bathroom, the telephone stopped ringing and the answering machine kicked in. Her father's voice boomed through the machine.

"Honey, call me when you get in. I just came back from Santa Fe and heard someone bumped off Duncan Morrell last night at The Hideaway. What do you suppose he was doing in that dive?"

The machine clicked off and Claire groaned, sinking lower in the water. She'd added dried flower petals and oils, being a firm believer in aromatherapy. *That dive.* She dreaded having to tell her father about last night.

Since suffering a stroke that had left him crippled, her father hadn't been in good health. If she became the prime suspect in Morrell's murder, her father would worry, and he might have another attack. She was all he had, and she knew how much he loved her.

She hoped the murder would be solved quickly, so she wouldn't have to discuss spending last night at The Hideaway. The longer the killer remained at large, the less of a chance she had of keeping her secret. She would become the source of even more grief to her father.

Lucy trotted in, her claws clicking on the black onyx floor. The retriever's dark blond fur gleamed in the candlelight. For aromatherapy, Claire had placed a half dozen magnolia-scented candles throughout the large bathroom. The light reflected off the vast sweep of mirrors, lining the walls.

"Don't worry," Claire told the dog. "I haven't drowned."

Lucy circled twice, then plopped down on the white rug beside the tub. She lay there, soulful eyes on Claire. She put one hand on the side of the custom-made tub that could have doubled for a swimming pool and started to get out. The telephone in the other room rang again, and she sank back, waiting to hear who was calling. Seconds later Seth Ramsey's voice came through the message machine.

"Claire, where are you? I would have called sooner, but I've been out at Max Bassinger's ranch."

Well, that explained why Seth hadn't called her today. Whenever Bassinger blew into town, Seth dropped everything to cater to the rich Texan with too much money and too much time on his hands.

"What happened last night?" Seth's voice continued to come through the machine. "I waited outside the restrooms but you just disappeared."

Claire sat bolt upright in the tub, sloshing the water over the rim. No. That wasn't how it had happened. He was supposed to be waiting for her outside the nightclub's restroom, but he hadn't been there when she came out. She had seen him going next door into the warren of adobe bungalows known as The Hideaway.

"Why is he lying?" she asked out loud. Not so fast, she cautioned herself. He had probably wandered into The Hideaway to look for her. After all, it was just steps from the club.

"That jerk Zach Coulter tracked me down at Bassinger's ranch," Seth rambled on. "I can't tell you how embarrassing it was. He wanted to know where I was last night when Duncan Morrell was murdered. Coulter asked if you and I were together. I told him that I went home without you."

Claire groaned, hardly hearing Seth telling her to call him when she returned. She let out a little water, then added more hot water. *Inhale . . . inhale deeply, take the refreshing aroma into the deepest part of your lungs.* Usually, aromatherapy worked, soothing and cleansing her mind, refreshing her spirit. Not tonight.

Lucy whined, a low-pitched sound that signaled her uneasiness the way other dogs alerted their masters by barking, then she trotted out the door. Claire rose in the tub and let the water sluice down her body as she remembered Bam Stegner in the gallery that morning. Zach had warned Bam, but she wasn't certain he'd really listened.

When she'd come home, she had turned on the burglar alarm, thankful for the state-of-the-art security system installed by the wealthy owner who had leased her the house. A second later the doorbell rang. Claire toweled herself off quickly, an eerie trickle of uneasiness sweeping over her.

The bell rang again, then again, impatient bursts of sound that echoed through the quiet house. Claire shrugged into a man-sized terry robe and cautiously walked up the long hall leading from the bathroom to the front door of the rambling hacienda.

"Who is it?" she called, wishing for a peephole in the thick plank door that dated back to the Spanish Inquisition.

"Zachary Coulter," came the gruff reply. "Open the door." His voice said he expected to be obeyed—immediately.

Zach Coulter. Twice in one day. Too much. At her side, Lucy was wagging her tail, her head cocked to the side. *At least one of us is glad to see him,* she thought as she punched the code into the security system's keypad.

She swung the heavy door open and Zach strode into the entry wall, Lobo at his side. This time he wore no hat, but he still seemed unusually tall. He overwhelmed her with his height, his size. His physical presence made her nerves pulse just as he always had. Anger, directed at herself, surged through her. *Hadn't the past taught her anything?*

He stood far too close, his eyes filled with ruthless determination. Her time was up. She would have to answer some very embarrassing questions. She tilted her head back, squarely facing him, not allowing him to detect how intimidated she felt.

She told herself she didn't care about not having a stitch of makeup on or having wavy hair curled even more than usual by the steamy tub. But she did care about not having anything on under the thick robe. His gaze sharpened, an even harder glint brightening his eyes as he stared at the deep V of her robe.

Zach sniffed, his nostrils flaring. "Smells like a French whorehouse in here."

"Magnolia, vanilla, and wild ginger—the finest ingredients for aromatherapy."

"That so?" He inhaled deeply, a grin spreading over his face. "What in hell's aromatherapy?"

"It's a way to relax, take the tension out of life by lighting scented candles and soaking in a tub filled with special herbs and oils."

"Works for me." His eyelids became heavier, his gaze more intent. He had a disturbingly sensual way of looking at her, or maybe it was just her imagination.

She knew exactly why he'd come, but she decided to bluff. "You want to talk to me? Is it one quick question I can answer, or should I put on some clothes?"

He contemplated her question a few seconds too long, letting his eyes drift from her tousled hair down . . . down a scant inch at a time until he was staring at her bare feet. She knew he was deliberately trying to provoke her, to make her say something sarcastic, but she didn't take the bait.

He finally said, "Put on some clothes."

She mumbled something about having a seat in the living room, then rushed down the hall to the master bedroom at the rear of the house. She pulled on jeans and an oversized cotton sweater in a deep shade of lavender. Oh, God, what am I going to do? The question kept repeating like an echo in a tomb.

The only answer was to tell the sheriff the truth about spending the night in The Hideaway. A man had been murdered. Her escapade, though embarrassing, was nothing compared to having a killer on the loose. And on some level, it served her right. She should never have allowed that stranger to kiss her.

Coyote comes out of the darkness. Beware the coyote. Tohono's words came back to her. Like most Native Americans, the old man laughed at the tourists who bought the T-shirts and posters with howling coyotes on them. While the wolf was noble, fierce and respected, the coyote was the symbol of cunning and deviousness. And evil, above all, evil.

As Tohono had warned, that dark force was now directed at her. She had no choice but to rely on Zach Coulter to find Duncan Morrell's killer. She had to tell the truth—even if it meant discussing what had happened last night with a man she despised.

She walked into the living room a few minutes later and found Zach asleep on the sofa, his booted feet up on the glass top coffee table. He'd taken the latest issue of *Architectural Digest* and placed it under his feet. His closed eyes revealed the long sweep of his eyelashes, and the angular planes of his face. A rasp of hair shadowed his jawline, proof his fast-growing beard was as dark as his black hair.

While some men appeared younger and gentler when sleeping, Zach did not. His expression was taut as if his guard was always up, yet there was a cold, intriguing dignity to his face. She realized he was a lone wolf, a man who allowed very few people to get close to him. A man with his own secrets.

His body was rock-hard, a mature masculine body well-honed by a tough life. Since this morning he'd unbuttoned another button on the chambray shirt. A wedge of dense, curly hair peeked out. His legs were impossibly long, every muscle defined beneath the soft denim that also emphasized the masculine ridge behind his fly.

She forced herself to look at his boots, which were buffed to a mirror shine. An unwelcome memory from the past intruded on the present with startling clarity. Even when Zach had been penniless, he'd taken pride in the way he'd dressed. True, he'd had little except well-worn jeans, but his boots had always been shined to a high gloss even when he hadn't had enough money to resole them.

Now, of course, he had money. He'd spent it on black sharkskin boots that were hand-made, the distinctive swirling insets of white sharkskin indicated they were expensive Tres Outlaws. His belt was black lizard with a unique hand-tooled silver buckle. Neither the boots nor belt were new, but they must be prized possessions because both were meticulously maintained.

She turned, thinking she should make coffee before

awakening him. It would give her time to carefully plan what to say. She moved away; his hand whipped out and grabbed her wrist, just as his eyes opened. Caught off balance, she bumped into the arm of the sofa. A split second later she was sprawled across his lap.

Nose to nose, they stared at each other. The intensity of his gaze was enough to take most women's breath away. She tried to yank her hand free, but he effortlessly restrained her. She glared at him, her instincts telling her to scramble off his lap, but the angle of her body and his tight grip made it impossible.

"Let go, you jerk."

He let out a low whistle, his breath lifting a strand of her hair. "Jerk? Am I supposed to be insulted? That's about the nicest thing you've ever called me."

"I could say something worse, but I won't lower myself."

"Temper. Temper," he responded, obviously enjoying baiting her.

She wiggled, pulling her arm, trying to twist free. Lurching sideways did no good either. He merely anchored her more firmly to his chest until her breasts were nestled against him. She tried again, squirming in his lap. A slow, sensual grin spread over his face as she struggled, getting nowhere.

"Honey, didn't anybody ever tell you not to move around like that unless you're looking for action?"

Shock arced through her like an electric current, and she froze, embarrassingly aware of the masculine contours of his body as it pressed against hers. Without thinking, she swung her free arm, intending to slap him. He blocked the blow, manacling her wrist in his large hand.

They stared at each other; the gleam of desire in his deep blue eyes was impossible to miss. Dammit, she wasn't some easy piece.

"I swear, I could kill you." She put as much bite into

her words as possible considering the strange but exciting feeling feathering up through her chest.

"I live in fear." He grinned, but didn't move.

No doubt about it. Zach Coulter had a rugged cowboy sexiness that appealed to most women. But not Claire; she knew better. She blistered him with one of her meanest stares.

"You're hurting me," she fibbed, trying to pull her hand away.

His mouth twisted, but it wasn't a smile. It was more of a grimace, then his expression changed from sensual to threatening, so quickly she might have imagined the charge of sexual energy that had arced between them a second ago. He effortlessly lifted her off his lap and plopped her down on the sofa beside him.

"I want the truth about last night," Zach said, "and I want it now."

Claire scrambled away from him, putting as much space between them as the small sofa allowed.

"I've busted my ass all day, tracking down leads. You lied to me."

She shook her head. "I never told an outright lie. I just saw no reason to go into the details of my private life unless absolutely necessary."

He glared at her with a look that said he didn't see the difference. A minute ago he'd been interested in sex, but he'd managed to channel that energy into a raw anger that frightened her.

"Where do you want me to start?"

He studied her with a steadfast gaze that assured her that he could detect anything she might omit. "Start with the bear. Khadafi may be the key to this murder. What do you know about his disappearance?"

"No one could do anything about the bear baiting," she said without hesitation. "I mentioned it to someone—"

"Cut the bullshit. I'm dead tired. Who did you tell?"

Claire held her ground. "I don't want to get anyone else in trouble."

"It'll remain confidential unless it figures into the killing. I'm the last person who wants Stegner to get back that bear."

"I asked Tohono what we should do about the bear. He said to spread the word. Putting money in the Maria Martinez vase in the Taos Inn and saying prayers to San Geronimo would help the bear."

"You're kidding? You actually got people to put money in that old pot?"

"It's a priceless piece. Since Maria's death—" she stopped, knowing Zach wanted facts, not a lesson in art. "I have no idea how much money was in the vase, but I contributed all I could spare, three thousand dollars. Angela, Vanessa Trent, Seth, and many others put money in the vase to rescue the bear."

Eyes that never missed a thing narrowed. "What did you think the money was going to be used for?"

"To pay someone to steal the bear. Then to keep Bam from finding it, the bear would have to be taken out of the United States, or something. I suppose it might have been taken to Canada. That's where there's a refuge for the bears taken from bear baiters in Oklahoma. Since the bears don't have any teeth, they need special diets, special care."

Zach nodded thoughtfully, his eyes never leaving hers. "Did you know the bear was being taken last night?"

"I received an anonymous phone call saying he would be gone before midnight."

"And you couldn't resist going to Hogs and Heifers to piss-off Stegner."

"Seth insisted he wanted to hear Flash and the Rusty Roots," she said, unwilling to admit Zach was right. She had wanted to taunt Stegner. "I decided that it might not be a bad idea to let everyone see me. How could I take Khadafi if I was in plain sight the whole time?"

"That was stupid. That bear weighs hundreds of pounds. No one would believe you physically stole him, but they sure as hell think you know who did."

"Going there wasn't smart," she conceded. "But I honestly have no idea who took Khadafi, and I don't know where he is. I'd still do it all over again. Someone had to save that bear."

For a moment the intense expression in his eyes softened. "The way you saved Lucy?"

Claire didn't respond. Lucy had been used as a live target by a man raising attack dogs. Claire had arrived with the authorities just in time to see the man turn a vicious attack dog on Lucy. While the police stood there, deciding which law he was breaking, she grabbed a gun from the man and shot the attack dog. Lucy would never be the same, her leg had been broken in three places, but at least she was alive. And out of that monster's hands.

Thinking about Lucy reminded Claire that she hadn't noticed either dog. "Where is Lucy?"

"They wanted to go out, so I let them go."

"No!" Claire vaulted to her feet. "The coyotes could get Lucy. Last week a pack dragged off Mrs. Sanchez's dog."

"Do you seriously think a pack of coyotes would take on Lobo?"

"No," Claire admitted, sinking back to her place on the sofa.

Zach's understanding expression faded, replaced by a world-weary frown. "Okay, so let's forget the bear for now. Tell me about your relationship with Seth Ramsey."

Under his inquisitive gaze, she bristled. "That's a little personal, isn't it?"

"Not when you lie, saying you were with him when you weren't."

"I didn't lie. I just didn't want to go into it, so I was a little evasive," she admitted, reminding herself not to sound guilty when she wasn't. "I've been dating Seth for the past few months."

"Do you usually spend the night with him after a date?"

The question seemed far too personal, but considering the fact that she hadn't stayed with Seth last night and that this might suggest a deviation from a normal pattern, she answered. "No. I've never been . . . intimate with Seth."

"Intimate?" Zach chuckled. "First you call me a jerk when you mean asshole. Now you say intimate. Can't you just say you aren't screwing him?"

She glared at him. "Obviously the women you hang around with talk like truck drivers. I answered your question. That's all I have to do."

Zach waited for a moment before saying, "Seth brought you but you didn't go home with him. He told me you disappeared a little after midnight. He waited outside the rest room for you, but you never came out. What happened?"

Claire drew in a calming breath, deciding to back up and give him the whole picture. Zach's brains were behind the buttons on his 501s, but he was all she had to work with. If he didn't find the killer, she was in real trouble. "We came to the club at about ten, and Seth immediately ordered drinks."

"They had a table waiting for you even though they had a line out the door to hear Flash and the Rusty Roots?"

"Yes. Seth had greased Bam's bouncer. We had a table near Angela Whitmore and her—ah—friend."

"Come on, Claire. I know Angela is your best client, but call a spade a spade. Carleton Cole is a young stud—young enough to be Angela's son." She shrugged, reluctant to concede the point, and he continued. "Okay, so what about Nevada?"

"He was near our table with two women. I didn't talk to him." She could hardly say the name of the artist she'd discovered without thinking how hurt she'd been when Nevada Murphy had left her for Duncan Morrell. "I felt fine until I finished my first drink, then—"

A mournful howl pierced the night, cutting off her explanation. The sound echoed though the silent hacienda, suspended in the air, reverberating long after the cry ceased.

Five

A second deeper howl filled the room with its haunting, soulful sound.

Zach rose. "It's just Lobo. He wants to be let in."

Grateful for the interruption, Claire followed Zach across the immense living room and into the foyer decorated in hand-painted Mexican tiles. The floor itself was Saltillo tile, and the red clay squares were cool under her bare feet. "I'd like to hear what Lobo sounds like when he's angry."

"No, you wouldn't." Zach swung open the antique door, its wide, thick planks hinged with hand-forged wrought iron.

Lobo trotted in with Lucy at his heels, wagging her tail. Once again, Claire was amazed. Lucy shied away from most dogs, but seemed to know Lobo would protect her, not harm her.

"Coffee?" Claire asked, stalling. It wasn't her style to prevaricate, but she'd found Zach's questions intensely personal, and she wondered how little she could tell him and still help him find the killer.

She led him down the hall and through the wide, arched doorway into the spacious kitchen. She flicked on the lights, which brightened the gourmet's paradise and artfully accented the ceiling of hand-hewn vigas, making the exposed wooden beams stand out against the whitewashed walls. *Latillas,* stripped wood saplings in a herringbone pattern, filled the spaces between the vigas. The decorator had accessorized the home with the finest examples of Native American arts and crafts available, pieces Claire would have been thrilled to have in her own gallery.

Harvest baskets hung from the high ceiling, their meticulously hand-woven designs formed by various grasses that had been dyed with bark and plants to duplicate the rich earth tones of the Painted Desert. Above the range a specially lighted, arched cove in the wall, a *nicho,* featured a folk-art carving of San Pasqual, patron saint of kitchens.

No doubt the decorator believed the Frederic Remington bronze sculpture in the living room was the showpiece in the home. But Claire secretly coveted the Navajo Yei blanket that hung on the wall in the breakfast area, its crisp red and black diamond pattern spotlighted by beams of light hidden in the ceiling.

Zach leaned against the island counter, and she wondered what he thought of the house. It was a world away from the Golden Palms, the trailer park across town where he'd been raised. She recalled sneaking him into her home when they'd been in high school. He had tried to be nonchalant, but she could tell he was awed.

This historic hacienda that she was leasing was much more impressive than her father's home, yet if Zach noticed, he didn't show it. His eyes flicked to one side for a moment, distracted by both dogs slurping from Lucy's water bowl. Once he spotted the source of the noise, his gaze returned to her. She self-consciously filled the Brewmatic with her favorite coffee, vanilla hazelnut.

Zach probably thought she had something to hide. Well, she did, but it had nothing to do with the murder. He had more testosterone than brains, but he was the sheriff. No matter how embarrassing it would be to tell him about last night, she had no choice.

She handed him a mug of coffee and stood nearby,

reaching for her own cup. Not a word had been said since they'd come into the kitchen and the silence enveloped the room.

Zach spoke first. "You claimed your first drink hit you hard."

"I felt woozy as if I'd had half a dozen drinks," she said, bristling at the word *claimed*, but silently conceding that he did have a good reason to doubt her. She hadn't been totally honest about her whereabouts the night of the murder. "My head was buzzing."

"What were you drinking?"

She hesitated a moment. "Tarantula juice."

"Oh, that's kick-ass smart. Stegner's house specialty— tequila, rum, and lime juice. Who the hell knows what else is in it? No wonder you were in the bag."

"I usually drink white wine, but Hogs and Heifers doesn't serve wine."

"It's not a wine crowd," Zach observed, his eyes searching her face in a way that made her even more uncomfortable.

"I thought dancing would help. You know, getting up and moving around, but when I came off the dance floor, I could hardly talk. I decided to go to the restroom behind the club to splash cold water on my face. Seth went to the bathroom, too."

"What time was that?"

"Three minutes after midnight. I distinctly remember because I thought to myself that Khadafi was free."

For a moment he regarded her intently, his eyes revealing nothing.

"When I came out of the restroom I felt worse, not better."

"Where was Seth when you came out?"

"He said he'd wait for me, but I looked around and didn't see him. It's so dark back there. I waited but he didn't come out of the men's room."

"Funny." Zach quirked one brow skeptically. "Seth claimed he waited for you but you had disappeared."

Claire stared at the two dogs, who were sitting nearby. She recalled Seth's telephone message. At the time she thought he'd gone into The Hideaway to search for her. Now she wondered what he was concealing. "I saw him in the distance and followed him into The Hideaway."

"You're positive it was Seth Ramsey? A lot of people came to see Flash and the Rusty Roots."

Claire nodded. "Seth turned. The moonlight was on his face. It was him."

Zach's expression remained unreadable, and she wondered what he was thinking. Didn't he believe her? How would he react to the rest of her story?

"Didn't you call to him?"

"I tried, but I couldn't talk. Honestly, not one word came out, so I kept following Seth. I knew by then I was really sick. I wanted to go home. Seth stopped in front of one of the bungalows."

"Really?" he said, his tone expressing his doubts. "Which one?"

Claire shrugged, then set the coffee mug on the counter. "I'm not sure. It's so dark back there, and by then I was really confused, stumbling around, anxious to get out of there. I heard a voice calling to me. I thought it was Seth."

She wavered, trying to decide how to tell him. Why, oh, why, did Zach Coulter have to be the sheriff? She didn't want him, of all people, to know she'd done something so foolish. An uncomfortably long moment passed as Zach took a swallow of coffee, waiting for her to continue.

"I went toward the man calling me. It was dark inside the room," she said, her voice dropping with each word. "I couldn't see a thing. I found the switch, but the lights wouldn't come on."

"When I searched the place, I didn't find any bulb in

that room. The windows are painted black and covered by blackout curtains," he informed her, his gaze narrowing.

She hesitated, reluctant to confess what she'd done. Go ahead. Tell him the rest and let him think what he wants. You don't care, do you?

"The man pulled me into his arms and kissed me. He kissed me several times," she said making it sound like simple kisses, not the erotic experience it had been. "My mind wasn't working quite right. It was a few minutes before I realized I wasn't kissing Seth."

Zach studied her quizzically for a moment. "You'd just seen Seth outside. How could you possibly think he was the man inside the room?"

"I-I can't explain. I was terribly confused." She swallowed hard, knowing this was just the beginning. How could she explain that the experience had been wildly erotic—and only looking back had she found herself frightened. At the time it seemed so . . . right.

"I wanted to push him away, but for some reason I didn't," she said, struggling to keep her voice from revealing her inner turmoil. "I wanted to tell him to stop, but my tongue felt like lead. One thing led to another and . . ."

"And?" Zach prompted, his expression sardonically amused.

"Well, you know . . ."

"No, I don't know." He grinned, feather-like laugh lines crinkling around his eyes. "I haven't a clue."

She refused to go into any more details. He knew exactly what had happened. She didn't have to paint him a picture. "The next thing I knew it was morning."

"All night, huh?" He gave her a knowing grin that made her want to whack him. "So, who was the lucky guy?"

Claire took a deep breath, then said, "I have no idea."

A suggestion of a smile played across his mouth, an infuriatingly sensual, arrogant grin. "You're telling me that you—Miss Holier Than Thou—slept with a total stranger?"

She looked him straight in the eye, determined not to let him rattle her. "I'm certain the drink had something in it. I would never have done anything so stupid otherwise."

Zach's expression said he had his doubts. "Didn't you ask his name the next morning?"

Claire shook her head. "He was gone when I woke up."

He gave her another look that telegraphed even more suspicion. "You must have some idea of what he looks like. Remember, he's your alibi."

She became increasingly uneasy. There was something more disturbing than usual in the way he was looking at her. She scrambled to recall any detail that might help. She was in real trouble here. All she had to work with were vague images of a very large man. "He had very big . . . equipment," she blurted out. "Really large."

"Equipment?" Zach repeated, arching one black eyebrow for a moment, then a slow smile spread across his face. It became a grin that emphasized his even white teeth. A second later he began to chuckle. The sound escalated into a full masculine laugh that echoed through the kitchen. Both dogs cocked their heads and stared at him. He tried to stop, managing to cut the noise, but his large frame kept shaking with mirth.

She realized what she'd said and wanted to die. "He was really large. A tall, muscular man. Very, very big."

Finally, he said, "Sweetheart, anybody ever tell you that it's not the size of the wand—it's the magician?"

She glared at him, the heat rushing up her neck. She knew her face was bright pink, which made her even more angry—with herself—with him.

"How am I supposed to find some dude with a really big—"

"Very funny. This is a murder investigation, and all you can focus on is . . ."

"A big cock," he finished with a grin. "Hey, you're the

one who brought it up. Can't you just see me going around town with a tape measure?"

She pushed away from the counter, both hands on her hips. "You vile creep, if I remembered anything more, I'd tell you. Do you honestly believe I want to be involved in this murder?"

"You're going to have to do better. I know it was pitch dark in there. That's the way customers at The Hideaway like it. But you must have some other impression—" he hesitated, studying her for a moment "—of your alibi. Try again. I'm not buying this."

She struggled to remember something—anything. An image came to her, an image she hadn't recalled until this second. Her thighs began to tingle and she squirmed as the erotic memory returned. "He had a beard."

"A beard. Now that's something to go on. What kind? A goatee like all the kids are wearing, or what?"

She thought a moment, trying to bring the image into a clearer focus. She felt herself blush as another even more erotic image of the mysterious stranger came to mind. "No, not a clipped beard, a full bushy beard."

"That's good. There won't be too many men around town fitting that description." He paused, looking across the room to the spot where the dogs were now curled up, their muzzles touching. "It should be easy to find him unless . . . unless . . ."

"Unless what?" she asked, more than a little unnerved by the memory of the bearded man kissing her.

"Unless he's one of the studs Stegner lets hang around to service women. In that case he could be from Santa Fe or Phoenix and long gone by now."

Claire had a vague recollection of the man talking to her, but she couldn't remember anything he'd said. Still, she had the impression of a good, gentle man. She reacted on instinct. "He's not one of Stegner's men."

"Okay, then I'm going to need a better physical description," Zach said. "Come here."

Although he was just a few feet away, she reluctantly
closed the distance between them.

"Shut your eyes," Zach said.

"Why?"

"Trust me, I need a little more information if I'm going
to find your . . . alibi."

She closed her eyes, having no choice but to trust him,
and Zach's large hands came down on her shoulders.
Through the lightweight sweater she felt the heat of his
palms and the strength in his fingers. A fluid warmth
spread through her, an annoying, dangerous feeling.

"Don't open your eyes," he told her, his breath whisking
across her ear. "Now put your arms around me."

When she didn't move, he lifted her arms to his shoulders, and she let them limply hang there. She struggled
to ignore the tingling sensation in the pit of her stomach.
She told herself it was relief; the worst was over. She'd
confessed what she'd done. But his rock-hard, inescapably
masculine body pressed against hers, telling her that wasn't
the whole truth.

"Hold me," he said.

Did he know what he was asking, what memories this
would bring? She hesitated, then linked her arms around
his shoulders. She could feel the sculpted muscles and
solid bone beneath his shirt. The last time she'd been in
his arms, Zach had been on the verge of manhood. He
was still slim through the hips, but he had a more powerful
torso than he'd had in his youth.

Yes, he was a man now. All man. The catch in her breath
took her by surprise. She had told herself that she didn't
remember what it felt like to have him hold her, but it was
all coming back to her in a dizzying rush. For the love of
God, don't do this to yourself, cautioned the sensible part
of her brain.

"Was the man taller or shorter than I am?" he asked, apparently unfazed by having her in his arms.

She squeezed her eyes tight, fighting to control the subtle, unwilling change in her body. Every heartbeat reminded her that his arms were around her, his hands resting lightly on the small of her back.

"Come on," Zach prodded. "Give me your gut reaction."

"Taller, much taller."

She opened her eyes and saw his head was bent down. He was so close that if she moved her lips would touch his chin, or cheek . . . or something. Rapidly escalating tension tightened every muscle in her body, and she became totally aware of Zach, so attuned to him that she could almost hear his heart beating. Certainly she could hear the soft rush of his breath and feel the heat of his body stealing through her.

"I'm six-four," he said, all business. He released her and took a half step back. "There are only a few men in town taller than I am."

"It has to be one of them," she assured him. "He was taller than you and more muscular."

His eyes narrowed speculatively and he frowned, his mouth becoming tight and grim. He studied her a moment, his gaze eagle-sharp beneath drawn brows. Something's terribly wrong, she thought. The warmth that had suffused her body just moments ago became a chilling apprehension.

Zach walked across the kitchen into the family room and stood near the kiva fireplace. He was nearly as tall as the rounded, triangular-shaped fireplace. He was right, she decided. Few men around Taos were as tall as Zach Coulter. Hands on his hips, he stared through the panoramic window at the mountains. The architect had designed the home to showcase the majestic bluff of Taos Mountain. At this hour nothing was visible except a vast sweep of darkness and a moonlit sky studded by glowing stars.

He stood there in silence, gazing into the night. Claire wondered what he was thinking. Nothing she recalled about the stranger seemed to lead anywhere. Except now Zach Coulter knew her secret.

Surely the stranger would come forward if he knew she was in trouble and needed an alibi. The whole night had been strange—and wonderful. She had been left with the distinct impression that he was a good person.

Why she believed that she wasn't sure. It was nothing more than a feeling based on . . . On what? Nothing. He could easily remain silent, not giving her an alibi.

"Claire, come here," Zach's voice cut through the quiet house.

She crossed the room and stood beside him, facing the darkness. The moon hung low over Taos Mountain, limning the peak with light.

"Tell me *exactly* what you remember after you went in that room." He leveled her with a look she couldn't decipher. "Everything."

What was he, some kind of pervert who got his kicks listening to details of other people's sex lives? "I told you everything. I don't see any point in repeating it."

"When did you take off your panties?"

Panties? All she remembered was waking up to discover she was stark naked and her panties were nowhere to be found. "I didn't. I-I mean . . . I don't know when or how it happened."

He nodded, looking at her a moment before staring into the darkness again.

"Most of the night is a blank," she assured him. "I was in that room for hours, but I only remember what I told you."

"Like an alcoholic in a blackout. You were functioning at some level, but now you can't remember anything."

"Wait a minute," she said, a surge of panic jolting her. She put her hands on her hips and glared at him. "Wasn't there some Jane Fonda movie about a woman who wakes up with a dead body next to her? She can't remember if she killed him or not? Don't try to pin Duncan Morrell's murder on me. I didn't kill him."

"I'm not accusing you of murder." He put one strong hand on her shoulder. "Let's go back to when you ordered the tarantula juice. Did you see who—"

"I didn't order it. Angela Whitmore at the next table was having one. As we came up, she insisted we try the tarantula juice. She added two more to her order. I didn't see who made them. I didn't even look."

Zach asked, "Where was Stegner?"

"Up by the band. He saw me, though. He looked right at me."

"Who ordered your second drink?"

"I don't know. It was just there when we came off the dance floor. I only took one sip. By then the first one had hit me hard."

He led her back to the sofa and nudged her down onto the cushions. "Have you ever heard of Rohypnol?" She shook her head, and he continued, "It's a new drug. It hasn't been approved for use yet, so doctors in this country can't legally prescribe it, but you can bring in enough for personal use from another country like Mexico."

"What does it do?" she asked, wondering where this was leading.

"The drug delivers a killer punch like you've had a dozen drinks instead of one. The pill itself is tiny, so it's easy to drop into a drink. It dissolves quickly and is tasteless."

She stared at him, too stunned to speak, her heart pounding as relief nearly knocked her to her knees to say a prayer of thanks. Her wild fling with a total stranger wasn't entirely her fault. The knowledge made her weak with gratitude. Yet she was frightened, too. Who would do something so vicious? "You think someone put one of those pills into my drink?"

He nodded, saying, "Police in Florida call it the 'date rape' drug because they had so many complaints of rape when guys dropped the pill into drinks."

"Seth would never—"

"I didn't say he did it, but someone wanted you stumbling around half out of your mind. Roofies—that's what the kids call Rohypnol—makes you appear to be a little drunk, but okay. The women report having trouble speaking and being confused about sizes and shapes as well as the sequence of events. They can't remember everything that happened come morning."

"Do you think I'm mistaken about the man's size?"

"Possibly. Things are always exaggerated in the dark. The stranger may well have been shorter and less muscular than you recall."

"I'm sure of the beard," she insisted, another flash of memory coming to her unexpectedly, and she hoped she wasn't blushing. Yes, he most definitely had a beard. "Why would anyone give me one of those pills?"

"If I knew the reason, I might be able to solve this case." He gazed across the room to where the two dogs were sleeping, curled up together. "I haven't had a single complaint of anyone getting a Roofie at Stegner's place. Nothing."

"Maybe the women were too embarrassed to complain." She studied her bare toe for a second. "It was really hard for me to tell you."

For an instant his gaze sharpened. "Did he rape you, Claire?"

"No," she said, shaking her head, reluctant to admit how thrilling the experience had been. After Zach had used the term "date rape drug," she recalled news accounts of other women's experiences with Roofies, and knew she'd been very lucky. "I don't remember everything, but I know I wasn't forced. At first I wanted to say no, but then . . ."

He let the word hang there for a long moment. "But? But what?"

"I didn't want him to stop. I was enjoying it too much," she admitted, her voice so low that she wasn't sure he could hear her.

"Really? You liked this well-hung dude." There was a curious expression on his face even though his intention was to bait her as usual.

She didn't respond, and finally, he said, "Roofies aren't in general circulation around here or I would have heard something. Several states have outlawed it, but it's not illegal to possess it here." He leaned closer, his expression frighteningly serious. "What I want to know is did someone know you were coming and bring Roofies, or was it unplanned?"

"I can't imagine why anyone would want to drug me," she said, bewildered.

"That's easy. They wanted to frame you for murder."

Six

Claire stared into the darkness beyond the soaring sheet of glass and knew Zach was right. She'd denied the possibility all day long, but the nagging fear had been there, lurking in the corner of her mind.

Beware the coyote.

By going to Bam Stegner's club, she'd allowed herself to be set up. She could have told Seth no, but she hadn't. She had agreed to the date immediately, welcoming the chance to taunt Stegner.

"What now?" she asked.

"Instead of butting your nose into everything, the way you usually do, I want you to keep your mouth shut. Not one word to your father, not one word to Seth Ramsey. The less people know, the more likely someone will trip up, and I'll be able to solve this case. But if you go around whining about Roofies and mysterious strangers, you'll tip off the killer."

She gritted her teeth to keep from protesting she wasn't a whiner, but she knew he was right. Don't give the killer even more of a chance to frame her. "Why are you helping me?"

"Do you really think I give a damn about what happens to you?" Zach asked. "I've got something to prove to To-hono and the others who stood up to your father. They got me the job as sheriff."

"And you have an election coming up next year," she said before she could stop herself.

His whole face contracted, every muscle hardening against the other. His eyes turned the steely blue-gray of a gun barrel. It was all she could do not to back up.

"I intend to solve this case. Don't get in the way, Claire."

With a few angry strides he crossed the family room and went into the entry. Lobo jumped up and followed him and Lucy tagged along. Claire walked behind, not certain what to say.

Zach dropped down to a squat and faced Lobo. He looked directly into the dog's eyes, then said, "You're staying here. I want you to—"

"Staying?" Claire cried. "What for?"

Zach ignored her, still speaking to Lobo. "Take care of Lucy and Claire. I'll be back for you." He rose to his feet, facing Claire. "You need protection. You've got Stegner pissed big-time, and someone's out to frame you for mur—"

"I have an alarm system and a gun," she protested.

"Stegner's a sneaky son of a bitch. He lost it this morning, but that's not like him. He'll get you when you least expect it."

She couldn't deny he was right. From the moment she'd heard Khadafi was going to be liberated, she knew Stegner would blame her. She had her guard up; she could take care of herself.

"Most people think that Attica was the worst prison riot in U.S. history, but they're wrong," he said, rising to his feet. "More men died during the riot at the penitentiary near Santa Fe. Know who was behind it?"

"Stegner?"

"Right. He eliminated all his enemies in that riot, guards and prisoners. But he was so slick, he was never blamed. Since then he's appeared to be clean. He doesn't want to go back to prison, so he'll strike when you least expect it."

"I knew that going in," she said, although she hadn't

known all the details of Stegner's past. "I don't want Lobo around. He's wild, unpredictable."

"Bull shit. Just talk to him like you would your own dog. Use regular obedience commands. Stay. Sit. Come. But pay attention to his signals. He'll bark if anyone is near. If he senses real danger—he'll growl low in his throat."

Taos was an unconventional town with many artists and writers who took their pets wherever they went. It was common to see two or three dogs waiting outside restaurants or shops for their masters. People wouldn't look twice at anyone with two dogs—unless one of them was Lobo. Being part timber wolf and having Zach for an owner had earned the dog quite a reputation.

What about her father? She could just imagine what Alexander Holt would say if he saw her with Zach's dog. It was bad enough that she was the image of her mother, but Zach could have been his father's identical twin instead of his son. If her father even suspected Claire was seeing Zach—for any reason—he would be humiliated the way he'd been when the whole town discovered Alexander Holt's wife had run off with Jake Coulter. She couldn't put him through any more heartache.

"Thanks, but—"

"Sweetheart, you don't have any choice," Zach informed her. "I'm taking care of you, like it or not."

His gaze narrowed and without moving his head, he scanned her body with the calculating appraisal of a man who mentally undressed women as a hobby. She was tempted to slap him, but thought the better of it as his eyes shifted to her lips and settled there.

She lifted her chin to look him in the eye and glared at him. It took a supreme effort, but she managed it. "First, you don't give a hoot what happens to me. Now you're determined to take care of me. You sound like a confused idiot."

Her scathing comment did nothing but encourage him.

He grinned with a maddening hint of arrogance yet the effect on her was shattering. It was all she could do to throttle the dizzying current racing through her. If she wasn't careful, he was going to kiss her. Just thinking about it made her pulse skyrocket. What was wrong with her?

She mustered the strength to say, "Get out!"

Zach cracked a laugh, startling her. "You're in no position to order me around. I'm in your life to stay. Count on it."

She took one small step back, then another for good measure. No denying it; her body responded to this man, overriding the rational objections of her brain. Too clearly she remembered what it had felt like to be in his arms, and some traitorous part of her wanted to be there again.

"You're not part of my life. As soon as the killer is found—"

He reached out and put his hands on her shoulders, and her body reacted with a surge of excitement as he pulled her flush against him. She twisted and shoved at his chest with both hands, but his arms shackled her.

"We're going to start where we left off," he said, a husky undertone to his voice. "It's been years, but I still remember how hot you were for me."

His comment shocked and disgusted her. Years ago, she'd come within a hair's breath of losing her virginity to Zach. The fiery crash that had taken the lives of both their parents had ended their relationship. At least something good had come out of the tragedy.

"Zach, you're the biggest jerk I've ever met." She braced her hands against his sturdy torso and pushed with all her might but couldn't free herself.

"You're pissed off big-time because you know I'm right. That's why you hightail it every time you see me coming. You haven't the guts to admit to yourself that you're just as hot for me as your mother was for my old man."

Fury erupted inside her with such frightening intensity

that she gasped, words eluding her. *How dare he?* She was
anchored to his chest, his superior strength imprisoning
her, the smirk on his face goading her. She had no choice.
She leaned over and bit his arm.

Big mistake!

He released her—for a second—then he grabbed her
again, twirled her around and pinned her against the door
before she could draw a breath. He was grinning at her,
but his eyes glinted and his nostrils flared slightly, betray-
ing his anger.

"Darlin', biting can be a real turn-on," he said. "Let's
head into the bedroom."

"Dream on!" She congratulated herself for sounding so
forceful, but a growing sense of alarm warned her that he
seriously expected . . . What? An affair? A one-night stand?
Something. Like a gunslinger notching his belt, Zach Coulter wasn't going to be satisfied until he could count her
among his conquests.

His smile vanished, replaced by an expression of icy con-
tempt. A cold knot of fear formed in the pit of her stomach
as he studied her. It was dangerous to cross this man, but
she refused to give into him. He raised his hand and took
a loose tendril of her hair between his fingers, his eyes
never leaving hers.

He didn't say a word, but his body was pressed against
her, every muscle taut, communicating barely restrained
anger. A flicker of apprehension coursed through her. She
kept staring into his compelling blue eyes, determined not
to look away and let him know she was afraid of him.

The silence lengthened. It couldn't have been more
than a few seconds, but it seemed like hours as she gazed
up at him while he played with her hair. The very air
around them seemed to be electrified as if they were in
the midst of one of the wild summer storms that ripped
through the mountains.

She wanted to bite him again, harder this time, but she

didn't dare. This murder had given him an advantage over her, and it was clear he intended to use it.

He slowly brushed the tendril of hair across her cheek. "Bite me again and you'll be *real* sorry."

She opened her mouth, a scathing retort on her lips, but something glistened in his eyes at that moment—unyielding determination. And a deeper emotion, which seemed to be frighteningly intense. She sucked in a calming breath, praying he'd just leave, but knowing he wouldn't.

He threaded his fingers through her hair, his hand slowly circling her head until his palm gloved the back of her skull. A slow heat unfurled in her belly, languidly spreading downward. Oh, Lordy. Don't let this be happening. Not with this man.

Say something. Do something. Get him out of here before he kisses you.

"I swear. You're going to regret this," she said in her most self-righteous tone.

He winked at her. "I live in fear."

He was massaging the back of her head now, his strong fingers gently moving against her. His touch was oddly soft and caressing, a sharp contrast to the muscular length of his body braced so intimately against hers. She could feel every firm, well-toned muscle. Suddenly, she couldn't look into his eyes any longer. Instead she concentrated on the hollow at the base of his throat where his pulse beat against the tanned skin.

One . . . two . . . three. She counted each pulsation, forcing her thoughts away from him and the incredible magic his fingers were working along the base of her skull. When she finally gave up and met his gaze again, his usually turbulent blue eyes were almost black, only a thin band of blue remained. Her heart was beating so hard she was positive he could hear it because he smiled, a slow sensual smile that sent a rush of heated longing through her.

"Don't," she murmured.

"Don't what?"

"Don't kiss me," she answered, her voice pathetically unconvincing.

Claire knew better, realizing full well she shouldn't allow him to kiss her, even as his mouth came toward hers, but she didn't turn her head away. Instead she waited, anticipating the kiss, her entire body charged with suspense. Desire coursed through her, sweeping away all rational thought. He kissed her roughly, one hand raking through her hair while the other pressed on the small of her back, arching her backward so that her breasts were flattened against his chest, his powerful body dominating hers.

True, she'd been kissed—many times—but only one man had used such sheer masculine domination, eliciting a dark, primal response from her. Zach. It had been years ago, of course, a summer she'd forced herself to forget. He'd been a boy then, gentler and manageable. No telling what this man would do.

Push him away, her mind ordered, but her body couldn't resist temptation. He teased her lips apart with the tip of his tongue, then surged inward. Shocked at her own passionate response to the touch of his lips, Claire returned the kiss, her tongue greeting his. The contact sent a bolt of sheer pleasure through her entire body and her pulse went haywire, throbbing in intimate, sensitive places.

Desire swept over her—and carried her away. She responded to the sensual movement of his body and the scorching heat of his thighs by running her hands over the steely muscles of his back and shoulders. Her hands explored while her tongue joined with his in a sensual parody of another more intimate mating.

"Damn, Claire," he murmured, lifting his mouth from hers for a moment.

She clung to him, savoring the male scent of his body and the smell of vanilla hazelnut coffee on his breath. And the feel of a swelling hardness thrusting against her. Oh, she knew she was going to bitterly regret this, part of her already did, but she didn't have the willpower to deny herself this pleasure.

"Damn, Claire, is that all you have to say?" she managed to whisper.

"We're past talking, babe. Way past."

He lowered his mouth to hers again and she willingly parted her lips, then daintily sucked at his tongue. His kiss, the feel of his body was the most erotic thing she'd ever experienced, his body the hardest, most powerful force. Yet it was the touch of his hands that enthralled her.

Sounds from outside dimly penetrated her senses. The lonely hoot of an owl, the chorus of crickets and the tick-tick of the clock in the hall. Traces of coffee and sweet scents from the aromatherapy lingered in the summer air. But she was so mesmerized by the sensations generated by his hands as he explored her body that she couldn't concentrate on anything else.

"I want you," he whispered. A low growl rumbled from deep in his throat. He cupped her bottom with both hands and brought her up on tiptoe against his stiff erection. "Hey, have you ever done it standing up?"

The crude question made her pull back slightly, but he wouldn't let her go. He held her firmly against the hard heat of his lower body. She sank her nails into his back and arched against him. An uncontrollable shudder of pleasure racked her body.

"Standing up?" she echoed like the village idiot. "Standing up?"

He pulled his lips from hers and mumbled something that must have been a curse. Eyes squeezed shut, he sucked in his breath and held it, his head tilted toward the ceiling. She reached up to pull his head down for another kiss, but he opened his eyes and released her.

"You're a real hot number, Claire. Like I said, you're just as crazy for me as your mother was for my old man."

With a smirk he blew her a kiss on the way out the door.

Twenty minutes later Zach was sitting in his Bronco outside Hogs and Heifers, watching. For what? He wasn't sure, but he damn well couldn't sleep. Not after that little scene with Claire.

It had taken every ounce of willpower to walk out on Claire, but he was proud of himself. He intended to play with her, give her a dose of the hard-to-get medicine that she liked to dish out. He laughed under his breath as a couple of drunks stumbled out of the nightclub.

It was easy to tease Claire. Just throw her mother's love for his father in her face. Like the rest of the town, Claire believed their parents' affair had been a short fling. Zach knew the truth. He smiled into the darkness and took a deep breath of the cool mountain air laced with the scent of pine. When the time was right, he was going to tell Claire what really happened between their parents.

He brooded in the darkness, barely hearing the raucous sound of the band playing in the club. After Flash and the Rusty Roots, they weren't worth listening to. His mind drifted back to Claire.

He could still feel her, soft and willing. He'd been aching to put his tongue, his lips on every delicious inch of her body. He'd start with the sensitive spot behind her earlobe and kiss his way downward, taking so much damn time that she'd be writhing beneath him.

Begging for more.

Then he'd part those thighs and show Claire that he could torture her with just his tongue. Heat pooled in his groin again. Jesus! Get your mind on something else.

"How did the murderer know Claire was coming to the club? He must have known. The Roofies were ready. Someone wanted Claire knocked for a loop," Zach muttered, then realized Lobo wasn't around. He was talking to himself.

Could have been coincidence, he thought. He wasn't a big believer in coincidences, but shit happened. Years ago, Claire had forgotten something and returned home in the middle of the afternoon. She'd caught her mother getting it on with Jake Coulter.

Coincidence. Deadly coincidence for their parents, he thought with an unaccustomed pang of regret that he thought he'd outgrown years ago.

That was then, and this is now. Was it just coincidence that someone slipped Claire a Roofie on the night Duncan Morrell was murdered? Probably not. He had a sneaking suspicion Seth Ramsey was hiding something. He was going to take a real close look at the cocky lawyer.

But first he needed to get a little more info on the Roofies. He decided to go into the club and stir things up. Inside, the Silver Bullet sign above the bar flickered like a flame in the wind, threatening to die and leave just the candles on the table to light the joint. The makeshift stage raised above the floor by two feet was deserted while the band took a break.

Zach eyed the dimly lit walls where posters from B-movies hung. Spaghetti Westerns mostly, but a few pre-dated the Eastwood era. Those went back to the old days when Native Americans were stereotyped. Indians were the bad guys. White men were the chosen ones.

"Coulter," Stegner bellowed from behind the bar the second he spotted Zach. "When are you going to get that fuckin' tape off those rooms? You're costing me money."

Zach sauntered up to the bar, deliberately taking his time. "The State Police's forensic team from Santa Fe should be finishing up tomorrow sometime. Until then, it's still a crime scene. It's against the law to take off the crime-scene tape and let anybody go into those rooms."

Stegner grunted and glared at him from behind the bar. Even in the dim light of the Silver Bullet sign, Zach could see how pissed Stegner was, but he didn't give a damn. Zach figured the guy was guilty of more crimes than he cared to count. If he had the resources of the SFPD, he'd have his fat ass in prison. As it stood, he'd have to be patient. One of these days, he'd catch Stegner red handed.

"Want a whiskey?" Stegner asked, his bare belly slopping over the bar.

Zach shook his head, keeping his face expressionless. The bastard knew damn well Zach never drank. Whiskey straight——cheap rotgut——had been his mother's favorite drink. Stegner knew it was the last thing he'd order.

"I have a couple of questions for you, and I want straight answers."

Stegner leaned against the counter where the bottles were kept. "More questions? Shit! You've been here three times already."

"It might take another dozen," Zach said, his voice level. No way was he going to let Stegner rile him. "Have you seen or heard of anyone around here selling Roofies?"

"Roofies? In my club?" Stegner looked at him with a slack-jawed stare. He was sneaky as hell, but Zach believed he'd caught him off guard.

"Yeah, Stegner. Here in your club."

The ridiculous spurs Stegner always wore clanged as he stomped over to the draft beer tap. "No Roofies around here, Sheriff."

Stegner's reaction confirmed Zach's suspicions. Someone with West Coast connections——probably Angela Townsend or her studmuffin or——. Aw, hell, the possibilities were numerous. Many of the people who had second homes here lived on the West Coast. Any of them could have brought in the drug.

The question was who had the motive and the opportunity to drop one into Claire's drink. She was a chick with balls bigger than most men's. She'd gotten herself in trouble rescuing Lucy. A little over a year later, she'd raised a real stink about Khadafi, and made Zach look bad because he couldn't do a damn thing about the bear.

And she'd brought to the attention of the art world the number of phony lithographs being passed off as the real thing. Yes, Claire Holt had more than her share of enemies.

But why would one of them slip her a Roofie?

Zach eyed the rattlesnake tattoo leering at him from the top of Stegner's shoulder. He let Stegner stew for a few seconds before saying, "I just thought you might have heard something about someone bringing in Roofies from California. You usually know everything first."

Zach had played to Stegner's ego, but it didn't work. Stegner merely shrugged, admitting nothing. Zach left, no closer to solving the case than he'd been that morning.

Seven

"Why did I let Zach Coulter make a fool of me?" Claire asked out loud even though only Lucy and Lobo were around. The dogs were in the back of the used Jeep she'd bought. They were half hanging out the window, more interested in keeping their noses in the wind than listening to her.

"You're so stupid," she muttered. She despised herself for allowing Zach to kiss her. She didn't give a rip about that lowlife. He was crude and into down-and-dirty sex, the exact opposite of what she wanted in a man.

You're as hot for me as your mother was for my old man.

"It's not true!" She slammed the palm of her hand against the steering wheel. But if she was totally candid with herself, there was a kernel of truth to it. Some dark, primitive part of her psyche responded on an instinctive level to Zach Coulter. Had the same compelling sexual attraction lured her mother into a short fling with the town stud, Jake Coulter?

Like mother; like daughter.

There. That was the bare-bones truth. Now deal with it. Refuse to give in the way your mother gave into . . . into what? She thought a moment, then came up with the right word. Temptation. The mother she'd worshipped had given into temptation. Claire promised herself she'd be stronger, learn from her mother's mistake.

She rounded the corner and saw The Rising Sun. On Sundays she opened the gallery at noon after having met her father at church and having had an early lunch with him. They had done this every Sunday since she'd returned home—until today. No doubt her father would be worried about her, which meant he'd appear at the gallery. And ask questions about Lobo.

She neared the gallery and saw her father's customized van parked at the curb. She drove around behind the adobe building and drove under the shade of a cottonwood, then rolled all the windows down and left the dogs in the car.

"You're a coward," she said to herself as she opened the back door of the gallery. She did not want to explain Lobo to her father. She loved Alexander Holt, and understood his pride because she'd inherited every ounce of it. The humiliation he'd suffered after her mother betrayed him still hurt him even after all these years. Seeing Zach Coulter, the image of his father, walking the streets of Taos only brought back the pain.

Alex Holt had given her mother everything, and had loved her with all his heart. But it hadn't been enough. She'd taken up with Jake Coulter, a man notorious for his affairs. Her father had been devastated when his wife had been killed in an automobile crash while running away with her lover. The exposure of their affair to the entire town had added humiliation to his grief.

Her father could be difficult and demanding, but she reminded herself how much he truly loved her. After her mother's tragic death, Claire had been inconsolable, blaming herself. Her father had comforted her, and for the next few years had been both father and mother to her.

Claire came through the back entrance to the gallery and saw her father's wheelchair stationed at the front door. At this angle she couldn't see his handsome face with his square jaw and full head of hair that once had been blue-black, but now was the color of burnished pewter. She saw the curve of Maude Pfister's broad hip as the woman stood in her usual place behind the wheelchair. Since her father had lost the use of his legs after a stroke five years ago, Maude had functioned as a live-in housekeeper.

Alex Holt never used the word nurse, unwilling to admit he was disabled, but that's what Maude really was. The actual housekeeping was done twice a week by a cleaning service, and Tía Sanchez came in to prepare the meals.

"Good morning." Claire tried for a cheery voice as she unlocked the front door.

"You missed church, honey," her father said as Maude lowered his wheelchair down the two steps into the gallery. "Is anything wrong?"

The older woman winked, her brown eyes crinkling at the corners. Maude was built like a tombstone with a square, flat chest and hulking legs, but she had a quick smile and a great sense of humor. She had to have or she wouldn't have lasted all these years with Claire's father.

"I didn't mean to worry you, Daddy. I overslept. Sorry."

He wheeled his chair over to Wild Horse, leaving Maude and Claire behind. He gazed at the bronze that been her mother's prize possession, a piece Claire knew he hated because it reminded him of everything her mother had achieved, then had thrown away for another man. Claire had kept it all these years and gave it the prime spot in the gallery because it represented the high standard of work she wanted in her gallery.

And it reminded her of the mother she'd loved and still missed even after all this time.

Whenever she looked at Wild Horse, she remembered the loving patience with which her mother had taught her young daughter about Southwestern art. Even though Claire was grown now, there was a part of her that remained a child who longed for the nurturing companionship of her mother.

What would have happened had mother lived? Claire wondered.

Finally, her father said, "I called you last night. You never called back."

Maude rolled her eyes upward as if inspecting the gray bangs that hung across her forehead. It was her way of saying Alex was in one of his moods. When he was in a snit, nothing could be done to appease him. Waiting him out was the only alternative and both women knew it.

"It was too late to call," Claire said, resenting her father's attitude. She refused to account for every move she made. Her father would overwhelm her if she allowed it.

She loved him and understood why he'd become so bitter. Fate had dealt him a cruel hand. First her mother betrayed him, then just as he was adjusting to life without her, a devastating stroke deprived him of the use of his legs.

He spun around to face her, pivoting the wheelchair with amazing dexterity. "Were you out with Seth again?"

Claire shook her head, saddened by the hopeful expression on his face. Nothing would make her father happier than having her marry Seth. Alex longed for grandchildren—especially a grandson who would one day inherit the bank.

A successful attorney, Seth was perfect in her father's eyes. But Claire had never been serious about Seth, and now that she knew he'd lied, she had no intention of going out with him again.

"You were working late again, weren't you?" Her father's tone was once more accusatory.

"Don't be hard on her, Alex," Maude spoke up. "Claire's business is as important to her as the bank is to you."

Her father's huff clearly said he had his doubts. He had tried to talk Claire out of reopening The Rising Sun Gallery.

He didn't want her following in her mother's footsteps. If he had his way, she'd be a vice president at the bank.

With a flash of red, Seth's Ferrari pulled up to the curb, and Claire stifled a groan. She itched to question Seth about his version of what had happened at The Hideaway, but she reminded herself that she couldn't. Not only didn't she want her father to find out about this mess, she had promised Zach that she would keep quiet.

Wearing a lightweight navy sport coat and tie, Seth breezed into the gallery. A smile spread across her father's face, but Claire caught Maude's slight grimace and realized the other woman didn't particularly care for Seth. By Taos standards, which were Western and extremely casual, Seth with his expensive sports car and Harvard ties, stood out like an orchid in a weed patch.

Seth might not have fit in with the local "look," but he had fit right into the business community. Alexander Holt, impressed by Seth's status as a Harvard law school graduate, had paved the way for the attorney who had practiced briefly in Los Angeles, before moving to Taos. Even with her father's help, establishing a lucrative law practice in Taos hadn't been easy. Most wealthy people came from other states where they already had attorneys, but Claire gave Seth credit for working hard and not relying on the money he'd inherited.

"Claire, you're all right," Seth said the second he saw her. "Whew! I've been so worried. What happened to you?" Then he spotted her father across the gallery and walked toward him. "Hello, Alex. What do you think of all the excitement?"

Claire braced herself. Her father hated surprises especially when they involved anyone close to him. He liked to believe those closest to him confided in him. She wished she'd had the opportunity to break the news to him.

"Excitement?" her father asked with a smile for Seth.

"You mean Morrell's murder? I'm just surprised someone hadn't bumped him off before now."

Seth's attention was focused entirely on her father, which wasn't unusual. "Why'd he have to get himself killed at The Hideaway? Now that creep, Zach Coulter, is on the case. I was out at Max Bassinger's working on a real estate contract and Coulter barged in, asking questions."

"I was dead set against giving that troublemaker the job," her father said. "He isn't worth a damn."

Claire couldn't resist; she despised Zach, but she refused to attack him behind his back when he was trying to help her. "Personally, I'm glad to have Zach Coulter on this case. Do either of you seriously believe Ollie Hammond is capable of conducting this investigation?"

"Well, the police chief did find the hit and run driver who bashed into Irma Pacheo's van," Maude put in. "Of course, the man's front fender was hanging half-off."

Seth frowned at Maude. Claire knew he didn't care for the woman, never really understanding her wry sense of humor.

Her father glowered at Claire. "Mark my words, Coulter will screw up this case. He hasn't got what it takes."

"That's the truth," Seth agreed. "He isn't even looking for the killer. He's just trying to drag innocent people into the mess like Claire and myself."

"What?" her father's voice boomed through the gallery like a volley from a cannon.

"Seth and I went to Hogs and Heifers to hear Flash and the Rusty Roots," Claire said, determined not to let Seth put his slant on the events. "The drink had hit me pretty hard. I went to the restroom, and when I came out, I couldn't find Seth."

"I looked everywhere for you. How did you get home?" Seth asked.

"A friend gave me a ride." Now this was stretching the truth. At dawn she'd hitchhiked home, catching a ride with a man who was delivering fresh-baked bread from the pueblo's famous outdoor ovens.

"Why on earth would you go to Bam Stegner's place?" her father asked.

"It was my idea." Seth's voice was smooth. "The Rusty Roots is the best band to play here in years. Half the town went to hear them."

Her father didn't look convinced, but since it was Seth's idea, there was little he could—or would—say to criticize.

"I read in this morning's paper that someone had stolen Bam Stegner's bear," Maude said.

Her father scowled, his brows forming a deep V. "Claire, you didn't."

"I swear. I did not take Khadafi, and I don't know who did."

Their conversation was interrupted by a couple interested in baskets from one of the pueblos. Claire explained that she had baskets, but since pueblo Indians weren't nomadic, they did not need woven baskets to carry their belongings the way the plains Indians did. Instead pueblo tribes crafted exquisite pottery.

She led them to the back of the gallery where she had a display of distinctive black and white pottery with intricate designs from the Acoma Pueblo. While the couple examined it, and the other pottery by the talented Diane Reyna from the Taos pueblo, Claire heard Seth and her father making plans for lunch. A few minutes later, they left, saying they were going to lunch.

As soon as the couple bought a modestly priced vase, Claire dashed out to get the dogs. Lucy was asleep, but Lobo's watchful eyes tracked her every move. When she went back into the gallery with the dogs at her heels, Nevada was waiting for her.

She mustered a smile, but the familiar surge of anger pulsed through her. She'd discovered Nevada, nurtured his talent only to have him desert her fledgling gallery for Duncan Morrell.

Nevada smiled at Claire, and she had to admit he was a handsome charmer who knew how to merchandise himself. His jet black hair was in long, sleek braids, which hung from behind his ears to the middle of his back like a Sioux warrior's. As usual, he wore leather jeans so tight they squeaked when he moved. The belt circling his trim waist was multi-colored woven horsehair with a silver buckle the size of a saucer.

His Navajo mother belonged to the Lost Hills clan, but she'd married a Cherokee blackjack dealer who was part Irish. They had lived in Las Vegas, so when their son was born, he was named Nevada Murphy. Always one who'd pursued commercial success with frightening determination, Nevada dropped his common last name when he began painting.

His warm blue eyes were a sharp contrast to his gloss-black hair and copper-colored skin. He used his eyes and his wide, disarming smile to get what he wanted. And Claire knew exactly what Nevada wanted—to be the next R. C. Gorman.

"How've you been?" Nevada asked with another smile.

"Fine," Claire said, recalling he'd barely nodded at her two nights ago when she and Seth had been seated near Nevada at Stegner's club on the night Duncan Morrell had been brutally murdered. Duncan's death had changed everything. She knew exactly why Nevada was here—smiling for all he was worth.

"Looks like Artistic Impressions is going to be closed for a while," he said. "I don't know if Duncan Morrell's wife will reopen it."

Claire shrugged, stubbornly refusing to give Nevada the opening he wanted.

"Next weekend is the Rodeo de Taos and Art Festival," he said, as if she weren't totally aware of the event which officially opened the tourist season. He looked at the gallery walls, then stated the obvious, "You don't have a showcase artist yet."

"I don't need one," she informed him. "I have a few Navajo wedding blankets I'll be hanging. I'm showcasing Jim Lightfoot's collection of drums."

"I'll help you, Claire," Nevada said quietly. "You can sell my oils."

She knew that this was as close as an apology as she was likely to get from Nevada, but it didn't change her mind. He was uniquely talented, and extremely marketable, but she refused to get involved with him. As soon as opportunity knocked, he'd dump her again.

"I can't help you, Nevada, but someone will. Try one of the other galleries."

"You need me," he said with more than a hint of sarcasm, "yet you won't help me. I did what I had to do, what was best for my career. You're just being stubborn."

"How many prints did you authorize Duncan Morrell to make?" she asked.

Nevada hesitated. She had warned him about Duncan's ethics. If Nevada authorized a hundred reproductions of an original, Morrell probably flooded the market with thousands. No doubt he'd pocketed the money without telling Nevada.

"I let him reproduce two dozen originals."

"Two dozen?" She tried to calculate how many Duncan might have reproduced legitimately, and how many more he undoubtedly counterfeited without Nevada's permission. "That's overexposure and you know it. Now each original oil will be worth less."

"Duncan thought—"

"Duncan Morrell only took care of himself," she insisted, once again amazed at Duncan's ability to charm people. Women adored him, even famous actresses like Vanessa Trent, she thought, recalling Vanessa's stricken expression when she'd learned Duncan had been murdered. Fools *were* born every minute.

Nevada's face turned sullen. "Most tourists can't afford originals. Prints are a gold mine."

"Not anymore. Now they're quicksand. Remember all those galleries the Beverly Hills Police department shut down because they were selling phony prints? The galleries eventually reopened, but who do you think got hurt? The artist."

"No one ever proved Duncan was involved in that scandal. He wouldn't ruin my career," Nevada insisted. "He was going to make me a star."

That was the trouble with Nevada, she thought. An ego the size of the *Hindenberg*. Duncan Morrell would have kicked babies aside to make a dime. Ruining Nevada's career by flooding the market with phony prints wouldn't have given him a second thought.

"I can't help you, Nevada. Maybe someone else will, but I need an artist with an unblemished reputation."

Zach waited behind the gallery, knowing Claire closed at five on Sundays. He had questioned Angela Whitmore and her studmuffin whose name was Carleton Cole, about Roofies. They had been at the table closest to Claire and had bought a round of drinks. Angela said she didn't know what Roofies were, and he believed her.

Cole claimed he didn't either. Zach would bet a month's wages the kid was lying. He had a California driver's license, so Zach had called a buddy on the SFPD and asked him to check various databases in the state.

Claire came out of the gallery, both dogs at her heels. When she turned to lock the door, Lobo spotted the Bronco and flicked his tail quickly, as close as the dog ever came to wagging his tail. Zach put up his hand as if halting traffic, signaling Lobo to stay where he was.

Turning, Claire saw him and stopped. He knew she was thinking about last night. He almost laughed, remembering the look on her face when he'd walked out on her. It was almost worth the sleepless night he'd spent.

"I need you to come out to The Hideaway with me," he told Claire when she walked toward her Jeep. "I want you to verify a few things before I take down the crime scene tape."

"All right," she agreed with obvious reluctance.

"I'll follow you home, so you can leave the dogs."

He drove behind her dusty green Jeep out of the plaza area of Taos and through a neighborhood where the yards were enclosed by coyote fences. The tall sticks had been broken off cottonwood trees, then hammered into the ground, providing crude barriers around the adobe houses. Clusters of wildflowers grew between the sticks along with clumps of rabbit brush, its bright yellow flowers in full bloom.

Claire turned down a gravel lane well-known in the area for its rambling haciendas surrounded by acres of meadows. The homes dated back to the previous century but had been purchased by wealthy people and modernized. It was the most secluded, exclusive part of town. Few coyote fences here. No, sir. High adobe walls cloistered these compounds.

Nothing like the Golden Palms trailer park where Zach had grown up.

He parked his Bronco, then waited in the shade of a towering cottonwood while Claire took the dogs inside. He leaned back against the seat and closed his eyes for a moment, wondering if he'd ever catch up on his sleep. He must have dozed off for a second. Suddenly, Claire was at his window.

"Lobo's gone wild!" she screamed. "He just attacked me!"

Eight

Zach was out of the Bronco in a second, not believing Lobo had actually attacked Claire. But her eyes were blazing, and she was trembling. He fought the urge to put a protective arm around her shoulders, knowing she wouldn't welcome it.

"He didn't bite you, did he?"

Claire shook her head, letting out a quick breath. "No, he didn't actually bite me. I went around to the front gate to pick up the mail. I'd forgotten all about it yesterday. As we were walking up to the gate, Lobo started acting strange. He growled at Lucy and she ran off across the road. Then for no reason, he began growling at me. I said, 'Easy, boy.' That's when he snarled and bared his teeth."

Suddenly, sweat peppered the back of Zach's neck. "Lobo was trying to tell you something." He walked around the oleander bush that had blocked his view of the adobe wall surrounding Claire's house. In front of the arched gateway leading into the yard was the mailbox. Lobo was standing between the mailbox and the gateway, facing the bushes across the narrow lane. A harsh growl rumbled from his throat directed at Lucy, who was cowering under a bush.

"Lobo," Zach called. "What's the matter?"

Lobo stopped growling and trotted up to him, but his hackles were up, raising his thick coat like a brush.

"He's dangerous and unpredictable," Claire said. "It's the wolf in him. He made friends with Lucy, then he turned on her in an instant. After what she's been through, the last thing Lucy needs is a huge dog terrorizing—"

"Quiet!" Zach dropped to his knees, so he could look into the dog's eyes. "You were trying to warn them about something, weren't you?"

Lobo looked past him, his eyes on Lucy. The retriever was crawling out from under the bush. Lobo growled twice, low guttural sounds that sent Lucy scrambling backward.

"That does it! He's dangerous." Claire stomped off toward the house. "You get him out of here."

In a flash of gray fur, Lobo was between Claire and the adobe wall, snarling and snapping at the air. She halted, leveling angry eyes at Zach. In two strides, he was beside her.

"Don't take another step." He grabbed her arm and pulled her away from the wall. "He's trying to warn you. Let me check it out."

The sun was slipping behind the mountains, casting warm light on the adobe wall, but cloaking the yard in long shadows. Zach put his hand on Lobo's collar and as he edged through the adobe archway into the yard, Lobo willingly came with him. Zach took two cautious steps down the tiled footpath toward the front door, inspecting the deep shadows and the bushes.

Nothing.

Zach looked over his shoulder at Claire. Naturally, she hadn't listened to him. She'd crossed the road, which was nothing more than a narrow, unpaved lane flanked by mesquite bushes growing wild. She was trying to coax Lucy out. Lobo saw what was going on and barked once. Lucy burrowed even further under the bush.

"You're afraid for her, aren't you, boy?" Zach said to the dog. "Something around here could hurt her, right?"

Lobo cocked his head and looked up at him. Dogs had

an acute sense of smell and hearing. Being a quarter wolf, Lobo's senses were even more finely attuned to danger than most dogs. What was bothering him? It didn't seem to be in the yard, and the house had a sophisticated alarm system, which hadn't been triggered. But he clearly wanted Lucy across the street.

Zach returned to the arched gateway, not certain what to tell Claire. As he passed the mailbox mounted on a post, Lobo halted, then took a step toward the mailbox, growling.

Claire walked up beside Zach. "Something's in there."

Zach stepped toward the fancy wrought-iron box, and Lobo blocked his way, snarling furiously. "It's okay, Lobo. I'm not going to touch it." He backed away and the dog stopped snarling.

Claire touched his arm. "A bomb? Do you think Stegner—"

"Ssssh." He saw Lobo's ears twitch, a quick contraction—nothing more. Most people would never have noticed it, but Zach knew what to look for. The dog heard, rather than smelled, trouble.

"The nearest bomb squad is in Albuquerque, isn't it? That's hours away."

"Damnit, be quiet. Let me think."

Claire stopped talking, but her expression said she didn't consider him mentally capable of adding two plus two. Zach ignored her, listening to the sound of the aspen's leaves, which fluttered with the rumor of a breeze. Somewhere a meadowlark called, but what he heard was the increasing silence typical of sunset when the birds stopped singing and the breeze became a memory. From under the mesquite bushes a few crickets were tuning up, but there was nothing threatening in those sounds.

The dog's ears cocked forward again, and Zach listened intently, guessing what Lobo's keen ears had detected. "Go stand by Lucy," he told Claire.

"Aren't you going to call the bomb squad?"

"Surprise me. Just once do what you're told without asking a bunch of questions." He grabbed her by the arm, and hauled her across the dirt road. Lobo followed, then positioned himself in front of the bush where Lucy was hiding, blocking her escape.

Zach rushed back to the Bronco. He kept a high-powered rifle in a rack attached to the ceiling, along with a pair of binoculars. In the glove compartment was the Glock he'd bought when he'd been on the force in San Francisco. He pulled out the gun, then jumped out of the car. He snapped a skinny branch off the cottonwood and hurried back to the mailbox.

This time Claire had stayed put, and both dogs were out of the way. He approached the mailbox, the long stick in his left hand, the gun in his right. The last rays of sunlight were on the large mailbox. He stood off to the side and hooked the stick in the latch. His hackles up, Lobo growled, standing on all fours in front of the bush.

With a flick of the stick, Zach snapped open the latch. A glistening blaze of brown and black shot out like a long streamer. A huge diamondback rattler, Zach confirmed his suspicions as it sailed through the air and landed on the dirt with a *thunk*. He fired, once, twice, but the damn thing was so fast and so pissed off that it was halfway across the road before the third bullet ripped its head off. Even then, it kept moving, sidling sideways toward Claire and the dogs. It stopped at Claire's feet, stone dead, its rattles still clicking . . . clicking.

"Oh, my God," she cried, her hand over her mouth, closing her eyes.

Zach shoved the gun into his belt and walked toward the snake. He breathed a sigh of pure relief. Damn all, he wasn't nearly as fast as he once was. He'd been in the country too long.

"Six rattles, a big one," he said, striving hard to sound

casual. "Guess he wasn't too happy cooking in the mailbox in the hot sun."

"He would have bitten me on the face or neck—"

"Then he would have hit the ground and attacked Lucy," Zach told her. "I guess Lobo doesn't look so vicious now, does he?"

"No," Claire admitted. "You're a very smart dog." She turned her hand outstretched, but Lobo had disappeared under the bush. He was licking Lucy's muzzle and she was licking him back.

"Look's like she's forgiven him." He gazed at Claire. "You might try saying thanks."

A strange, faintly eager look flashed in her eyes for a moment, but he couldn't tell what the look meant. "Thanks, I—"

He decided her guard was down and put his arm around her. Claire jerked away as if the damn rattler had bitten her.

"Bam Stegner did it," Claire insisted. "It's just the sort of sneaky thing he would do."

"Okay, hot shot, try proving it."

The fire was back in Claire's eyes, even more intense now. "Stegner gets away with so much. It's sickening. Obviously, you can't do anything about him, so I'm going to—"

He was in her face in a second, grabbing both arms and hauling her so close their noses bumped. "Listen to me. You're not doing a damn thing. I have plans for Stegner. I'll take care of him."

"How? What are you going to do? I want to be in on it."

Zach didn't have a clue about how he'd fry Stegner's ass, but he'd think of something. The trouble with swearing to uphold the law was that—too often—the law didn't work. Yet when people took the law into their own hands, all hell broke loose. Still, anger burned, welling up inside him from some dark, primal place. There was no stopping it with words or arresting it with common sense. His feelings for Claire had nothing to do with reason.

She would have been bitten by a deadly snake on a country road where no one would find her until the poisonous venom paralyzed her or killed her. Sometimes he thought she was the only woman on earth who was right for him; at other times, he hated her, despising her snobby attitude.

Still, he dared anyone to try to hurt her. Bam Stegner had crossed that line, and now, nothing but revenge would appease Zach. But he'd be damned if he'd let Claire know how he felt.

"What are you going to do?" she prodded in an irritating way that implied he didn't have the balls to take on Stegner.

"I'll let you know when the time comes. Now put the dogs in the house. We're going out to The Hideaway."

Claire was certain she appeared calm as Zach drove into the parking lot at Hogs and Heifers. She'd fed the dogs and changed into jeans while Zach had dumped the rattler into the trash bin. Time had done little to calm her; the tightness in her chest remained along with a heightened sense of tension. She could still see the deadly snake hurling out of the mailbox.

She ought to thank Zach and sincerely tell him how much she appreciated what he'd done, but the words wouldn't come. After the way she'd behaved last night, wantonly kissing him and pressing against his virile body like some two-bit hooker, she might give him the wrong idea if she was too nice to him. And, to tell the whole truth, she was afraid to let down her guard. Being cold was the only way she could cope with Zach Coulter.

She grudgingly admitted he wasn't all bad. True, he was crude and often vulgar, but he had a few good points. He thought on his feet. Had it not been for Lobo's warning and Zach's skillful handling of the situation, the rattler would have bitten her.

"Is Bam here tonight?" she asked as they pulled into the parking lot.

Sunday evening at Hogs and Heifers wasn't the club's busiest night. A few dusty pickups were parked in the asphalt lot where weeds flourished between the cracks. It was early yet; she was positive Bam's diehard crowd would appear later.

"Stegner's in Santa Fe picking up a new stereo system. He figures he'll attract a lot of tourists this summer." Zach put the car in park and came around to her door, a gesture she found oddly gallant considering. She leaped out of the car before he could open the door. "Let's go around back to the restrooms," he said, as her tennis shoes hit the ground.

Long shadows darkened the path around the side of the club to the disgusting excuse for a restroom that Claire remembered from her one—fateful—visit to the club.

Zach stopped outside the wooden door with the crudely painted picture of a fat pig wearing a ballerina's tutu and a sleek heifer with breasts like soccer balls. Disgusting. And so like Bam Stegner who reduced all women to stereotypes—fat pigs or willing bimbos with huge boobs. Claire ignored the Hogs and Heifers sign and faced Zach.

The growing darkness and the shadows concealed his expression except for the glint of his blue eyes. She had the unsettling feeling that he was thinking about the way she'd kissed him last night. Every time she looked into his eyes for more than a second, she was reminded of that scorching kiss. She intentionally studied the toes of her sneakers.

"Okay," Zach said. "You were standing here when you came out of the restroom and looked for Seth. Do you remember what you saw?"

Claire struggled to concentrate, but it was hard with Zach standing so close. She peered into the deepening shadows made even darker by the shade from the cottonwoods towering over The Hideaway. The sun was nothing but an afterglow on the horizon, the moon visible above Taos Mountain. With the disappearance of the sun, the temperature had dropped, the summer more of a promise than a reality as was usual in June.

"It was cool like it is now, I remember that," she told him. "I glanced around, but didn't see Seth. I looked over there," she pointed toward the shed visible in the distance, partially concealed by a thicket of trees and brush.

"Did you go near the bear's shed?"

"No. It was after midnight. I knew Khadafi was gone." She closed her eyes a moment, trying to remember what had attracted her attention. She struggled to straighten out her thoughts but everything was muddled. "I heard a laugh. A man, I think. I walked toward the first bungalow."

"Where did you see Seth?"

"He was standing down there by the fifth adobe," she said, clearly recalling the image of him, the moonlight catching his blond hair as he stood by a crumbling adobe bungalow.

"You're sure? Bungalow number five?"

"Positive. See how it's at an angle?" She pointed toward the fifth bungalow. "He was standing in front of the door talking to someone inside."

"Who?"

"I couldn't see. The person was in the shadows." Claire waited while Zach evaluated what she said, noting the bright yellow crime scene tape around bungalows two and three.

"What happened next?" Zach asked.

Claire walked toward a cottonwood whose lowest branches were far above her head. "I walked this far and felt dizzy. I leaned against the tree and closed my eyes.

Then I heard a man calling my name. I assumed it was Seth. Later I realized my mistake."

"Come on," Zach said. He led her to the bungalow and tore away the strip of yellow tape that was across the door to number two. He motioned her into the room, but she held back, unwilling to actually look at the room again. She remembered it from the cold light of early dawn when she'd awakened alone.

Zach snapped on the light switch, flooding the small room with glaring light. The bed was nothing more than a cot with a tattered chenille spread that had slipped between the bed and the cracked plaster wall that was thirty years overdue for a fresh coat of paint. A single window, its glass painted black, was flanked by heavy plastic blackout drapes. The chair was covered in fabric that might once have been a bright rust but now had faded to a tan with darker stains splotching the seat.

Claire closed her eyes for a moment, struggling to imagine herself in this dingy room with the mysterious stranger. Despite the disgusting setting, it was a powerful, erotic memory. Then a complete blank as if she were looking into a black hole.

"I tried the lights," she said weakly, opening her eyes. "They didn't work."

"The forensic team from Santa Fe put in the bulb," Zach told her. "Your wallet was found between the bed and the wall, caught in the spread."

She remembered awakening and seeing her purse in the chair. It hadn't occurred to her to check for her wallet. "Where were my panties found?"

"On the back doorknob inside the bathroom."

She groaned out loud, not needing to walk into the small bathroom. Too well she remembered the tiny room with nothing more than a rust-stained sink and a toilet tank without a lid. "I went to the bathroom before I left. I didn't see my panties."

"Did you look?"

"The place was so filthy. There was a cockroach on the sink. All I wanted to do was get out of there. I think I would have seen them, but I guess I didn't."

Zach looked at her strangely for a moment, then said, "Too bad you didn't bother to check for your wallet."

Nine

Zach glanced sideways at Claire, who was seated beside him. She hadn't said anything since they'd left The Hideaway. Seeing that filthy room and realizing what she'd done—with a total stranger—had badly upset her.

For too long now, Claire had acted bitchy, waltzing around town with her snoot in the air, pretending never to notice him. She thought she was too good for him; she always had. Years ago, she'd liked him, but he'd always known part of his appeal was being dirt poor and having a bad-ass reputation.

Now, Claire thought he was a crude bastard, an image he deliberately cultivated by cursing and doing his best to disgust her. Seeing that room in The Hideaway had reminded her of what she'd done, so she could hardly priss around acting so superior. She'd made love to a man she couldn't remember.

And she'd willingly done it.

Zach almost laughed out loud. He stared into the headlights of an oncoming car, but his mind wasn't on the traffic. It was on Claire. He could smell a faint trace of floral perfume, the unique brand she dabbed behind her ears and on the pulse point at the base of her neck.

He took a deep breath, inhaling the provocative scent and imagining the other places she'd sweetened with perfume. The thought alone made his body respond with a rush of heat. He could just see her on his bed, her sexy body naked on the tangled sheets, her wild blond hair across his pillow.

With a quick glance sideways, he saw the gentle rise and fall of her breasts. Her nipples thrust against the sort fabric of the blouse which was knotted at the waist. He could almost taste those tight buds and smell the sweet perfume laced with spice that she sprayed between her breasts. Untying that blouse and claiming every inch of her luscious body with his mouth would be his first move.

His heated groin muscles contracted with an upward surge. Christ! What she could do to him even if he wasn't touching her. He struggled to be rational. For the hundredth time he wondered what made this woman so appealing.

She didn't give a rat's ass about him. Never had. Never would. So? Who cared? Claire was a challenge. That's all she'd ever be to him. Any man crazy enough, stupid enough to love her would get his balls cut off in a New York minute.

"Zach," Claire said unexpectedly, breaking into his thoughts. "Ah . . ."

He sat up straighter, the hard heat in his jeans making him uncomfortable. Aw, hell. Why deprive himself just to tease Claire? Last night he'd proved how hot she was for him. Tonight, he'd get her where she belonged—beneath him.

"Did you find . . . ah . . . anything else in that room besides my wallet and underwear?"

It took a split second for him to realize what she wanted to know. When he did, he let her dangle, hardly able to resist the urge to laugh. "A few cigarette butts beneath the bed. They looked old, but the crime lab will let us know for sure."

"That's all?"

He deliberately took his time answering as he guided

the Bronco around the corner onto the narrow lane where Claire lived. "The tecs vacuumed the room, collecting evidence. They probably picked up a lifetime's worth of fibers and hair and God only knows what else."

"Was there anything in the wastepaper basket?"

Again, he almost laughed. Prissy Claire. Why couldn't she just come out and ask? "What wastepaper basket? The Hideaway is a no-frills joint."

"Oh-h-h," she moaned.

"What did you think they'd find?"

"Well . . . I . . . was hoping they would find ah—you know—a prophylactic."

He jerked his head toward her. "A prophylactic?"

"A condom. Surely, you've heard of them. Maybe you're even smart enough to know about safe sex."

He pulled into her driveway and slammed on the brakes. There were times he'd like to lift her skirt and tan her cute fanny with his bare hand. She was so damn uppity and had a tongue that doubled as a lethal weapon.

He turned off the motor, then faced her, leaning close, and she plastered herself against the door. "Sweetcakes, I know exactly what prophylactic means. I'm just blown away by the way you talk. You sound like a Sunday-school teacher. Why didn't you just say condom or, better yet, life jacket. That's what they're calling condoms these days."

"Life jackets? That's, that's—"

"Appropriate, wouldn't you say?" He edged a little closer, silently cursing the console space between the seats. "Why don't you just come out and ask me what you really want to know? Did you have unprotected sex with a stranger?"

She swallowed hard and slowly shook her head. "If you didn't find one, I guess I must have."

"One?" He put his hand on her shoulder. She tried to pull away, but her back was already against the door. "Suppose it had been me in that dark room with you? For damn sure I would have screwed you over and over and over. A case of life jackets wouldn't have been enough."

She grabbed his wrist with both hands and pried his hand off her shoulder, saying, "You're disgusting."

"True. It's hereditary," he said and was rewarded with a slight squint, which meant she was royally pissed. God, he loved teasing her. He ran one finger slowly along the strip of bare skin exposed by the blouse knotted at the waistband of her jeans. She squirmed, trying to move away, but there was nowhere to go. He traced the soft flesh across her midriff with the pad of his fingertip, moving a fraction of an inch at a time, then back again so slowly his finger barely moved.

"Don't—"

"No one can touch you, princess, least of all me. Is that what you're trying to say?" He flattened his whole hand against her bare skin, shoving his fingers up under the blouse. Her shocked gasp made him smile, and he grinned even more when she tried to stare him down. He didn't move his hand, even though his fingertips were temptingly close to the edge of her bra. Instead, he cupped his palm against the curve of her rib cage, savoring the softness of her skin and the heat rising to warm his hand.

"Stop calling me princess," she said, but the quaver in her voice gave her away. He was getting to her, and that sent a bolt of arousal lancing through him.

"You're right," he said, moving his hand slightly upward until his fingertips touched the bottom edge of her bra. "Princess sounds like some icy-cool type. That's not you, Claire. You've got the hottest pants in town. Screwing a total stranger—"

"It was the Roofie. You said so yourself."

True, but he was having too much fun baiting her to admit it. "Last night, I kissed you and you were all over me like a bitch in heat. You're just like your mother—so hot for a Coulter you can't keep your hands off me."

For a second, he thought she was going to punch him. Instead, she turned and coolly reached for the handle to open the door. He shackled her wrist with his free hand.

"You're not going anywhere until I say so."

"Let go of me—now."

His response was to move his other hand up a little until the soft fullness of her breast brushed his knuckles. "You know, last night you tried telling me what to do. Didn't work, did it?"

"You creep. What do you want?"

He released her, taking his hand off her rib cage and letting go of her wrist at the same time. "You know exactly what I want, so stop fighting me. You're in no position to give me a bad time unless you want everyone to find out your panties and wallet were found at the murder scene. Imagine how upset your old man would be. It'll probably put him six feet under."

"This is nothing short of blackmail," she said, shock and anger underscoring every syllable.

"True," he said with a reckless grin as he reached for the knot holding her blouse together. "Works for me."

He expected her to try harder to talk him out of it. After all, Claire was the type who could talk to a cigar store Indian for hours. But she didn't say a word as he untied the knot, then worked his way upward quickly unbuttoning the blouse.

He should have been ashamed of himself, but he wasn't. He'd wanted her so much, for so long that nothing was going to stop him from proving to Claire that at least on a sexual level, they were meant for each other.

He brushed the blouse aside to expose a lacy black bra. It was one of those Wonderbras that pushed up her breasts, making the cleavage even deeper. Her breasts weren't huge, and they weren't pumped full of silicone. They were smallish, but nicely rounded with pert nipples that stretched the lace. Sexy as hell.

He touched the clasp holding the bra together. "Hey, my favorite, a front loader."

"You jerk. You're going to regret this. I can't stop you now, but when the murder is solved, I'm going to fix you."

He grinned; she was so damn cute when she was pissed. "Fix me, huh? Sounds like a winner. I want you to fix me right now."

He grabbed her hand and shoved it down to his crotch. That got her. She let out a gasp that could be heard across the border in Texas.

"What do you think, babe? Bigger than the guy you screwed in The Hideaway?"

Her eyes narrowed and she squeezed her fingers around the turgid heat of his sex. His heart soared, then settled back to jackhammer against the wall of his chest. He was more than a little surprised. He'd expected her to be totally grossed out, but there was a teasing glint to her eyes. She squeezed him again, harder this time.

"No, you're smaller, much smaller than the sexy man in The Hideaway."

She was lying through her teeth, but he didn't call her on it. Amazing. Claire Holt had more guts than he'd thought. He was positive this crude move would send her flying out the Bronco's door screaming for her daddy.

"He had the most incredible technique," Claire informed him as she slowly moved her hand up and down. "He wasn't like you. He was sweet, sensitive, and unbelievably sexy. The perfect lover."

He yanked her hand away from his erection. His little stunt had backfired. Instead of being upset, she was trying to turn the tables on him. And it was working. If she had kept moving her hand, he would have lost it like some horny teenager.

"I thought you didn't remember very much about that night."

"I don't." She gave him a coy smile. "But I had the

distinct impression that he was a very good person as well as an accomplished lover."

If he hadn't been so close to losing control, he would have laughed. But rather than let her get the better of the situation, he hauled her into his arms. He kissed the curve of her neck where she had sprayed perfume. It tasted as sweet as it smelled, and he brushed the tip of his tongue across the soft skin.

She didn't put her arms around him, but she let him kiss her. He took his sweet time, nibbling his way downward while his hand roved up to cradle her breast. He stroked the nipple with his thumb until it was a tight, hard bead straining against the lace fabric.

Claire tilted her head to one side with a sharp intake of breath followed by a soft sigh. Who in hell did she think she was fooling? He smiled inwardly as he turned his attention to the other breast.

When he'd coaxed the other nipple into a firm peak, he thrust his tongue into the hollow between her breasts. Then with agonizing slowness, he withdrew it, then edged it into the narrow channel again. The rasp of his tongue against the tender skin elicited a shudder from Claire. Suddenly, her arms were around him, her nails digging into his back.

"You don't want me at all, do you?"

"You're blackmailing me into this, you bastard," she muttered.

"Bastard? Watch it, Claire. Next thing you know, you'll be using four-letter words like a truck driver."

There was just enough moonlight filtering in from the window to see her close her eyes and catch her bottom lip between her teeth as he cupped her breast in his hand, the taut nipple hard against his palm.

"You're not a very good liar," he whispered into her ear. "I'd give anything to see how you act when you admit you're crazy about a man."

She didn't respond, and she didn't open her eyes either. Her breasts were rising and falling more rapidly now, the moonlight playing softly across the pale skin and filmy black lace. God, he loved those Wonderbras. Her breasts were thrust upward, all lush fullness and impressive cleavage. Again his tongue delved between the pliant mounds, then he slowly withdrew it only to plunge back again with even more force. The move was intended to suggest another, more intimate penetration.

"Your breasts are really sensitive, aren't they?" he commented as he unhooked the clasp on the bra.

"Yes," she whispered softly, taking him by surprise because he hadn't expected her to admit it. "Very sensitive."

His blood beat against his temples and the swelling hardness confined by his jeans ached to be set free. But with those physical reactions came a primitive elation that he remotely acknowledged as masculine pride. He had her number, all right. And she had his, came an echo from some distant part of his brain.

He ran his hand over her bare breasts. Freed from the contraption known as the Wonderbra, they were smaller, with a less pronounced cleavage. But still, they were the sexiest, most erotic breasts he'd ever touched. The nipples jutted upward, dusky-rose in the moonlight and begging to be kissed.

He lowered his head and took one hard nipple into his mouth, applying a touch of suction as he ran his tongue over the tight bead. Claire arched against him and furrowed her fingers though his hair. The sensation of having her in his mouth—finally—was exactly as he had imagined. Only better. He never knew he could be this aroused. The iron heat of his sex was almost painful now, but he wasn't going to rush something he'd waited so long to get.

He lifted his head and stared into her eyes. They were wide open and dark with desire. Her lips were parted, her tongue peeking out from between her teeth. She was aroused and slightly awestruck, and that sent another heady surge of excitement through him.

He whisked the pad of his thumb over the damp nipple that he'd been kissing. "When I touch you here, you feel it some place else, don't you?"

Again she surprised him by answering, "Yes . . . yes."

"I'm real good at blackmail," he said. "An expert."

He sounded cocky as hell, but he didn't care. He had her number. She knew it; he knew it. Yet something was missing. He was suddenly consumed by a yearning ache for her to kiss him.

He hadn't kissed her tonight, having chosen instead to make his point another way. He could kiss her now, and she would respond by passionately kissing him back. But the desire to have her kiss him had nothing to do with sex. Longing rose, swift and sure, from some place deep inside him, revealing a galaxy of uncharted emotions that he refused to fully explore.

He could say he was blackmailing her, and on some level he was, even though she willingly responded to him. He had an emotional, gut-level need for her to make some gesture to him. He gazed at her, more than a little shocked at his feelings, and time halted, seconds fragmented and became a full minute while neither of them moved or said a word.

Under his breath, he cursed himself. Since his first sexual experience at the age of thirteen, Zach had controlled his feeling for women. Only one had gotten to him—and had gotten the best of him. Claire.

He'd be damned if he'd let it happen again. So what if she didn't kiss him. Who cared?

Wonk! Wonk! The sound of the Bronco's horn cut through the still night while its headlights flashed off and on. Aw, hell, Zach silently cursed as Claire pulled away from him.

"What's wrong?" she asked, covering her bare chest with her arms.

Zach struggled to ignore the thrusting pressure of his arousal as he flicked on the radio. "There's an emergency. When the radio's off, the car's specially wired to alert me."

By now she had her bra hooked and was buttoning her blouse. Talk about bad timing. He picked up the transmitter and gave his call sign, then waited to see what the night dispatcher thought was so damn important.

"We've got a Code 49 here at the station," the dispatcher informed him.

"Code 49?" Zach repeated, certain he must have misunderstood. This was a secret code used to circumvent the numerous hackers who loved to listen to the police radio calls. When something needed to be kept top secret, Code 49 was used. The only other time he'd heard it was the night Duncan Morrell had been murdered.

"That's right, Sheriff. Code 49. Get back to the station."

Facedown on the cool floor of her pantry, Angela Whitmore eyed the sleek vibrator that Carleton Cole had stuck between the two bottles of extra virgin olive oil that she'd had flown in from Italy last week. She hadn't bothered to try either of them, she thought as Carleton worked on her, smoothing rose petal lotion over her naked body.

Nothing was working anymore. Nothing seemed to alleviate the profound boredom that weighed her down like a slab of concrete. Cooking, her great love, no longer seemed worth the effort. And kinky sex with young hard bodies, once an obsession with her, now made her irritable.

Carleton tried so hard to please her that it was embarrassing. True, she craved kinky sex, but being slathered with rose lotion on the limestone floor of her pantry, surrounded by bags of jasmine rice and chains of dried garlic, was not her idea of great sex.

What was? She had absolutely no idea—anymore.

Except for art, nothing interested her. She adored collecting Southwestern art. In the long run, it would prove to be much more rewarding than sex with men young enough to be her sons. But would it pull her out of this profound funk?

"How do you want it babe?" Carleton asked.

Angela hadn't realized they were quite at that stage yet. Actually, she much preferred the vibrator, but didn't say so. Carleton had been so touchy since the night Duncan Morrell had been murdered. Undoubtedly, he regretted investing his meager savings in the prints Duncan had touted. She'd warned him to invest only in originals, but, of course, Carleton hadn't listened.

"Doggie style," Angela said over her shoulder. She couldn't bear to look at him and wished he'd just disappear like so many other young studs who'd waltzed through her life, but she didn't have the heart to throw him out just after he'd learned his last dime had been invested in phony prints that weren't worth the price of the paper they'd been printed on.

Mercifully, it was over in seconds. Carleton helped Angela to her feet, then solicitously wrapped her in the silk robe that he'd tossed over a bag of rice. She followed him as he went out of the pantry and down the hall into the music room. He quickly punched a button. The CD he loved started playing.

Oh, God, Angela thought. Did she have to hear that Charlie Daniels' song again? How much fancy fiddle playing and "fire on the mountain, run, boy, run" could she take? The last line of that phrase always bothered her.

The devil's in the house of the rising sun.

It reminded her of Claire Holt's Rising Sun Gallery. Claire was having a tough go of it. Her gallery had been so promising until Nevada deserted her. It still had some very nice David Tzuni jewelry and pueblo pottery, but Claire was desperate for an artist.

Perhaps Claire needed financial assistance. Angela knew Claire had enough pride for a dozen women. She'd refused to take money from her father. A wise decision, Angela decided, remembering her own father's domineering attitude. He'd rejected more suitors than she cared to remember. No one was good enough for his daughter.

Now that her father was dead, Angela had more money than she could spend, but she could still hear his dire warning. *They're only interested in your money.* She didn't doubt he was right as she watched Carleton Cole tapping his bare foot to the music.

Buck naked he was as gorgeous as an Italian statue. But not nearly as interesting. Tomorrow she'd ditch him and see if Claire needed a loan or help or something.

"I'm going to have blue balls for a week," Zach muttered under his breath as he shouldered his way through the door into the station. He couldn't believe his damn luck.

"What in hell's the Code 49 all about?" he asked the night dispatcher.

Toby Clements had worked the night shift for thirty years, outlasting five sheriffs and countless deputies. His bald head glistened under the fluorescent lights as he tipped his head sideways toward Zach's office. Through the open door, Zach saw a man with salt and pepper hair sitting at his desk with his feet up on the memo tray.

"A Feebie," Melvin said, his voice low.

"FBI? Crap!"

There were several FBI field offices in the state, more than the population or the number of crimes justified, but any felony committed on an Indian reservation automatically became a federal crime. Then the Feebies coordinated their efforts with the tribal police—not the sheriff.

"He's not just any Feebie," Melvin added. "He's the Gallup SAC."

"The SAC? Christ!" Duncan Morrell's murder had to be the reason the Special Agent in Charge of the Gallup office was here. But why Gallup, not Albuquerque? Gallup was a smaller, less important field office.

Zach had the uneasy feeling that Claire Holt was in a lot more trouble than he'd realized.

Ten

"You're in my chair," Zach informed the SAC as he strode into his office.

"Sorry," the agent replied. He came to his feet and stood aside while Zach plopped down. "I'm Special Agent Brad Yeager from the Gallup office."

"Yeah, who'd you cross at headquarters to get banished to the res?"

Yeager barked a laugh, but Zach saw he'd struck a nerve. The agents assigned to the reservation posts were usually green rookies who could count on several years of mind-numbing boredom before they were reassigned to more active, interesting positions. Not many crimes were committed on the reservations. When something happened, it was usually handled by the tribal police, who were Native Americans and had the trust of their people, leaving the Feebies to sit around and push paper.

"I read your murder book on Duncan Morrell." Yeager sat in the chair opposite Zach's desk. "Very impressive. We don't usually see small-town sheriffs using homicide procedures so effectively, but then, you were a top-ranked homicide detective, right?"

Zach was pissed but tried not to show it. He always kept "the book" right on his desk where T-Bone, his deputy, could add to the notes on the crime, but he hadn't anticipated a Feebie would waltz in and read it. But then, what did he expect? He'd worked with the FBI on a couple of cases. In his experience they were an arrogant bunch.

"Yeah, I worked homicide in San Francisco. What's your interest in the Morrell case?"

Yeager studied him a moment, his expression serious. "The bureau's been investigating Morrell in connection with a print fraud scam. Now he turns up dead. It's entirely possible one of the members of the counterfeit art ring killed him."

"Is the FBI going to be officially involved in this case?" Zach prayed the answer would be no. If the Feebies horned in, he wouldn't be able to protect Claire.

Yeager smiled, or tried to. The gesture came off as more of a quirk of the lips. "Not officially—yet. The counterfeiters are costing the artists and gallery owners millions. We'd like to put this ring out of business. Why tip them off by telling them the FBI has an interest in this case?"

Zach nodded, hoping he didn't look as relieved as he felt.

Yeager scooted his chair forward and rested his arms on the edge of the desk. "Let me level with you. I know you resent having the FBI around, but I can help you. I've been with the force for over fifteen years." Yeager tried another smile; this one worked better. "You were right. I got crosswise with the brass in Quantico. I want out of Gallup. This is my chance. Let's work together to put this ring out of business and catch a killer."

Zach nodded slowly. This was an offer he couldn't refuse. He had nothing more than a green deputy and the State Police crime lab in Santa Fe. With the FBI's resources, he'd have a much better chance of solving the case. "Thanks, I could use the help."

"What's your gut instinct on this?" Yeager asked. "Who killed Morrell? That Holt woman?"

A cold knot formed in the pit of Zach's stomach. He

did not want Claire to be a suspect. "No. She didn't kill
Duncan Morrell."

Yeager raised his eyebrows. "Hell hath no fury like a
woman scorned. Morrell stole her prime artist. According
to your notes, she's just about two steps from bankruptcy.
Kill your main competitor and get back the artist."

"Nevada offered to come back to Claire Holt, but she
refused to represent him," Zach said, silently blessing
Claire for mentioning Nevada's visit to her gallery.

"Really? That still doesn't eliminate her. According to
your notes, there was very little in the room where Morrell
was shot, but next door you found the Holt woman's wallet."

"True, but she was probably in there for a quickie.
That's what goes on at The Hideaway."

Yeager didn't look convinced, but Zach didn't elaborate.
There was only so much that he was going to tell about
what happened to Claire in that room.

Yeager took off his jacket and rolled his cuffs up to his
elbows. "Maybe we should start with the bear. Stealing him
was the first crime committed that night. Do you think
they're linked?"

"They're not connected," Zach said emphatically.

"I take it the bear was a cause celeb around here. Cham-
pioned by Claire Holt, right?"

"Yes, she made a lot of noise about the bear, but she
didn't take him."

"No? Do you know who did?"

"Let's just say that someone told me where Khadafi is,"
Zach hedged. This was getting sticky. He didn't trust
Yeager enough to tell him the whole truth. Nothing was
more dangerous than a Feebie trying to resurrect a career.

"Where is the bear?"

"Where no one can touch him without causing a major
political incident."

Yeager chuckled. "He's on the reservation somewhere.

Clever. The Indians have gotten so touchy about their land, no one would dare to try to take anything off the res."

"And no one in Taos wants the bear returned to Bam Stegner. So don't even think about—"

"Hey, don't look at me." Yeager held up his hands as if surrendering. "The FBI doesn't need any more bad press. I'm not interested in giving a toothless, malnourished bear back to an ex-con like Stegner. It would serve the son of a bitch right if he disappeared like the bear."

"True," Zach mumbled, a plan forming in his mind. The bastard had planted that rattler in Claire's mailbox. Zach refused to let him get away with it, but until this moment, he didn't have a good idea about handling Stegner.

"Okay, forget the bear. Let's concentrate on motives. Who wanted Morrell dead?"

"Good question." Zach raked his fingers through his hair. "Half the town had reason to kill him. Bad real estate deals, inflated prices for art, get-rich-quick schemes that made Morrell rich, but no one else. You name it."

"What about his wife? Your report says they were in the midst of a bitter divorce."

"Her alibi checked out," Zach answered, reaching for the murder book. "I just haven't had time to enter it."

"I'm a numbers man," Yeager explained as Zach made the entry in the spiral notebook. "Statistics say murder is a crime of passion or a crime of greed. If we rule out the wife and the Holt woman, then we're left with greed. That's what I'm banking on anyway. Greed involving those phony prints. Either one of his partners bumped off Morrell or someone was upset about getting stuck with worthless lithographs."

"Makes sense, but I'll add another possibility. Nevada Murphy. He authorized Duncan Morrell to produce a limited number of lithographs of his oils. Evidently, Morrell produced thousands. It's damaged Nevada's reputation, and prices for his originals have plummeted."

"He's the logical candidate," Yeager agreed, "but your murder book says he has an alibi. Two women tied him to the bedpost. Didn't untie him till dawn."

Zach shrugged as if to say: Go figure. He was having a hard enough time trying to get one woman into bed—let alone two.

"The FBI checked a number of Nevada's prints," Yeager informed him. "They have phony certificates of authenticity and the artist's signature. It takes state-of-the-art laser equipment to reproduce the certificates and the artist's signature. You don't report finding that equipment when you searched Morrell's house."

"No, and his wife claims she doesn't know a thing about it."

"Okay, what about the other suspects?"

"I started with the people I knew were at the club earlier that evening like Angela Whitmore. She's a wealthy art collector with a taste for buff studs young enough to be her sons. Her latest, Carleton Cole seemed suspicious to me. He'd recently invested in some of Morrell's prints, and they turned out to be phony. I'm running his name through the data bases in California. You could help by getting on this immediately."

Yeager reached for his jacket and pulled out a small notepad. He jotted down the information.

"Then there's Seth Ramsey. His account of what happened that evening and Claire Holt's version aren't the same. It's just a vague feeling I have, but something hits me wrong about Ramsey. He doesn't have an alibi either."

Claire stared at the gallery's inventory list. Sparse, she thought, determined to keep her mind off Zach Coulter and the little scene in his Bronco the previous evening.

What she had to offer wouldn't be very impressive on Friday night when all the galleries were going to have open houses to celebrate the beginning of the Rodeo de Taos. Cowboys from all over the Southwest came to compete, attracting hordes of tourists. To take advantage of the influx, the galleries staged the Art Festival, keeping their shops open Friday evening and serving refreshments.

Claire had arranged for a selection of treats from Tortilla Flats, and had hired one of their bartenders to make their trademark Cuervo Gold Margaritas. But the best food in the world couldn't make up for not having a premier artist.

Maybe she'd let pride get in her way. Perhaps she should have taken Nevada back and dealt with his print situation later. Well, it was too late now. Lowell Hopkins, owner of the River Spirit Gallery across the plaza had snapped up Nevada.

Claire had a marvelous selection of jewelry, including some really fine Old Pawn. The jewelry had been made for the Indians' own use and was at least half a century old. When times were bad, they had pawned it for cash. The detail in the silver and the fine turquoise made the Old Pawn more valuable than most of the modern jewelry.

But Claire was always on the lookout for fresh new talent. Tonight she'd be featuring jewelry made by David Tzuni. He had creativity and a fine eye for detail. She had no doubt that one day his jewelry would be as coveted as Old Pawn.

She ran her pencil down the list of kachina dolls that she was offering. The elaborate wood carvings had originally been made by the Hopi Indians as religious art, but now they were collectors' items. Even though souvenir shops sold cheap kachinas for a few dollars, Claire carried only the best. They were sculpted from a single root and hand painted. Of the four hundred kachina spirits, more than half were available at The Rising Sun.

She was checking through her list of rugs and *yei* blankets, trying to reassure herself that she would have enough to interest people, when Suzi appeared at the entrance to the alcove that was her office. Her part-time worker knew little about Southwestern art, but she was cheerful and eager to learn.

"There's a man out here." Suzi kept her voice low. "He says Quentin Reynolds sent him. Should I know this Reynolds guy?"

"No. He was one of my art teachers at U. of A. He's managed a lot of galleries over the years," she said, rising.

She walked into the main room of the gallery, then halted so quickly that Suzi bumped into her. It couldn't be! A man with a full, bushy beard was studying Wild Horse. He was so interested in the bronze that he didn't notice her.

The man wasn't as tall as the one she remembered from that night in The Hideaway. He wasn't as powerfully built either. This man had a lean, almost gaunt look, not at all the image she had, but considering the effects of a Roofie, her mind might have exaggerated certain things. But not the beard. She was positive about the beard.

She pulled Suzi into her office before the man looked over and spotted them. "Call the sheriff," she whispered. "Tell him a man with a beard is at The Rising Sun Gallery. He'll know what I mean."

Suzi looked puzzled, but reached for the telephone as Claire left. In the main section of the gallery, the bearded man was now inspecting a Cochiti drum. He tapped lightly on the rawhide stretched taut over the small, hollowed-out log.

"Beautiful sound, isn't it?" Claire said as she approached. "Hypnotic, really. You should hear the Corn Dance at the Cochiti pueblo when they're beating dozens of these drums at once." She came to a stop beside him and extended her hand. "I'm Claire Holt, owner of the

Rising Sun Gallery. I understand you're a friend of Quentin Reynolds."

He shook her hand. "I'm Paul Winfrey."

Close up, Claire saw the man had dark brown eyes. His full beard was several shades darker than his eyes, the color of his hair. He was an attractive man, but he didn't have that distinctive strength of personality and presence she always associated with Zach Coulter.

"I took a one-day workshop from Quentin Reynolds. I told him I wanted to live in Taos, and he suggested I contact you," Paul said.

"Really? You're an artist?" Claire folded her arms across her chest to keep from trembling and looked down at her toes. An artist. She'd been praying for one, and now, in a blast from the past, her mentor had sent one. An artist who could very well have been the stranger in the dark room. "When did you get in town?"

"Thursday evening," he said, and she stopped staring at her shoes and met his gaze, realizing he had been in town on the night she'd gone to The Hideaway. "It took me a while to find a place I could afford. I'm renting a trailer at the Golden Palms."

Claire took another look at the flashy cowboy boots she'd put on that morning. The Golden Palms. She immediately saw the dusty dump of a trailer park whose only saving grace was a tall pine tree. Zach Coulter had grown up in a rusted old trailer at the rear of the Golden Palms. Calling it a dive would have been the ultimate compliment.

"Where is Quentin these days? I haven't heard from him in some time." Claire intended to contact her old friend and see what he knew about this man.

Paul shrugged. "I don't know. He's on the road, I think, lecturing to aspiring artists. Teaching a class here and there."

Claire slowly nodded, disappointed that she couldn't speak personally with Quentin, but she believed Paul was telling the truth. Quentin Reynolds was a gifted teacher with a unique ability to spot talented artists. He'd lost his battle with the bottle several years ago. Last she heard, he was drifting around, getting work where he could.

"Miss Holt, here's a message for you," Suzi said as she walked up and handed Claire a note.

Claire quickly read it and silently applauded Suzi's creative way of letting her know the sheriff was in the field. He couldn't possibly get here in time to question this man about The Hideaway. She thanked Suzi and stuffed the note into her pocket.

Was this the same man, or was this merely a coincidence? It was possible that this man had spent a night or two at The Hideaway. It was almost as cheap as the sleazy rental trailers at the Golden Palms. It was also possible that he'd had sex with her and left while it was still dark, never getting a good look at her. If that was the case, she didn't want him to find out who she was.

She wanted that night behind her forever, knowing she had made love to a total stranger. And enjoyed it—what she could remember anyway. She'd been lucky. Most women had terrible experiences when someone slipped one of those pills into their drinks. Roofie or not, she'd done something that would always shame her.

"Do you want to see my paintings?"

He was looking at her strangely, obviously puzzled by her reaction. He brushed his bangs back from his forehead with an impatient thrust of his hand. She had the impression that he was a proud man. By hesitating and not asking to see his work, she'd offended him.

"Of course, I'm dying to see your work. I drifted off there for a second, wondering about Quentin. He's helped so many people. I just wish someone could help him."

"You're right," Paul said. "He turned my life around."

Claire smiled at the quiet sincerity in his voice, excitement building. Could Quentin have sent her the artist she'd been praying to find? "Let's look at your work."

"They're out in my truck," he said. "I'll get them."

She watched through the gallery window as he hurried out to a dusty blue pickup that was nothing more than rusted metal held together with Bondo. The front fender was attached to the grill with baling wire. He returned to the shop with two rolled-up canvases under his arm.

"Two? That's it?"

"I'm just getting started." He unrolled one canvas and spread it out over the glass case where she kept jewelry, then quickly rolled the second out beside it.

Claire looked at her silver-spangled boots, telling herself not to expect too much. Alcohol might have pickled Quentin's brain by now. Two canvases did not make a body of work necessary to launch an artist. Six to ten was bare minimum. She eased her eyes open and peeked at the first one.

It was a cowboy on a horse, his hat pushed back slightly to reveal his face. This was a very familiar gesture. Cowboys considered it rude to hide their eyes when speaking to a lady. This man was handing a bunch of purple wildflowers to a woman on a palomino. His expression was so charged with longing that it made Claire inhale sharply.

It was an emotional painting, but cloaked in mystery. The woman's face was turned away just enough to conceal her features. And it was impossible to tell if the man was returning after a long absence and offering the flowers as a token of his love, or if he was leaving the love of his life forever.

The other oil painting was equally as moving. It was a man and a woman walking into a meadow in the high country. A brilliant blue sky domed overhead and aspens dressed for the fall in shimmering gold covered the hills, but it was their expressions that riveted the viewer. Were they affirming the love known only to soul mates, or was some unseen force driving apart two people who could love only each other?

Stay calm, Claire told herself. This isn't a body of work. It wasn't even close. Yet here was the uniqueness, the raw talent it took to be a world-class artist.

Paul was now staring down at his boots, and she knew he was nervously awaiting her judgment.

"Your work is fabulous, truly fabulous. I need to ask you a few questions before deciding if I can represent your work," she said, and his smile vanished. "Where have you shown your work?"

"Nowhere."

"Have you allowed anyone to reproduce them as prints?" she asked, then held her breath.

"No. These are all I have."

Thank you, Quentin, and bless you wherever you are. "I'll represent your work," Claire said, realizing this was the opportunity of a lifetime. In the form of a bearded man.

Eleven

Paul Winfrey hadn't been gone for more than ten minutes when Vanessa Trent bounced into The Rising Sun. If possible, the blond bombshell was more beautiful than ever. The morning after Duncan's murder, the actress had been stunned by news of his death, but judging by the smile on Vanessa's face today, she'd gotten over it.

"Wow! Your gallery looks different. You must have changed it for the Art Festival," Vanessa said.

"Yes. Tomorrow night's our big night. I hope you're planning to come." Claire would have to stay up all night to rearrange the gallery—again—to properly display Paul's paintings, but she didn't care. This was the artist she'd been waiting all her life to discover.

"I wouldn't miss it," Vanessa assured her. "I'm a little nervous, though. Do you think there'll be trouble?"

"Trouble? What are you talking about?" Claire asked, knowing Vanessa tended to be overly dramatic.

"Gang trouble like in LA. A gang of chokes got Bam Stegner."

It couldn't have happened to a nicer guy. Then a prickle of unease waltzed down Claire's spine. "A gang of chokes? You must mean *chukes.*"

Vanessa rolled the baby blues and jiggled her breasts, a gesture that had made her a prime-time queen. "That's it. *Chukes.*"

"It's Latino slang for bad boys. Around here, a gang just means a group. Did they cause problems at Hogs and Heifers?"

This time Vanessa kept her eyes wide as she whispered. "No. The *chukes* kidnapped Bam Stegner, beat him up, then tossed him into a ravine out by the pueblo."

"Is he all right?"

"Yes. He's at the tribal clinic." Vanessa shrugged. "The first thing I did when I heard about it was call the sheriff. I'm out in that big hacienda all by myself. I want more protection. Those *chukes* could try to kidnap me."

In a heartbeat, jealousy, the green-eyed monster as old as time itself, shot through Claire. Vanessa would use Bam's troubles to get Zach Coulter's attention. Not only was she drop-dead gorgeous, but Claire understood the power that Vanessa wielded on a different level. Who could resist making love to a woman that millions of men had seen on television and dreamed about luring into their beds?

Fine. Let the actress have Zach. It would keep him away from her. Somehow the thought did not console Claire. The elation she'd experienced at finding a talented artist evaporated.

"I wouldn't worry, if I were you," Claire said, her tone as level as she could make it. "We've never had gang problems. I don't think you're at risk, and I'm positive they won't do anything to disrupt the Art Festival."

"Speaking of art," Vanessa said, the *chuke* threat apparently forgotten. "You don't have any paintings to show, do you?"

"Tomorrow night, I'll be showing a brand-new artist's oils."

"Really?" The actress appeared more flustered than interested. "Well, I want to help you. I have a number of lithographs you can sell."

"Nevada's," Claire guessed.

"Yes. I bought quite a few from Duncan Morrell."

Claire hesitated, not wanting to offend a potential customer. Having *the* Vanessa Trent at her gallery during the Art Festival would certainly help business. And the actress raked in a bundle between her TV show and personal appearances. She should be investing in original art like Paul Winfrey's.

"Lowell Hopkins across the plaza at the River Spirit Gallery is representing Nevada now. You should give him the opportunity to sell those lithographs."

Vanessa's lower lip went into a pout that had undoubtedly served her well over the years. "But Claire, you and I are friends. I hardly know Lowell Hopkins."

She isn't much of an actress, Claire thought. Obviously, Vanessa had already offered the lithographs to Lowell. He'd owned the River Spirit Gallery for years. He was too shrewd a businessman to risk his reputation by selling questionable lithographs.

Actually, she had been shocked to learn that Lowell had taken on Nevada. In the last few years, the fifty-something man had surprised people several times. It all started when he married a woman half his age. He accompanied Stacy to local bars like the Neon Cactus. Claire had seen them at a table near hers the night Seth had taken her to hear Flash and the Rusty Roots.

"I'm sorry I can't help you, Vanessa. Too many of Nevada's prints are of questionable authenticity."

"How can you tell without seeing them?"

"Even if I saw them, I couldn't tell if the certificates were forged or not. Laser scanners are so sophisticated these days that they can duplicate a certificate and an author's signature. It takes special equipment to tell the real ones from the fakes. That's why I'm dealing strictly in original art. Charcoals, watercolors, acrylics and oils, but no prints."

"You're saying Duncan cheated me." Vanessa's baby

blues weren't primed for a photo opportunity now. They were narrow with barely concealed anger. "He would never have done that. He adored me."

"I'm sure he did." Vanessa was the type of woman men flipped over. But how was it that Duncan Morrell managed to fool so many people? Nevada was convinced Duncan would never harm him either. That must have been the secret of his success. Duncan possessed a good-ole-boy charm that made people feel special. Then he took them for all they were worth.

Obviously, Vanessa was among Duncan's conquests. She'd been distraught at the news of his death. Come to think about it, this was the first genuine emotion Claire had ever seen the actress show. True, Vanessa was a world-class drama queen who played every moment for all it was worth, but Duncan's death had stunned her.

"Vanessa, if you wish to sell those prints, take them to the Art Institute in Santa Fe. They have a machine that can verify the certificates. They'll give you a letter saying the lithographs are legitimate."

"Good idea," Vanessa said as she turned and hurried out of the gallery.

The actress was in such a rush that she didn't notice Zach Coulter parking his Bronco in front of the gallery. Claire stifled a groan, remembering she'd had Suzi call him about the bearded man. Now, though, she didn't want Zach bothering Paul Winfrey.

If he had been the stranger at The Hideaway, he'd certainly given no indication he knew her. Forgetting the whole thing seemed to be the best plan. She certainly wasn't going to tell anyone else about that night. It was bad enough she'd had to tell Zach Coulter.

Zach sauntered through the door, thumbing his Stetson to the top of his forehead. Just like the cowboy in the picture, she thought, except this man wasn't bringing flowers. Even so, her pulse thrummed at the sight of him.

"Okay, so where's the dude with the beard?" Zach asked, with a maddening hint of irreverence.

"He just left, but it was a false alarm," Claire replied as Lobo and Lucy trotted out of the back room to greet Zach. "I'm certain he's not the man from The Hideaway."

She was extremely conscious of Zach's virile appeal. Each time she saw him the pull was stronger and stronger. Her feelings for him were intensifying, and she didn't like it.

"What makes you think he's not the man?" Zach leaned against the jewelry case, a relaxed pose that was somehow sexy. With one hand he patted the dogs who were brushing against his long legs. He was looking at her with what appeared to be a casual gaze, yet his eyes were sharp and assessing. No doubt, he'd mentally stripped her down to her bra and panties—if he'd stopped there.

Claire looked at the toes of her boots, then realized she had spent too much time today staring at her shoes. It was a nervous habit, one she'd tried unsuccessfully to break. She made herself look up and meet Zach's gaze.

His eyes were as blue as the mountain sky, but the shadows under them said he wasn't just tired. He was exhausted. She noticed a small cut near his left eye. It hadn't been there last night. The knuckles on one hand were scraped raw. She was positive both his hands had been fine last night.

"I heard some gang roughed up Bam Stegner," she said, and was instantly annoyed at the breathless sound of her voice.

"He's got a few bruises and a broken jaw," Zach said. "Sounds like a drug deal gone bad. What do you think?"

"I think you did it. Bam made up the *chuke* bit because he's embarrassed or scared or both."

"*Moi?*" he said with a naughty little boy's grin. "Take the law into my own hands? Go on, you can't believe that."

Her gaze locked with his, and suddenly, the rest of the

world seemed very far away. There were the usual noises from the busy plaza and the smell of fry bread in the air, but somehow the sounds were muffled and the aroma was faint. This had happened to her before, she recalled. There was something so compelling about Zach that the rest of the world disappeared when she was around him.

He chose that moment to treat her to one of his engaging, sexy smiles. She battled the urge to smile back, but that didn't diminish the charged connection between them. If anything the sexual chemistry intensified.

Get a grip, Claire. Get a grip!

She knew if she gave in to the forbidden impulse to surrender to this man that she might very well lose her heart. To women like Vanessa Trent and men like Zach Coulter sex was a game. He used sex to tease Claire and threatened to blackmail her just to get what he wanted. Obviously, to him, sex was fun; it was a challenge, but didn't involve love or commitment. Claire never had been able to separate the two. Maybe that's why she had so much trouble handling Zach. She had made love to few men. Those she had, she truly cared about.

Had Zach ever loved anyone, she wondered. She had seen him around town with different women several times in the year that she'd been back. She didn't know anyone who'd actually gone out with him, but she couldn't help hearing gossip about him. Everyone seemed to think he was "exactly" like his father, and Jake Coulter had been notorious for his affairs.

The word "exactly" bothered Claire because her father always told her she was exactly like her mother. But she wasn't. She had her own distinct personality. She sensed that Zach was his own person, too. But she had to admit he had the same virile appeal his father had possessed.

Just thinking about the way Zach had kissed her made her angry with herself. Why, she'd let him undo her bra. Allowed him kiss her breasts. Heat inched up her neck at the memory and a shiver of longing ran through her like a dangerous riptide.

"Earth to Claire. Come in, Claire." He waved his hand in front of her nose. "I asked you what makes you think this guy with the beard isn't the man in The Hideaway?"

Claire shrugged, thankful to be discussing the case again. "I can't say why exactly, but my sixth sense tells me Paul Winfrey is not the man."

"Where's he from?"

"I got the impression he'd drifted from one job to another. Then he met an old friend of mine who teaches art," Claire said, unable to keep her excitement out of her voice. "Paul's the artist I've been hoping to discover. He's ten times more talented than Nevada. I'll be featuring his work tomorrow night at the Art Festival."

"Great," Zach replied, but the word sounded flat. "Did you check him out with your friend?"

Claire explained about Quentin's problems, then added, "Despite his drinking, Quentin really knows talent."

Zach stood up straight, crossed his arms and stared hard at her. "Doesn't it strike you as suspicious that this bearded man suddenly appears? No past history. No personal references. Nothing."

"His work speaks for itself."

"Yeah. Ted Bundy and John Wayne Gacy were artists."

"Paul Winfrey is no serial killer. He's a man who's just discovered his true talent, and I intend to be the one to bring his genius to the public's attention."

"Then you won't mind if I check out the genius. Where's he staying?"

Claire hesitated, then said, "Paul's on a tight budget. He rented a trailer out at the Golden Palms."

For an instant his gaze sharpened, and she wondered what he now thought about his old home. These days, Zach lived on the opposite side of town. She'd never seen his home, but anything was a step up from that trailer park.

He gave Lobo another pat saying, "I'm outta here. I have a couple of stops to make."

Claire watched him leave and climb into his Bronco. Undoubtedly one of his calls was Vanessa Trent. Let her have him, she told herself, but there was a sour feeling in the pit of her stomach.

By the time Zach drove along the weed-choked road into the Golden Palms, he was all kinds of pissed. The reverence in Claire's voice and the light in her eyes when she told him about this Paul Winfrey had gotten to him. She was nuts about the guy. He'd bet anything, she thought he was the "perfect lover" from her night in The Hideaway.

What a crock!

He'd lost all sight of reason when it came to this woman. Last night after he'd left the Feebie, he'd found Bam Stegner. It had taken a couple of punches and one solid left hook to persuade Stegner to leave Claire alone.

What a hoot! Stegner had covered his ass with some wild story about being kidnapped by a gang of *chukes* from Santa Fe. Zach had a few bruised ribs, knuckles that hurt like hell, and a small cut on his cheek, but it was worth it. Claire would be safe from that bastard. Not that she would thank him for it. She had too much pride and latent hostility for that.

Visiting the Golden Palms didn't improve Zach's mood. Why in hell would anyone name a dusty gulch with one lousy pine tree the Golden Palms? Must have been a sick joke.

The joke was on him, Zach thought as he brought the Bronco to a stop in front of Rufus Allen's double-wide trailer. How he hated this place. When he was a kid, he used to pretend he lived on one of the big ranches outside of town. He dreamed he had two horses, a pack of dogs and the meanest tom cat west of the Pecos.

And parents who loved each other.

The reality had been much different. His father had spent most of his time roaming the hills taking photographs, and his mother didn't care about anything except the bottle.

He walked through Rufus's cactus garden. It hadn't changed much since Zach had been a kid. Even the weeds looked the same. He knocked on the screen door. No doubt, Rufus had his fat butt planted in front of the television as usual. The manager lived to watch soap operas.

"Well, lookie here. Zach Coulter, you old dog, you," said the fat man with the grease-stained T-shirt.

Just hearing Rufus made Zach feel like a kid again. A poor, mixed-up kid, acting tough to hide his insecurities.

"I'm looking for Paul Winfrey," Zach said.

"Did he do something?: As usual, Rufus was suspicious, but then, thirty-odd years as manager of the Golden Palms had given him reason to be suspicious.

"He's doing business with a friend of mine. I just want to meet him."

"He rented number seventeen over yonder."

Before Zach could thank him, Rufus lumbered back to his soap opera. Zach walked across the park with a quick look at the space where he'd grown up. Another trailer was there now, and wash was hanging from a line, indicating someone had a baby. Still, Zach could see himself there, hoping his father would come home and knowing his mother would pass out any minute.

The single-wide that Winfrey had rented was by far the worst trailer in a park that had more than its share of used, sorry-looking trailers. It was the kind of place most people never escaped from. Once you sank this low, you gave up.

Already Zach felt sorry for Paul Winfrey, but that didn't mean he was going to let him get too close to Claire.

The bearded man who answered the door was shorter than Zach and thirty pounds lighter. As usual Zach hadn't bothered with a badge, but the man gazed at him with more than a hint of caution.

"I'm Zach Coulter, a friend of Claire Holt."

The wariness vanished, replaced by a flash of teeth in the thick beard. "I'm Paul Winfrey. What can I do for you?"

Zach quickly sized up the man, a habit from his days on homicide. New clothes, cheap but brand new. New boots, too. Zach had a thing about boots that dated back to his Golden Palms days when he'd had to go around with holes in his boots. Winfrey's boots were new, but dirt cheap. The seams would split before the first snowfall.

Dilapidated pickup, new cheap clothes, a trailer at the Golden Palms. Zach would bet his life that he knew why this man was so vague about himself.

"I'm the sheriff. I kind of like to get to know the new-comers," he said with a friendly tone, but at the word sher-iff, Winfrey's eyes narrowed slightly. "It helps prevent problems."

"I can assure you, Sheriff, I won't be a problem. I'm just a struggling artist. Claire's given me a break."

There was a slight crack to his voice and so much heart-felt sincerity that Zach almost slapped him on the back and wished him good luck. But first he had to know the truth.

"How long have you been out of prison?"

Winfrey turned and retreated into the trailer. Zach fol-lowed him, noting the cot that made beds in The Hideaway look like the Ritz.

"Once a con, always a con. There are no second chances."

"I didn't say that," Zach replied, feeling like a mean son of a bitch. "I just want the truth."

Winfrey faced him and stroked his beard. "I spent fifteen years at Vernon State Prison for second-degree murder. I killed a man in a fight in a bar when I was barely thirty. I served my time. I'm starting over."

Again there was the ring of truth in his voice and unmistakable sincerity. All Zach could think was—there but for the grace of God, go I. He'd been in plenty of fights in his time. He'd lived in this hellhole, too.

"Looks like you're making a great start. Claire believes in you, so you must be a winner."

Winfrey rewarded him with a smile.

Zach wished him luck and left. He hurried toward his Bronco with a quick glance at the space where he'd grown up. He stopped, looking at the reddish dust swirling around his favorite boots. Aw, hell. He could imagine himself living in this prison called the Golden Palms. Maybe Alexander Holt had done him a big favor. If Claire's father hadn't all but run him out of town, Zach might still be trapped here, going nowhere.

It had been a long uphill battle to make something of himself. Rented rooms in rundown boardinghouses, macaroni and cheese night after lonely night, blankets that were too thin on beds that were too hard. And when he'd graduated from the police academy—first in his class—no one had been there to be proud of him.

Zach gazed at the space where his trailer once had stood, wondering what his father would have said. Jake Coulter was proud of Zach's talent. He never expected Zach to become a sheriff, but he would have understood that a man had to support himself. If you were ever getting out of a place like this, you had to earn money.

Zach knew he was good at what he did. He might have chosen to be something else, but life hadn't given him much choice. Paul Winfrey didn't have much choice either.

He turned and strode back to Winfrey's trailer. Through the screen door, he saw the man at the small counter, opening a can of Beanie Weanies.

"Hey, Winfrey, there's a widow just outside of town," Zach said. "She travels most of the year and needs a house sitter. You interested?"

Twelve

Claire gazed out of The Rising Sun's window at the brightly lit plaza. The summer sun had drifted behind the tall mountains, cloaking the plaza in shadows even though the last rays of light glowed between the ridges of the buttes. Twinkle lights outlined the trunks of the graceful cottonwoods while piñatas hung from the higher branches. Marachis were playing in the gazebo in the center of the square. Later a rock band would take over and there would be dancing.

Her gallery looked as inviting as the plaza, she thought. It had taken her most of the night to rearrange it. Now Paul Winfrey's two oils had the prime spot directly in front of the door.

She tapped her foot to the beat of the guitar and squinted hard to see if there were people in Lowell Hopkins's gallery across the plaza. Most of the guests she expected to be interested in Paul were still at private cocktail parties. She couldn't tell if any of them had arrived at the River Spirit Gallery yet. Of course, Nevada would be inside with Lowell, waiting for customers to pay court.

With Duncan Morrell out of the picture, Lowell Hopkins was her main competition. She truly believed that Paul Winfrey was the find of the decade, a cut or two above Nevada. But what would everyone else think?

She had put exorbitantly high prices on Paul's paintings.

Was she asking too much? She'd justified the price to the horrified artist, telling him no one had seen art of this caliber in years. She wanted everyone to know how much she believed in his work.

It was a calculated risk, and she knew it. The paintings might not sell. If she later reduced the price, it would diminish the artist in the eyes of the art community and make it impossible to sell his paintings. Should that happen, she would be forced to close her gallery.

She heard Suzi greeting Paul and realized he'd come through the rear entrance where Lobo and Lucy were waiting. It was going to be too crowded tonight to keep the dogs inside. She'd told Paul to come at eight. She checked her watch and saw he was right on time.

"What do you think?" he asked rather sheepishly.

She hardly recognized him. Paul had shaved his beard and trimmed his hair. He was wearing different clothes. His jeans were of soft Tencel denim that looked old even though they were brand new. His chambray shirt was nicely cut and accented by a bolo tie with a hand-tooled silver clasp. His belt had a similar silver buckle. But it was his new cowboy boots that really shocked her. They were black snakeskin with the unmistakable cut-work design of Tres Outlaws.

Where did he get the money? She had advanced him a little cash for art supplies. Had he used the money for clothes? She resisted the urge to scold him. After all, image was the name of the game. Artists with a shtick were adored by the public. Competing on Nevada and R. C. Gorman's turf, Paul Winfrey was taking on two extremely popular Native American artists—the big leagues.

"You look terrific," she told him.

"He reminds me of Clint Eastwood," Suzi put in.

Paul shuffled his feet, but Claire agreed with her assistant. Paul did remind her of the actor in his younger years. Lean and rangy with rough, masculine features. Was he the man from The Hideaway, she wondered for the thousandth time. Her sixth sense told her that he wasn't, but a niggling doubt remained. What had happened to the bearded man?

"Zach says the public wants a star, so give them a star," Paul replied with a shrug that telegraphed insecurity.

It was the absolute truth; once, the art world hadn't been that way, but times had changed. Struggling artists were perceived as unsuccessful. "I guess you and the sheriff have gotten friendly," she said.

She had expected Zach to check out Paul, but obviously, they'd established some sort of a relationship. Sheesh! The last thing she needed was Zach Coulter telling her artist what to do.

"Zach's great," Paul said with a smile. "He got me a new place. I'm staying at Sylvia Henley's home while she's off in Europe. He lent me some money and helped me pick out the right clothes."

Claire attempted a smile but she was secretly upset. Every time she turned around, there was Zach Coulter. Of course, she hadn't seen him last night. She'd been at the gallery until dawn, but he hadn't called or come by to tell her what happened when he went to see Paul.

He must have gone out to Vanessa Trent's home to protect her from the *chukes*. Not that she gave a darn. Then she reminded herself to be totally honest. She'd made that pact with herself when she'd come home. Despite everything, some small part of her did care about Zach Coulter.

Paul broke into her thoughts. "Tell me what I'm supposed to do."

"Mingle with the guests and talk about yourself. Nevada goes into a whole number about his Sioux ancestors and how their spirits inspired him." The routine was so phony that it made her gag. Most people, especially women, went for it.

Paul looked at her strangely for a moment, then said, "Could I talk to you privately?"

"I'm outta here," Suzi said. "I'll take care of the couple who just walked in."

Claire led Paul to the back of the gallery where she had her office, an ominous feeling dampening her earlier excitement.

"Zach told me to tell you the truth," Winfrey said, and Claire waited, holding her breath. "I was in prison. That's where I met Quentin Reynolds. He came in one weekend to teach an art class."

Claire was too stunned to say a word. An ex-con. People would never buy his art, if they knew he had committed a crime. Oh, Lord, what was she going to do? The silence that followed was more than awkward. Noise filtered into the alcove from the gallery. People were arriving, happy chatter filling the air. The blender whirred as the bartender made margaritas. Neither of them said a word.

She stared down at the toes of the vampy sandals she'd selected for this special night, finally asking, "What were you in prison for?"

"Second-degree murder," Paul replied.

Murder, she thought, the worst possible crime. Why couldn't it have been bad checks or something that would be easy to explain away?

"Didn't Quentin think this would be a problem?" she asked, more thinking out loud than asking a question.

"Oh, yes. Quentin warned me, but he said that you could help me if anyone could. I wanted this chance so much that I wasn't going to tell you about my past. Zach said it was bound to come out eventually, so I should deal with it now."

She turned toward the rear entrance where Lucy and Lobo were poking their heads through the open door. "Let me think."

"I didn't mean to kill him," Paul said. "I punched him

and he went down. His head hit the side of the brick building."

"What were you fighting about?" she asked, ready to grab at any crumb of information that could be helpful.

"He wouldn't sell me back the mare I had sold him."

Great. A fight over a horse could cost this man a future as a renowned artist. A horse. She loved animals and had put herself at risk several times to help them, she thought, as she gazed at Lucy and Lobo.

She recalled rescuing Lucy from that terrible man. She could easily have misfired and hit him instead of the pit bull. At any given moment your life could be turned upside down. Unbidden the image of her wonderful mother in Jake Coulter's arms came into her mind.

Yes, at any given moment your life *could* be turned upside down.

"Why did you sell your horse if you wanted to keep her?"

"I needed the money." Paul's gaze was level, but there was an underlying current of emotion in his tone. "I thought he was going to ride her. Misty could run like the wind, and she had a soft mouth. Just a flick of the reins and she'd turn on a dime."

"What did he do with Misty?"

"He had several strings of mares that he kept in a miserable, hot barn in stalls not big enough to turn around." With every word the disgust in his voice intensified, and she saw that he could be scary when he was angry. "Misty was pregnant, her belly bulging with a foal. She should have been outside getting air and light."

"Why wasn't she?"

"It wasn't just Misty who was carrying a foal. They all were, and every damn one of them was in the dark in a box of a stall. He had them urinating into buckets. He collected the urine and sold it to a lab."

"To make Premarin," Claire said, the light dawning. She'd read about this in several animal rights publications she received. Urine from pregnant mares was used to make the estrogen replacement drug.

"Yeah. The worst part was the guy didn't give the mares enough water. That would have made them urinate more and it would have been more expensive to ship to the lab," he said with undisguised bitterness. "The mares were so thirsty their lips were cracked, and they'd fight like stallions over the one pan of water they were all forced to share."

"There's no excuse for the way they treat those mares," Claire said, fighting the lump swelling in her throat as she imagined horses being abused like this. "The drug can be made from plants or synthetically produced in a laboratory."

"I studied up on Premarin when I was in prison. I had plenty of time on my hands." He was frowning hard now and shaking his head. "They can make it in the lab, but they still torture mares. It's cheaper."

He'd certainly pushed the right button with her, she realized. Her next thought was that Zach had clued him in. He knew about her brush with the law to rescue Lucy. She had spearheaded the drive to get Khadafi away from Bam Stegner even though she hadn't been the one to actually steal the bear.

"I'd sold everything I had. My truck, my saddle and tack. I hocked the watch my daddy left me, just to raise the money to save Misty, but the jackass refused to let her go."

The raw emotion in his voice and his heartfelt words tore at Claire. This man had tried to help a beloved animal who was suffering cruelly. His efforts had backfired and he'd gone to prison. To hell.

"Do you know what the worst of it was?" he asked. "I never knew what happened to Misty. I'd lay awake at night in my cell and pray that she was free somewhere. Running in a field of clover, that's what I wanted to believe.

"But I knew it wasn't true. There's too much money in that kind of operation. Someone else took it over, I'm sure. Misty stayed chained to the wall, her belly bloated with one foal after the other. All the time she wondered why I'd done this to her."

Claire understood completely. She had spotted Lucy in a pen, next in line to be torn apart by pit bulls. She would have done anything, taken any risk to help her. If Lucy had died, she would never have forgiven herself.

Then she thought about Khadafi. She'd heard a rumor that Bam was using the bear for bear baiting. She had gone out to his club and found the bear chained to the wall of a shed behind the club.

The bear had cowered as she approached, but when she kneeled down and spoke softly, he had gazed up at her with big brown eyes that pleaded with her to end his suffering. The poor thing was toothless and so starved that it was almost too weak to eat the blue corn mush she had brought in a bowl.

How did bear baiters get any pleasure out of beating up a creature so defenseless, so weak?

She would have done anything, taken any risk to help the bear. But Tohono had stepped in, showing her another way. She had spearheaded the crusade to gather money to get the bear away from Bam Stegner. But someone else had broken the law to free the helpless bear. Paul hadn't been so lucky.

"If I ever get my hands on some real money, I'm going after the drug companies who look the other way while mares are tortured," he said, and she had no doubt he would do it.

"Here's what we're going to do," Claire said, quickly before the swell of tears in her eyes became the real thing. "Tonight don't mention anything about prison. If people ask you about your past, concentrate on what you did in the years before you were convicted. By the end of this summer, you will be launched as a premier artist. Then you'll call a news conference and give the details about your past.

"We'll play up the animal cruelty stuff. We'll get Zach to give the law-enforcement angle and tell how he helped you start over. Let's turn this into a positive not a negative."

The gratitude in Paul's eyes for her understanding and support made her smile at him with tender reassurance. But she knew this wasn't going to be easy. Too many ifs. If she could launch his career before anyone discovered the truth about his past. If she could manage to convince the public he was a good man despite having killed someone. If he stayed out of trouble with the law.

"Claire, I don't mean to interrupt—" Suzi poked her head around the corner "—but Tohono's here."

"It's all right. We've finished talking." She gave Paul another encouraging smile. "I want Tohono to meet Paul."

As she walked out into the gallery, Claire saw a few people had arrived and had margaritas. They were clustered around Paul's painting, discussing it. She looked over her shoulder while Paul awkwardly straightened his bolo tie.

Claire went up to Tohono who was standing apart from the group of tourists, studying the painting. "This is a pleasant surprise. I didn't expect you."

He turned to her, a slow smile spreading over a weathered face that was a testament to his will and wisdom. "Ah, Claire. I came especially to meet the new artist you have discovered and to see his work."

Claire managed to return Tohono's smile, but it was a struggle. Having a new artist was supposed to be a surprise. Only two people knew about it, Suzi and Zach. Since Tohono and Zach were very friendly, Zach must have told him. Criminy! Every time she turned around, Zach was there.

"Tohono, this is Paul Winfrey, the artist I'm featuring.

I wish I could tell you I had discovered him, but an old friend, an art teacher, sent him to me."

Paul extended his hand. Neither man said a word as they shook hands. Claire waited but did not speak. It was Tohono's turn to say something, and it would be considered rude by Native Americans for her to speak before he did.

Instead of addressing her, Tohono spoke to Paul. "I find your paintings most unusual. Both make the viewer ask questions. What is happening? What are these people thinking?"

Did that mean he liked them? Claire wondered. With Tohono, it was hard to tell. Years as governor of the pueblo, dealing with the white man, had made him master of the poker face.

"This I like," Tohono said to Paul. "Art that makes us question ourselves. You are very talented."

Claire wasn't sure whose smile was wider, hers or Paul's. As pleased as she was, she longed for an art connoisseur to plunk down money to buy a painting. Tohono had more power than most men, but his net worth didn't put him in a league with art collectors. Even if it did; the Taos pueblo was unbelievably conservative. They refused to install electricity or running water. There was no place for a white man's painting.

"I'm glad you appreciate my work," Paul said with a shy yet genuine smile that Claire knew would go over well with the public.

"I must be going," Tohono said. "These old eyes are no longer the eyes of the eagle. My pickup has to find its own way to the pueblo when it is dark."

He nodded to Paul and headed toward the back of the gallery. Claire went with him, realizing he must have parked in the lot behind the gallery. When they came up to the back door, the dogs jumped up, wagging their tails, and Tohono stopped. He looked at Claire with the world-weary eyes that had experienced so much.

"Claire, did you not heed my warning? Beware the coyote."

"I've thought a lot about what you've said, but I didn't understand exactly what you meant. Coyotes are tricksters and they're evil. Are you warning me that a friend or someone I trust is trying to hurt me?"

"My people believe the coyote was created at the same time The Great Spirit created the first man and woman. From the very beginning Coyote was in trouble. The first couple were carefully taking stars out of the blanket and arranging them in the night sky. Coyote came along and shook the blanket as a joke." He pointed upward where crystal-clear stars were just beginning to emerge in the mountain sky. "Look at the mess he made. There is no order in the heavens."

Claire had heard this story before, but did not commit the white man's sin of interrupting before an elder had finished his story, or saying she was familiar with the tale. Tohono was a wonderful person, but he was born to the Talking Water clan. She could very well be here all night listening to Coyote myths.

"Coyote has the unique ability to change shapes," Tohono continued in the measured pace he used. "He can be a man, then a woman—whatever suits his needs. Look at those around you, Claire. Ask yourself who does not wish you well, man or woman. Perhaps both."

She didn't want to insult Tohono by saying this was perfectly obvious. "Who do you think shot Duncan Morrell?"

Tohono looked up at the night sky with its haphazard arrangement of stars caused by Coyote. "A *chindi* killed the evil man."

"What?" she cried, then remembered who she was talking to before saying this was ridiculous. Tohono was a leader who deserved respect. He was trying, in his own way, to tell her something. She just wasn't getting the message.

Before she could stop him, Tohono walked across the parking lot to his pickup. He opened the door, stopped, and looked up at the night sky that spread wide and dark above the mountains, the stars nothing more than blazing pinpricks of light. From a nearby bluff a coyote's howl rose to the moon half-hidden behind a peak. Then from another ridge came a few yips that became a full-throated howl.

Two coyotes, Claire thought as Tohono drove off. Could two people have been involved in Duncan Morrell's murder?

Thirteen

Angela Whitmore walked into the River Spirit Gallery and was surprised to find so few people. She had deliberately missed the cocktail party before the Art Festival. Cocktail parties bored her, especially parties where the same people saw the same people and talked about the same things. Over and over.

Was it any wonder she was so . . . so what? Maybe she needed counseling. What she was experiencing went beyond simple boredom. She was adrift on an uncharted sea. She didn't know where she'd been, or where she was going.

Lowell Hopkins spotted her and came toward her with a solicitous smile on his face. Can it, Lowell. She had two of Nevada's originals already. They were worth less than half of what she'd paid Claire for them. She could thank Duncan Morrell for that. He'd printed so many lithographs of questionable authenticity that Nevada's reputation was in shambles. Why would Lowell bother to take on such an artist?

Before Lowell could reach Angela, he was intercepted by a beast of a woman in a dress that must have been designed by Omar the Tent Maker. Judging by the delighted smile on Lowell's face, the fat woman had pots of money.

"Good evening," a masculine voice came from behind her.

She turned and found Seth Ramsey offering her a glass of champagne. One look at the huge bubbles told her how cheap it was. *The finer the bubbles, the finer the champagne.* It was her father talking to her from the grave. Too often, especially lately, her father's elitist words kept haunting her.

"You look lovely as always," Seth told her as she took the glass.

"Thanks," she said, knowing Seth could bury the world in East Coast BS. Taking care of Taos was no problem. What did Claire see in him, anyway? He was pretty, almost too well-groomed. She suspected he had been a mama's boy.

"Where's your a-a-a . . . friend?"

"Carleton's over at the Neon Cactus," she said, glancing around the room. Stacy Hopkins, Lowell's wife, was nowhere around. She was probably in the back room of the Neon Cactus where they kept the kegs of beer, getting it on with Carleton. The two had been making eyes at each other for weeks.

So what? It was Lowell's problem. Any man who married someone young enough to be his daughter, deserved what he got. For her part, she had insisted Carleton go to the bar. The last thing she wanted was him tagging along while she attended the Art Festival.

"I missed you at the cocktail party," Seth said.

Angela staged a smile, taking a half step back. While she'd been thinking about Carleton, she had failed to notice Seth had moved closer. He was smiling at her in that haughty way of his. "Cocktail parties are a bore."

"You're right. It was deadly dull. I needed someone interesting to talk to." He gave her a look that said she was the "interesting person" he'd been waiting to see.

She gazed off across the gallery to let him know he

bored her. For cripes' sake, he was dating one of the few people she could call a friend. Did he seriously think she would be interested in him if he were seeing Claire? Probably. Some men were all ego.

"Notice how few people are here? The Last Supper," Seth said, using the industry term for a poorly attended show. "Claire's got some hot new artist. Everyone's over there. They aren't on the munchie circuit, making the rounds of the other galleries the way they usually do."

"Really?" Angela silently cursed her decision to come here first, then make her way around the plaza, dropping by the other galleries, but going to The Rising Sun last because she wanted to stay there until it closed. Afterward, she planned to talk to Claire about some sort of a joint venture.

"Should we go over together?" Seth asked. "Max Bassinger is with me."

Angela had met the fabulously wealthy Texan. Short, built like a fireplug with a bald head and watery blue eyes. She didn't care how much money Max had. He gave her the creeps. What she wanted to do was ditch Seth and beeline over to Claire's gallery. But before she could open her mouth, Lowell Hopkins appeared at her elbow.

Max Bassinger took a swig of champagne. Sickly sweet, bubbly puke. Give him Johnny Walker Black Label any day. While he toyed with the glass, his eyes never left Seth Ramsey, and heat built in his gut, warming him like a shot of fine whiskey.

Max was a self-made man and damn proud of it. Starting in the oil fields, he'd worked his way up. He'd parlayed his successful oil venture into a fortune, then he'd bailed out before oil hit the crapper. Investing his megabucks in the emerging computer software business, he'd struck another geyser.

He knew what he wanted; he knew how to get it; and he didn't give a shit what people thought. Trouble was Seth Ramsey did. Right now, he was coming on to that red-headed broad, Angela Whitmore, because she had big-bucks.

He gave a derisive snort that caused the woman next to him to move away. Angela Whitmore wasn't worth a fart. She had made her money the old-fashioned way. She'd inherited it.

It was money Seth was after, Max knew. Seth had run through his trust fund. He had expensive tastes that required moolah. Seth intended to marry Claire Holt and get his hands on her father's money.

But Claire was a frigid bitch. Seth had been dating her for months, yet she wouldn't go to bed with him. Max had told Seth that it was obvious Claire wasn't interested in him. Seth refused to believe it, but he was hedging his bets, sugaring up the redhead.

Seth coveted money and respectability. He wanted to run for senator. That's why he was hovering over the woman who was at least ten years older. Angela Whitmore had a fortune, but she was notorious for preferring muscular young bucks. Max couldn't fault her there.

The heat in his gut intensified as he gazed at Seth and recalled the night in The Hideaway. It had been tricky to lure Seth into that pig sty of a room. Mighty tricky. But worth all his trouble.

"Ouch," he muttered, then rotated his shoulder to work out a kink, but the dull ache persisted. What the hell? He'd taken his heart medicine. It wasn't another spell, was it? The ache suddenly disappeared, and he took a deep breath, promising himself that he'd take his medication regularly.

"Hi, there," a woman said, and he turned to find Stacy Hopkins beside him.

"Howdy," Max replied, almost laughing out loud be-

cause he'd just been thinking about how he'd used Stacy
to entice Seth at The Hideaway.

"Have you, like, got anything for me?" Stacy asked in
her breathy voice as she cocked her head to one side. Her
long, black hair fell across her bare shoulders and he was
treated to more than just a glimpse of her sweet tits.

Max wondered if Lowell Hopkins had any idea what his
wife was really like. For a second, he toyed with taking her
into the back alley and letting her relieve the ache in his
groin with those pouty lips. Been there; done that. He put
his glass down and walked away from her without another
word.

He headed toward the group now clustered around Angela as if she was some highfalutin queen. Time to blow
this joint and get a real drink. Max came up behind Seth
and stood close, pretending to listen to Hopkins as he
spouted off about Nevada's talent.

Max slipped his hand down Seth's tight butt, fondling
the sleek curve for a fraction of a second, then he
squeezed. Hard.

Again. Extra hard this time.

Always let 'em know who was the boss.

There were so many people in The Rising Sun Gallery
that they had spilled out onto the sidewalk in front of the
shop. Paul Winfrey was a hit, and Claire couldn't help smiling. But she had a problem. Nobody had bought either
painting. They stood around discussing them, but no one
had come up with the money.

It's still early, she assured herself. The clients most likely
to afford a high-priced painting had yet to arrive. She con-
soled herself by watching Paul. In his own quiet way, he
was working the crowd. He seemed to have no trouble
making conversation without discussing his past.

"Don't look now," Suzi said as she nudged her way through the crowd.

Vanessa Trent swept into the gallery, and the throng parted to allow the actress to enter. She wore a black silk blouse cut Western style, with long fringe swishing from the sleeves. Each strand was studded with tiny silver beads. The same high-gloss silver detailed the lapels of the blouse and trailed down the front, accenting her impressive cleavage.

She wore black suede jeans that were simply cut, adorned only by a black crocodile belt with a buckle the size of a satellite dish. Her cowboy boots were black crocodile studded with the same silver beads that were on her blouse.

The effect was breath-takingly dramatic. The black was a perfect foil for the long, blond hair fluttering across her shoulders. Claire couldn't help feeling a twinge of envy as a hush fell over the crowd.

"Oh, my," Vanessa said, halting in front of Paul's paintings.

Claire wended her way between people and came up beside the actress. "Isn't Paul Winfrey's work absolutely moving?"

The only sound in the room was the whir of the blender at the bar where the bartender couldn't make margaritas fast enough. Everyone waited for Vanessa Trent to pass judgment. Claire scanned the room and met Paul's steady gaze.

Vanessa Trent knew how to play the moment. She let Claire's question hang in the air as she stared at the painting of the cowboy handing the woman the bouquet. Finally, she turned to Claire, tears misting her eyes, but not spilling over to ruin her mascara.

"He's fantastic! Look at how he's captured her feelings. The man has hurt her badly, and now he's trying to make up. Of course, she isn't going to take him back. She's learned her lesson. He's history."

People nearby, especially the men, murmured their agreement. Chatter resumed gradually, fueled by the arrival of a noisy group. Claire wasn't shocked by Vanessa's interpretation of Paul's work. The actress was extremely self-centered, and undoubtedly saw herself as the woman in the painting.

But the point of view was clearly the man's. Thought-provoking emotion etched every line of his face while the woman was turned away just slightly, her face indistinct, concealed by shadows. It was impossible to tell if she was rejecting him or assuring him that she loved him dearly.

"It would be a perfect addition to your collection," Claire told the actress.

Vanessa moved away from the paintings, saying, "My financial manager has advised me to divest myself of the art I have before acquiring more."

It was a backhanded way of saying she had no intention of buying one of Paul's paintings until Claire helped her get rid of Nevada's lithographs. Claire smiled, nodding. She refused to trade Paul's masterpiece for lithographs of questionable authenticity.

"I'm simply parched," Vanessa announced. "What I wouldn't give for a margarita." In an instant five men were stampeding their way toward the bar. "I called the sheriff about my personal security after those *chukes* kidnapped Bam Stegner," Vanessa said, her voice so low that only Claire could hear her. "What do you think the sheriff did?"

The flicker of envy Claire had experienced when the beautiful actress arrived increased until it became the dull ache that she recognized as full-blown jealousy. She could just imagine Zach discussing "security" with this woman. "What did he do?"

"He sent some doofus deputy with the ridiculous name

of T-Bone. He checked all my locks and windows, then recommended getting a security system."

Claire almost smiled. "You need to get a rottweiler. They're real protection."

Two men arrived with margaritas, and Vanessa allowed them to pay court. Claire slipped away, wondering where Angela Whitmore was. She was a client who had enough money to acquire one of Paul's paintings. She looked toward the entrance and saw Maude Pfister guiding her father's wheelchair into the gallery.

People moved aside as Alexander Holt passed, his head held high. She knew that his pride suffered a blow each time he had to go out in public, relying on Maude. Claire hurried over to them, and quickly kissed her father's cheek.

"Quite a crowd," commented Maude with her usual happy smile.

"The other galleries looked deserted," added her father. He wasn't smiling, but he seemed happier than she'd seen him in some time.

"At the eleventh hour, I found a new, talented artist," she told her father. She looked around, and saw Paul nearby. She motioned for him to join her.

"Where did you find him?" asked her father.

"An old friend sent him to see me." She deliberately avoided mentioning Quentin's name. Her father had never liked her mentor. Quentin had been instrumental in Claire going into the world of art when her father had expected her to come to work at his bank.

"Paul," she said, as he came up. "This is my father Alexander Holt, and Maude Pfister."

"Howdy," Paul extended his hand and smiled.

Maude greeted him warmly, but her father's greeting was less enthusiastic. Alexander scrutinized the artist with the eyes of a father evaluating a prospective son-in-law.

Sheesh! Would her father ever be happy until she married and gave him a grandson?

"Are you from around here?" her father asked.

"No, sir," Paul replied. "I was born in Tennessee."

"Really? You don't sound like it."

Paul smiled, or tried to. Claire knew how intimidating her father was. Being confined to a wheelchair made him feel like less of a man, and he became even more authoritative, a slightly threatening edge underscoring every word.

"I've worked hard to get rid of my accent, sir."

Claire smiled at Paul, saying, "Come on, Daddy. I want you to see how talented Paul is."

People moved aside as Claire led her father and Maude up to the two paintings while Paul followed a few steps behind. Claire watched her father study the painting of the cowboy offering the woman the bouquet. Every muscle in her body was tense, awaiting her father's judgment.

Why did she let him do this to her? As childish as it seemed, she still thought of him as the larger-than-life father who had taken over when her mother was killed. A bond between them formed, their grief binding them to the image of a laughing, loving woman who had been devoted to her family.

A shared memory linked them and sometimes stood between them. Claire's father never ceased to remind her of how much she was like her mother. Opening the gallery had increased the tension between them about this, but she didn't care.

Be honest with yourself, whispered some inner voice. Her father's opinion did matter very much. She wanted to be a success, to validate her chosen career in his eyes. In her mind, it was a way of making up to him for all the misery she'd caused.

She stood beside him, gazing at the painting, but her mind drifted back over the years to the day when she'd unexpectedly returned home from school. Her mother and Jake Coulter had been naked on the living room rug in front of the fire. The mother she'd loved had been on top of Jake Coulter, riding him with her head flung back, her wild, blond hair streaming down to her bare buttocks. Claire had stood dumbfounded as Jake Coulter climaxed, bucking upward, his face grimacing as if someone had stabbed him.

Claire had run straight to her father. And ruined all their lives.

She inhaled a stabilizing breath. That was then; this is now. She could not make up for what she'd done. All she could do was go forward and try to make her father proud of her.

Her father pivoted in the wheelchair, looking up at her. "How could you?"

It took her a full second to realize her father wasn't on her wavelength. He wasn't reliving the past. For some reason, he was upset about Paul's painting.

"Daddy, what are you talking about?"

Her father didn't answer, instead he turned to a very puzzled Maude. "Let's get out of here."

He rammed his way through the crowd. People reacted as quickly as they could, moving aside for the wheelchair, sloshing margaritas over each other. Claire followed, muttering her apologies. Alexander Holt shot through the door and across the sidewalk to his van parked in the handicapped space.

Claire rushed ahead and stood between her father and the van's door. "Tell me why you're so upset."

He glared at her, his hands shaking as he clutched the wheelchair. "It's bad enough that I have to see that scum, Zach Coulter walking the streets of my town, looking exactly like his father. Then you insisted on reopening your mother's gallery."

What did this have to do with his reaction to the painting, she wondered. She'd heard this litany dozens of times. She didn't want to ruin the best night of her career by listening to it again.

"Don't you think the whole town knows?" he shouted so loudly that several people on the sidewalk looked their way.

"Knows what?" Maude asked, a quaver in her voice.

"That painting mirrors my life. I gave Amy everything she wanted. I loved her with all my heart."

The unchecked emotion in her father's voice brought tears to Claire's eyes. She looked to Maude for help, but the older woman was crying, silent tears slipping down her broad cheeks. With a flash of insight, Claire realized what she should have known all along. Maude Pfister loved her father even though he was still crazy about a woman long dead. A woman who had chosen another man over her child and her marriage.

"When Amy was packing to leave with Coulter, I told her I would do anything if she'd just stay with me. The whole town knows that I'm the cowboy in the painting, offering a woman all I had to give. But she just turned away."

Claire dropped to her knees beside her father, so she could look into his eyes. She couldn't imagine her proud father begging her mother to stay. She couldn't imagine loving someone so much that your pride no longer mattered.

She stroked her father's hand, realizing with surprise how frail he'd become. She couldn't bear to see him suffer like this. He didn't have many years left, and she wanted those that he did have to be happy ones.

"The emotional impact of Paul's work is staggering. Everyone interprets it in a different way. No one associates you with the cowboy, but yourself."

"I thought the man was leaving the woman," Maude added, her tone wistful. "The flowers were a parting gift."

Claire smiled at the older woman, but her father stubbornly averted his face and stared off across the plaza.

"Vanessa Trent thought the man was trying to make up to the woman, but she was finished with him. Everyone agreed with her." Personally, Claire thought this was how self-centered Vanessa saw herself—ready to reject any man who dared to cross her.

Without another word, her father wheeled away and Maude slowly followed, throwing an apologetic look over her shoulder. Claire resisted the urge to run after her father. More and more, she sensed his problems were psychological, and nothing she did improved his frame of mind.

Fourteen

From across the plaza at the open-air café, Tortilla Flats, Zach saw Alexander Holt's van pull away from The Rising Sun. He checked his watch, deciding to give Brad Yeager another three minutes. The FBI agent already was ten minutes late.

As he toyed with his Coke, Zach saw Claire walk into the plaza and sit on a bench. Weird. With all the people in her gallery, why would Claire want to be alone? Because that jackass of a father said something to upset her.

Didn't Claire see what a selfish bastard Alexander Holt was? Of course not. Your parents had a special place in your heart, he reflected. No matter what, you loved them.

Too well, Zach remembered his youth. He'd loved his father, even though Jake Coulter had been so absorbed by his photography and his affair with Amy Holt to spend much time with Zach. His mother had been a different story. She'd devoted herself to her son—when she wasn't drinking. Trouble was, the bottle was more interesting than her child. But he'd loved her just the same. When she wasn't drinking, she was the best mother in the world.

How different his parents' lives would have been—if he hadn't been born. He'd been conceived in the back seat of a Chevy when his parents had been in high school. His father had done the honorable thing and married his mother, sacrificing a scholarship to college.

The marriage had been doomed from the first, but somehow Zach always blamed himself. Was that what Claire was doing now, blaming herself for something beyond her control? Zach was ready to toss a couple of bills on the bar and go talk to Claire when Yeager walked in.

"Wow!" Yeager said. "This is some celebration."

Zach gazed out at the plaza where vendors were preparing tamales and blue corn taquitos for the tourists who were slowly drifting out of the galleries. The aroma of roasting chiles and piñon wood filled the summer air along with the sounds of the rock band tuning up. In another hour, people would be dancing and stuffing their faces. Tortilla Flat's outdoor bar was brimming with chattering people.

Only Claire Holt was alone.

"It's the beginning of the tourist season," Zach told Yeager. "I have my hands full. I put on my badge for the first time since last year's rodeo. I activated four reserve deputies and the Mounted Patrol to handle the problems."

Yeager leaned against the bar, ordered a Red Dog beer, then asked, "Are you expecting trouble?"

"Nah. We'll have a lot of drunk Texans. They'll want to fight. The deputies and the volunteers on the Mounted Patrol will help me toss 'em in the drunk tank and let 'em sleep it off."

Yeager's eyes lit up—proof positive the SAC had been at the FBI's Gallup post way too long. He missed the action. "Tell everyone that I'm in from Gallup to help you if you need it. That way people won't be suspicious about me being around."

"Right," Zach said as he noticed Angela Whitmore join Claire on the bench in the plaza. "What did you find out?"

Yeager moved closer, his beer clutched in one hand. "Duncan Morrell was killed by a single shot to the temple at close range. The bullet came from a .25 caliber automatic, a gun easily concealed. It could have been in a woman's purse, or in a small duffel bag."

Zach thought of Claire's wallet being found in the room next to Morrell's. Incriminating. Sweat peppered his upper lip, but he cuffed it off with his shirt. Jesus H. Christ, leave Claire out of this.

"There were traces of fiber in the wound."

"A homemade silencer," Zach said. "Someone put a pillow or something to his head before pulling the trigger. That explains why no one heard the shot."

"You didn't find the pillow or anything with blood."

"Nope. I had the mounted patrol comb the area searching for the murder weapon. They would have picked up anything bloody."

Yeager grinned, obviously pleased with himself. "I have the list of major investors in Morrell's lithographs. Number one investor. Wanna take a guess?"

Shaking his head, Zach shot a quick glance sideways. Beyond the patio of Tortilla Flats, he could see Claire and Angela talking on the bench. No, he did not want to guess; he wanted to be with Claire.

Yeager chuckled. "Nevada Murphy was the number one investor."

"Really? Nevada planned to make a killing on his own lithographs. Interesting."

"The number two investor was—now this is a stunner— Vanessa Trent."

Zach nodded, thinking he'd never met the actress, but she'd called the station after Stegner blabbed around town that *chukes* had kidnapped him. Zach had seen Trent's show once or twice. Mindless drivel. The actress strutted around, jiggling boobs way too huge to be original equipment.

"Almost as big an investor was Seth Ramsey." Yeager took a swig of beer while Zach twirled his glass, clinking the ice against the side. "And get this, Ramsey is tap-city."

"Why am I not surprised?" Cocky little prick, Zach thought. Ramsey tooled around town in a Ferrari even though he was nearly broke. "Was there anyone else at The Hideaway who'd invested and had a motive to kill Morrell?"

Yeager drained his glass and motioned to the bartender for another. "Way, way down the list of investors is Carleton Cole."

Zach conjured up a mental image. Buff but brain-dead. He was perfect for Angela Whitmore. Zach stole a glance sideways and noticed Angela and Claire were still on the bench, talking.

"Let's discuss the body," said Yeager.

Body. Zach's muscles responded instantly, thinking of Claire's soft body. He could almost feel her beneath him. He noticed Yeager studying him with a puzzled expression and Zach managed to appear interested.

"Good thing you had them save Morrell's vital organs and tissue samples," Yeager told him. "He had ejaculated within half an hour of being killed."

"Really? We didn't find any condoms. No visible semen on the body either."

The bartender slid another beer across the bar to Yeager. The agent caught it, took a sip, then said, "A special forensics team went over the body. If they say he'd had sex, they're dead-on."

"We've interviewed all the personnel at The Hideaway. No one reported any woman in the area."

"Except for Claire Holt."

It was all Zach could do to keep his face expressionless. He didn't trust Yeager enough to talk to him about Claire. "I checked. She has one gun registered, a .38."

"That doesn't mean she couldn't have used another gun."

"I'm not buying it. Claire Holt is not the type to murder anyone in cold blood."

Yeager drained half the beer. "True. We had our criminal profiler go over the case. The profiler doesn't rule out a woman, but the killer could be a man with repressed sexual impulses or something."

"What in hell is that supposed to mean?"

"It means a bull-dyke who still goes for men, or a man who's a switch hitter."

"They could tell that from the evidence at the murder scene?"

Yeager shrugged. "They've been amazingly accurate in other cases."

"I know. I worked with a profiler in San Francisco. He analyzed crime scene photos and the physical evidence, then came up with the perp's criminal behavior pattern. When we caught the serial killer, he fit the description. But I didn't pick up on any clues at the murder scene to indicate a woman committed the crime." Zach shook his head. "A pervert? Nothing there either."

"The odds are against it being a woman. Men are more often the killers."

"Crimes usually come down to greed or passion," Zach said. "You think this was a crime of passion."

"Not necessarily. Just because Morrell recently had sex doesn't mean that it was a crime of passion. Perhaps this situation merely provided the opportunity for the killer."

"Then we're back to square one," Zach said.

"This is where we double-check alibis to rule out suspects. What about that actress who invested heavily in Morrell's prints?"

"Vanessa Trent missed her flight, and didn't arrive in Taos until after Morrell was killed." Zach stole a look at Claire who was still out in the plaza talking to Angela.

"How's Carleton Cole's alibi?"

"Up in the air. Cole took Angela home about midnight, then went to his room. No one can verify his whereabouts at the time of the murder," Zach told him. "Now that I know he invested in those prints, I'll take a closer look."

"What are you going to do about Seth Ramsey?"

Zach couldn't help smiling. Alexander Holt was so high on the prissy lawyer. "I say squeeze him. Hard."

Max Bassinger sauntered into The Rising Sun Gallery beside Seth Ramsey. Four shots of Johnny Walker in a plaza-side bar had improved his attitude, and he was feeling mellow. He enjoyed being with Seth. He'd analyzed their relationship and knew what attracted him to the blond man besides his good looks.

They were complete opposites. Max had been born a stone Okie in a shack with an outhouse behind it. He'd never finished high school, but he had street smarts up the ole wazoo.

Seth had been born with a silver spoon in each hand, a flock of servants to wait on him. Private schools all the way, then Harvard and Harvard Law. Now he was catering to Max like he was a king.

And Max loved it. How far he'd come.

The bright lights inside the gallery soured his disposition. What a mob scene. He wanted to return to the opulent hacienda he had renovated. And get naked.

On the far side of the gallery, he spotted Vanessa Trent. He imagined making love to the famous actress.

Women were useful, he decided. For as long as he could remember, Max had been attracted to both sexes. He accepted himself for what he was. Bisexual. It worked for the ancient Greeks. Sex was sex. Limiting yourself to one gender was boring.

As Max headed toward the bar, he came face-to-face with Vanessa Trent. He had seen her television show maybe twice. It played up her incredible tits. Unexpectedly, Vanessa Trent smiled, a sensuous bewitching smile.

"Hello, again. How have you been?"

It took Max a second to realize the actress was speaking

to him, not to Seth. He knew he was stick ugly; women were only interested in his money.

"We met last year at the Talbotts' party," she continued.

He didn't respond. Instead, he let his eyes wander down the graceful slope of her jaw to her neck. Then lower. He blatantly inspected the exposed breasts that would have had most men drooling. But then he wasn't most men.

He'd run into the actress several times, not just at the Talbotts' party. She'd never stopped to give him the time of day. So why now? Simple. The conceited bitch wanted something.

"Someone told me that you'd totally renovated the old Sanchez hacienda. I understand it's a showplace now," Vanessa cooed. "I'd love to see it."

Max studied Seth out of the corner of his eye. There was more than a flicker of interest. The actress turned him on. Max was about to blow her off, but if Seth wanted another group grope, why not?

Claire sat on the plaza bench beside Angela, gazing at the gazebo where the band was setting up. She'd been talking to Angela for some time, explaining her father's unexpected reaction to Paul Winfrey's painting. She'd half expected Angela to jump up and storm into the gallery to see the controversial work, but she hadn't. She seemed genuinely interested in Claire's troubles, and Claire realized Angela was a better friend than she'd first thought.

"Your situation is very similar to what I went through with my father," Angela confessed. "He had a great deal of money and wanted to tell me what to do and how to live my life. Every time an eligible man came along, he would insist the man was only interested in my money."

"How did you handle it?"

"Mr. Right came along in the form of a tennis pro. Papa hit the roof. 'That man's only after your money.' He convinced me to drop him." Angela gazed at Claire, her brown eyes concerned, and Claire could see how hurt she still was. "It took years for me to get over it."

"What happened to him?"

"He found someone else. The last I heard, they were happily married with three kids." Angela shrugged as if it didn't matter, but Claire knew better. "I learned to live with what my father said because it had the ring of truth to it. I have more money than I can spend. That's what men are interested in, so I've learned to play along. I go for young guys I have no intention of ever marrying. A feminist version of love 'em and leave 'em."

Claire's heart went out to her friend. What a way to live your life. To have everything but no one to share it with. "My father says I'm just like my mother. I guess that has the ring of truth to it, too. I look like her. I love finding talented artists and displaying their work."

"All you'd have to do is take up with Zach Coulter"— Angela stopped. Obviously something in Claire's expression had alerted her. "Small towns thrive on gossip. I heard all about your mother running away with Jake Coulter."

The ring of truth. Claire was more like her mother than she cared to admit. She was hopelessly attracted to Zach, but it was a relationship without a future. She could never take him home to her father—not that he'd want to go.

"Oh my God, Claire! You're not!" Angela cried when Claire didn't say anything. "You're not involved with Zach, are you?"

"It hasn't gone that far yet."

"Well, I can't say that I blame you. If he were younger, I'd go after him myself." Angela slammed her palm against her forehead. "I'm sorry. This situation isn't funny, is it?"

"I don't know what makes Zach so attractive. If I became involved with him, he'd throw me over in no time."

"What makes you say that?"

"Zach has a reputation for taking out women just once, then dropping them."

Angela considered this for a moment. "I wouldn't pay too much attention to gossip. The Sheriff may just not have found the right woman."

"Possibly," she conceded, "but if I went out with Zach, my father would be mortified. He might have another stroke."

Angela held up her hand. "I have a suggestion. Go for a one-night stand out at Zach's place where no one will see you. Satisfy your curiosity, then find someone you can take home to your father. That's what I would do."

It was a tempting idea, but she wasn't sure she wanted to risk it. Would one night with Zach Coulter be enough?

"I'd better get back to the gallery." Claire rose, smiling at Angela. "Thanks for listening to my troubles. Come with me. I'd like you to see Paul's work. I want your opinion."

Zach Coulter shouldered his way into The Rising Sun Gallery with Brad Yeager at his side. Being a head taller than everyone gave him the ability to spot Ramsey right away. "He's the blond-haired guy standing next to Vanessa Trent."

Yeager craned his neck. "By God, it's *the* Vanessa Trent. She has a set of knockers that won't quit."

Zach didn't bother to look around the gallery for Claire. He knew she was still in the plaza with Angela Whitmore. But he couldn't help comparing Claire and the actress. Give him Claire any day. Better yet, any night.

"Who's the old, bald runt with them?" Yeager asked.

"Max Bassinger, the billionaire from Texas. He lives here part of the year. Ramsey's his attorney. Run a check on Bassinger, will you?" Zach moved forward as Seth headed to the bar. "Let's take Ramsey out back and question him alone."

Zach tapped Seth on the shoulder just as he came up to the margarita bar. "I'd like to have a word with you."

Seth shot him a hostile glare that might have intimidated some men. "You've questioned me twice. I'm busy getting Vanessa Trent a drink."

"Out back—now—unless you want Vanessa to see you arrested."

"What for? I haven't done anything."

"Obstructing justice. You didn't tell me that you had a motive to kill Duncan Morrell. You invested a bundle in his lithographs and lost your ass."

A dull flush shot up Ramsey's face, and Zach saw that he'd scored. With Yeager at his side, he led Ramsey through the crowd to the back of the gallery. Lobo and Lucy were sitting just outside the rear entrance. Zach gave his dog a pat and let Lobo lick his hand while he positioned himself so the light over the door shined directly in Ramsey's face.

Pointing at Yeager, Ramsey went on the offensive, a bullshit lawyer tactic. "Who's he?"

Yeager pulled out his wallet and flipped it open to show the official FBI seal and his photo ID as Zach said, "Special Agent Yeager is down from the Gallup office to help me with rodeo problems."

Seeing the Feebie ID shook Ramsey. "What do you want to know?"

"You had a reason to shoot Morrell. You don't have an alibi," Zach said.

"I say arrest him, get a warrant, and tear his place apart," Yeager put in, following the plan they had to squeeze the smarmy lawyer. "You'll find the murder weapon."

"I did not kill Duncan. Sure, I was angry because he sold me those lithographs, but I'm rich, I—"

"You're lying," Zach yelled. "You're maxed out on your Visa. American Express cut you off."

Ramsey glared at Yeager. "The FBI must be in on this case. You wouldn't have access to those records."

"Why would I call in the Feebies?" Zach hedged. "Brad's up in Gallup bored silly. He's doing this for fun, right Brad?"

"Yeah. Not much happens on the res," Yeager responded, then he waited a minute. When Ramsey didn't speak, Yeager told Zach. "Read him his rights."

"Just a darn minute! You can't arrest me."

Darn? Zach grinned. What a wimp. "You have the right to remain silent—"

"I can prove I didn't murder Duncan Morrell. I have an alibi."

Zach slanted a glance sideways at Yeager. The bluff had worked. "I interviewed you twice and you said that you looked for Claire Holt, couldn't find her, then went home. Are you changing your story?"

Ramsey's face was even more flushed than before, having turned the color of an eggplant. Boy, this was going to be good. Zach could just feel it. "You'd better tell me the whole truth this time, and don't you dare leave out a single detail."

Seth raked his fingers through his hair, ruining the too-perfect line, then said, "I waited for Claire, but she didn't come out. I had picked up the key to number five. I was going to take her down there."

As Ramsey hesitated, Zach saw Yeager was confused. "The Hideaway doesn't have a front desk. The keys are in boxes," he explained. "You slip in ten bucks and take the key. If the key is missing, you know the bungalow is in use."

"I walked out there to say I'd be there as soon as I found her . . . but I went in and didn't come out."

"Was there a party in number five?" Zach asked.

Ramsey tilted his head upward and the glare of the light revealed the sweat coating his brow. "You could say that."

"Get more specific," Yeager told him. "You're in deep shit."

"Look, I've been seeing Claire Holt for months. Her father is crazy about me, but I've never gotten to first base with her. Max Bassinger suggested slipping half a Roofie into her drink to relax her, then bring her down to number five."

"You little prick!" Zach cocked his arm, ready to give him the same punch that had leveled Bam Stegner.

"Zach," Yeager cautioned. "Don't touch the suspect. Let's do this right."

Zach could barely control himself. "A Roofie can make a woman helpless."

"I didn't mean any harm," Ramsey whined. "I just thought that if Claire made love to me, she'd like me a whole lot more. It was just half a pill. She was still talking. She seemed okay to me."

"So what was Bassinger going to do?" Zach asked. "Watch?"

"Of course not. He was just holding the room until we could get there."

Yeager asked, "What went wrong? You never came back for Claire."

Ramsey looked down at the dogs, sitting by Zach's boots. "Stacy Hopkins was in there stark naked giving Max a blow job. I couldn't drag Claire into a scene like that. I went in and shut the door."

"Who was laughing?" Zach asked, remembering Claire had heard laughter.

"Max hooted and said I was too uptight. He's my best client. I didn't want to alienate him. I stayed in the room and watched. Stacy couldn't get enough . . . so I let her take care of me." Seth's voice was dropping with every word until it was hard to hear him over the sound of the band in the plaza. "The three of us were in that room going at it until dawn."

Fifteen

Claire and Angela became separated at the front entrance of The Rising Sun Gallery. It had been crowded when Claire had left with her father, but now there was a throng in the gallery, and just one clerk to help. What had she been thinking? This was no time to be sitting in the plaza, feeling sorry for herself.

Claire saw Suzi at the sales counter frantically writing up an order. Their gazes met, and the freckled-faced blond rolled her eyes heavenward. Claire was on the way over when she spotted Zach at the back of the gallery, coming in the rear door. He must have come by to check on Lobo, she decided. He was smart enough to know that the Art Festival was going to be a mob scene, and the dogs were better off waiting out back.

As he shouldered his way through the crowd, his eyes on her, Claire saw he was dressed entirely in black. Midnight black denim jeans emphasized the length of his legs, and the long sleeves on his black chambray had been rolled back to the elbows to expose powerful forearms. Tonight, Zach was wearing his badge. It was pinned to the pocket of his shirt, but the silver star was slightly off-center, as if he'd put it on as an afterthought.

Recalling the way she'd let him kiss her last night, a flush of heat warmed her neck and cheeks. With it came the advice Angela had given her. What harm would there be in having a fling, then finding a suitable man to take home to her father.

"You look like Darth Vader in cowboy boots," she said.

He smiled, an adorable, sexy smile that would have convinced anyone that he had just received the ultimate compliment. "I came by earlier to tell you I'd checked out Paul."

"Really?" she said, as if she couldn't have cared less, but she was secretly pleased. "Suzi didn't—"

"She was with a customer, so I didn't stop." He gave her a slow once-over that stripped her down to her birthday suit. "Great outfit."

She shrugged as if the compliment didn't matter, but it did. She'd spent a lot of time deciding what to wear. The baby-soft deer suede dress had a deep V-neck and a wrap skirt. The rich green, tinged with a hint of blue reminded her of the high-country meadows at dawn. The color offset the bright turquoise corn necklace that had been hand crafted and polished to enhance its natural color.

"Quentin Reynolds gave me this necklace," she said a little too quickly, but the way he was studying it so closely made her stomach flutter. "Corn is the staple of the Pueblo Indians, you know. It's sacred, and giving someone a corn necklace symbolizes lasting friendship."

"I don't need any history lessons. I grew up around here the same as you." He was staring into her eyes so intensely now that it made her weak. And warm. Perhaps deer suede, even though it was lightweight and perfect for high-country evenings, was too heavy for a gallery crowded with people. And Zach Coulter was standing far too close.

"I take it Paul wasn't the man at The Hideaway," she said to get the conversation back onto business, and he nodded. "I told you he wasn't the one."

She lowered her voice and leaned closer to him, explaining what she'd decided to do about Paul's prison record. Then she added, "Thanks for befriending him. He told me that you lent him the money to buy good clothes and new boots."

"Glad to help. Every man needs two things in life, a good pair of boots and a good woman."

There was something in his low, husky tone that made her believe this was an intimate comment, but she chose to tease him a bit instead of allowing him to become too personal. "Boots? That just goes to show you the gap in intelligence between the sexes. Who's man's best friend? A dog. Now, a woman is smarter. Diamonds are a girl's best friend."

He smiled again, but it was more of a smirk this time. "You're after money, huh? Guess I'd better try a little blackmail."

Blackmail. The word alone brought back the image of him kissing her breasts and heat pooled in secret, intimate places. The look on his face made her pulse skyrocket. She managed a comeback, but it was an effort. "Threatening me again? Why don't you just grab me by the hair and drag me back to your cave?"

"Don't give me any ideas." He winked with a grin. "You're so easy to blackmail, no telling what you'd do if I got you back to my cave."

Obviously, Zach thought he was God's gift to women, and she was only encouraging him by flirting with him instead of using her earlier tactic of being cold. Tonight she didn't feel like being cold and sarcastic. She was elated at showing Paul's art and thrilled to have so many people in her gallery.

She put her fingertip on the silver star pinned to Zach's shirt. It was warm, having absorbed the heat from his body. Her pulse surged for a second before settling back into a faster than normal pace.

His dark brows slanted downward as he looked at her hand almost resting on his chest. Her own eyes were drawn to the open V-neck of his shirt where an intriguing tuft of hair had edged its way out. She had the absurd urge to unbutton his entire shirt and run her fingers through the crinkly hair on his chest.

"Feels good, doesn't it?" he asked, his voice a shade shy of a whisper, carrying with it a sensual undertone.

For a second, she thought that he had read her mind and was telling her just how good his chest would feel, but then she realized he was talking about the badge where her finger was still resting lightly.

She yanked back her hand, her words coming out in a jumble that she hoped made sense. "I've never seen you wear it."

A smile glimmered softly in his eyes as if he knew exactly what she'd been thinking. "I put on my badge during the rodeo. Folks around here recognize me, but it doesn't hurt for strangers to know the law's around."

"I'm surprised you're in town with so many cowboys and tourists out at the rodeo arena, getting drunk."

His eyes narrowed and a frown marred the angular planes of his face. "I'm here on official business. I need to talk to Max Bassinger."

She smiled with more enthusiasm than she felt, amazed she'd wanted him to say that he'd come just to see her. "He was out front a minute ago, cooling off, I think."

He let her words hang there without responding while his gaze slid down her body a scant inch at a time. She waited for the familiar anger to come, but it seemed to have been tempered by Angela's outrageous suggestion. A damp patch of moisture formed between her breasts as she wondered what it would be like to give in to her baser instincts and make love to this man.

A smile tugged at the corner of his lips as he moved his head and his thick, dark hair shifted across his brow. He winked at her, saying, "Later."

Claire heard Suzi calling to her, but she watched Zach move through the crowd toward the entrance. She was very, very tempted to take Angela's advice. One night. What could it hurt?

But then she remembered the tears in her father's eyes and the anguish in his voice. Just seeing Zach Coulter upset him terribly. If he even suspected she'd succumbed to temptation—the way her mother had—and made love to Zach, he'd be crushed.

It would prove that she was exactly like her mother.

Vanessa Trent intercepted Zach before he reached the front door, and Claire watched them talking, although there was too much noise in the gallery to hear what they were saying. An unfamiliar sensation of anxiety replaced the happy feeling she'd had just moments ago.

Zach and Vanessa. Both tall, both dressed in ebony. A perfect match, she thought, like two sleek thoroughbreds. Vanessa smiled, then tilted her head just slightly as she laughed, an extremely provocative gesture.

Zach responded with a smile that Claire had never seen. It was a wide smile that revealed a set of perfect teeth beneath those sensual lips that usually smirked at her in a knowing, teasing manner. The grooves bracketing his mouth deepened and the lines fanning out from his eyes appeared. It was a masculine smile, the kind of smile reserved for a drop-dead gorgeous woman.

Zach walked away from the actress, and now Vanessa was smiling a self-satisfied smile. Did he tell her that he'd see her later? Undoubtedly. Claire tamped down her feeling of envy. She had what she wanted, a first-rate artist and a successful gallery.

Max Bassinger stood outside The Rising Sun Gallery, looking through the window at Claire watching Zach Coulter. He'd just witnessed the little scene between the two of them.

Interesting. Mighty interesting.

No wonder Claire Holt wouldn't sleep with Seth. Who could blame her? Zachary Coulter was a real stud who was built like a fullback, but moved with the athletic agility of a running back. All man.

A man's man.

Max had only spoken to the sheriff once when Coulter had stopped him on a country road, claiming he'd been speeding. Max had denied it, of course, even though the speedometer on his Viper read 120 mph when he'd heard the siren. The sheriff had given him a ticket, hardly saying a word.

But Max was an expert at reading people. The first time he'd met Seth Ramsey, Max had known it would take a little effort, but he could have him. He'd used a ploy that often worked. Bring in a sexy woman and let her make love to you both. Separately, then together.

Hands everywhere, legs everywhere, arms everywhere . . . tongues everywhere. Suddenly you were doing something that you'd never dreamed you'd do.

And getting off on it.

Wanting more.

On that backwoods road, Max had sized up Zachary Coulter while the sheriff was writing the ticket. Nah, Coulter wasn't the type to allow a group grope to become a two-man show. He wasn't the kind to even consider sharing any woman with another man.

But there was no law to keep Max from fantasizing about it.

"It's a damn sight cooler out there than it is in here," Zach said as he came up to Max.

Max nodded, a little surprised that the sheriff had sought him out. He kept his eyes on Zach's face, but that didn't mean he'd missed the black denim outfit, especially the way the jeans clutched his sex like a lover's hand.

"Yeah, cooler," Max agreed as he let his eyes drift over the group inside the gallery for Seth. He'd disappeared over ten minutes ago when he'd gone to get the blonde bimbo a drink. Max had been so absorbed with trying to guess why Vanessa Trent was coming on to him that he hadn't seen where Seth had gone.

"I need to verify a few facts," the sheriff said casually. Too casually.

"Shoot," Max said just as nonchalant, but his brain kicked into high gear. Seth had disappeared; it was not like him to let his meal ticket out of sight. Something was wrong and the sheriff was involved.

"On the night Duncan Morrell was murdered, I need to know where you were, who you were with and the time frame."

Max kept a smug smile off his face. *God, he was good.* Seth was involved in this. Evidently, the sheriff had learned that Seth had lost heavily in Morrell's investment scheme. That gave him a motive to kill.

"I went out to The Hideaway at a little before midnight," Max said slowly as if he was having trouble recalling exactly where he'd been and what he'd been doing. Just the opposite was true, of course. It had taken him weeks to find the right bait—Stacy Hopkins—then set the hook and reel in Seth Ramsey. "I met a couple of friends in number five."

"You have one of the most impressive homes in Taos. Why would you meet friends in such a dive?" Zach asked.

The question took Max by surprise, yet it pleased him. Since selling his oil business, he'd had little to do except sit on his ass and watch his assets grow. Restoring La Casa del Sol had been fulfilling in a way that he hadn't expected. He was inordinately proud of taking a run-down, two-hundred-year-old hacienda and restoring it to its former glory.

"There was a certain lady involved," he said in a careful tone as if he didn't suspect Zach Coulter knew exactly who the "lady" was. "She had come to the club with her husband, but he was leaving early. Seth was already there, so why make everyone drive out to my place? It was easier to meet in The Hideaway. Sometimes cheap motels are more fun, don't you think?"

That got him. Zach's eyes narrowed slightly. "Why would Stacy Hopkins agree to meet you and Seth?"

God, he was good, Max told himself yet again. Zach knew exactly who was in the room. Then what was it that he *really* wanted to know? "Look, Sheriff, I don't want to get anyone into trouble," Max said as he stalled for time, trying to figure out what was going on here.

"Everything you tell me is strictly confidential. I don't care about people's sexual escapades, I'm just interested in finding a cold-blooded killer."

"Stacy's a candy nose," Max informed him, attempting to sound as if this fact was being dragged out of him when he didn't give a damn what happened to her. "Give her coke or money for coke and she'll do anything. I gave her money to party with us. Threesomes are real fun, ya' know."

He didn't say that he'd paid her way more than it was worth. He'd watched Seth for weeks and noticed his interest in Stacy. From then on it was easy. He'd paid Stacy to perform, then get out on cue, so he could have Seth to himself.

"I need to know what time each of you left bungalow five."

That's what this was all about. Time and motive. "Ah, shucks, we were having so much fun. Next thing I know the sun is peeking through the itty-bitty slit in the blackout drapes. It was just after five-thirty when we left."

"Exactly who left with you?"

Seth could have come up with an alibi just by saying he'd been with him, Max decided, but Seth hadn't. The wussy was too ashamed of what he'd done to admit it. People should accept each other for what they are. But no,

Seth coveted respectability and still hankered to marry a rich woman so he could have the best of both worlds.

Max was tempted to blow Seth's cover, but decided against it. Lying for Seth only gave him more power over him. "We all three left together, but everyone had their own car. Seth drove out to my place. I had some contracts I wanted him to go over."

Zach asked a few more meaningless questions, assuring Max that he'd read the situation correctly, then went back into the gallery. Max waited until he was out of sight before walking across the plaza.

There weren't very many people in the River Spirit Gallery. Those who were there were clustered around Nevada and Lowell Hopkins. Stacy was wandering around the back. As usual she looked bored, having no interest in her husband's business. Max went around the side of the building into the alley and opened the back door. He walked through the dark storeroom and peeked into the gallery. Stacy was just a few feet away, her back to him.

"Stacy," he said in a voice just loud enough for her to hear. "I have something for you."

The brunette slipped through the door. Even in the dim light from the alley, he could see that she was pretty in an earthy, sexy way. He understood perfectly why Seth found her so attractive.

"Thanks for your help the other night," Max said as he guided her out the back door and into the alley. He pulled a tiny box out of his pocket. He snapped it open, showing Stacy what appeared to be a well-known brand of headache medication.

"What have you got there?" Stacy asked in that breathless voice of hers.

"Something special. Put one under your tongue, honey."

She popped the tablet into her sweet mouth. She was real good with those lips. And that tongue. Whoa!

While the capsule dissolved, he pulled out his money clip and peeled off five bills. He held them up to the light. "Samuel P. Chase, sweet lips. Secretary of the Treasury. Naturally, he put himself on the thousand-dollar bill."

He folded the money and tucked it into her bra, making certain he ran his hand over the soft globe until he found the nipple. Her eyes were narrow slits now, the high-grade coke laced with a few goodies, had kicked in. She leaned against the building, her breasts thrust upward, breathing hard through those pouty lips.

"The money's yours, honey. You earned it." He let his hand drift downward to her crotch. She didn't protest; he knew she wouldn't. Once you were hooked, you lived for that high. And nothing else mattered.

"Just remember one thing," he said, as he fondled her. "You were with Seth and me until dawn. We all left that room together. Got it?"

Stacy nodded, but he wasn't certain that she understood. He probed lightly with his fingers, pressing into the soft silk fabric of her dress.

"Tell me exactly what you're going to tell the Sheriff when he asks."

It took a few minutes for Max to give her instructions about what to say while Stacy parroted back her answers before he was satisfied that she'd verify their story. By the time he'd finished, he had her dress up and her panties in his pocket. He was rock hard. He took her, standing up against the wall in the back alley, enjoying every second of it.

Sometimes there was nothing like a woman.

Sixteen

"Bassinger's a liar," Zach told Brad Yeager as they drove the Bronco out to the rodeo arena to keep a lid on things. "I don't know what tipped me off, but my gut instinct says the sleazeball is lying."

"What would Bassinger have to gain by lying?"

"Beats me. I'll double check his story with Stacy Hopkins tomorrow, but she'll probably back him up." Zach was pissed big-time; he'd been dead certain Seth was guilty. He had been waiting, just dying to gloat when Alexander Holt heard the news. And Claire. He had planned to tell her personally.

Ramsey was a helluva lot sleazier than anyone suspected. He'd slipped a Roofie into Claire's drink. Then he'd left her, knowing she was under the influence of a dangerous drug. Anything could have happened to her.

"I'll pull the file on Bassinger," offered Yeager, breaking into his thoughts, and Zach promised himself that he would fix Seth Ramsey the first chance he got. "I'm going to take a closer look at Lowell Hopkins, too. Everyone seems to think it's odd that he took on Nevada."

"You know what else strikes me as really odd?" Zach pulled onto the blacktop road that led to the rodeo arena located on the outskirts of the reservation. "Nevada let some women keep him tied up for hours. That's his alibi."

"People go for that S and M stuff." Yeager shrugged as if it wasn't any big deal.

Zach's scalp pricked at the thought of being tied up and sweat peppered the back of his neck. He knew—first hand—how it felt to be tied up. No way did he equate being helpless with great sex. But he didn't share his private feelings with Yeager.

"Speaking of S and M, want to torture yourself?" Zach asked. "Vanessa Trent's worried about being kidnapped. Why don't you go out there and look over her security arrangements?"

"Hey, thanks!" he said. "I'm perfect for the job."

They drove the rest of the way in silence. Zach's mind was on Claire, not the murder or Vanessa Trent. Tonight, for once, Claire had been almost friendly. She'd thawed just a tad and he planned to take advantage of it. If his luck held, there wouldn't be any fights that his deputies couldn't handle. He wanted to get back before the gallery closed. There would be dancing in the plaza and then the fun would really begin.

Dumping Vanessa Trent on Yeager was a brilliant move. Maybe the flashy actress would want to add an FBI agent to her list of conquests. Sure as hell, Zach wasn't going for it. Vanessa was nothing more than a slut with a body created by some pricey Beverly Hills plastic surgeon. Did she really think those boobs looked natural? She should check into a clinic and seek treatment for silicone dependency.

Some men went for the silicone bit. A glance sideways confirmed Yeager had a shit-eating grin on his face. No doubt he was anticipating the "security" advice he was going to give Vanessa Trent. The actress didn't want advice; she wanted to get laid.

He found Vanessa's interest in him demeaning in a way that he could never have explained. Zach never fully understood, but had long since learned to accept that women thought he was sexy. Adding a badge made him even more appealing to certain women. That was what the actress was after, a man with a badge.

Not Zach Coulter without a badge.

He had no interest in bed hopping. Okay, okay, he'd spent more than his fair share of time in various women's beds, but at this age, he'd gone beyond simply screwing. Now, he wanted more than a quick tumble.

He wanted the whole enchilada. A home. The family he wished he'd had when he was growing up. But did he think he was going to get what he needed from Claire? Hell, no. Her old man still had the power over her. The scene in the plaza this evening proved that. Holt could pitch a fit and Claire would tell Zach to go to hell.

So why was he torturing himself? The answer was as simple as his returning home. Something compelled him to give it a try.

Angela had deliberately lagged behind Claire and hadn't gone into The Rising Sun Gallery. She'd been anxious to see the paintings that had kept the majority of people from wandering from gallery to gallery as they usually did during the Art Festival. Claire had been so upset about her father that Angela hadn't wanted to disappoint her if she couldn't get excited about her new artist.

Face it. Nothing excited her anymore. Not cooking. Not sex. And she didn't want to have the rug pulled out from under her entirely by discovering she no longer had enthusiasm for art. What would she do then?

She wandered next door into the nearly empty Tallchief Gallery that specialized in Native American jewelry. She could always use another piece of hand-crafted jewelry, she thought, but when she looked into the cases, she couldn't decide on anything. Every piece reminded her of something she had, even though most were one-of-a-kind.

Embarrassed for the owner who was hovering at her elbow, anxious to make a sale, Angela selected a silver pendant. She handed him her Visa and waited. She was out on the sidewalk heading back to Claire's gallery when she dropped the small box as she tried to shove it into her purse. It hit the bricks and the pendant tumbled out.

From the shadows a man emerged, quickly retrieving the box and pendant. "You dropped this, ma'am."

There was no word on earth—even the most vulgar term—that upset her more than "ma'am." It made her feel old and she freaked whenever one of her young studmuffins used it. But coming from this stranger with the warm brown eyes and shy smile, it seemed right. Anyway, he was older himself, and rather handsome in his own way.

His face was thin, almost gaunt, and his thick brown hair was cut stylishly short, nearly hiding the gray along his temples. His tall, lean frame wasn't the type of body that normally attracted her. But he had a down-to-earth, likable air about him that appealed to her.

"What is it?" he asked as he carefully placed the silver pendant in its box again.

Angela had to take another look to recall just what she'd bought. "It's the Crow Mother Kachina."

"Beautiful," he said. "Really beautiful."

His comment seemed to refer to the pendant, but the way he looked at her when he said it made her wonder. "It's kind of sad, actually. The Crow Mother is the mother of all Kachinas according to the Hopi people. During the ceremonial bean dance, she selects the war heroes who will sacrifice themselves for the good of the tribe during battle."

"Why would you buy something so depressing?" he asked with the same shy smile.

Until that moment she hadn't realized that she must have subconsciously selected the pendant because she was depressed. Of course, she couldn't say that to a total stranger. "The craftsmanship is superb. I couldn't resist."

"It is beautiful," he said, but again, he wasn't looking

at the pin. Each time he gazed into her eyes, he kept staring at her longer.

He was coming on to her, she decided, but he wasn't
her type. Not only was he too old, he was slender. She
preferred young buff males. Still, he did have something
elusive that attracted her.

"Did you visit The Rising Sun Gallery?" she asked just
to keep the conversation going.

"Yeah. It's really hot in there. Too many people. I need
space."

"Well, what did you think about the featured artist?"

The stranger shuffled his feet and shrugged. "He's okay,
I guess."

She looked into his earnest brown eyes and saw a flicker
of some indefinable emotion. Obviously, he was just a tourist and didn't know much about art. Was he alone, she
wondered, then quickly asked herself why she cared. "Well,
I've got to go. Thanks."

She hurried toward the entrance of the gallery where
clusters of people were sipping margaritas. As she went in,
she looked over her shoulder and saw the stranger on the
sidewalk staring at her.

It was another five minutes before Angela finished greeting friends and edged her way through the crowd and was
close enough to see the paintings. She blinked once . . .
twice just to make certain she wasn't imagining this.

Oh, my, God!

Both paintings, especially the one of the cowboy with
the bouquet, struck an emotional cord. A lump rose in
her throat and she swallowed hard, reminding herself to
analyze this art as a professional. Emotional paintings
weren't necessarily great paintings.

Fabulous use of color, she thought objectively. The artist
had taken the softer hues of the high country, inspired by
the early morning light on the sugarloaf mesas and shadowy canyons. Those moody hues, his flawless use of pastels,

and unerring perspective were an astonishing meld of creative elements that few artists had mastered.

Unique brushwork, too, she noted. It was sharp in places as if the paint had been applied with a blade, yet in other areas the strokes were feather soft. No ordinary art-store brush had touched this canvas, she decided. The artist had made his own.

Angela wasn't certain how long she stood there enthralled by work so unique it defied description. There was an air of mystery and longing and loneliness that spoke to her because it echoed what she was feeling. She was on the verge of tears, yet for the first time in weeks, she was happier than she had ever been.

Art, her great love, had not deserted her, after all.

"What's the woman thinking?"

Now long had Claire been standing beside her, Angela wondered. "Who knows? That's the great strength of this artist's work. It defies one single interpretation."

"He's obviously from the new school of contemporary realism."

"True," Angela agreed, unable to suppress a note of sadness as she recalled what Claire had said about Alexander Holt's reaction to the painting with the bouquet. Thank God her father was dead, Angela thought, remembering too vividly how he'd yank her chain the same way Claire's father did.

"I'll take both of them," Angela said without dickering, which wasn't the least bit like her. "Now, I want to see—she squinted to read the name scribbled in the right-hand corner—"the rest of Paul Winfay's works."

"Winfrey. Paul Winfrey," Claire corrected her. "This is it for now. These are the only paintings he's completed."

"You're presenting a new artist with just two paintings?" Angela was dumbfounded. She'd followed Claire from the gallery in Arizona where she'd been manager to her own gallery and knew Claire was too savvy to represent an artist without a body of work to substantiate his talent.

"Paul's just started. He has a brilliant future."

"You can't seriously expect me to invest this amount of money when the artist doesn't have other works," Angela retorted, her anger and frustration mounting. "The more he sells, especially to museums, the more my investment will be worth. Otherwise, I have two expensive paintings by a nobody who may never pick up a brush again. I won't be able to resell them."

"Then don't buy them," came a masculine voice from behind her.

Angela whirled around, self-consciously realizing she had been shouting at Claire, and people were staring at them. The stranger she'd met outside had spoken those words. Apparently, he was the artist. Unbelievable. She would never have pegged him as the arty type.

"Tell me about yourself," she demanded, barely conscious of the people moving closer to catch every word. "What have you been doing that you wasted your time when you should have been painting?"

He reached over and took her hand. The gleaming seven-carat diamond on her finger had been a gift from her father—when she'd broken off with the tennis pro. The Piaget watch with its diamond band had been her gift to herself for her fortieth birthday.

"You know, ma'am, some of us have to work to keep a roof over our heads." He dropped her hand as if it were a poisonous snake. "A friend gave me two pieces of canvas and four colors of paint."

"Don't tell me you painted these"—she waved her hand toward the wall—"by blending just four colors?"

"Yes, ma'am. I couldn't afford a brush, so I used a yucca quill."

The astounded buzz that followed his words mirrored Angela's own amazement. Someone would have to desperately want to paint to create works like these. In her entire life, nothing had touched her as much as his work. Not even the death of her father. She had everything; the artist had nothing.

Nothing but talent that money could never buy.

Angela orchestrated a smile, her chin tilted up just slightly as she turned to Claire. "Put sold stickers on both paintings." She slowly faced Paul. "Come on, I'm going to buy you a drink. A man of your talent needs a mentor."

Seventeen

"What do you think is happening in Paul's painting?" asked Claire as she walked up to Zach.

It was late now and the gallery was almost empty after the Art Festival. Most people had drifted into the plaza to dance or had gone to one of the nearby restaurants. She hadn't noticed Zach return to the gallery until she spotted him admiring her prize bronze, Wild Horse.

Zach turned and looked at her. For once he didn't inspect her body in that arrogant, insulting way of his. Instead he smiled, an adorable smile that canted slightly to one side. But it wasn't anywhere near the devastating grin he'd unleashed on Vanessa.

"How in hell would I know what Paul Winfrey had in mind?" he asked.

She bristled, telling herself that his cussing made her angry. Be honest, Claire. Be honest. She was upset because the cute grin he had for her was nowhere near the magnitude of the smile he'd bestowed on the actress.

"Don't you have an opinion?"

He grinned again, more of a smirk this time, but she didn't smile back. Forget Angela's advice. This man was trouble with a capital T.

"I haven't a clue," Zach said. "I'm wondering how this artist managed to show the fine hairs in Wild Horse's headdress."

"That's the secret to crafting a great bronze," she said, very proud of her mother who had spotted the Colin Ashcroft bronze long before the artist became world renowned.

"No thought about what Paul's painting means?" she asked as Zach continued to study the bronze.

Finally, he looked over his shoulder at the painting, then at Claire. "The cowboy loves her, but all he has to offer is himself. Does she love him enough to accept the flowers he picked . . . and accept him for what he is?"

His eyes never left hers during the explanation, and she knew there was some hidden meaning to what he was saying. Suddenly, the gallery seemed too empty and too dominated by Zach's masculine presence, all six-feet-four-plus of him. Every time they were alone something happened. She bridged her torso with her arms to combat a shiver of anticipation.

"What do you think it means?" he asked.

She hesitated to say what she thought. She'd heard so many interpretations of Paul's work that she was confused. "My first impression was the woman loves him. She honestly loves him, and she's touched by the wildflowers he's brought. She turns away to keep him from seeing the tears of happiness. It's the kind of painting that means something different to everyone. That's what makes it so powerful."

He looked back at the painting, then turned his gaze to her. She told herself not to let her guard down, but it was difficult. There was something boyish in his expression that reminded her of the young Zach Coulter the bad boy who hid his sensitive side from everyone but her. She had defied her father for the first time and had secretly met Zach, night after night, convinced she loved him. Well, she'd been a kid then, too young to know the meaning of true love.

"Should I lock up?" asked Suzi.

Claire blessed the interruption and glanced around. Everyone had left except the three of them. No doubt, Suzi was anxious to get out to the plaza where the band was now playing. "Go on. I'll close the shop. You were a tremendous help tonight. Thanks. There'll be something extra in your paycheck."

"Who bought Paul's paintings?" Zach asked as Suzi left.

"Angela Whitmore took both of them. She's decided to become his mentor. They're over at Tortilla Flats having a drink." She scrambled for something else to say, conscious of being alone with him. "People loved Paul's work. I would have sold both paintings in the first ten minutes, if I hadn't put such a high price on them. He was an instant hit."

"Paul's a good guy. He deserves it." He was silent for a moment, then his dark gaze moved over her face. "Everyone deserves a second chance."

The suggestive undertone to his voice warned her to keep the conversation light. She opted to ignore the remark, waving her hand at the near-empty display cases. "Look at this place. Red dot heaven. People bought everything in sight. I have a lot of cash. I need to take it to the night drop at the bank."

"I'll walk over with you."

She started to protest, but changed her mind. The night drop at her father's bank was around the corner from the plaza on a dark side street. Normally this wouldn't have concerned her, but the town was filled with strangers. The last thing she wanted to do was risk losing the money that would be a giant step toward getting her out of debt. No one would dare take on Zach Coulter.

She brought Lucy and Lobo inside and locked the gallery, then dropped the keys in her pocket. "Boy, I have a lot of cleaning up to do, not to mention restocking."

Outside, the band blasted rock music up to the star-filled sky. A blue corn moon sulked between mountain peaks, creating pools of shadow and light. A full moon like this meant warm summer days which would make the corn grow tall, promising a bountiful harvest.

Tonight the air was soft and filled with the mouth-watering aroma of chilis roasting on piñon grills and tamales steaming in blue corn husks. Claire's stomach rumbled, and she realized that she hadn't eaten all day.

Zach walked beside her, but he hadn't said anything since volunteering to accompany her to the bank. He put his hand on the small of her back to guide her through the crowd in front of a sidewalk café. She tensed, as the warmth from his palm seeped through the summer-weight suede.

She clutched the deposit bag under her arm, aware of a lightness that made her slightly giddy and the chill prickling down her arms. Was this the way other women responded to Zach? Undoubtedly. He was the talk of the town, she reminded herself—just the way his father had been.

Never forget it.

"The weirdest thing happened." She was jabbering nervously and she knew it, but if she could keep talking, she could overcome her body's involuntary reaction. "Tohono stopped by to see Paul's paintings. I asked Tohono who he thought killed Duncan Morrell. What do you think he said?"

His arm was around her waist now, touching her lightly, guiding her through the crowd, but there was something possessive—and reassuring—about his touch. A dangerous warmth was invading her body, and she had to steel herself against it.

He gazed down at her, a hint of mocking laughter in his eyes. "I give. Who does Tohono think murdered Morrell?"

"A *chindi*."

"A ghost?" Zach chuckled as they rounded the corner

and walked down the dark side street. "What do you expect? Tohono's part Navajo and comes from the Talking Water clan. They love to spin a yarn, particularly tales about ghosts. When something isn't easily explained—like this murder—they blame it on a *chindi*. It's Tohono's way of copping out. Believe me, he has an opinion about who committed the crime."

"Well, the killer might as well be a ghost. Nobody saw anything. No one even heard the shot," Claire said, but Zach didn't comment. Whatever he knew, he was no longer sharing it with her.

Acting on a hunch, she asked, "Who was the man with you tonight?"

A half beat of silence. "Brad Yeager is the Special Agent in Charge of the FBI field office in Gallup. He's a friend who's in town to help with the rodeo crowds."

Claire smiled inwardly, his words confirming her suspicions. Zach was keeping information about the case to himself because the FBI was in on the investigation. She wasn't a bit surprised. The lithograph fraud had been simmering for sometime, ready to boil over and tarnish the entire art community.

"Maybe this will be like Manby's murder," she said, referring to a turn-of-the-century case that was never solved. "Arthur Manby was just like Duncan Morrell. He'd bilked so many people that there were more than a dozen prime suspects. Any one of them had reason to cut off his head and leave it on the fireplace."

Zach didn't take the bait. Without commenting on the similarities between the two cases, or telling her anything, he held open the night deposit box.

She dropped the pouch into the slot. Wait until morning when the teller counted the cash, tallied the checks, and added the credit-card receipts to the total, she thought. Her father would *have* to be impressed by The Rising Sun's success. Then she wondered if she would ever be able to please him.

She suppressed the niggling feeling of anxiety that always came when she thought about pleasing her father. Nothing she was going to do short of giving up the gallery and coming to work at his bank was likely to make him truly happy. But if he would just once be a tiny bit encouraging, she would be satisfied.

They walked back toward the plaza, Zach's hand still on her waist. People filled the square and the street, which had been blocked off for the event. The band began fiddling a country tune that sounded vaguely familiar.

"Listen to them butcher that song," commented Zach. "They aren't Flash and The Rusty Roots. Why even try to play 'The Devil Went Down to Georgia?' It's a crime."

"I knew I'd heard that song somewhere. They were playing it the night someone put a Roofie in my drink. One line says something about the devil being in the house of the rising sun. I laughed then, but I'm not laughing now. Duncan's dead and I'm one of the suspects."

"It's one of my favorite songs—played right. The Charlie Daniels' Band does it best," he responded, again dodging any reference to the case.

"Really? I didn't know you liked Country Western music." Claire looked up at him.

His eyes were so blue, so compelling, and the lashes framing them so dense that together they tempered the angular planes of his face. His eyes spoke to her and always had. At times they seemed to see straight through to her soul, silently communicating with her in a way no one else could. It was just Zach's special brand of magnetism, she reminded herself.

"There's a lot about me you don't know, Claire."

She wasn't touching that one. She forced her gaze away from his and looked at the brightly lit plaza. People were dancing, laughing, having a great time. She'd be dancing on air herself but Duncan Morrell's murder hung over her, dampening her spirits. Knowing the FBI was involved should reassure her, but instead it gave her a very uneasy feeling.

"I just wish the man with the beard would turn up and give me an alibi," she said. "In a way, I hoped it was Paul because I really could use an alibi. But when I saw his work and discovered how talented he was, I didn't ask him. I don't know if I could work with him if he'd been the man at The Hideaway."

"Claire, I told you earlier. Paul is not your stranger."

Zach's words were reassuring, yet something in his tone troubled her. *Coyote waits. Lurking in the shadows.* Tohono's ominous warning came to her suddenly. Could there have been two people involved in Duncan's death?

She shuddered, remembering her archrival had been killed in the bungalow next door to the room where she had been that night. What had happened to the stranger? Why hadn't he contacted her?

"Let's get one of Manuelito's chiles rellenos," Zach suggested.

She knew better than to spend any more time with Zach Coulter, but the thought of one of Manuelito's chiles stuffed with meat and cheese made her stomach overrule her brain. They stood in line at Manuelito's stand. She looked up and found Zach smiling at her. She couldn't resist; she returned his smile.

"Hey, two of my favorite people." Manuelito greeted them, his gold-capped front tooth twinkling. He didn't look one day older than when Claire's mother had brought her to his stand when she'd been a youngster. "My special, no?"

They both said "Yes" in unison, then laughed. Zach pulled out his money clip, and Claire started to protest, but remembered that all she'd brought with her were the keys in her pocket.

Finding an empty park bench was out of the question, so they ate standing up. All around them other people were eating or listening to the band who had given up on country music and had gone back to rock. Nearby a woman was making balloon animals for children. Just beyond her, a sidewalk artist was sketching charcoal portraits for tourists.

"H-m-m-m," Claire murmured as she dabbed at her lips with the napkin. "No one, but no one makes a better chile relleno than Manuelito."

"True. All the years I was away, I kept trying to find rellenos like Manuelito's."

She looked at him a moment, more than a little surprised by his comment. Had Zach missed Taos the way she had? She couldn't imagine why he would want to return to a place that had so many unhappy memories, but the unique pueblo, the soaring mountains, and the quaint town had a special magic that lured people.

It would be easy to ask him why he'd returned, but she didn't want to get too personal. Last night he'd made it clear that he intended to make love to her. At the time she'd been tempted to give in to ensure his silence. But Tohono's reference to a *chindi* triggered the realization that this case was going to take longer to solve than she'd anticipated. With the FBI investigating, her involvement was certain to be exposed.

A ghost hadn't killed Duncan; a flesh-and-blood person had. Coyote. A clever, tricky person, who wasn't going to be caught easily. The longer it took, the less chance she had of keeping her involvement secret. She might as well tell her father and brace herself. There was no reason to hurt her father by getting involved with Zach.

Ollie Hammond sauntered through the crowd, greeting everyone with a smile, but when he saw Zach, the police chief's brow furrowed. His immaculate uniform and erect bearing heralded his military background and rigid personality. Zach's black outfit with the badge off-center made a sharp contrast, but a welcome one. There was sómething friendly, yet protective, about a casually dressed sheriff.

"Shouldn't you be out at the rodeo grounds in your own territory?" Ollie asked.

There was such obvious dislike and outright animosity in the police chief's voice that Claire was tempted to tell him to drop dead. Ollie was the most bigoted man in town, the perfect stereotype of a racist law officer. For years he'd had a sign on the door to his office. *No Dogs or Indians Allowed.* The city fathers finally insisted Ollie remove it, but he hadn't changed his attitude.

Zach's expression was cold and closed. "I'm off duty until midnight."

"Yeah?" Ollie hooked his thumbs in his belt and glared at Zach. "What have you done to find those *chukes* who roughed up Bam Stegner? Nothin'. You're not even looking for Morrell's killer either."

Zach tensed, his eyes narrowing slightly. She knew how explosive Zach's temper could be. A thought flashed through her mind. What would it be like to live your life with people always *expecting* you to fail?

Ever since Zach had been a young boy, people had thought the worst about him. True, he'd been a hellion, responding with his fists to older boys who teased him about his mother's drinking. When his father was killed, the chip on Zach's shoulder became a slab of granite. No matter what she thought of him personally, she was proud that he'd made something of himself, beating the odds.

Now the whole town was waiting and watching, judging him on how he solved one miserable case. Arthur Manby's murder had happened over seventy-five years ago, but people still condemned the sheriff who failed to solve the case. She didn't want Zach adding to his problems by getting into a fight with Ollie.

"Of course, the sheriff is investigating." Claire moved

closer to Zach. "He was just going over the information I gave him earlier."

Ollie grunted, clearly surprised she was involved. Obviously, he'd thought she was standing near Zach because the plaza was so crowded.

"Yeah, well, Coulter hasn't got what it takes to solve this case," Ollie told her, then he turned and shoved his way through the throngs of tourists.

Zach started to go after him, but Claire grabbed his hand. "Let's dance." She tugged and he moved with her toward the gazebo area where people were dancing.

"You don't have to defend me, Claire," he said, allowing her to lead him around a group of children eating cotton candy with their fingers. "I'm used to taking care of myself."

She looked over her shoulder. "I'm taking care of you, the way you took care of Bam Stegner for me."

"What in hell are you talking about?"

She stopped and he bumped into her. Their hands were still linked, but now his large hand had closed over hers and their fingers were laced together. "Come on, Zach. How stupid do you think I am?"

"Aw, hell. Now that you mention it. I think you're—"

"Zach, be serious. *Chukes* did not beat up Bam Stegner. You did." She pointed to the small cut near his eye, then to the scabs on his knuckles. "Don't deny it."

"I took off my badge and got Bam out to the reservation where the tribal police have jurisdiction," he admitted. "It was a fair fight. One on one. Bam landed a few good punches. I've got a cut and a bruise and a few cracked ribs, but he won't be pulling any stunts on you like that rattler."

"You promised you'd let me—"

He put a finger on her lips, silencing her. "No, Claire. I never promised. You tried to tell me. What you don't understand is that men like Stegner respond only to power.

Why do you think he made up the story about *chukes?* He wants everyone to believe it takes a whole gang to get the best of him. Otherwise, he loses face—and power."

She gazed into his eyes, not knowing how she truly felt. Part of her was grateful—and touched—that he'd gone to so much trouble for her. On another level, she was disturbed. This meant that she owed him something, and she was dead certain what he'd want in return.

"Thanks," she finally said, hoping her voice concealed her mixed emotions. "I'm truly grateful."

The band was just finishing a song, the final notes obliterated by a round of applause from the crowd. The band wasn't very good, but it didn't seem to matter. The townspeople loved a good time and the tourists had fallen under the spell of a blue corn moon in an extraordinary village that hadn't changed much since the days of the Conquistadors.

The band began to play again, soft, lilting sounds, which were a sharp contrast to their earlier songs. A slow number, Claire realized as Zach pulled her to him, his arms encircling her.

His powerful body was hard and warm against hers, and she was disturbingly aware of every masculine contour. Earlier that evening, his badge had felt warm to her touch. Now it was positively hot as it pressed against her breast. Suddenly, her mouth was as dry as sandpaper, her throat just as rough.

She knew better than to relax her body, the way his strong arms were demanding. She kept her spine rigid as his hand roved across the small of her back. He was moving to the slow cadence of the music, his thighs brushing intimately against hers. She concentrated on staring over his shoulder at the other dancers, attempting to forget she was in his arms.

Impossible.

Zach Coulter had a virility that beckoned every female,

she reasoned. Claire, for all her resolve, wasn't as immune to sexual magnetism as she had believed. To keep herself from wantonly pressing against his to-die-for body, she tried talking.

"Who taught you how to dance?" The words came out with a croak.

He disarmed her with an even more adorable grin than he'd given her at the gallery. "My mother taught me. She was a wonderful person . . . when she wasn't drinking."

Claire managed what she hoped was an approving smile. Despite all the shame his mother had caused him, Zach had loved her. Claire could still remember him trying to raise the money for a decent funeral. His loyalty and love left her unexpectedly touched.

She should have had the guts to shove her father aside when he had blocked her from giving Zach the twenty-dollar bill she had clutched in her hand. That day had been so long ago that it seemed like another person who had stood at the bank's door staring at Zach as he walked through the blizzard into total darkness. She should have run down the street after him.

But she couldn't. She had been afraid, frightened to hurt the only parent she had left. And some part of her had been angry with Zach for not telling her about their parents' affair. She'd been wrong; she could see that now with the vision possible only when you were an adult.

But she couldn't change the past. Nothing could.

She glanced over Zach's shoulder at the couples dancing around them. The area was so packed that it was almost impossible to move, but Zach swayed to the beat, one leg flexing slightly, nudging between hers. Goose bumps prickled across the back of her arms and languid heat spread through her body.

She took a deep breath, but it didn't help. Inhaling merely filled her lungs with the citrus scent of his after-shave. He placed her hand on his badge, its heat instantly warming her palm. His hand now free, he lightly fluffed her hair aside and touched the back of her neck.

His thumb slowly traced across her bare skin, forcing her to relax a bit. Beneath the silver star, she felt the solid, steady *thump-thump* of his heart. She was thankful for his superior height. She didn't have to look him in the eye so he could see how attracted she was to him—despite everything.

"Who taught you how to dance?" Zach asked, his warm breath stirring wisps of hair along her cheek.

"My father," she said without looking up at him.

"Really? That's interesting."

She felt his voice vibrate against the badge pressing into her palm. She looked up at him, and the warm glow she'd been fighting suddenly flared into something more when she met his gaze. His smoldering blue eyes bore into her with breathtaking intensity.

They were barely moving now, not even pretending to dance as the crowd tried to dance to the slow song. *Nothing can happen here. We're surrounded by people,* she told herself as he continued to stare at her. Thankfully they all seemed to be tourists, and weren't paying any attention to them.

His large hand rested for a moment on the small of her back. Then, it edged lower and lower and shockingly lower still. Claire noted the sheen making his eyes even more intense and the enlarged pupils as his hand cupped her bottom. She lowered her gaze to the sensual outline of his lips, so inviting, so dangerously close.

Don't let him kiss you, she warned herself. *And whatever you do, don't you kiss him first.*

She put her head on his shoulder to avoid temptation. Before she knew it, the hand cradling her buttocks pressed her closer and slightly upward until she was flush against his hard, jutting shaft. *Oh, my.*

She spoke, telling him to let go, but no sound came

from her lips. Heat flooded her, pooling where he had so intimately joined their bodies. She tried to resist, she honestly did, but the urge to move against him was too strong.

She rotated her hips just a little. He felt so-o-o good. A little more. And more. Mindless, shuddering passion coursed through her as she brushed her yearning body against his. A depth charge of desire shot through her with knee-weakening intensity.

Without realizing she'd moved, she discovered both her arms were linked around his neck. His arms were loosely circling her waist. Oh, mercy! She was the one who was wantonly rubbing against him. Not that he seemed to mind.

His breath was hot and fast against her ear. The unmistakable gleam of desire glistening in his eyes, evident even beneath slightly lowered lids.

"Claire, baby, I hate to tell you this, but the dance is over."

She should have been angry at his teasing tone, but she wasn't. He made no move to release her, and she didn't let go of him either. The crowd milled around them, talking and waiting for the next song.

"Claire, over here," she heard a familiar voice calling. She pulled away from Zach and saw Maude Pfister elbowing her way through the crowd. Immediately, Claire knew something terrible had happened to her father.

Eighteen

Angela gazed across the table at Paul Winfrey. They'd been at Tortilla Flats for over two hours having dinner, and now they were finished. She'd tried to get him to talk about himself, but he had little to say. Apparently he'd led a dull life, drifting from town to town and living off odd jobs.

Boring. Positively boring.

That's how she would normally view a man of his age who hadn't been to the Galapagos Islands or gone to Nepal to view the total eclipse of the sun—or done something equally unusual. Young studmuffins were an exception, of course. She never expected them to be interesting.

But Paul Winfrey fascinated her. Everything about him intrigued her from his rangy cowboy's body to the quiet way he spoke. There was a power and depth to him that she found intriguing.

She was excited, truly thrilled for the first time in years. She wanted to help him have a stellar career. He had to be what? Forty-something. Her age or even older. He'd almost squandered his talent.

"What made you take up art?" she asked.

Across the table, he took a sip of his coffee before saying, "Quentin Reynolds gave a one-day workshop. I didn't have anything better to do than take it. He encouraged me to paint . . . seriously paint."

"Really? I know Quentin well. I mean, I knew him when

he was managing the Buck Head Gallery in Aspen. I bought several paintings from him. They're in my home in Scottsdale."

She struggled to conceal her excitement. They'd been talking all this time, and Paul hadn't mentioned Quentin Reynolds. Before becoming a hopeless alcoholic unable to hold down a steady job, Quentin had been one of the leading authorities on Southwestern art. He knew a winner when he saw one.

"Quentin scraped the paint off two old canvases he had and gave them to me," Paul said. "That's why I only did two paintings."

His brown eyes were serious, charged with some inner emotion she couldn't quite read. She assumed he now knew he had talent and wanted to paint from dawn to dusk.

The waiter arrived with the check and Angela plunked down her American Express Platinum card. Paul's eyes narrowed slightly, and she realized he was a bit old-fashioned. Unlike the young studs who expected her to pay, Paul was embarrassed by it.

"I've been exposed to Southwestern art my whole life. My father was a well-known collector. After his death, I continued to collect. Now I have one of the best collections in this country." Actually, she was downplaying it. She had the best private collection, a fact few would argue. "You have tremendous talent. I want to help you. I can take care of things for you, so you won't have to do anything but paint."

"What's in it for you?" he asked.

"I'll have the thrill of seeing your work and knowing I helped," she said as the waiter returned with the bill. She added a hefty tip, then scribbled her name. "I'll want the right to buy any paintings I like, of course."

His dark eyes roved over her face, the way they had all evening. Each time they lingered longer on her lips. A prickle of awareness, of sexual tension ignited. It had been there all along, she decided, but her elation over his art had relegated it to a subtle undercurrent.

He put both elbows on the table and leaned toward her. "Do you get a kick out of buying people?"

"I don't buy—" She gazed into his eyes and saw he was baffled by her offer. He continued staring at her, and she was forced to admit that she did indeed buy men. She craved young hunks with hard bodies. But this was different; this was about art, not sex.

"I just want to help," she assured him.

He rose slowly from the table and pulled out her chair. None of her studmuffins would have been as gentlemanly. They left the crowded restaurant in silence with him guiding her, his hand firm against the small of her back.

Outside the night was cool and laced with the sweetish scent of smoke from piñon grills, the way it often was in the mountains in the summer, but there was a softness to the air that she had never noticed before. The band was playing a disgustingly bad version of "The Devil Went Down to Georgia." She ought to know. Carleton Cole played it all the time.

"I like that song," Paul said. "My daddy could fiddle like that. Truth to tell, he was a hell of a fiddler."

"You loved him very much, didn't you?" She had already questioned him about his family and had discovered his parents were dead. He had no one except distant cousins that he'd lost track of. In many ways they were alike. She had no family except for a great-aunt who had Alzheimer's.

"Both my parents were great," he told her with his usual sincerity. "I wish they could see me now."

"You're going to be even more of a success when I help you."

They stepped around the corner, then down the dark alley where Angela had been forced to park her convertible because of the crowds. The top was down and the Mercedes silver hood glistened in the moonlight.

"I don't want that kind of pressure."

She stopped, thinking at first he was joking. His earnest expression said he meant every word. "I want to help you, so you're free to paint. That's not pressure."

"I don't intend to paint yet," he informed her in a tone that told her he'd given this a good deal of thought and knew what he wanted. "I want to live a little. Get a first-class mare to ride. I don't want some rich woman riding herd on me, telling me to paint."

Riding herd? Dammit. Dammit all the way to hell. No wonder Paul Winfrey had drifted around. He was one of those flitty types who had God-given talent, but was too lazy to use it. Obviously, he needed her. She mustn't over-react or she'd frighten him away.

"All right," she said, her tone smooth as if he hadn't just insulted her. "I won't press you to produce, I swear. I just want to help. Let me take care of things."

He moved closer, staring hard at her now, and her breath quickened. She felt alive, really alive. She did not want to lose this man. She could make him a household name. She was dead certain of it.

"Don't mention me painting again, promise?"

Agreeing to this was like stabbing herself in the heart, but if she wanted to direct his career, she had no alterna-tive. Later, she was positive that she could change his mind. "I promise."

A slow smile spread across his face, and her body re-sponded with a thrill of pleasure. She longed to see him happy, to have him be a shining star among artists.

He closed the distance between them, saying, "I'll let you take care of me. Here's what I need."

With amazing swiftness, he pulled her into his arms, his lips came down on hers. His kiss was gentle, almost tenta-tive, as if he hadn't kissed many women and wasn't sure of himself. After all the cocky studs she'd been around, this kiss was refreshingly sweet. It took only a second for him to gain confidence. She parted her lips and his tongue nudged its way inside.

Paul's body was surprisingly strong, she thought as she slipped her arms around him. He didn't have the muscles the young hunks did, but then he didn't work out six hours a day. Her hands explored the curve of his back as she returned his kiss.

She was unexpectedly breathless, her pulse racing. How long had it been since she'd reacted this way to what was a very simple, no-frills kiss? She leaned against the hood of the car, her knees no longer willing to support her.

He pulled back a fraction of an inch. "I wanted to do that when I first saw you outside of the gallery."

"Really?"

"I didn't think I could make it through dinner."

He kissed her again with such simplicity and heart-wrenching tenderness that she felt the sting of tears. They were banished in a second when she realized he was fully, awesomely aroused.

With just a kiss or two.

She edged her hand between them, then closed it around his penis. A low growl of pleasure rumbled from deep in his chest. She wriggled her hand into his jeans and beneath his underwear. His shaft was hard and pulsing with heat. She ran the tip of her finger over the smooth, rounded tip, detecting a hint of moisture.

She was damp herself, she realized, more than a little stunned at the discovery. Her whole body was on fire for this man. It usually took much longer—and lots of kinky sex—to arouse her. Lately, nothing had worked.

He would have kept kissing her all night if she'd let him. She unbuckled his belt and was working on his pants. "Let's do it on the hood of my Mercedes. I've had sex *in* a car, but never *on* a car."

He gazed at her with an odd expression. Apparently, he didn't see how erotic the high gloss hood of her car was.

"No, Angela." He ran his hand up the slope of her waist to her breast, then caressed the raised nipple with the wide pad of his thumb. "You're going to take care of me, remember? I want a big bed with crisp white sheets." He gently squeezed her breast, lifting it slightly as he planted a tender kiss just under her ear. "I want soft pillows and music on the stereo. I want to make love to you over and over and over, but I'm not cheapening you by doing it on the hood of a car."

Zach checked his watch and saw it was just past midnight. Claire had left him to go to the emergency room to be with her father a little over an hour ago. Zach had called to check on him, but the doctor hadn't decided just what was wrong with him. Don't let it be anything serious, Zach thought, imagining how much it would upset Claire. Not that he gave a rat's ass about the old coot, but he knew Claire truly loved him.

"You know what puzzles me about this case" Brad Yeager said, interrupting his thoughts.

They were sitting in Zach's Bronco in the parking lot of the rodeo arena watching the cowboys mill around. No one was drunk enough yet to warrant an arrest. Okay, so many were way over a breath-analyzer limit, but as long as they didn't get into a fight or attempt to drive, Zach refused to arrest them. Drunk cowboys at rodeos were a given.

"Why did Duncan Morrell go to The Hideaway for sex?" Yeager asked. "He had a great house, and it was empty. His wife says she left him because he had flipped over some bimbo and wouldn't give her up."

A spurt of excitement jolted Zach. "Really? I didn't know that. Who is it?"

"Thelma Morrell doesn't know. Her husband said he'd met the love of his life, and she could just take a hike. Apparently, he'd had numerous affairs over the years, but this one was important enough for Duncan to leave his wife and risk splitting their assets."

The flare of hope faded. This wasn't the break in the case he'd been hoping for. "Morrell was the ultimate con artist. Women went for him big time. Even after he fleeced them, they still loved him. But if he'd suddenly met someone who rang his bell, why go to The Hideaway for a night of hot sex?"

"It had to have been unplanned," Yeager said. "Vanessa Trent was supposed to meet him, but she missed her plane."

"And she'd invested heavily in Morrell's phony lithos. You don't suppose she was having an affair with him?"

"Nah, she's hot and heavy with some producer. I went out there a while ago to check her security. Know what she wants? To screw someone with a badge."

"Why am I not surprised?" Zach said, smiling inwardly.

" 'Course, I didn't want to be a number in her little black book, so I didn't take the bait."

Zach hooted, then high-fived Yeager. "Me either."

"I don't think you're off the hook yet, buddy. She wants you to give her a second opinion on her 'security.' I told her I'd pass the message on."

Zach watched a group of cowpokes butt shoulders, a precursor to a fight. Aw, hell, he didn't want to haul anyone to jail tonight. He wanted to go off duty and see Claire. He was breaking her down, bit by bit, day by day. One kiss at a time. But he *was* getting somewhere, wasn't he?

Yeager broke into his thoughts. "Thelma Morrell suspected Duncan had a thing for Stacy Hopkins."

"Do you think she's the woman Morrell fell for?"

"Nah, Seth said Stacy was with them at The Hideaway until dawn," Yeager reminded him. "Why would she be making love to two men—at once—while her lover was in a nearby room?"

"It doesn't make sense, but I'll double check with Stacy tomorrow."

"I turned up something else interesting," Yeager said while Zach watched the milling crowd of cowboys near the stalls, knowing a fight was minutes away. "Carleton Cole is an alias for one Edwin Shumski. He has a rap sheet thick as a Bible."

"Hot damn!" Zach couldn't help smiling. With luck this would break open the case. "What was Shumski in for?"

"Petty crimes mostly, but let's keep our eye on him."

Nineteen

Her father was on a gurney waiting to be taken in for tests when Claire arrived at the hospital. A lump formed in her throat, and she swallowed hard, then tried to give him an encouraging smile.

"I'm okay, honey . . ." His voice drifted away, leaving so much unspoken, but she detected the anguish in his eyes. She realized her own fear was dwarfed by his. He needed her now in a way that he had never needed her before.

When he had suffered the first stroke, she had been living in Scottsdale, managing a gallery there. By the time she arrived home, the crisis was over, and her father had put up a brave front. But the front was gone now.

He closed his eyes, yet she doubted he was resting. He didn't want her to see how frightened he really was. Pride etched every plane of his face, and even his unnaturally pale skin didn't disguise it. She took his hand and gently squeezed his trembling fingers.

She gazed at him and the years slipped away . . . away.

Suddenly, she was a small child again, reaching up, up for her father's hand. He clasped her small hand in his, and she saw the love in his eyes as he said, "You look so pretty today, Claire. I swear, you're the image of your mother."

Mentioning her mother made Claire study the shiny tips of her new Mary Janes, guilt pricking at her. Even though her father was devoted to her, deep in her heart, Claire loved her mother more. She didn't know why exactly; she simply felt closer to her mother.

In those days her world was perfect and she believed nothing could go wrong. Daddy would fix everything. Foolishly, she'd still believed this myth when she'd discovered her "perfect" mother wantonly making love to Jake Coulter.

She had run straight to the bank and barged into her father's office. He'd listened, his face expressionless as she explained what she'd seen.

"I'll take care of it," he assured her.

After school, she reluctantly went to her ballet lesson, then returned home. The house was dark, and the usual sounds were not coming from the kitchen. Good, she thought, going up the stairs to her room. She did not want to face her mother. She felt like a rat for having tattled, but she was furious. How could her mother let a man like Jake Coulter touch her?

Worse, she'd been enjoying it. The image of her naked mother, head flung back, hair streaming down to her buttocks was seared in Claire's brain.

Inside her room, she plopped down on the bed, then noticed the envelope propped against her pillow. She stared at it, afraid to even touch it. Minutes passed before she found the courage to open it.

Darling Claire,

I'm leaving Taos with Jake Coulter. Your father will explain the details. I know you're upset, and I ask your forgiveness. I pray that one day you'll understand.

There is perfection in art, darling, but not in life. Please keep Wild Horse, my favorite bronze, as a symbol of the happy times we shared. I love you and I want nothing but the best for you.

All My Love,

Mother

Claire wanted to ask about the "details" but didn't. Her father returned home that evening a solemn, shattered man.

Late that night Claire was staring at the ceiling, unable to sleep. She'd sobbed for hours, muffling the sounds as best she could with her pillow. Why upset her father even more? Now her eyes were dry and itchy, her nose raw and sore. Anger still burned inside her coupled with disbelief.

Her mother had deserted them for the town stud. Unbelievable.

Her fury intensified every time she thought about Zach Coulter. She hadn't spoken to him since she had caught their parents together, but her sixth sense told her that he'd known all along. Why hadn't he told her? If she'd been warned, she would have been prepared. She might not have run so recklessly to her father.

She might not have driven her mother away.

But there had always been a mysterious side to Zach, an aura about him that seemed dangerous and made him even more attractive. Now, though, she recognized this secretiveness for what it was—a destructive force. He could have forewarned her, but he'd chosen to remain silent.

A crunching of tires and a flare of headlights sent her flying to the window overlooking the driveway. Thank God. Her mother had come to her senses and returned home.

The sliver of a moon perched high above Taos mountain revealed a black and white police car parking in front of their house. A prickle of anxiety became a thundering drumbeat of fear as Ollie Hammond emerged from the car. The chief of police was above making routine calls; everyone in town knew that. Something was terribly wrong.

She threw on her robe and yanked open the bedroom door. The lights were on in the hall and her father was standing there, his eyes squeezed shut. The doorbell rang, cutting through the silence like the crack of a rifle. She gazed at her father, silently pleading for him to make her world perfect again.

But those days were over. Her father wasn't even capable of moving. Only when the doorbell rang again and she grabbed his hand, did he follow her downstairs. Claire was the one to switch on the lights and open the front door.

"What is it?" she asked Ollie, her voice pitched so low she could hardly hear it.

Ollie had taken off his hat and tucked it under his arm. He walked into the entry, saying, "You'd better go to your room, Claire. I need to speak with your father."

"No! Tell me what's happened to my mother!"

Ollie looked at her father, then took a deep breath. "Alex, there's been a terrible accident—"

"Is Amy still alive?" her father whispered.

Ollie slowly shook his head. "Their car was hit by a semi-truck. Amy and Jake Coulter were killed instantly."

"No!" Claire cried. "It can't be true!"

Ollie didn't look at her. Instead he put his hand on her father's shoulder. "There's no mistake. I went out to the scene myself. Amy's gone."

Her father said nothing, letting Ollie's heavy breathing pulse through the foyer. Finally, her father turned away. Without another word, he mounted the stairs, leaving Claire standing beside the chief of police.

The cold, cruel reality of the situation swept over her as Ollie muttered something about being strong for her father's sake before he backed out the door. She stood alone in the foyer staring into the family room where she had spent so many wonderful hours with her mother. Scalding tears seeped from Claire's eyes, blurring everything around her.

It's all my fault. Why didn't I keep my mouth shut? Why didn't Zach warn me?

Everyone in town—except Zach and his mother—attended Amy Holt's funeral. Claire forced herself to be strong. Her father was so quiet, so unlike himself that she was truly afraid for the first time in her life.

She didn't dare look in the casket, fearing she would

break down, but when everyone left, she tiptoed up to her mother's coffin. She was almost overwhelmed by the cloying scent of the hundreds of flowers sent by friends. Peeking into the mahogany casket lined with white silk, Claire saw her mother for the last time.

Her mother had on more makeup than she ever would have worn and every hair was in place. Even if she didn't look natural, her mother appeared serene. Claire prayed she was at peace and with God the way the minister had claimed. But Claire had her doubts.

Amy Holt had been young, far too young to die such a violent death. Had she felt much pain? Claire wondered. What had been her last thoughts? Had she forgiven Claire for what she'd done?

"Oh, Mama, I'll never forget the wonderful times we had. I promise, I'll make you proud of me. Just forgive me, please. I love you so much. I never meant for this to happen."

She had no idea how long she stood beside the casket talking to her mother for the last time. There were so many things she longed to say. So many questions she had planned to ask her mother. So much she needed to share with her mother. But time had run out. Now, there could only be good-bye.

"Mommy, you'll always be with me in spirit, won't you," Claire whispered. "I love you and bless you for all you did for me."

She leaned forward and pressed her lips to her mother's cheek. The skin was as smooth as she remembered, but cold, lifeless. Her mother's cheek had always been warm. It was only then that the reality of her mother's death struck her. Memories. That's all that remained of her warm, vibrant—loving—mother.

Memories. Nothing more.

"No! No!" she screamed, the sound echoing though the empty church. She sobbed hysterically, unable to control herself. Her father walked up and stood beside her, his back straight, silent sobs racking his body.

"We're ready for you now," said a nurse to her father.

The voice jolted Claire back to the present, cutting off the emotional onslaught of memories.

"I'll be waiting with Maude," Claire assured her father as they wheeled him down the hall. Somehow the faraway look in his eyes reminded her of that day when they'd stood crying beside her mother's coffin. The day the father of her childhood had disappeared forever.

Claire stared up at the clock in the waiting area outside the emergency room. One thirty-two. She and Maude had been at the hospital for over two hours. What was taking so long?

Her father's health hadn't been good since his stroke. The tight feeling in her chest increased until she was out of breath. The same sensation gripped her every time she thought of losing her father the way she'd lost her mother. She truly loved him, and even if they had their differences, he was her father and he was devoted to her.

After her mother had been killed, he willingly accepted the role of both father and mother, never begrudging the time it took from his work. He'd supported her emotionally and encouraged her to be anything she wanted to be. It was only when she decided the world of art—her mother's love—was what she wanted to do with her life that her father had become difficult.

Oh, he'd always been a bit possessive and domineering at times, but she could handle him. Whatever his faults, he was her father, and she couldn't imagine life without him.

"Alex claimed it was just indigestion," Maude said as they waited in the reception area while Alexander Holt underwent tests. "I insisted he go to the emergency room. You just can't be too careful."

"Good thinking," Claire responded.

A commotion in the hall near the admitting station interrupted their conversation. Claire looked through the double door and saw Zach Coulter strong-arming two men with cuts and bruises. Zach didn't look much better. His black outfit was mottled with dust as if he'd rolled on the ground, and one sleeve was torn. He looked up and saw her, then rolled his eyes and grinned.

Obviously, he'd broken up a fight and now had to see that two of the men received medical attention. She watched him talking to the admitting nurse, thinking this wasn't a job that challenged Zachary Coulter. He'd never really had a chance to explore his options.

Maybe a self-made man was a stronger, better man. No matter how infuriating Zach could be, she knew he would never have left her at The Hideaway to fend for herself. She was in a mess now, and she could blame the man her father worshipped—Seth Ramsey.

Zach let the nurse lead off the two men, then turned toward her. Claire rushed across the room into the admitting area. The last thing she wanted was to have Maude hear their conversation and report back to her father.

"How's your father?" Zach asked as she came up to him.

"They're still running tests." She scanned Zach's face, a little surprised at the concern she saw. He looked terrible himself, tired and cut up and covered with dust, but he seemed worried about her. "Are you okay?"

He smiled, his laser-blue eyes searching her face. "Sure, it was just a fistfight that turned into a brawl. Brad Yeager and the Mounted Patrol took the rest of the bunch to jail."

She followed him as he began walking toward the exit. "I'm glad the FBI agent was there to help you," she added, not knowing exactly what to say. How could she tell him that seeing he'd been in a fight worried her? His job was dangerous, yet he took that risk for granted. It frightened her, but even more frightening was her own reaction.

She was beginning to care what happened to Zach.

He shouldered his way through the swinging doors with just the slightest wince. Outside the air was slightly cool yet soft, summer in the mountains, a time when the lower elevations hit triple digits. The moon had risen above the majestic peak of Taos Mountain, casting light across the dark parking lot.

"Claire, where are Lobo and Lucy?"

She reluctantly admitted, "Still in the gallery. I've been so upset, I forgot them."

"It hasn't been that long. They're okay. Give me the key and I'll get them. You may be here all night. If you can leave, spend the night at your father's place with Maude. You'll be safe there."

Claire pulled the key ring from her pocket. "Thanks. I-I- . . ."

He reached for her and without a thought she moved into his arms, her head coming to rest on his sturdy shoulder. He smelled of dust and leather with a faint trace of soap, a masculine smell. His strong arms were reassuring and comforting. Unlike other times he'd held her, there was nothing sexual about this embrace. He was dusty and dead tired, yet he wanted to help her.

"Your father will be all right," he whispered, stroking the back of her head with his large hand.

"I hope. He's all I have," she replied before she realized Zach had no one. He'd been alone since he was seventeen. She felt ashamed of herself for not being braver.

Her mother's death had been almost unbearable, but her father had taken good care of her. Zach had lost the one stable parent in his family. He'd been forced to become an adult overnight. How could she complain about being alone to this man?

He tipped her chin up so he could look into her eyes. "It's going to be all right." A frown furrowed his brow and he was silent for a moment. "Word of your father's illness will get around. If Seth Ramsey shows up, don't have anything to do with him."

"Why? What's wrong?"

"I can't discuss it," he said, hugging her again. "Just trust me."

He held her a minute, then said, "I've got to run. I'll pick up the dogs, then head back to the station. Call me there when you get word on your father."

Claire watched Zach get into his Bronco. He waved as he drove out of the parking lot, and Claire waved back. She liked him; she honestly liked him, she thought, as she watched his taillights disappear in the distance. He was cocky and irreverent, but he was a far nicer person than she had wanted to believe.

She forced herself not to remember too much about the day they'd met years ago. No recalling the sweet, earthy scent of the high mountain meadow. No recalling the purling of the stream over the smooth stones along the creek bed as it formed a pool. No recalling how Zach looked, his shirt off, standing with his back to the summer sun.

As if it were happening all over again, Claire could feel the cool mountain breeze and the sun blazing overhead, its hot rays filtering through the pines and shimmering off the aspens' leaves as she came down the trail to the shallow pool formed by the stream. Rounding the bend, she spotted Zach Coulter leaning against a fallen log next to the pool.

She halted with a jerk; dust from the trail swirled around her sandals. His head was down as he concentrated an whittling something in his hand. She took a half step backward determined to head back up the trail before he saw her.

"That's it, Claire," he called. "Turn tail and run."

Anyone with half a brain would get away from Zach Coulter as fast as possible. He was constantly in trouble in school. A chip off the old block, her father claimed. A boy who needed love and attention, her mother told her.

Whatever the case, Claire steered clear of him. She'd

caught him watching her several times that spring. He
stared at her with unnerving boldness, not caring when
she coolly looked through him.

"I'm not running," she fibbed.

He stopped whittling and shoved the piece of wood into
his pocket, but he didn't put away the knife. "You're scared
of me. Admit it."

Never one to ignore a challenge, Claire walked forward.
"That's ridiculous."

"Then come over here and talk to me." His gruff voice
projected hostility and something else she couldn't quite
identify.

Common sense said to run, but she refused to let him
have the satisfaction of frightening her away. She had to
admit that she was a little curious. The boys she knew were
tame, predictable. Zach Coulter had been suspended for
smoking. He'd been sent to juvenile hall for joy-riding in
one of the Tribal Police squad cars.

Then there were the girls. No one in her crowd would
be caught with the likes of Zach Coulter, but there were
several wild girls who bragged about going out with him.
Even though few girls were brave enough to be seen with
him, all the girls watched him.

And wondered.

"What are you doing?" she asked as nonchalantly as
possible considering the fluttering in her tummy.

He shrugged as if it should be obvious to any idiot that
he had been swimming in his cutoffs and now he was whittling, the sharp knife still in his hand. His gaze meandered
from her bare toes, which were curled against the bottom
of her sandals, roaming upward, taking in legs that were
too long and too thin to shorts that suddenly seemed to
reveal more of her thighs than proper. She stared right
back at him as he inspected the T-shirt that did nothing
but emphasize embarrassingly small breasts.

His eyes met hers, and he smiled, his lips canting just

slightly to one side. It was an adorable grin, the type meant to lure girls. Of course, she knew better.

"Is the water cold?" she asked, knowing she sounded foolish, but needing to say something to fill the uncomfortable silence.

"At first it's cold, then you get used to it." He twirled the knife between his fingers. The sharp blade reflected the light, sending sparklike flashes toward her. "You goin' in, or are you going to talk it to death?"

She resented his attitude. Zach had a recklessness about him, a way of goading people that she didn't like. He made her feel off-balance, defensive. "I'm going in, of course."

She kicked off her thongs and waded into the water. It was so cold she shuddered, and she would have bolted for the grassy bank except he was watching her. The stones beneath her feet were smooth and slick. She teetered to one side, nearly falling. She managed to regain her balance, then waded around in the water, pretending not to notice Zach.

Suddenly, he began to chuckle, a deep sound that escalated into a rich masculine laugh. She ventured a look in his direction and saw him standing in ankle-deep water, his hands on his hips, his head cocked to one side as he laughed at her.

She tried the haughty tone that worked on other boys. "What's so funny?"

It took a minute, but he did manage to control himself. "You. You're kickass funny. You probably did come all the way up here to prance around with all your clothes on."

"Of course," she responded without thinking. "There's no place to change into a suit."

This time Zach roared, a loud laugh that frightened the birds out of the brush along the stream's bank. He slapped his bare thigh just below the spot where his cutoffs ended and his tanned legs began to show.

"Suit? Hey, babe, nobody uses a suit."

Heat prickled the back of her neck and inched up her

cheeks. She kept her eyes on his face, but couldn't help noticing his cutoffs weren't soaked the way they would have been had he swum in them. They were damp, wetter in some places than others. Oh, mercy. Had she not stopped to watch an eagle catch an updraft and soar up the ridge to Taos Mountain, she might have come upon Zach Coulter in his birthday suit.

He grinned as if he knew what she was thinking. Sure-footed despite the slick rocks, he strode out to her. "Isn't it a pain in the ass being Miss Goody Two-Shoes all the time?"

She bristled at his vile language, but reminded herself that he was merely trying to bait her. She mustered a smile. "I like being good. Do you like being bad . . . so bad no one wants to be seen with you?"

His expression didn't change; his eyes didn't flicker, but she sensed an invisible current of anger in the still summer air. She looked down, cursing the tongue that got her into trouble too often, but her toes were concealed by the water. The blade of the whittling knife gleamed, catching a bar of sunlight filtering through the pines.

Every wild story she'd heard about Zach whirled through her head. He was a troublemaker, possibly even dangerous. What was she doing alone with him? She swallowed hard, mesmerized by the razor-sharp blade on the knife. She could scream until Christmas, but no one was around to hear her except the squirrels.

With a flick of his hand, he snapped the knife shut, then shoved it in his pocket with the piece he'd been whittling. "You'd better get out of here while you've got the chance. I'm so bad, no telling what I might do."

Her mother's words whispered through her head as she waded quickly toward the bank. *Zach only does those things to get attention.* More often than not, her mother was right. She had no reason to believe Zach would harm her.

She reached the bank and sat down to put on her sandals. When she finished, she remained sitting. Zach was still in the water, his back to her.

He had a man's body, she thought. Tall. A fullback's shoulders. Powerful legs. She remembered how he'd grown up over one summer. He'd been just another one of the boys in the grade ahead of her that spring. He'd returned the following fall, intimidatingly big and with an attitude.

What had happened over the summer, she wondered. People said he'd spent the summer camping in the mountains with his father and taking pictures. Would that turn him into the town's bad boy? It didn't seem likely. Something else must have happened.

"What are you whittling?" she asked.

He turned, obviously startled to find her still there. His expression sullen, he stalked through the water and up to the bank where she was sitting her knees together and drawn up to her chin. She told herself the *thud-thud* of her heart was due to her bravery and not the sight of Zach stretching out on the grass beside her, his legs splayed, his bare heels digging into the soft grass.

He poked his hand into his jeans pocket, stretching jeans that were indecently tight, and it occurred to her that he had nothing on beneath the faded denim. Worse, he didn't care. He hadn't bothered to button the top button.

Not one of the boys she knew would be so bold. But then, none of the boys she knew were half as interesting. He pulled his hand out of his pocket with a shy smile, and she amazed herself by smiling back. He showed her a small chunk of a cottonwood root, the kind Native Americans used to make kachina dolls.

"An eagle," she said the minute she saw the nose.

His eyebrows snapped together. "It's a wolf."

"Oh, yes. Now I see," she rushed to tell him even though she personally thought the nose would never suit a wolf. "I just had eagles on my mind." It took her a few minutes to make up for her mistake, but by the time she'd told him about the eagle she'd seen, his expression had softened. It was clear he shared her love of nature.

They continued talking through the afternoon, and by the time the sun dropped behind the mountains, Claire was already plotting ways to see Zach, yet keep her parents from finding out. He guided her down the trail as shadows darkened the forest, taking her to the turnout on the fire road where she'd left her bike.

"Meet me up there tomorrow," he said, a demand, not a request. Still, there was a tentative note to his voice as if he didn't expect her to agree.

"I'll bring a lunch," she responded a little too quickly.

He mumbled something about counting on it, then hurried off before she could change her mind.

That night she lay in bed, staring out at the star-filled sky. Was Zach looking up at the same sky, she wondered. Was he thinking about her?

Probably not, but she couldn't stop thinking about him. She knew things about him that others didn't know. He wasn't as bad as he liked everyone to believe.

And he could be hurt.

Her comment about no one wanting to be with him had struck a nerve. Then he'd been insulted when she thought his wolf was an eagle. Zach Coulter could act as tough as he wanted, but he had a soft, caring side that few people saw.

"Claire! Claire!" someone called, bringing Claire out her reverie. What was she doing thinking about the day she'd gotten to know Zach Coulter?

It was far, far better to remember where that day had led them. To a place called loneliness, where their young love had not survived the disaster of their parents' death— a place where heartaches lasted a lifetime.

Twenty

"Claire, Claire," Maude called to her, and Claire turned around. "The doctor will be down in a minute to give you a full report. Alex is going to be all right."

Claire embraced the older woman, relief surging through her, and Maude bear-hugged her. A trace of guilt accompanied the knee-weakening sensation of relief. She'd been out here, mooning over Zach Coulter when she should have been inside waiting for word on her father.

"Claire," Maude said as they walked inside, "I don't like to say anything, but your father would be so upset if he had seen you dancing with the Sheriff. I have to admit I was stunned to see how close he was holding you." Maude slowed her pace. "You looked as if you were enjoying every second of it."

What could Claire say? She had been dancing—if you could call it that—with Zach. She knew better, yet she'd done it. Even now she experienced a flutter of excitement recalling that erotic dance.

"It's none of my business, Claire. I wouldn't mention it except I don't want your father to be upset."

Something in Maude's tone brought a flash of insight. "You love him, don't you?"

"Yes," she admitted, her warm eyes mirroring heartfelt emotion. "I had hoped one day, Alex might . . ."

"Marry you?" Claire blurted out, realizing too late she sounded shocked.

Maude turned a dull red, and Claire realized she'd embarrassed her. "I know I'm not much to look at. I'm nothing like your mother, but I really care about your father."

Claire cursed her too quick tongue as she put a hand on Maude's shoulder. "You're the best thing that's happened to him in years. So what if you're not like my mother? She brought him nothing but grief."

"You saw his reaction to that painting. Alex still loves your mother. He always will."

Yes, Claire silently conceded as they began walking again. Her father refused to put the past behind him. He had a terrific woman who loved him, but he clung to a memory. He simply would not get on with his life.

"I'd be thrilled if you married my father," Claire told Maude. "I think you're wonderful."

Inside, Dr. Nelson greeted them, looking very tired. "Alex was right. He ate something that didn't agree with him. I'm letting him go home, but he's to stay in bed until Monday."

They asked a few questions about his diet, then Alexander Holt wheeled into the room. He smiled at her and seemed so grateful to see Claire, making her feel even guiltier about Zach.

"It was nothing to worry about, honey," he said as she kissed his cheek. "Just Maude overreacting. I told her it was the tamale pie."

"She did the right thing. It's better to be safe than sorry."

"Don't worry so much about me, Claire," he said, but she could see that he was happy she was concerned.

They walked down the corridor, her father beside them, and Claire stole a glance at Maude. Claire had often wondered why Maude didn't quit the way the others had. She was upset with herself for not having guessed Maude had fallen in love with Alexander Holt. If only her father would permit himself to be happy, to let another woman take Amy Holt's place.

What would it be like to be so hopelessly in love with someone, she wondered, looking at Maude. She was a good woman who deserved to have a man love her. But Alexander Holt was as blind to her love as he was to many things.

"Claire's showing was a tremendous success," Maude informed Alex. "I went by the gallery to find her and saw red dots on everything but the dogs."

"Dogs? Did you get another dog?" he asked Claire.

"No. I just have Lucy. I was taking care of a friend's dog."

"Good. You don't need another dog."

She held the door open for them, noticing her father hadn't asked who her friend was. He hadn't congratulated her on The Rising Sun's success either. Without missing a boat, he rambled on about how he hated to miss the Fosters' champagne reception, but he promised the doctor he'd stay in bed. The party was held on the last Sunday evening of the Taos Rodeo and Arts Festival. The snobbish Fosters included only the wealthy locals and visiting celebrities like Vanessa Trent with a few artists thrown in for "color."

What did her father see in those people? Sometimes she didn't understand him at all.

Angela snuggled in Paul's arms, her head against his chest. They'd made love three times—always in the missionary position—but Angela hadn't minded. There was something so endearing about the way Paul made love. He put everything he had into each kiss, each caress. The more he made love to her, the more he seemed to need to make love to her.

"What would you like to do tomorrow?" she asked, hoping he'd suggest a trip into Santa Fe to buy art supplies.

"I'd like to go up in the mountains and ride on those trails."

Don't push him, she reminded herself. "We can rent llamas at the trekking station. That'll be fun."

Even in the dim light, she saw the surprise on his face. "Llamas? I meant a horse. A nice mare that likes the wind in her mane."

"Of course, but mares are so ordinary. The llamas have been quite a hit. Wouldn't you rather try something new and exciting?"

"No." His fingertips coasted across the rise of her breast, and she knew he was going to make love to her again. It was almost as if he'd spent a lifetime on a deserted island. "I'm a simple man. I want to ride a horse, not some newfangled animal."

One of his hands stole between her legs and gently stroked her. Angela closed her eyes, thinking she'd get rid of Carleton Cole when she returned to her home. Paul could move in, then she'd be in a better position to encourage him to paint.

Oh, she had to admit that an added plus was his insatiable sexual appetite. He wasn't young, and he wasn't buff, but she didn't mind. His talent and the earnest way he made love more than offset those liabilities.

In one smooth stroke he was deep inside her. He paused, levered himself up on his forearms and gazed into her eyes. "Take care of me, Angela. Take care of me."

Claire unlocked the plank door of the hacienda she was leasing, telling herself not to be so skittish. Since leaving her father and Maude, she'd been looking over her shoulder. Expecting what?

She didn't know, but the incident with the rattler and

the fact that someone seemed to be trying to frame her for murder made her anxious. Well, more than anxious. She was jumpy probably because she was alone. For the last year, Lucy had been at her side, but Zach had both dogs.

She should have spent the night at her father's the way Zach expected her to. She would have, but she didn't want to be around her father. Usually, his attempts to dominate her made Claire keep her distance. Tonight was different. Until now she hadn't realized how truly selfish and insensitive her father was.

A wonderful woman loved him, yet he couldn't accept her love. No, he'd rather wear his love for her mother like a thorny crown. He reveled in his unhappiness, rejoicing in suffering, Claire decided.

Claire loved him, but she didn't know how to help him. His uncharacteristically emotional outburst tonight signaled a deep-seated psychological problem. He needed counseling, but she could just imagine what he'd do if she suggested it.

She wandered through the rambling hacienda, trying not to check for someone lurking in the shadows. After all, the alarm system said no door or window had been opened. When she had turned on a light in every room, she went into her bedroom.

She undressed and climbed into bed, but sleep was impossible. Not only were the lights on—a problem, for sure—but she was too keyed up. She was uncomfortable without Lucy. She looked up the number of the sheriff's station.

She asked for Zach, and he came on the line with a gruff, "Hello."

"You said to call." Claire cursed herself for giving in to such a stupid impulse.

"How's your father?" he asked, his voice much friendlier now.

She wanted to say: he's a mess and I don't know what to do. "It was a false alarm. He had severe indigestion."

"That's a relief. You're spending the night at his house, right?"

She made a noise that she hoped would pass for a positive response, hating to tell an outright lie. "I'm in bed."

"That sounds like more fun than I'm having. I'm sitting here watching a bunch of drunks puke up their guts."

"You have a way with words." He was so crude, she thought. Why was she the least bit attracted to him?

He chuckled, a low, husky sound that was somehow provocative. "Okay, babe. I should have said that these dudes we arrested for fighting are now getting sober and they're upchucking all over the place. That's a drunk tank for you."

"Poor Lucy. I'd better come get her." She was positive she could sleep if Lucy was in the house.

"Nah. She's busy right now licking Lobo's"—he muttered something she couldn't quite hear—"Now she's licking harder. Her tongue's right on his—"

"Private parts." Lordy, the man was so crude.

"Actually, Claire, she's licking his paw. Her tongue's right between his toes. It looks like a shard of glass from the bottle some drunk busted over my head cut Lobo. It must have been in my hair and fell out."

"Someone broke a bottle over your head," she mumbled, embarrassed.

"Yeah, so leave Lobo's 'privates' out of this." He laughed and she had to laugh, too.

"I think I should come get Lucy."

"You're safe right where you are. I don't want you driving at this hour," he said, and she heard noise in the background. "Hold on a minute."

Before she could tell him good-bye, he put her on hold. It was a full minute or more before he came back on the line. "I'm in my office now. Both dogs are with me, and you're staying put. What I want you to do is think about where Duncan Morrell hid the laser scanner and equipment to produce those phony lithographs."

"It wasn't at his house?"

"Nope, and it wasn't at his gallery either. His wife claims she never saw the equipment."

"How big do you think the setup would be?" she asked, excited he was discussing the case with her again.

"Laser scanners are much smaller than they used to be. Storing the prints after they're produced is the problem. They'd have to be rolled and placed in special cylinders for shipping, right?"

"Right." She had no idea why he was consulting her, but she was glad to be included. No one wanted this case solved more than she did. If the bearded man wasn't going to give her an alibi, then she had to let Zach help her.

"You could probably have the setup in a space the size of a garage," he said.

"What makes you think it's around here?"

"A check of Morrell's credit card activity for the past year shows one trip to Los Angeles a month ago."

"He visited Vanessa Trent and sold her a number of lithographs. She told me so."

"Okay, but that's the only trip he took. It only stands to reason that the prints are being produced here, but where?"

"In the last place anyone would look," Claire said automatically. "Out at the pueblo or in one of the churches."

"You're joking."

"Of course, but it's someplace where you wouldn't normally look."

He was silent, obviously searching for the answer, she decided, imagining him at his desk. His long legs were up on the desk, his booted feet crossed at the ankles. No doubt, he'd wiped his boots, but dust still splotched his black jeans.

"The last place anyone would look," he repeated thoughtfully.

There was an intimacy to their conversation that hadn't been there until tonight at the hospital when Zach had closed the distance she usually kept between herself and most men. Now they were—what? Friends? Lovers?

Well, not lovers yet, but Zach had to believe they soon would be. After that dance tonight, what else could he think? She shuddered, experiencing equal parts anticipation and dread. On one level the thought excited her, yet it frightened her, too.

Her father's health and psychological state were fragile. The last thing he needed was to discover his daughter was involved with Zach Coulter. Yet she needed Zach's help. She had the uneasy feeling that she was being drawn deeper and deeper into the Morrell case.

"Claire, do you have any idea who Duncan was in love with? His wife tolerated his affairs for years, but he was leaving her for someone."

"No. He came on to anything in a skirt, and he got plenty of action. It was always a mystery to me what women saw in him. Even Vanessa Trent went out with him, and she was terribly upset by his death." An odd thought occurred to her. "If Duncan was in love with someone special enough to divorce his wife after all this time, then what was he doing in a sleazy room at The Hideaway?"

Twenty-one

Zach watched the River Spirit Gallery from the shade of an ancient cottonwood in the plaza, waiting to catch Stacy Hopkins alone. But Lowell Hopkin's wife showed no sign of coming out of the gallery. Great, Zach thought. He was wasting time he didn't have.

He'd rather be across the plaza seeing Claire. They'd had two conversations—at the hospital and on the phone—without fighting. Claire was slowly beginning to treat him better.

He wished he'd had time to wait for her this morning. He dropped off Lucy and Lobo, leaving the dogs with Suzi. Claire hadn't yet arrived at the gallery, and he couldn't blame her for sleeping in. What he wouldn't give for a decent night's sleep. Since Morrell's death, Zach hadn't had more than three hours sleep a night.

He wanted to spend time with Claire, but he couldn't until after the rodeo tomorrow. Getting through today should be easy, but Saturday nights during the rodeo were tough. Judging by the hell-raisers from Texas who'd started the brawl last night, he was going to have his hands full tonight. Then Sunday would be a cakewalk. The rodeo finished in the late afternoon and the cowboys hit the road, heading to the next rodeo. Another sheriff's problem.

All he had to do, he reminded himself as he kept his eye out for Stacy, was to keep a lid on the drunken brawls.

The last thing he wanted was for a fight to become a major incident involving dozens of cowboys. Then he'd have to call on the chief of police for assistance. A prick like Ollie Hammond lived for the opportunity to tell everyone Zach couldn't handle the sheriff's job. He hadn't needed to call on Hammond last night, but it had been damn close.

Tonight he would patrol the rodeo grounds. He'd waited too long last night before breaking up the fight. He'd delayed because his mind had been on Claire. He couldn't make that mistake again.

He shouldn't even be here now. Morrell's murder should go on hold until after the roughneck cowboys and low-lifes that followed the circuit left town. Ollie Hammond and people like Alexander Holt were waiting, just dying for him to screw up. Still, he wanted to question Stacy about the night Morrell died. His sixth sense had kicked in when he'd interviewed Bassinger. The son of a bitch wasn't telling the truth.

Just as Zach had given up and was leaving, Stacy came out of the gallery and hurried over to her car. Zach crossed the plaza and hopped into his Bronco. He followed Stacy out of town, then stuck his hand out the window and plopped a portable police light with a magnetic attachment onto the roof of the Bronco. He hit the siren and pulled her over the second she left the city limits and drove into his jurisdiction.

"Was I speeding, Sheriff?" she asked, all breathy and wide-eyed when he came up.

"Yep. Get out of the car."

Stacy threw open the door and swiveled to the side, slowly swinging out one spectacular leg. Her short skirt was already hiked up far enough for him to arrest her for indecent exposure, but she made sure she paused before swinging out the second leg so he got more than just a glimpse of her neon pink panties. Sniffling, she stood up and jiggled to make her skirt fall into place. The movement made her breasts sway.

"I hope I'm not, like, going to get a ticket . . . or something."

Or something, Zach thought. He'd busted Stacy once the previous year outside Tía Juana's for buying coke. She'd come on to him—big time—letting him know she was willing to trade sex to get out of trouble. He didn't take her up on the offer.

Not that he hadn't been tempted. Stacy Hopkins had an earthy sensuality that turned on most men. Feminine with a bod that wouldn't quit—and so willing. She was the opposite of Vanessa Trent whose every move was staged for a camera.

Zach stood to one side so the direct sunlight was on Stacy. "I have a couple of questions about the night Duncan Morrell was murdered. I understand you stayed at the club after your husband left. You went next door to The Hideaway, correct?"

Stacy looked at the jack pine nearby. The sapling was half bent; it wouldn't survive a cruel winter. "Yeah, I was over there for, you know, a while."

"How long is a while?"

"I'm not sure . . . exactly." Her nose twitched.

"Stacy, a man died that night. Think hard."

She gazed a him for a second, her brown eyes troubled, then she looked back at the sad little pine. "I was there until dawn, but please don't tell anyone."

"I'm not interested in giving you trouble. All I want to do is find a killer." He sensed her reluctance, but he wasn't sure how to persuade her to talk. "I never mentioned anything about that night in the parking lot of Tía Juana's, did I? I told you if you got treatment, I'd let you by that one time."

She swiped at the back of her nose with her hand. "You were awesome, totally awesome."

"Then why don't you level with me now? Unless you're directly involved in the murder, no one will ever have to know."

She licked her bottom lip, her tongue provocatively moving over the lush fullness. But she didn't say a word.

"Who were you there with? Can they corroborate your story?"

She shrugged, jiggling her full breasts. Zach was struck with how differently Claire would have handled the situation. Her hands would have been on her slim hips, her chin out, daring him to question her.

He was forced to play his trump card. "Stacy, I have a friend from the Gallup FBI office. He's unofficially helping me with the case. If you don't come clean with me, I'm turning your name over to him, and I'll have to tell about the incident at Tía Juana's. Could be that deal was part of a drug ring, and the FBI should look into it."

"You're lying." The words were angry, yet had an undertone of fear.

"I believe you met Brad Yeager. He said he walked through your husband's gallery last night."

Stacy's eyes narrowed slightly. Her pupils were dilated, and from the way she kept sniffing, Zach knew she needed another hit. Her nerves were probably like a dozen live wires. And she was undoubtedly experiencing the paranoia that came with addiction to cocaine. *Everyone is out to get me. Coke is my only friend.*

"I'm your friend, Stacy. I told you to get help."

"I did. Lowell sent me to a rehab center in Arizona. It cost a fortune. I was all right for a while then I . . . I don't know what happened. I just . . . like . . . messed up. You know, slipped."

"I'll help you again, if you want me to," he responded.

"Someone's already helping me," she informed him with a smile. "I've finally met the right man, someone who understands my problems and loves me."

Zach shook his head. Obviously, Lowell Hopkins had better find a good divorce attorney. "Who?"

"Carleton Cole. He's totally buff and way cool. He's going to leave that old bag, Angela Whitmore. We're moving to San Francisco."

Zach smiled as if he thought this was a match made in heaven. Secretly he believed Stacy was making a huge mistake. Cole was an airhead. How could he help Stacy? No doubt, she'd end up on Frisco's streets turning tricks to support a drug habit.

"Stacy, do you know Carleton Cole well enough to leave your husband—"

"I know all about his prison record. He changed his name, too. You know, he has, like, a bod to die for. Edwin Shumski didn't fit him." She stared at the jack pine again, her head turned away from him. "I love him, truly I do. He's into fitness and heath foods. You know, stuff like that. He can help me."

Zach could see he wasn't talking her out of leaving her older husband for the buff young hunk. Hell, Cole just might be able to help her. Stranger things had happened.

"Does Carleton know you were at The Hideaway with two men?"

Stacy slowly turned to face him. Her doe-brown eyes were luminous with tears. "Please, don't tell him. I did it for Carleton, but he wouldn't understand. He invested all his money in Nevada's prints, but, something, like, went wrong. Duncan Morrell wouldn't give him back his money." One tear broke loose, trembled on her long lashes for a second, then dribbled down her cheek. "Max Bassinger offered me a lot of money to get Seth into that room. I did it because I love Carleton."

"Lucky guy." Zach barely got the words out. Did this woman seriously believe love was a reason to prostitute herself? She was so friggin' screwed up that Zach didn't know how to reach her.

"I won't tell Carleton, if you're up front with me, Stacy.
I need details about what went on that night." She nodded,
sniffing and swiping at the tear on her cheek with the back
of her hand. "What time did you go into that bungalow
with Bassinger?"

"I met him there after Lowell went home. It must have
been, like, somewhere around midnight."

"Tell me what happened next. Don't leave anything
out."

"It was weird, freaking weird," she said, lowering her
voice as if someone besides the squirrels were listening.
"Max gave me half a line of coke. I took it. You know, just
to get me through it. Then he turned off the lights and
opened the door enough so he could see what was going
on outside. He waited until Seth came into sight before
making me get on my knees and . . . you know."

Zach nodded. "Go on."

"Then I was supposed to get into bed with Seth," she
said, disgust in her voice. "It went according to plan. Max
jumped in, too. It was supposed to be, like, one of those
ménage things. You know, three people doing it. Max told
me that I was supposed to get Seth ready, then slip out of
bed." She shook her head. "I thought Seth would never
go for it. He's been, coming on to me for months, but he
didn't even notice I was gone. It was, like . . . yuck."

Bassinger using Stacy to lure Seth into his clutches? Like,
yuck—was a gross understatement.

"What time did you leave that room, Stacy?"

"A little before one," she said with an impish smile.
"Max paid me five thousand dollars to lie to you and say
I was with them until dawn, but it isn't true." She smiled
again, gloating this time. "I made enough money off Max
for Carleton and I to go away together."

Hot damn, Zach thought. This was the break he'd been
praying for. Seth Ramsey had a motive to kill, but no alibi.

"What did you do after you left that room? Did you see anyone or talk to anybody?"

Stacy shook her head just a little too vigorously, her hair slapping her sculpted cheeks. "I went right home."

"Lowell will vouch for that?"

"No, he was asleep."

Stacy was lying, he decided in an instant. Somehow he'd been born with a built-in bullshit detector. He'd known Bassinger was lying, and now he was dead certain Stacy was telling only part of the truth.

"Stacy, unless you tell me the whole truth, I'm going to make certain Carleton finds out about this."

"I told you what happened," she protested.

Stacy wasn't a good liar. Bassinger had been far better. Zach crossed his arms over his chest and adjusted his legs so they were wide apart. It was a belligerent stance, one he'd often used while working homicide in San Francisco. Good cop—bad cop was a common interrogation technique. He always insisted on being the bad cop because his superior size physically intimidated people. Now he had to play both roles himself.

"I swear," she said, but she didn't sound the least bit convincing.

He stood, staring at her for a full minute, the blistering midday sun eating through his shirt until moisture peppered his back. He decided to bluff. Hell, it had worked with Seth, hadn't it?

"I know for a fact that you did not leave at one o'clock. Someone saw you. Now—"

"O-o-oh," she moaned. "You found the man with the beard. I thought he was some bum on his way to Santa Fe because I never saw him again."

The bearded man. What in hell was she talking about? It was all he could do to keep a straight face. "I think you'd better tell me everything."

"Could we, like, go over into the shade?" she asked.

He led her into the pines and found a fallen log not too far from the road. He sat and patted the rough bark beside him. Stacy gingerly sat down, then tugged at her short skirt so the bark didn't dig into her thighs.

"Look me in the eye, Stacy, and tell me exactly what happened."

"I did leave that room at one," she said slowly, despair in her voice. "I got into my car and saw Bam Stegner talking to Duncan. I waited until Bam left and caught Duncan before he got into his Jaguar. In the past, he'd . . . you know, come on to me and I thought maybe I could persuade him to give Carleton his money back on that print investment."

She took a deep breath and closed her eyes for a second. "He said he'd get a key to one of the bungalows and we could discuss it. Like, I'm no bimbo; I knew what he wanted, but I figured this would be nothing after that total gross out with Max and Seth. I thought I could really help Carleton."

Stegner and Morrell, interesting. Then Stacy, possibly the last person to see Morrell alive—except the person who murdered him.

"How long were you in there with him?" he asked, wondering just when she'd spotted a man with a beard.

"I kept trying to bring up Carleton's investment, but Duncan only wanted to . . . you know."

"What time did you leave?"

Stacy looked down at some suspicious-looking mushrooms growing along the base of the log. "We both fell asleep. Like, I don't know how long we slept. A noise woke me—a creaking sound. I saw a flash of light and realized someone must have opened the door and seen us. I, like, totally panicked when I realized it was morning. I left without waking Duncan."

"What time was that?"

"My watch said twenty minutes until six. I rushed to my

car, praying whoever saw me with Duncan wouldn't tell Carleton. That's when I saw the man with the beard. He was coming out of the woods beside the club carrying his sleeping bag. I hid behind Duncan's Jaguar. I watched him get into a totally trashed pickup and drive off. I didn't think he saw me, but I guess he did."

The last thing Zach had expected was to discover Paul Winfrey had been near the murder scene. Jee-sus! He never mentioned being at The Hideaway.

"Stacy, was there a pillow on the bed?"

"In The Hideaway? Are you kidding? There was a scuzzy throw. That's all."

Interesting. The killer brought a gun and a pillow.

"Did Duncan use any protection?"

"Get real. You can't rely on men. When Max paid me to meet him, I put a box of life jackets in my purse."

"Did you take the used ones with you?"

Stacy grimaced, one side of her lip rising a fraction of an inch. "They were yucky. I left them on the floor. Why would I take them?"

Christ! The killer had done a major cleanup at the murder scene, removing evidence of Duncan's fling with Stacy. Why?

Twenty-two

Max Bassinger opened the door of his hacienda and saw Zach Coulter and another man. From what Seth had told him the previous evening, he assumed it was the FBI agent, Brad Yeager. He was right. The cocky prick flipped open his wallet without saying a word, showing Max his FBI seal and photo ID.

"You weren't telling the truth about who was with you at The Hideaway," Coulter said. "I can arrest you and haul you in, or you can level with us now."

Max sized up the situation in an instant. That candynose Stacy had cracked. He should have expected it. Coulter was a whole helluva lot smarter than your average sheriff. He would have sensed Stacy was lying.

"Arrest me?" Max said with his most ingratiating smile. "What for?"

Coulter's expression remained grim. "Obstruction of justice."

"Read him his rights and haul him in," Yeager said.

Max had never been arrested, and he wasn't going to let some stupid bitch get him in trouble. "Whoa! You don't have to arrest me." He threw up his hands and shrugged. "No big deal. I fudged on my story. Stacy Hopkins left sometime around one. Seth and I stayed in that room—sleeping it off—until dawn."

"Exactly what time did you leave?"

Max didn't like the Sheriff's uppity tone. He'd fix him as soon as he got the chance, and he'd take care of Stacy, too. Now just wasn't the right time.

"It was ten minutes till six when we walked into the parking lot. Seth got into his car and I followed him out to my place."

"Did you see any other cars?" Yeager asked.

"I recognized Morrell's Jag. There were a couple of other cars. One of them had a rental sticker on the bumper."

"Did you see anyone else around?" Coulter wanted to know.

"Down the road, I saw Claire Holt in a van with an Indian driving."

"Really?" Yeager said. "Did—"

Coulter cut off the FBI agent. "You can't be sure it was her, can you?"

Of course, it had been Claire Holt. No doubt about it at all. Claire had spent the night at The Hideaway. Max had told Seth about it, and they'd had a belly laugh. What a riot! The uppity bitch probably had been forced to hitch-hike home.

"Kinda' looked like her," Max hedged. "Coulda' been someone else."

Coulter quickly changed the subject, confirming Max's suspicions. He was hot, real hot for Claire Holt. He did not want her linked to this murder. Fine, Max thought, smiling inwardly.

Claire Holt had been at the murder scene. When pay-back time came—Max could hardly wait—he'd use this info to fix the bitch and the cocky sheriff.

They asked a few more questions, then left. Max walked back to his study to call Seth. They were going out again tonight with Vanessa Trent. Seth had better hope the blond bombshell didn't find out Seth was bisexual. The bitch gave new meaning to the word *vain*.

She honestly believed every man she met adored her.

He wouldn't have wasted a second on the broad, but Seth had the hots for her. Vanessa kept coming on to Max, which really frustrated Seth. Max saw right through the bitch. She wanted money from him. She hadn't yet mentioned it, but that's what she was after.

Max picked up the telephone and punched the automatic dial button numbered one. After two rings, Seth answered.

"Get your sorry ass out here. I have a contract for you to go over."

Max slammed down the receiver without waiting for an answer. He dropped into the leather chair and put his feet up on his desk. He loved having Seth at his beck and call. He was getting hard just thinking about it.

From the second-floor window, Angela saw the sheriff drive up to her home just as the sun was setting. She was headed downstairs to see what he wanted when the telephone rang.

"Hi," Claire said. "How did it go last night?"

"Fine," Angela responded, but of course, fine did not cover it. "Paul is not just another cowboy in Calvins, pretending to be an artist. He is extremely talented."

Extremely. And awesomely easy to arouse.

"Did you take him to Santa Fe to get art supplies?"

"No. He wanted to go riding."

"He really loves horses."

"True," Angela said, wondering how Claire knew such an intimate detail about Paul. The doorbell rang before she could ask. "I've got to go. Someone's at the door. I'll see you at the Fosters' reception tomorrow night."

Angela hung up and walked downstairs, thinking she should have told Claire that Paul had moved in with her. It had been surprisingly easy to get rid of Carleton Cole. She usually kissed off a young hunk with a new car. Carleton had bluntly asked for cash instead. All she had to do was write a check, and he was history.

Paul could use her guest house to paint. Not that he'd showed any sign—yet—of wanting to paint. They'd spent the afternoon riding in the high country. She was going to be stiff and sore for days, but it had been worth it. Paul had been so happy, stopping at every scenic spot and looking at the wildflowers.

She paused in the hallway, realizing Paul had answered the door. She couldn't see them, but she could hear Paul talking to Zach Coulter.

"I wasn't hiding anything, Zach. You never asked me if I had been at The Hideaway. I was there from nine o'clock on. I saw a poster saying Flash and the Rusty Roots would be playing. I couldn't afford to go into the club, so I took my sleeping bag and a hot dog and a beer that I bought at the Stop n Go and sat in the woods, listening. I slept under the stars. It was a beautiful night."

Angela smiled to herself. How like Paul. He loved being outdoors, studying the plants and trees almost as if seeing them for the very first time.

"A man was killed at The Hideaway. Why didn't you tell me that you'd been there all night?"

Zach's disappointed tone surprised her. He was usually cool. Too cool and remote for her taste.

"I'm sorry, Zach. I didn't want to get involved with the law. I'm sure you understand why not."

"After you met me, why didn't you mention something?"

"I didn't have anything to tell."

"Anything, any little detail might help solve this case."

After a pause, Paul said, "About midnight, between songs, I heard a clinking sound. I peeked through the trees. I couldn't believe my eyes. Two men were loading a bear into a pickup. They drove off without turning on its lights. Then the tall man walked back toward The Hideaway, humming 'The Devil Went Down to Georgia' along with the band. That's all I saw."

Zach said something about seeing Paul later, then left. Angela stood in the hall out of sight, wondering why Paul didn't want anything to do with the law. And why hadn't the sheriff gotten a description of those men who stole the bear? Not that she wanted them caught. She'd put a lot of money into the vase to make sure Khadafi got away from Bam Stegner.

Angela walked around the corner and asked Paul "Did you see the men who took the bear?"

He hesitated a beat, then grinned. "I can't rightly say what they looked like. It was real dark."

She smiled back. He knew exactly what they looked like. He didn't want Stegner to get his bear back either. That instant she knew he was a very special man, and she was at risk of losing an essential part of herself—her heart.

"Speaking of dark," he said before she could ask if he had a reason to avoid the law. "Let's go upstairs and pull down the shades. We have time for a little fun before we head out to the rodeo."

"How's Daddy doing?" Claire asked Maude as the older woman opened the front door.

"He had a little trouble sleeping last night." Maude stepped back so Claire could come in. "He just got up. He's in the morning room reading the Sunday paper. He'll be glad to see you."

Claire followed Maude down the wide hall of the rambling hacienda where she'd grown up. She knew every turn in the thick adobe walls, every architectural detail from the hand-hewn vigas supporting the roof to the kiva fireplaces in the corners of the bedrooms. How happy she'd been growing up here, believing her parents were the perfect couple. They'd been completely in love, or so it had seemed to her young, hopelessly romantic mind.

"Hello, Daddy," she said, bracing herself. Last night she'd decided that she couldn't wait any longer. She had to tell her father about the incident at The Hideaway. The way the case was dragging on, the details were sure to come out. She didn't want her father hearing about it from the town gossips.

"Hey, you look pretty this morning," her father said as he lowered the newspaper. "Did you come from church?"

Her father always acted as if missing a Sunday service was the path to eternal damnation. Just wait until he heard her story. "Yes. Reverend Butler gave a wonderful sermon on the sins of the flesh."

He nodded approvingly, his pewter-colored hair gleaming in the sunlight filtering through the windows. "I had some trouble sleeping last night. Maude talked with me until I finally drifted off." He looked over at Maude and smiled.

There was something in his smile that told Claire that the two of them were sharing her father's bed and probably had been for some time. She should have guessed as much. Despite his disability, her father was an extremely handsome man. Maude had outlasted his previous "assistants" because she'd fallen in love with him. Why couldn't her father let go of the past and love Maude instead of just sleeping with her?

"Maude said I was out of line last night," her father said with uncharacteristic tenderness in his voice. "You have a real winner with that Winfrey fellow. Your show sold out, and I didn't congratulate you." He looked over at Maude and she beamed her approval. "I'm real proud of you, honey."

She'd waited so long to hear him say those words. Her stomach had that curious weightless sensation she always developed when she was excited. But she wasn't as happy as she'd anticipated. Maybe it was because Maude had to persuade her father to congratulate her. Why couldn't he have thought of it himself?

"Thank you, Daddy." She kissed his cheek, putting aside her doubts. At least he was acknowledging her success. "You don't know how much it means to hear you say that."

He pulled out the chair beside him. "Have a cup of coffee with us before you go to your gallery."

She desperately needed to get to the gallery and restock as best she could, but she couldn't run out now. She'd waited too long and worked too hard to win her father's approval. Maude poured her a cup of coffee from the silver urn on the sideboard as Claire sat beside her father.

"I know I've thrown your mother at you too many times," he said, raw emotion in his voice. "Because you look so much like her and are interested in many of the same things she was, I tend to think you inherited all her faults."

Claire was tempted to ask which faults. She didn't recall any vices or terrible habits. All she remembered was a happy, smiling woman. Not a day went by when she didn't miss her.

"If running that gallery is what you want to do, Claire, then I have to accept it. I've worked my whole life to build a business. When I die, it will be sold to strangers."

He couldn't just congratulate her, could he? No. Ho used the gallery to segue into his usual guilt trip. If she wouldn't accept a position at the bank, the least she could do was marry the proper man and give her father a grandson.

"Seth Ramsey called to see how I was," her father rushed on. "He's such a nice young man, and he's crazy about you. If you married him, I'd make him vice-president of the bank."

She listened to him drone on about Seth's endless virtues. Zach had specifically warned her about Seth, not that she intended to have anything to do with the creep. If he had waited outside the restroom, he would have been able to get her home safely. To make matters worse, the jerk had lied, claiming he'd waited for her.

"Daddy, I have no intention of going out with Seth again," she said as she stirred her coffee. "There's something I have to tell you."

Maude took the seat opposite Claire and listened as she told them about the night at The Hideaway. By the time she'd finished, all the color had leached from her father's face.

"You had unprotected sex with a total stranger." He was so shocked that he could barely whisper the words.

"It was the Rohypnol," Maude put in. "Lots of young women have been victimized—"

"She had no business going out there in the first place," he snapped.

Claire almost mentioned how strongly Seth had urged her to go, but she didn't. Nor did she explain yet again that his protégé, Seth Ramsey, had left her. She took responsibility for what had happened. She might privately fault Seth's conduct, but she accepted responsibility for her own actions. She had no business going out to Bam Stegner's club.

She directed her comment to Maude. "My experience wasn't nearly as traumatic as what has happened to other women. The man seemed very nice. Sweet. What I can remember is pleasant."

"I hope you're not pregnant." Her father's voice was a broken whisper.

"Now, Alex, women don't get pregnant from one-night stands."

Being pregnant had not entered her mind, but she had worried endlessly about catching some dreadful disease, maybe even a life-threatening disease.

Her father must have misinterpreted her silence. Color flooded his face, turning the chalky white skin to a mottled red. "You wouldn't have a baby without being married, would you? You wouldn't do that to me."

Why did her father always think in terms of himself?

"Daddy, the point is Duncan Morrell was murdered in the bungalow next door to where I was. We were enemies. Everyone knows about our feud over the prints he reproduced. I'm afraid I might be blamed for his death."

"Can anyone prove you were at The Hideaway?" her father asked. "You said the bearded man vanished. Just don't tell anyone."

"My wallet fell out of my purse. The sheriff found it. He knows I was there."

Her father's startled intake of breath was followed by a sad shake of his head. Maude stared into her coffee as if reading tea leaves. Although Claire hadn't said Zachary Coulter's name, it hung in the air between them like a poisonous gas.

"I've seen Coulter strutting around town just the way his father did," he said, venom in every syllable. "He'll use this murder to get to you the way his father conned your mother, claiming he wasn't just any two-bit photographer who took graduation pictures for a living. Oh, no. He was an artist—the next Ansel Adams."

She knew her mother had been planning on exhibiting Jake Coulter's photographs. Then the terrible car crash had killed them both. For the thousandth time she asked herself why she hadn't just kept her mouth shut? Why had she run to her father?

"Zach isn't using this to get to me," she protested, but she had to admit there was an element of truth to what her father had said. Zach had used the murder to force his way into her life. And she seemed powerless to resist him. "I'm not positive, but I think the FBI is in on the case. I hope it'll be solved quickly."

"They'll take it out of Coulter's hands," her father said.

"He can't even handle the Saturday night rodeo crowd. There was another big fight last night."

Claire hadn't heard from Zach yesterday, not that she expected to. He needed to be out at the rodeo arena the whole time. She'd hardly slept last night for thinking about him. She'd told herself not to worry, but he'd had a bottle broken over his head the night before and had been cut and bruised. When she'd finally fallen asleep, she'd been jolted awake by a dream about Zach that had been so erotic she blushed whenever she thought about it.

"Honey, I don't want you to worry," her father said, gruff affection in his voice. "The FBI will find the killer. Until they do, you keep quiet. Go to the Fosters' reception tonight and act like nothing's wrong. Explain to them why I'm not there."

By the time nine o'clock rolled around, the last thing Claire wanted to do was to go to the Fosters' reception. Every year Arnold and Muffy Foster had a champagne and dessert bash to celebrate the opening of the season. Of course, the season meant different things to different people. To Claire and the other merchants it was the time of year when tourists flooded the city, spending money in the shops. To wealthy people, the season revolved around the Santa Fe Opera and an endless succession of parties.

She locked the shop and turned to walk down the block to the reception. Zach Coulter was standing behind her. He had a bruise on his jaw and a small cut on his upper lip, and he looked dead tired. He'd just shaved, she guessed, and his hair was so shiny that he must have showered after leaving the dusty rodeo arena. He'd taken off his badge and was dressed in navy trousers and a white polo shirt that looked brand new.

"I heard it got rough last night," she said lightly, masking her inner turmoil with a deceptive calmness. She had no idea what she was going to do about Zach. Not only did she care about him, now she found herself worrying about his safety.

"Could have been worse," he said, as if it had been nothing more than a minor scuffle, but she knew better. "Where are the dogs?"

"Out back in my Jeep," she said. "The windows are down and it's cool tonight. I'm just sticking my nose into the Fosters' reception, then I'm going home."

Something about him seemed different, she reflected. She remembered what her father had said about Zach using the murder to get close to her. No denying it. He'd done just that.

There was a certain ruthlessness to him, but he had his good side, too. She wanted to give him a chance, to see what he was really like aside from memories which were years old. Her father would pitch a fit. It wouldn't have worried her so much except he seemed unstable at times. One day he was hysterical about Paul Winfrey's painting, then the next day her father was rationally telling her how proud he was of her.

"How's your father?" he asked, breaking into her thoughts.

"He's fine, thanks." She smiled up at him, not knowing what to say and he smiled back. She looked down at her shoes, searching for words, and noticed Zach had on his best black lizard boots, and they were buffed to a high gloss.

"Claire, I was wondering if you wanted to go to Sacred Grounds for coffee?"

The question took her by surprise. Was he asking her out on a date? Of course he was, and he was just a little shy about it. It dawned on her that he must have rushed home after the rodeo and cleaned up—for her.

Her pulse skittered alarmingly. Be honest with yourself, Claire, cautioned an inner voice. She'd returned home, promising herself that she would deal honestly with her problems, not run away from them. If she were dead honest, she had to admit that she wanted to spend time with Zach.

True, she was attracted to him physically. Why bother to deny it? Yet beyond Zach's virile appeal was something . . . more. She had never known anyone with his strength of character and determination. He'd made something of himself, and she had to admit she was proud of him.

But she wasn't ready to be seen with him—yet. She had to deal with her father first, prepare him somehow. He was emotionally vulnerable, she decided, recalling his reaction to the painting. And his heath was fragile.

Then it occurred to her that Zach might be cleverly luring her back to his place or hers for sex. Well, what did she expect? She had wantonly thrust her body against his while they'd been dancing. When the dance was over, she hadn't been able to let go.

Every time they were together, they came closer to making love. If she was alone with him tonight, she knew *exactly* what would happen. But he wasn't asking her to go anywhere that they would be alone. Sacred Grounds was a popular coffee bar. It would be very crowded after the rodeo.

"I can't go for coffee," she said quickly, realizing she'd paused too long and an embarrassing silence had developed. "I've got to go to the reception."

He studied her a moment with reproachful eyes that missed nothing. "Is that what you really want to do?"

Of course, it wasn't. She would love to go to Sacred Grounds and talk to him while sipping a cappuccino. "I promised my father I'd go and give the Fosters his regards," she said, every word sounding hollow even to her own ears. "It's the first of their receptions he's missed."

They were in the shadows of the portal overhanging the shops, but across the plaza she saw couples she recognized going into the Taos Inn for the party. Most of those people wouldn't be thrilled to see her with Zach Coulter. They were

the establishment—wealthy and accepted. Her father's
friends.

She had no doubt most of them would snub Zach, if
she brought him to the reception. An odd thought struck
her. The majority of the people the Fosters had invited
lived in estates outside the city limits in Zach's territory.
They would gladly let Zach protect their homes, their lives.

But he wasn't welcome at their parties.

It was an ugly double standard, she thought with disgust.
How did it make Zach feel? He didn't seem to notice or
care. She suspected that he'd developed this attitude long
ago when his mother had been the subject of scorn and
ridicule. Maybe he'd deliberately protected his inner feelings by becoming the town bad boy who always landed in
trouble with both feet.

She'd always been accepted because she was Alexander
Holt's daughter. Zach had never had the protection of a
respected family. He didn't need it today, but once, when
they'd been younger, he must have been lonely and inse-
cure. Now, though, he was a man, a man accustomed to
being alone.

"Please walk me over to the reception," she said, not
wanting to leave him.

He fell in step beside her, matching his long stride to
hers. But he didn't say anything. What was he thinking?
Was he angry with her for going to the party instead of
accepting his invitation?

"Hello, there," Angela Whitmore said as she came
around the corner nearly colliding with them.

Paul Winfrey was beside her, his arm around Angela's
waist. She glanced at him for a second and knew that Paul
had taken the place of Carleton Cole. Claire would have
applauded her friend's choice except Paul was her discovery. She did not want him wasting his valuable painting time
on sex.

Paul and Zach exchanged a few words while Claire tried

to decide what to do. Paul had not been invited to the party. He was coming as Angela's guest. The hosts certainly wouldn't mind if Claire brought someone. If it had been anyone but Zach Coulter, she would have suggested he join them.

By leaving Zach now, when it was obvious that Angela was bringing someone who hadn't been invited, Claire was rudely snubbing Zach. He'd helped her when she'd needed him, finding the rattlesnake, then taking care of Bam Stegner. How could she be like all those other snobs, accepting Zach's protection as sheriff—yet cutting him dead socially?

Zach looked down at her, his expression intent, and she knew that he was waiting for her to invite him along. She tried a smile, hoping to communicate that she liked him. He didn't return her smile. Instead he waited, watching her.

If she were brave, she'd roll the dice and walk into the party on Zach's arm. Muffy Foster would call her father the next morning—if one of the other town gossips didn't beat her to it. Claire didn't want her father to find out that way.

She needed to think this over carefully. If she entered into any kind of relationship with Zach, she owed it to her father to discuss her feelings with him. He was too emotionally fragile to let some shrew break it to him unexpectedly.

Paul held the door to the Taos Inn open for Angela. "After you."

It was clear Paul thought Zach was going to the party with her. Zach waited, his eyes on Claire. She gazed down at the tip of her shoe, then forced herself to look directly at him. Was he waiting for the words that would change things between them and set their relationship on a new course? She suspected he was. He'd taken the first step by asking her out tonight.

An uncomfortable silence hung between them, magnified by the sounds from the plaza and the chatter coming from the hotel lobby. Even worse, Paul was holding the door open, expecting them both to follow Angela inside.

"I'll see you later, Zach." Claire turned her back on him and walked through the door before he had a chance to say anything—even good-bye.

She rushed into the lobby and immediately encountered friends who inquired about her father. Claire angled her body so she could look out the window as she woodenly mumbled a reply. Zach was walking away, his shoulders squared. Something about his stride reminded her of the day he'd walked out of her father's bank without getting the money to bury his mother.

He'd been little more than a kid back then, having lost both parents within a year's time. But no one took pity on the town's bad boy who couldn't raise enough money to properly bury his mother.

It was clear that he had loved Sally Coulter—despite her problems. There was a depth to Zach, a capacity to love and understand people that no one gave him credit for having. He'd been a hell-raiser and that's how the town saw him even now. No one took the time to look beyond his image to discover the real person.

Going door to door, asking for money to bury his mother, promising to do any menial job to pay back people must have taken every ounce of Zach's pride, but he'd done it. He'd raised a little money, yet not nearly enough. He had been forced to come to the bank and beg her father.

After the accident that had killed both their parents, her father had blasted Jake Coulter. True, he'd been driving the car, but the accident wasn't his fault. The truck had blown a tire and hit them. To hear her father tell it, Jake was a worthless creep who had all but murdered Amy Holt. Of course, he wasn't going to help Jake Coulter's son.

Claire had been in the bank, doing homework at an empty desk when Zach had come. She had wanted to give

Zach all the money she had, but her father refused to let her. Zach never heard her arguing with her father, and Zach never looked back to see her watching him as he disappeared into the blizzard.

Claire should have gone after him even though she couldn't give him enough money to really help. A show of support had been what he needed. But nobody was there for him.

Not then; not now.

Suddenly, she felt even more depressed than she'd felt that day years ago. And thoroughly disgusted with herself.

Twenty-three

Zach walked away from the Taos Inn, cursing under his breath. Unfuckingbelievable! Claire treated him the way she would one of the low-lifes that hung out at Bam Stegner's. He was so friggin' fried that he felt like putting his fist through a brick wall.

Claire wanted him—no denying it. But when it came to being seen in public with him, the princess drew the line. Why did he bother? He had wound up things at the rodeo a few hours ago, then had rushed home to shower and shave, so he could see Claire without looking—and smell-ing—like five-day-old roadkill. He should have gone to bed. Christ knows, he needed sleep. The last two nights had been hell.

"You're such a stupid ass," he muttered to himself. Why had he come to see Claire? Hadn't he gotten enough of that uppity establishment crap when he'd been a kid? Yeah, right. He thought they couldn't hurt him. *They* couldn't, but . . . well, Claire could.

He'd made something of himself, and he was damn proud of it. Yet Claire had the ability to make him feel like a worthless teenager with a drunk for a mother and a fa-ther . . . and a father who would rather waste his life wait-ing for Amy Holt than try to make something of himself.

Why couldn't he just let Claire go? Cursing himself un-der his breath, he decided this had to be some kind of sick obsession. Concentrate on solving the murder, he told himself. Avoid Claire Holt entirely.

"Sheriff! Oh, Sheriff!"

Vanessa Trent was sashaying up the side street toward the plaza. Her blond hair fluttered as she tried to hurry yet still look sexy. The fire-engine red sheath she wore kept her from walking very fast. The mile-high heels didn't help either—especially on cobblestones laid down centuries ago.

Aw, hell. Just what he didn't need. He stood on the corner and waited until the actress came to a breathless stop beside him.

"I want to thank you for sending that to-die-for FBI agent to check my security," she told him, sweeping her long lashes up, then slowly, slowly down.

"Glad to help," he said. He was all kinds of pissed, and the last thing he wanted to do was to play games with Vanessa.

"Have you been able to find Duncan's killer?" she asked, moving so close her breasts brushed his arm.

He could see the actress was more interested in coming on to him than in Morrell's killer. She was one of those women who automatically assumed her pretty face and sexy body would get her whatever she wanted. Whoever she wanted. He wasn't interested in her—and he never would be.

"We're closing in on the killer." Zach believed Stacy Hopkin's information would crack the case.

"Really?" she said with one of those dramatic wide-eyed poses intended for a camera. "How exciting. Will you be making an arrest soon?"

"Hard to say."

"Could you double check my security?" She lowered those spidery-looking lashes and tilted her head to one side. "I was a close friend of Duncan's. The killer could be after me, too."

Hell, that was a stretch of anyone's imagination. Was

she really so self-absorbed? "You lost a lot of money investing with Morrell, didn't you?"

She pulled back, a genuine look of shock replaced her sultry expression. "I bought several of Nevada's prints from Duncan. I did not lose any money—not one cent."

Lowell Hopkins had refused to buy the lithos from the actress. Then she'd tried to sell them to Claire, who'd also declined to sell them for Vanessa. How long was Vanessa going to go on kidding herself? Morrell had taken her to the cleaners the way he had so many others.

"Were you involved with him?" he asked, wondering if she could be the mystery woman Duncan was leaving his wife for.

"Of course, not. Everyone knows I'm going with Treveyan Farrell, the producer of my show."

Everyone did not have this fascinating tidbit of information, but then, Vanessa Trent saw herself as the center of the universe. Undoubtedly, she thought she was too special for Morrell to have conned. Zach stepped off the curb. "I'll drop by sometime to double-check your security," he said to pacify her.

He drove around to the back of The Rising Sun Gallery where Claire's car was parked beneath a cottonwood. Lobo stuck his head out the window the second Zach drove into the lot. His fangs were bared, but when he saw Zach, the dog wagged his tail.

"Miss me?" Zach said to Lobo when he'd gotten out of the Bronco and had gone over to Claire's car.

Both dogs were wagging their tails, but only Lucy was trying to lick him. Lobo had never been much of a licker, but he was wagging his tail harder than he usually did.

Zach reached his hand inside and unlocked the door. "Come on, boy. We're outta' here. Bam won't bother Claire. She's on her own now. She doesn't need us."

Lobo jumped out the second Zach opened the door. He had to grab Lucy's collar, or she would have leaped out, too. He hustled back to his car, telling himself that he was finished with Claire Holt.

His father had been forced to meet Amy Holt on the sly because she was married. Okay, that was their problem, not his. There was no reason Claire couldn't be seen with him. Except Alexander Holt.

He opened the back door of the Bronco for Lobo, but the dog didn't hop in the way be usually did. The dog was still by Claire's Jeep, gazing up at Lucy.

"Lobo! Come here."

The dog ambled over to the Bronco, looking over his shoulder the whole way. He jumped into the back like an old man suffering with arthritis. Great! Just what he needed. His dog was crazy about Claire's lame retriever.

Lobo was still hanging out the window, looking back at town when Zach rounded the bend to the small house he'd purchased on the edge of the Kit Carson National Forest. Like his office, the house had a panoramic view of Taos Mountain. Groves of aspens and pines flanked the house, and a meadow of wildflowers and clover cut a wide swath down to a stream that meandered across his property.

The house wasn't much, as houses went, but it was all his. He had a studio out back where he puttered in his off hours. He hadn't been out there in weeks, and he really missed it. Maybe tomorrow.

As he pulled up, he saw Brad Yeager's BUCAR, government-issue Ford, parked in the driveway. Yeager had made himself at home. He was sitting in one of the two bent willow chairs on the porch facing the mountain. His feet were up on the railing, his heels hitched over the hand-hewn oak bar.

"What's happening?" Zach called as he hopped out of the Bronco and held the door for Lobo.

"I have a little information for you. I tried to catch you before you left the rodeo arena, but you were outta' there like you had a hot date."

"Don't I wish," Zach said as he dropped into the chair beside the agent.

Yeager rocked back, balancing on the two rear legs of the chair. "Not much on Max Bassinger except he's richer than Midas and a switch-hitter who leans toward men. He reminds me of an old Elvis song about a 'burnin' burnin' hunk a love.' Bassinger fits the description, right?"

Zach tried to laugh at his friend's joke, but it was hard. After the scene with Claire, it was difficult to laugh at anything. "What about Vanessa?"

"The boob-tube queen—no pun intended—is flat broke." Yeager stopped to laugh at his own joke. Zach tried to chuckle, but he was still so pissed at Claire that he sounded like he was choking on a piece of meat. "Vanessa tried all year to raise money to form her own production company. She wants to get into the movies, but Hollywood doesn't think she's a good enough actress to carry a film."

"That must be why she invested in Morrell's print scam. He touted it as a double-your-money overnight deal."

"She'd been living with the producer of her show, but he moved in with one of those blondes from a beach show."

"Hold it," Zach said. "Vanessa just told me that she was living with that guy."

"She's lying. He moved out months ago."

"Why would she lie about it?" Zach wondered out loud.

"Because she's in love with herself. Her ego won't let her admit the guy dumped her," Yeager said. "I could tell that when I checked her security."

"True, but is she lying about other things?"

"I'd say her career has plateaued, but she's determined to get to the next level. Too bad she has a solid alibi. She missed her flight and pitched a fit because the plane left without her. She had to buy a coach ticket on one of those cattle cars that fly into Albuquerque. She arrived the following morning—after Morrell was murdered."

"Did you check to be sure she actually came in on that flight?"

"No, but I can. I doubt she would lie about it. Vanessa Trent is not the kind of woman who gets on a plane without passengers recognizing her."

"All we'd have to do is call one male passenger to verify her story. It's probably not worth the effort. I think Stacy Hopkins is the key."

He had given Yeager a rundown of what Stacy had told him before they went to talk to Bassinger. Zach had taken care to omit any mention of the bearded man, Paul Winfrey.

He hadn't mentioned Claire's fling with a man who also had a beard, not wanting anyone to think Paul had been the man in that room with Claire. Even though he was furious with Claire, he knew she hadn't killed Duncan Morrell. Why drag her name into this?

"Here's my theory," Zach said, his eyes on Yeager to gauge his reaction. "Someone was looking for Stacy or Duncan Morrell. They opened the door and saw them buck naked together and went ballistic. The killer had a gun and a pillow of some sort in the car. He went to get it."

Yeager nodded enthusiastically. "If Stacy hadn't left when she did, she might have been killed, too."

"Exactly. This isn't about money. It's a crime of passion. Mark my words."

Yeager let out a ragged breath, blowing upward and lifting his hair off his forehead. "It's linked to the print fraud, I swear."

Zach knew Yeager saw the print scam as his ticket out of Gallup, but he didn't agree that it was the motive for murder. He humored Yeager, though. The guy was all right. Without his help last night, Zach might have been forced to call on Ollie Hammond for assistance when a bunch of Texans decided to mix it up with some good old boys from Oklahoma.

"Want a beer?" Zach asked and Yeager nodded.

Zach unlocked the door to his house and the FBI agent followed him in, nodding with approval at the few pieces of Santa Fe style furniture Zach had been able to afford. He knew the room with its wood floors and stone fireplace had a Southwestern look that was definitely masculine.

He handed Yeager a bottle of Red Dog out of the six pack he kept for company. He reached for a Coke for himself, knowing Yeager would never miss even a small detail. By now he must know Zach never drank.

"Yeager, maybe we're missing the obvious. This is an art colony. Homosexuality is a given. Now we've got switch-hitters." He popped the tab on the can of Coke. "What makes you think Duncan Morrell was leaving his wife for a woman?"

Claire wandered through the crowd in the D. H. Lawrence room of the Taos Inn, sipping champagne. The Fosters really knew how to throw a party, she silently conceded. The best champagne, Cristal, and sinfully delicious chocolate desserts flown in from Paris. The people were another story. They were boring snobs for the most part. Few lived in Taos full-time. Most of them came only for the season.

She kept her eye on Paul and went up to him the second he went to refill Angela's glass. "I hear you're staying out at Angela's."

Paul's endearing grin told the whole story. "Staying" did not cover what was going on. "She's taking care of me."

"Are you getting any painting done?"

Paul stared into the champagne glass that he was awkwardly holding. For a second she tried to imagine Zach with a champagne flute in his large hand. She almost giggled, but the image of him walking into the night—alone—was too painful.

She should have gone to have coffee with him, or she

should have brought him into the party with her. Why did she care what these people thought? She didn't belong here. These were her father's friends and wealthy people with second homes who waltzed in and out of town on a whim.

Claire, get a grip, she reminded herself. She owed it to her father to warn him before she went out in public with Zach. The only solution was to go to her father and explain her feelings. He wouldn't like it, and she doubted he would accept her decision, but at least she would have fore-warned him. Going out with Zach was bound to make the town gossips rehash their parents' love affair.

Paul answered her question, interrupting her thoughts, "I want to live some, have some fun, not paint. Quentin Reynolds came to teach the workshop when I had a year left to serve. I painted before I left prison—when I didn't have anything better to do."

Claire mustered an encouraging smile. She understood, but that didn't mean she liked this. She was off to a suc-cessful season, but if she didn't have more paintings to sell, the gallery would be in trouble again.

"I've had so much interest in your work, Paul. There've been calls from all the art magazines and dozens of collec-tors."

"You've been great to me, giving me a chance and all. So I don't want to lie to you. I'm just not interested in doing any painting right now."

Stifling a groan, she almost asked what he was interested in, but his gaze swept across the room and came to rest on Angela. Claire had never seen a smile like the one An-gela beamed at Paul. Certainly, she never looked that way at one of the studmuffins.

"Don't worry about it," Claire said, being as upbeat as she could. "You'll feel like it again. A man of your talent has more than two paintings in him."

She was mentally preparing a pep talk for him when Vanessa Trent swished up. The actress was wearing a red sheath with Western detailing, a Hollywood version of a cowgirl.

"Claire, I've been looking for you. I just left the sheriff. He tells me that he's about to arrest someone for Duncan's murder. Who is it?"

"How would I know?" Why would Zach confide in this woman and not mention anything to her?

"I saw you walking down the street with him a little while ago. I assumed he'd told you."

"He didn't say a word about the murder."

"Really?" Vanessa's tone implied Claire was lying.

Before Claire could say anything, the actress spotted Max Bassinger and Seth Ramsey coming into the party together. She swanned across the room, hips swaying, and sidled up to Max. Remembering Zach's warning about Seth, Claire went to say good-bye to the Fosters. She'd been here long enough.

"Claire," Seth grabbed her arm, intercepting her before she reached the hosts. "How's your father?"

"Fine." The word came out like a curse. She couldn't help blistering him with her drop-dead glare.

"Look, Claire. I'm sorry I accidentally left you at The Hideaway."

"Accidentally?" She bit out the word, stunned he would say anything so stupid. She turned away from him, fearful of what she might say. She couldn't imagine any gentleman not caring more about what happened to his date. Her father might be impressed by Seth's pedigree and Harvard education, but she wasn't. He was a Class-A heel.

"Come on, Claire. Give me another chance."

She faced him again, barely resisting the urge to toss her champagne in his face. "I wouldn't have another thing to do with you if you were the last man in the universe. What you did was inexcusable."

"Coulter told you, didn't he? He hates me because I'm everything he's not. I knew he'd use this against me."

Claire bit down on the inside of her cheek to keep herself from blurting out something that would indicate Zach hadn't told her anything.

"Honest-to-Pete, I thought half a Roofie would relax you, Claire. You're always so uptight. How did I know you'd get sick?"

She turned away, passing her half-full champagne glass to a waiter for a refill to hide her stunned expression. Seth had put the pill in her drink. Hundreds of times, she'd mulled over the events of that fateful evening, suspecting everyone from Bam Stegner to Nevada. Why hadn't Zach told her? Oh, he'd warned her to stay away from Seth, but she deserved more than a simple warning.

"What do you mean, you didn't know I would become ill?" She turned back to Seth, a full glass of champagne in her hand. "Roofies have been all over the news. They call it the date-rape drug."

"It's just a sedative. I was careful. I cut it in half. You didn't even get a full dose." The pathetic whine in his voice was doubly insulting. Was he so conceited that he honestly expected her to forgive him?

"You could see I was out of it, yet you left me." She knew her voice was rising with every word, but she couldn't help herself.

Seth quickly looked around as heads turned in their direction. He lowered his voice, so only she could hear. "I thought—I mean, I assumed a friend had given you a ride home."

"Seth Ramsey, you are nothing but a sniveling wimp and a liar." She grabbed his belt and yanked his pants back, then she dumped the champagne into his underwear.

Twenty-four

Claire was inside her car before she realized Lobo wasn't beside Lucy. The retriever whined, a forlorn expression on her face. Zach must have taken Lobo. The wolf-dog would never go with anyone else.

She gave Lucy a quick pat. "Don't worry. You'll see Lobo soon. We're going out there."

She was driving far too fast, the accelerator floored. Just wait until she saw Zach. Not only had he failed to tell her an arrest was imminent, he'd deliberately kept quiet about Seth. True, he'd warned her to stay away from the creep, but he hadn't told her Seth had been the one to put the Roofie in her drink.

She braked hard, almost missing the turn leading down a dark road toward the Kit Carson National Forest. She'd never been to Zach's house, but she had a good idea of where it was. She checked the names on a couple of mailboxes and didn't find Zach's. Near the end of the road, she spotted a longhorn's skull bleached white by time and the elements. Across the forehead in black letters was Z. COULTER.

She drove down a narrow drive flanked on one side by sapling aspens interspersed between towering pines and firs. On the other side of the dirt road, the full moon revealed a meadow of wildflowers that swayed as a gusty summer breeze funneled down the mountain ridges.

Ahead was a small ranch house with a light glowing from a window.

"I don't know if he's home or not," she told Lucy. "He might have one light on a timer. It's darker than blazes out here."

As she pulled up, her headlights caught the silhouette of a man sitting on the porch, staring out across the meadow at Taos Mountain. Why was Zach alone in the dark, she wondered. She got out of the car and Lucy hopped out behind her. Lobo dashed up to greet them, tail wagging, but Zach didn't look her way.

The dogs nuzzled each other, then Lobo led the retriever toward the moonlit meadow. Before Claire could stop them, they were loping across the grass, heading toward a stream.

"Zach," she called, bounding up the steps to the porch. "Why didn't you tell me Seth had put the Roofie in my drink?"

She sounded like a shrew, but she couldn't help it. All this time, she'd been thinking the pill had been put in her drink as part of a plan to frame her for Duncan's murder. She'd spent sleepless nights wondering and worrying. If she hadn't found out on her own, just how long would Zach have let her agonize?

Zach slowly turned to face her. He'd taken off his shirt and slacks and was now wearing jeans he'd owned for at least a decade. His good boots were off, and his bare feet were propped up on the rail in front of him. The dim light filtering through the window from inside the house highlighted one side of his face, leaving the other in a shadow. His contemptuous expression would have made most people cower, but she wasn't leaving until she had some answers.

"How'd you find out? Don't tell me the wuss admitted it."

The sarcasm and latent anger in his voice was even more

frightening than the cold glint in his eyes. Still, she refused to allow him to put the fear of God in her. She stood squarely before him, her back to the railing where his bare feet were resting.

"Seth confessed because he thought you had already told me," she informed him. "Why didn't you tell me? You should have."

"This is a murder investigation." He all but snarled as he spoke. "Until the killer is caught, the details are confidential."

"You had no trouble bragging to Vanessa Trent that you were about to make an arrest in the case."

He jerked his feet off the rail and was towering over her—all six-four-plus of him—before she could even *think* to move aside. "What in hell are you talking about?"

She tilted her head back to look him in the eye, resenting once again the way he used his size and height to intimidate her. "Vanessa said you personally told her an arrest was imminent."

"That's crap. I said we're closing in on the killer—nothing more. Vanessa just toots her horn to get attention."

"Well, I don't know why you couldn't have told me."

"Because you didn't bother to ask. If you had, I would have told you what I told the blond bimbo. We have some promising leads. We're working on it."

She tried for a stern come-back, but it was hard because his arguments made perfect sense. He shouldn't be discussing the details of the case with anyone. And he had warned her to stay away from Seth.

She couldn't meet his hostile gaze any longer. Force of habit caused her to look down at her shoes. Instead she found herself staring at the most impressive set of pecs she'd ever seen. Tanned and clearly defined. And shadowed by dark hair that formed an arrow where it met the open button at the top of his jeans.

"Is there anything else you've conveniently forgotten to

tell me that I should know? You've probably found the bearded man, which means I have an alibi and can stop losing sleep over it. Come on, Zach, tell me. You owe me that much."

Sparks flickered in the depths of his eyes, coloring them a deeper, more intense blue. For a second she thought she'd gone too far. He put his hands on the railing, placing one arm on each side of her, then he leaned down so they were nose to nose. "Claire, get one thing straight. I don't owe you a damn thing."

There was such unchecked fury in his voice that she was stunned. Leaving him so abruptly in front of the Taos Inn had been an unforgivable thing to do. She was thoroughly ashamed of herself, and she would be the first to admit it, but he apparently had taken it more seriously than she'd anticipated. She should apologize—somehow—but she knew he'd never admit that she'd hurt his feelings.

And she had no idea how to say she was sorry to Zach Coulter. Why not? It was the decent thing to do, yet the words wouldn't come.

"You're right. You do not owe me a thing. I'll just get Lucy and go."

Zach didn't move. She was trapped between his rock-hard body and his arms on either side of her. His mouth was a grim line of bitterness that matched his sullen expression.

"Is that all you came for, Claire, to chew me out?"

She knew exactly what he was suggesting. Sex. He had a one track mind. She had no doubt he was capable of some frighteningly primitive sexual acts. Women like Vanessa Trent would be willing to oblige him. Claire had been tempted herself, but now she knew better.

Tonight it was easy to leave him. His unbridled anger constantly flashed in his eyes and etched every word like acid. This was a man she did not know and did not care to know. An instinct for self-preservation told her to leave immediately.

"Lucy," she called over her shoulder. "We're going."

The blasted retriever was nowhere in sight. She didn't have to turn around to know Zach hadn't moved. She could feel the heat of his body all around her. The fine hair on her arms reacted to his nearness, and there was an unmistakable weightlessness in her chest.

"Lu-cy! Lu-cy!" she yelled over her shoulder.

"Stop squawking, Claire. You'll bring down the mountain lions."

She swung around to face him again and found his eyes level with hers. The tension between them was so electric she almost expected sparks. They glared at each other, their breathing harsh in the still night air.

Silently challenging her, he leaned imperceptibly closer, his hands flexing on the rail beside her. His eyes glittered in the moonlight, the cobalt blue reduced to a thin hoop around his pupil. He brushed his body against hers. "This is what you came for, isn't it, Claire?"

His blatantly sexual gesture disgusted her. This man would never balk at anything others might consider crude or raunchy. "Let . . . me . . . go."

"No." His jaw flexed with anger. "I'm sick of playing cat and mouse with you. You want to get laid, but you can't stand to be seen with me, right? Right. So, this is how it's going to be. We'll do what our parents did. We'll screw each other's brains out every chance we get—and keep it secret."

Rage engulfed her, white-hot and fierce. Without thinking she lashed out, ramming one clenched fist into his stomach. It was rock hard, causing a jolt of pain to shoot up her arm, but she caught him by surprise and he jerked back. She bolted across the porch and down the steps, her feet thudding on the wooden planks. Making a split-second decision, she sprinted toward the meadow to get Lucy. Once she had her dog, she was never going near Zach Coulter again.

"Lu-cy! Come here!"

The retriever dashed out of the woods, Lobo at her side. Claire rushed across the tall grass, waiting to grab Lucy's collar. She heard Zach thundering up behind her, running full speed. She veered left, instinctively racing back through the meadow to her car. He was gaining on her, so she cut left and charged toward the stream.

Dumb move! She was getting farther and farther away from her car. She pivoted, looking over her shoulder, and saw he was nearly upon her. She reversed directions, but he was as agile as a cheetah and just as fast. He was so close now that she could practically feel his breath on the back of her neck.

Her heart pounding in her throat and her breath coming in ragged pants, she changed course again, but he'd cut her off, blocking her way. She tried to dodge him, ducking to the right. Her foot caught on a rock and she pitched forward.

Zach lunged for her, attempting to break her fall. He managed to grab her, both arms circling her, but he was off-balance. They tumbled to the grass, Zach taking the brunt of the fall, landing on his back.

For a moment she was so winded that all she could do was gasp for air, filling her lungs with the sweet scent of clover and the fresh smell of soap on his skin. Her senses were pummeled with myriad impressions. A star-filled sky. Tall meadow grass. Two dogs watching them curiously, obviously thinking this was some kind of game.

Then she realized her face was against his bare chest, and she felt the rapid *thud* of his heart beneath her ear. For a moment she was too stunned to react, then it dawned on her that she was intimately sprawled across his body, his arms locked around her.

"Are you okay?" he asked, his breath warm against the top of her head.

"I'm fine," she whispered, holding herself rigid.

Instinctively she clung to him, not moving, but totally aware of every inch of his body where it touched hers. She was nestled between his legs. The fall had bunched her skirt up around her thighs, but she could still tell she had an awesomely aroused male beneath her.

The physical contact set off a chain reaction. Her stomach tumbled into one long free fall while her pulse beat in her temples so loudly she couldn't think. Deep muscles quivered, carrying a clear physical message to every part of her body.

She tried to resist; she honestly did. But a raw, primal need she'd denied too long overwhelmed her. She allowed her body to soften and mold itself against his. She nuzzled his bare chest, where the crinkly hair tickled her nose. Before she knew it, she was kissing his chest, tasting him.

Yes, tasting him.

He'd obviously showered recently. The clean scent of soap still clung to his skin. But the sprint across the meadow had developed a fine sheen of moisture that tasted slightly salty. The almost uncontrollable urge to taste every inch of his magnificent body overwhelmed her.

Then she found a flat nipple concealed beneath a whorl of hair. With her tongue, she circled the tiny nub once . . . twice. A low groan rattled in his chest as he reached down to stroke the exposed back of her thigh. He yanked the skirt aside and his hand burrowed under her panties before she realized what he was doing.

"Christ," he muttered as his fingers traced the curve of her buttocks.

In a heartbeat, he'd rolled over, his large body now covering hers. He stared down at her, his lips temptingly close. He studied her for a moment, and she wished he would kiss her. Don't give me time to think, she silently pleaded.

"This is what you want, isn't it? You want sex. Right, Claire?"

His words jolted her. Passion evaporated, again leaving her angry with herself. What was she doing on her back in the middle of some meadow with him?

"Let me go." She shoved at his shoulders, but he effortlessly restrained her.

"We both want this, so why do you keep fighting me?"

"I need to," she said before she could stop herself. "I don't know why."

He pulled back and looked at her with the kind of pitying expression reserved for mental basket-cases. "Let's get something straight, princess. I've never used force on a woman."

"I didn't mean that . . . exactly."

"What in hell did you mean?"

She shrugged—or tried to—but it was hard. His body was half covering hers, anchoring her firmly against the grass. And the pressure against her thigh told her he was becoming more aroused by the second.

"You want to play rough. Okay, I get it now." He kissed her roughly, his mouth slanting across hers and his tongue plunging inward with an impatient thrust. His hands were under her now and his fingers dug into her tender flesh as he shoved her upward against his erection.

"There's no stopping now, princess."

She scored his back with her nails as they kissed ravenously, their tongues battling each other for control of the situation. He nipped at her lower lip; she bit his. He rolled to the side to hike up her skirt even more, and she took advantage of the movement to scramble on top of him. His legs imprisoned hers, trapping her against his lower body even though she was in the superior position.

He flipped her over onto her back again, manacling her hands with one of his like a steel cuff. With his free hand, he managed to yank off her skirt, the soft cotton tearing as it gave way. The cool night air washed her heated skin. He gazed down at her exposed lower body, his eyes narrowing as he inspected every inch in the moonlight.

She took advantage of the momentary diversion by rocking to one side, then she managed to roll, taking him with her. Now she was on top again. Yes! She undid two of the buttons on his jeans.

He bucked, his whole body convulsing like some wild bronco. She hung on, her arms locked around his neck, her legs entwined with his. The throbbing heat of his sex thrust against the juncture of her thighs.

The power in his body as he thrashed beneath her was like a wild animal—almost frightening. An unbelievable turn-on that reminded her of an X-rated version of king of the hill.

The next second she was gazing up at the stars again. His powerful hand lashed out and imprisoned both of her wrists, shoving them above her head. *Pop. Pop. Pop.* The buttons on her favorite blouse dropped into the grass as he stripped it away with his free hand.

She refused to surrender, even though he'd removed most of her clothes. Not to be outdone, she grabbed at his jeans, using her feet to force them down his hips. She only succeeded in getting his pants just to the point where a dark tuft of hair confirmed what she suspected. He wasn't wearing anything under the tattered jeans.

She had no clothes left except her bra and panties. He held her down and mounted her. She was panting hard now, vaguely aware of the damp grass beneath her bare skin and loamy smell of the meadow. And the two dogs hovering nearby—watching.

"I won, Claire. Admit it," he said as he unhooked her bra and brushed the cups aside.

He gazed at her bare breasts, and she should have been embarrassed. But she wasn't. If anything the tussle had emboldened her. "I'm not conceding this battle yet."

Flat on her back, looking up at his body sheened by moonlight, she was suddenly struck speechless by how powerful he appeared at this angle. His shoulders appeared wider, the muscles bunching as he held her down. His thighs, clamped against hers, held her captive.

"Know what your problem is," he asked, a bead of moisture running down from his temple. "You're so damn cold, daring any man to touch you. But you're wild at heart, really wild." The fascinating droplet lingered on the square edge of his jaw for a second, then dropped onto her cheek. "The wilder the woman, the more fun the ride."

"I'm more than you can handle," she said just to taunt him.

He ignored her, staring at her breasts. A quick peek confirmed they were resting softly against her chest. Her nipples jutted upward, dark and hard in the silvery light. And aching for the touch of his tongue.

He bent over and coaxed one stiff peak into his mouth, sucking hard. He grazed it with his teeth, gently but erotically until she was squirming beneath him. He was straddling her, his knees bearing most of his weight, and one of his hands still held her wrists above her head.

King of the mountain. Well, there was no question who had won that little game. He had her right where he wanted her, and it seemed he was going to take the rest of the night to play with her breasts, no matter how much the rest of her body ached with need.

"Give up?" he asked a few agonizing minutes later.

She wanted to give up, to go on to the next level—to feel him inside her, but her stubborn streak refused to admit it. His eyes were dark with desire, the lids heavy, but there was something else in his expression, some indefinable emotion. Suddenly, it became hard to swallow. She'd never had a man look at her in quite that way.

She heard herself whisper, "I give up."

He chuckled, a low, raspy sound. "Promise to do exactly what I say?"

Obviously, he was prone to the usual male obsession with submission. So big deal; she'd indulge him. "If you insist," she said, deliberately trying to sound disgusted. Secretly, she was thrilled, anticipation building by the second.

"Stop fighting me," he said. "Try a little tenderness."

Tenderness? It seemed like an odd thing for him to say. She never would have suspected wrestling with him would be so arousing. Yet unquestionably it was. Every fiber in her body tingled with longing, moisture building in private places.

"Oh . . . all right. I'll stop fighting."

He released her hands and rocked backward until he was sitting on his haunches, looming over her but no longer actually holding her down. "Darlin', I never had any woman try to take off my pants with her feet. Let's see what you can do with your hands. Go for it."

Without hesitating, she reached for the two buttons on his fly that she hadn't been able to get undone. Heat rose through the fabric to scorch her fingertips. The first button popped out of the hole easily, but the second was held securely in place by his burgeoning erection. He growled, low and deep in his throat as she struggled with it. He finally shoved his hands into the waistband and yanked down his jeans.

On more than one occasion she'd felt him and knew this part of his body was as impressive as the rest, but nothing could have prepared her for seeing it. His erection sprang free from the confining jeans and thrust outward at her, hard and thick and long.

And proud. In that moment, she knew the one word to characterize Zach. Proud. Even as a kid, cast in the role of the town's bad boy, he'd walked with pride. That same pride was etched in the firm line of his jaw and the confident set of his shoulders. In his magnificent erection.

Impulsively, she leaned forward and kissed the flared tip. It was smooth, but velvet soft, and oh, so warm. His body shuddered and he reached for her as he kicked his jeans aside. Holding her, he angled himself across her body.

"See?" she tried to joke. "I am too much for you to handle."

"Wrong, Claire. I have your number."

His hand inched along her stomach until he reached the moist patch of curls, then dipped downward, finding a very sensitive spot under her panties.

She sucked in her breath, lifting her hips as he traced his finger in slow circles. Moaning, she bit her lip, savoring the waves of pleasure racking her body. This was torture, pure exquisite torture.

He jerked the panties down over her hips to her ankles. She fluttered her legs, forcing them lower, then kicked the panties aside.

"I have your number, Claire," he repeated.

Her brain was searching for a smart comeback. Suddenly, he was kissing her *there*. His tongue found the same spot his finger had just been. He applied a little suction as he lolled the tight bud with his tongue. His tongue stroked and teased, working miracles. Her pulse staggered, then surged at a breakneck speed until rational thought was impossible.

She was dimly aware of the thick ridge of his sex pressing against her thigh, a promise and a threat. She'd never made love to a man so large, so powerfully built. Arching upward, her hips instinctively sought his as his expert caresses sent rippling waves of pleasure through her entire body.

"Hurry up, Zach."

She was ready, more than ready, Zach thought, but he tweaked her again with his tongue, then blew hot breath across the wet curls as he lifted his head. This was exactly where he wanted her, on her back, blond hair flung across the grass. Okay, okay, so he'd mentally pictured her on his pillow. What the hell? She was into rough stuff, and now they were buck naked in his meadow.

"Hold that thought," he said gruffly, reaching for his jeans.

The two dogs were nearby, tongues hanging out, watching. "Don't you two have anything better to do? Go chase rabbits."

He found the small foil packet he'd put in his pocket earlier. He'd won the bet with himself. He'd known Claire would come to him after the party. She refused to be seen with him, but she wanted him to screw her. Okay, he could live with it—or maybe he couldn't.

His feelings for this woman were unbelievably complex. It was sexual, sure, but it went way, way beyond the physical. He wanted—oh, hell—he couldn't express exactly what he was craving where Claire was concerned.

He'd asked her to be tender, but she hadn't. Instead, she'd been astonishingly passionate. Her undisguised need for him was arousing, sure, but he wanted so much more from her.

And he had the disturbing suspicion he was never going to get what he wanted. Right now it didn't matter. He'd worry about the future—and his pride later.

He tore open the package, silently cursing. The damn thing was gooey and too small, but he managed to get it over his turgid shaft. He parted her legs with his knee, then settled himself between her smooth thighs. He released a harsh breath and nudged his cock into place. She was ready, hell more than ready, but the fit was tight.

"Is this hurting?" he asked.

She shook her head, flinging her hair from side to side. "Don't you dare stop."

With each thrust of his hips, his shaft probed deeper and deeper. He groaned, his body taut with strain, his lower lip caught between his teeth. A scant inch at a time, he coaxed himself forward, stretching her, stretching her. Loving every second.

Her body gloved him so damn tightly that he thought he'd lose it just getting inside her, but he made it. He gave another little forward nudge just to be dead certain he was in to the hilt. Then he willed every muscle in his body to freeze until he had control of himself again.

He rocked his hips once . . . twice . . . three times, and she cried out with wild pleasure. He desperately wanted her, but he needed it to be good for her. A night she'd never forget. She might not walk down the street with the likes of him in broad daylight. But at night there would never be anyone else for her but him.

He pulled back by degrees, slowly withdrawing until only the tip of his sex was inside her. It was exquisite torture, but he managed it.

"What are you doing?" she protested.

"I'm giving you a dose of your own medicine. You've been teasing me with your hot, sexy body. Now it's my turn." What a smart-ass. He was dangerously close to losing control.

He flexed his hips and burrowed in again, discovering her muscles had adjusted to his size. They were still tight, hugging his sex like a closed fist and making him shudder with desire, but he could more easily glide in and out.

"Harder," she cried, bucking upward.

He gave her what she wanted, jackknifing his hips again and again and again. He clamped his teeth together so hard his jaw ached, determined to hold back and not let himself go until she was satisfied. He took off, zooming into high gear, gathering speed as he went.

"O-o-oh, Zach—yes!" she cried, her eyes squeezed shut. Her whole body shuddered with pleasure, then went limp.

He kept pumping, loving the feel of her, loving being inside her. Not wanting this to ever end. His release came in one long hot wave that was so gut-wrenching in intensity that he threw back his head as it shot up his spine into his skull. His head tingled from the aftershock of his climax, and every muscle lost its ability to support him.

Pitching forward, he remembered just in time to take the brunt of his weight with his forearms or he'd crush Claire. He hovered over her, breathing like a racehorse, every pore in his body throbbing with pleasure.

Gathering her in his arms, he rolled onto his back. Their bodies were still linked, his sex pulsing contentedly deep inside her.

He couldn't help smiling up at the stars and winking at the glossy white moon riding the night sky. "Okay, babe. How was that for wild sex?"

Twenty-five

Max Bassinger lay on his side across his enormous round bed naked except for a loosely tied maroon silk robe. The fabric was perfect for cooling his heated loins, he thought as he gazed up at the mirrored ceiling and smiled. He snipped off the tip of a Havana Noir, a top-grade Cuban cigar that he had rolled and banded by Davidoff for his personal collection.

He hadn't opened his humidor for over a month. Fuck the doctors and all their crappy advice. He took his heart medication as directed. So what if his only exercise was in bed? It was still exercise.

He flipped the bitter end of the cigar over his shoulder and sucked on the freshly exposed tobacco. Sweet, so sweet. Like the scene before him.

Vanessa and Seth were next to him on the bed. He'd rather be alone with Seth, but after that bitch poured champagne on Seth's cock, embarrassing him in front of "everybody who was anybody," Max had to boost Seth's ego.

Just before the champagne dousing, Vanessa had been pitching Max on some half-assed film she wanted to star in. Damn was he good, or what? He knew he was fat and giving sixty a hard shove. No way Vanessa was interested in his bod.

On the other hand, Vanessa was proving she would do

anything for his money. Not that he'd been crass enough to suggest trading sex for dollars. But when the Cristal soaked Seth's Jockey shorts and left a humiliating wet patch all around his fly, then ran down his legs to drench his Cole Haan loafers, Max had rescued Seth.

Everybody in the entire joint had heard Claire Holt yell, "You're a sniveling wimp and a liar!"

Seth had stood there dumbfounded while the bitch flounced off like some high falutin princess. The whole scene had been so damn funny. After a long moment of shocked silence, people began to laugh, including Max.

But the mortified expression on Seth's face had forced Max into action. He'd grabbed the actress by the arm and propelled her across the room, knowing the tight dress and big tits would distract people. They were out of there seconds later.

Max had told Vanessa that Claire was a vengeful bitch bent on destroying Seth because he'd tossed her over. Then he hinted that the two of them could show Vanessa a real good time—while discussing her film project.

"Sniveling wimp," Vanessa was saying. She had Seth on his back, her sleek rump in the air as she serviced him. "Claire doesn't know anything about men."

She sucked on Seth; Max sucked on his hand-rolled cigar. Vanessa Trent was so conniving and utterly ruthless. She might as well have been a man. Had she been packaged like Zach Coulter, people would have been afraid of her. But the surgeon's scalpel and God-only-knew how much silicone had turned her into a beauty. If you cared for a bottle-blonde look with a plastic bod.

Seth absolutely, positively did. The kid perked up—wet pants and all—the second Max had mentioned a threesome. He lit the cigar, letting the tip burn just slightly. Vanessa was now dangling her boobs in Seth's face.

Max took a long drag on his cigar, letting the sweet, hand-cured tobacco flood his lungs. He was enjoying this much more than he expected, heat surging through his groin, then clenching like a tight fist. Seth was a toy, a human toy—a novel experience. Why hadn't he thought of this before?

Max intended to keep the kid around for a long, long time. Seth was so easy to manipulate now that Max understood him perfectly. Seth got off on respect. He wanted to be a state senator, but he didn't have the money to run for office. He had hoped to wheedle it out of Alexander Holt.

Once Max understood the kid's needs, he made dead certain Seth Ramsey knew what Max Bassinger craved. He blew the smoke up at the mirror, thinking of how astonished Seth had been when Max had written him a check for half a million dollars to get his campaign rolling.

Seth had been all over him—literally. What was half a mil to Max? He had billions and nothing to do with it. Then Max had opened his safe and shown Seth the bearer bonds he kept for a lark. Instant cash. Anyone could sell them and get money. No questions asked. Pocket change— worth a couple of mil. Enough to fully fund a senate campaign.

That cinched the deal. From then on Seth had been all his. Max's toy. Why Seth had bothered to try to make amends with Claire and end up with a wet sticky dick eluded Max.

Vanessa moved off Seth, looking at Max, homing in on his crotch. "Sweetie, don't you want to get in on the fun?"

"I'm having all the fun I can have." The biggest kick of all would be telling Vanessa that he had no intention of backing her film. She was trying so hard to please, to cover the cunning mind beneath the silicone veneer.

Blind ambition.

Max studied the gold band with his initials on the cigar, and adjusted his position. He'd been on his side, his head supported by his bent arm. Now he had a cramp. Changing his position didn't seem to help much.

But watching Seth did. He now had the actress face-down and was running his tongue along her spine. Vanessa was moaning to beat the band. Lousy acting, Max thought. Why piss away good money on any film of hers?

But if she pleased Seth, really pleased him, Max might reward her with a bone—one of his smallest bearer bonds worth ten grand. She could sell it the next day and start looking for another sucker.

He scooted himself up to the headboard, then leaned over and dropped the five-hundred-dollar cigar into the ashtray. Damn thing had made him nauseous. He sucked in a deep breath to clear his lungs. That helped settle his stomach, but the pain in his shoulder was worse, much worse.

Why had he lain on his side for so long? He should have rolled onto his stomach to watch them. He glanced over and saw the show was now in high gear. Seth was nipping at the bimbo's butt while holding a fistful of hair so her head was facedown in the pillow. She was turned away from Max and slightly to the side with just enough room to breathe.

Seth was the picture of ecstasy, loving every second. When it came to women, Seth had a cruel streak. He was really getting off on hurting Vanessa a little. All in the name of hot sex, of course.

The pain inched down Max's arm, but he ignored it, thinking of how much fun he'd have later. Making Seth pay for enjoying this. Some people might have said Max was perverted, he reflected. Not so. Poor people were per-verted. Rich people were kinky.

Kinky and . . . the breath stalled in his lungs. An explo-sion of white-hot pain seared through his chest and shoul-der, down his arm to scorch his fingertips. His heart! Something was wrong! He glanced at the bedside clock.

Just after midnight.

In a one-horse town like this, would a doctor be in the emergency room after midnight? Could he get there in time?

"Seth!" he cried, a strangled sound he hardly recognized as his own voice.

Seth looked over at Max, all smiles. Max struggled to cry out again, but his lips were too contorted with pain to form the words. The severity of the situation registered on Seth's face—thank God.

Seth's smile vanished, and Max managed to reach his hand toward him for help. Seth glanced down at Vanessa whose head was still facing away from Max. Evidently she hadn't picked up on the distress in his tone when he'd cried out to Seth. She kept moaning like an actress in a cheap porn flick.

Help me, Max silently cried, mouthing the words. Seth levered Vanessa's backside up, then entered her from the rear, a look of unadulterated pleasure on his handsome face. He turned his head slightly and blew Max a kiss.

Claire glanced up at the digital alarm clock on Zach's nightstand. Almost four o'clock. When had she arrived here? Before ten, she thought. How many times had they made love?

She lay very still, staring into the darkness and knowing if she moved, Zach would be on her again. The thought alone caused a flutter in her tummy and a familiar heat languidly crept through her. It had been a night of sex, as primal and raw and uninhibited as she could imagine.

Wild sex.

Tell the truth, Claire. You loved every second. Tonight for the first time in her life, she'd let herself go. True, she had initially fought Zach with that king-of-the-mountain game, finally yielding in total surrender to his superior strength.

Why had she initiated that silly game? She searched her brain, yet couldn't explain it to herself. It must be some sort of control issue, she decided. Zach was so strong and physically able to dominate her. She must have needed to be in control. She couldn't come up with a better explanation.

But there was one thing she was certain about. Making love to Zach was like taking a narcotic and telling yourself that once would be enough. She was hooked, plain and simple.

Okay, so what are you going to do about it?

She had been waffling for some time, teetering between wanting him and hating him. He would deliberately bait her with some crude remark or action, and she would fall for it. It was a stupid, adolescent way of approaching a relationship. And that's what she wanted from Zach—a real relationship.

But how did he feel? What did he want?

She looked over at Zach, his face barely visible in a slanting bar of moonlight coming through the window. He didn't relax as he slept, she thought, remembering him catnapping on her sofa just last week. If anything his expression was more stern, worry etching the masculine planes of his face.

What troubled him even in his sleep?

She glanced down at his arm slung possessively across her rib cage just below her breasts. The soft underside of her chest rested on his tanned forearm. Bronze against opal white. The contrast fascinated her; everything about him fascinated her.

Yet on another level, he frightened her because she didn't understand him. A relationship founded on sex didn't leave much room for understanding. She reminded herself to follow Angela's advice and get this man out of her system. It was going to take longer than one night, so she needed to keep her emotional barriers up.

Sex and nothing more. It worked for Angela—for years. Yet the thought depressed Claire terribly. This wasn't how she saw herself at all. She wanted a home and a family.

Two or three children would be perfect. A dog. A couple of cats. But most of all she wanted a man who would make a good father, a man who would want to share the kind of family life she wanted.

She reached over and caressed Zach's cheek, wondering if any woman could tame Zach Coulter enough so he would remain true to her instead of skipping from bedroom to bedroom the way his father had. She lightly touched the stubble along his jaw.

With a flush of warmth that centered between her legs, she recalled the rasp of his beard against her breasts. Between her thighs.

Oh, Lordy, what had she gotten herself into this time?

As if sensing her mental hesitation, Zach moved in his sleep. His arm tightened, pulling her against his solid torso. His warm breath fanned across her breasts. She could feel his heart beating strong and steady against her body. What would it be like to wake up every morning with Zach holding her?

She snuggled closer, and he whispered her name in his sleep with an aching tenderness that took her by surprise. He was so intense about life, so passionate when he made love. It was difficult to believe such a man existed who could make her cry out with pleasure and bring tears of utter happiness to her eyes. Now she knew what had been missing her whole life.

The echo in her soul that crept into her mind in the early hours just before dawn. The voice in her mind that knew her innermost thoughts. The mirror of her heart, reflecting hidden desires and secret fantasies.

Zach Coulter.

He was her destiny and always had been, she thought, looking back to her youth. Tonight, her life had changed forever, her very existence had been altered by the experience. And telling herself anything else would be a lie.

She shivered in his arms . . . wondering what would happen if he knew she was falling in love with him.

Bah-ring! Bah-ring! The telephone beside the bed shattered the stillness. Zach sat bolt upright and shook his head, staring at her as if she were a ghost. He hesitated a moment as if he couldn't believe she was there. Then he reached out and touched her face with his fingertips, a surprisingly affectionate gesture.

Bah-ring! Bah-ring! Zach grabbed the telephone with a gruff, "Coulter, here."

Claire watched as he cradled the receiver against his shoulder and switched on the lamp. She pulled the sheet up to cover herself.

"Aw, shit," he said as he slammed down the receiver. He was out of bed, striding across the room, totally oblivious to how magnificent he looked without a stitch on. "Max Bassinger dropped dead of a heart attack."

"I can't believe it!" Claire cried, stunned. "I just saw him at the Fosters' reception tonight. He seemed perfectly healthy." She thought a moment, remembering something someone had said at the gallery. "I heard he had a heart condition, but it wasn't supposed to be life threatening."

Zach pulled on his jeans without bothering with underwear. "Yeah, well, your buddy, Seth Ramsey was there when it happened. He called Ollie Hammond."

"Why? Max's hacienda is miles outside of town in your jurisdiction."

Zach buttoned his shirt. "Beats me."

"Seth is up to something." Claire jumped out of bed, the top sheet tucked under her arms, and retrieved his badge from on top of the dresser. She pinned it squarely on Zach's shirt, imagining him confronting Ollie Hammond. She smelled big trouble.

He stared down at her, and she had the insane urge to lure him into bed again. She did not want him to fight with Ollie Hammond. Her sixth sense told her there was something terribly wrong.

"Call Brad Yeager at the Fifth Pueblo Hotel for me," he said as he opened the door. "Tell him to get out to Bassinger's pronto."

"Be careful," she cautioned.

Zach looked over his shoulder, an adorable smile on his face. He continued to smile at her until the suggestion of a boyish dimple appeared, tempering the rugged planes of his face. "This shouldn't take long. Don't go anywhere. I'll be right back."

She called the hotel and gave Brad Yeager directions to Casa del Sol. Then she prowled around Zach's small house, turning on the lights. Both dogs had awakened when Zach left and were now waiting by the front door. She let them out and they flew down the steps and out to the meadow.

She hadn't had much of a chance to inspect Zach's home last night, so she carefully looked around the living room. Beautifully buffed wood floors offset a Navajo rug that was an excellent reproduction. The Santa Fe style furniture consisted of a leather sofa in a rich shade of sage and a single chair in a slightly darker hue.

The wooden coffee table appeared to be part of a barn door from a ranch. Numerous brands had been seared into the wood with branding irons. The Lazy Z, Twin Peaks, the Double J. Displayed squarely on the center of the table was a bronze.

It was a great horned owl perched on a limb. The branch soared out from a solid base then stretched across the entire table. The owl was perfectly balanced on the tip of the limb, suspended high over the coffee table. It was an amazing feat of engineering, but it wasn't nearly as impressive as the owl itself.

The bird appeared to have been captured alive rather than cast in bronze. Truly amazing. She looked at the base to see who the artist was. There was no signature on the base. Unusual.

Artists, even rank amateurs, signed their pieces. She pondered the question, then recalled what her father had told her about Jake Coulter. He'd fancied himself to be another Ansel Adams. He'd spent days in the mountains taking pictures of animals. Her father had passed him off as nothing more than a womanizer who hung around her mother using his photography as an excuse.

Could he have been a talented photographer and gifted artist as well?

Twenty-six

Angela walked into her kitchen at a few minutes before seven, Paul at her side, having returned from a sunrise horseback ride in the hills. The housekeeper had breakfast ready; the smell of hot tortillas and bacon filled the air.

As soon as Paul had this horse thing out of his system, she was positive he'd use the guest house she was secretly converting into a studio. She'd ordered brushes from Florence and contracted with a New York company to purchase the finest archival paper. Wait until Paul saw the thousands of tubes of paint gathered by her special source in Paris.

"What are your plans for today?" she asked casually as Maria, the housekeeper, served her special blend of eggs and bacon laced with Chimayo red chili and cheese rolled in blue corn tortillas. The locals called them breakfast burritos; Angela called them divine.

Angela mentally crossed her fingers but Paul's answer was the same as it had been since he'd moved in. "I'm going to shower and get the trail dust off."

He grinned and her heart couldn't help kicking up a beat. He'd lather her up—to take care of that nasty trail dust—and they'd make love standing in the shower, the water sluicing over them. The man had an appetite for sex that outdistanced any of the young studs she'd known.

Angela didn't mind. No young hunk had ever made her feel this way.

With Paul she felt safe in ignoring her father's dire warning—he's only after your money. Sure, Paul took what she offered, but with such genuine gratitude and enthusiasm for life that she couldn't fault him. It thrilled her to see him happy.

They were enjoying the burritos when Angela glanced at the television on the counter and saw Max Bassinger's face on the screen. "Please, turn up the TV, Maria."

CNN featured a perky reporter with a perpetual smile who was doing her best to look sad. "We are distressed to report the untimely death of oil tycoon and financial genius, Max Bassinger. He died last night of an apparent heart attack in bed at Casa del Sol, his hacienda in the exclusive art colony of Taos, New Mexico. Beloved by millions, Max—"

"Beloved?" Angela cried. "The man was a creep. If he hadn't been so rich—"

"Wait," Paul interrupted, "they're going live to Casa del Sol."

The newscaster, ever upbeat, chattered on about Max's rags-to-riches story as the camera panned across the opulent hacienda Max had renovated.

"Casa del Sol," Angela scoffed. "It should have been Casa del Muerto—house of death. It was built by Indian slave labor. The original owner bought the slaves right down on the plaza where they had an Indian slave market. After the hacienda was finished, the jerk got what he deserved. His horse threw him and he broke his neck. Since then the place has been cursed. One bad thing after another. The Indians claim *chindis*—that's what they call ghosts—haunt the place. The ghosts undoubtedly are the Indian slaves who died of heat and thirst, building a hacienda so grand it rivaled the plantations in the old South."

"Interesting," Paul commented as the camera revealed

the mob in front of the mansion. "How did all those reporters get here so fast?"

Angela shook her head. "There's Zach and Ollie Hammond. I wonder why Ollie's there? Casa del Sol is in Zach's
jurisdiction."

The CNN reporter on the scene took over from the announcer, saying there would be an interview with Vanessa
Trent, a close friend of Max Bassinger's who had been
with him when he had been stricken.

Angela gave the busty actress high marks for getting
tears to run down her face without ruining her makeup.
But why was she wearing such a sexy dress to talk about
Max's death? With that much exposed cleavage, corn
flakes across America were going to become soggy while
men hung on every word Vanessa uttered.

"Dear, dear Max," Vanessa gushed, dramatically brushing tears off her cheeks. "He adored me. He was backing
my first film, you know."

"Is that what you were discussing when he died?" asked
the reporter.

The question caused a fresh spate of tears and Seth Ramsey stepped into camera view to put his arm around her.
Another man Angela didn't recognize moved up from behind the actress so she was now being supported by two
men.

"She's faking it," Paul said as the camera angle widened,
bringing into view Ollie Hammond, Zach and the FBI
agent. "Zach's not buying it either."

"Earlier we discussed my-my movie," Vanessa played out
the moment. "Then Max, well, he"—she looked to Seth
for support and he smiled sympathetically—"came into
the room where Seth and I—" Another dramatic pause
"Well, we were . . . you know, making love. Max came up
to us before we noticed him."

"Seeing us making love was too much for him," Seth

interrupted and the camera jerked to the side to catch him. "Max collapsed onto the bed."

"Wait a minute," Angela cried. "The announcer said Max died in bed. Now Seth claims Max collapsed *onto* the bed."

"The other reporter was in Atlanta at CNN headquarters. The reporter here in Taos didn't hear what the announcer said," Paul told her. "That's all."

"It sounds fishy to me. Someone doesn't have their story straight."

Paul's brow furrowed into a deep V. "Do you suppose all three of them were in bed together?"

"Anything's possible," Angela assured Paul, suppressing the urge to lean over and kiss him. Until he'd come along, she'd been into kinky sex. A *ménage à trois* wasn't that far out, but Paul seemed shocked.

The reporter spoke loudly to be heard over Vanessa's fresh burst of tears. "We have been speaking with television star Vanessa Trent and state senate candidate, Seth Ramsey. They were with Max Bassinger when he suffered a fatal heart attack."

"Senate candidate?" Angela said. "Since when?"

"Since he had the opportunity to get free television time," Paul responded. "Unless the three of them were all in bed together. Then he's toast."

"Maybe," Angela conceded, "but it's getting harder to shock people. Americans re-elected a president even though he had been implicated in numerous extramarital affairs. I don't think it matters that much anymore."

"Miss Trent," the reporter said, his voice stern. "Why did you fail to call the authorities until two hours after the death?"

"Hot damn!" Angela slapped the table. "This is why I watch CNN. First on the scene, first to ask tough questions."

Vanessa sniffed, then paused, ever the drama queen. "I-I

didn't want to tarnish Max's image as a beloved philanthropist. I—we"—she gazed fondly at Seth, who lapped it up with a flavor straw—"wanted to consult Murray, my manager. Poor, poor Murray wasn't at home. It took almost an hour to find him."

The camera zoomed in on "poor, poor Murray" who did not look poor at all in his Armani suit with the cuffs rolled up to the elbows and a titanium earring.

"She called poor, poor Murray, and he reminded her how Hugh Grant became a household name. That's why there are so many reporters here," Paul said. "Poor, poor Murray saw to it."

"You're right," Angela said. "Murray's one of those spin doctors who put the best light on everything for their clients. He told Vanessa the world would be fascinated that she'd been in bed with a man when another man came upon them and dropped dead of a heart attack just seeing her make love. He convinced her this will help her movie career."

The reporter was now moving over to question Zach. Angela had to admit that central casting couldn't have provided a more fitting sheriff. Tall and powerfully built with dark whiskers shadowing his masculine jaw. He looked dead tired, but projected an inner confidence that was reflected in his eyes, a tribute to the badge pinned on his chest.

"Sheriff, I understand you have some questions about the time of death?"

Zach looked right into the camera, and Angela imagined women across the country steaming up their television sets. "To me it appears Bassinger was dead for much longer than two hours."

"That's why Seth Ramsey called me." Ollie Hammond poked his face in front of the microphone. "Coulter's still green. I've been chief of police for thirty-six years. I say Bassinger died exactly when Miss Trent said—at 2:00 A.M."

"I agree with the sheriff," Brad Yeager said and the camera cut to him. The reporter scrambled to retain control of the interview, introducing Brad Yeager. The agent then continued, "I believe Max Bassinger was dead at least three, maybe four hours—not two—when we arrived. The FBI's forensic team is going to perform a complete autopsy."

At ten o'clock Claire was walking across the plaza to her father's bank, knowing he'd be upstairs at his desk. It would take more than the scare on Friday night to keep her father away from work. From down the street, a low rumble like distant thunder became a teeth-rattling roar. A dozen or more scary-looking men circled the plaza on Harleys. Leading them, on his chrome and crimson hog, was Bam Stegner.

He was wearing a black leather vest, without a shirt, of course. Naturally, he was wearing spurs. They were gleaming silver with stiletto points like lethal weapons. A shudder went though her. Just what Zach didn't need—a gang of Hell's Angels. Wasn't it enough that Zach had to deal with Duncan's murder and the mysterious circumstances of Max Bassinger's death?

Bam Stegner spotted Claire and he gave her a leering grin, but his eyes telegraphed pure hatred. She had no illusions about what he would do to her if he ever got the chance. She waved as if they were old friends and kept walking.

She rushed into the bank and smiled at the tellers she'd know for years as she hurried upstairs. The second she walked into her father's office, she knew he'd heard from the Fosters.

"Claire, how could you cause a scene like that? Muffy Foster was totally mortified. She suffered another of those migraines that send her to bed for days."

"Good for Muffy." She pulled out the chair in front of his desk. "I didn't come to discuss the party. I want to talk to you about Zach Coulter."

He looked away, clearly stunned, his stern expression hardening. "That bastard. Look at the trouble he's causing by claiming Max Bassinger was dead a lot longer than Vanessa and Seth say."

"Special Agent Yeager agreed with him," she responded, trying to keep her tone level, but it was hard. Where Zach was concerned, her father refused to see anything good. With Seth, it was the complete opposite.

"At the Fosters' party last night, Seth confessed he'd put the Roofie in my drink. He knew I was out of it because he gave me the pill, but he didn't bother to see I got home safely. I'm just lucky a nice man found me. It certainly could have been a lot worse, but Seth didn't care."

He father aged visibly as she told him, slumping forward in his chair and slowly shaking his head. "Seth did that?" He seemed on the verge of tears. "Seth isn't good enough for you. I'd hoped but . . . well, seeing him with Vanessa Trent and knowing the two of them are involved disgusted me."

"Something's strange about their story. Zach will get to the bottom of it."

"No, this case will prove Coulter's worthless," he insisted. "So what about the sheriff? You wanted to talk about him. He isn't trying to pin Morrell's murder on you, is he?"

"No, Father, he's not."

She took a deep breath, thinking of how she'd walked away from Zach last night to go to the Fosters' party. She should have taken him into the party with her. He'd been hurt, and she couldn't blame him.

She inhaled a calming breath, hoping . . . no, praying she wasn't just being impulsive. She had mulled over the situation and had decided that telling her father was her only choice. True, nothing might come of her relationship with Zach, but keeping it secret wasn't fair to him.

Zach had made something of himself, yet most people believed he was the town bad boy when they saw him. Or they remembered his father. Few people knew the real Zachary Coulter. Last night, Claire had seen another side of him, a very frightening side. But it was really an echo of the hurt and frustration he was experiencing.

Everyone deserves a second chance. He said that to her once, and she'd chosen to ignore it. Well, she wasn't ignoring it any longer. She promised herself to give their relationship a chance.

"I'm seeing Zach Coulter. I wanted to tell you myself. I didn't want you to hear it from some old gossip."

She'd expected her father to be so shocked that he might have another stroke, or so angry that he would shout loudly enough to be heard out at the pueblo. Instead, he leaned back in his chair and nodded, slowly releasing his breath as if he were in pain, but taking great care to hide it.

"I knew it. I sensed it when you talked about him the other day. It reminded me of your mother telling me how talented Jake Coulter was and how she intended to exhibit his photographs."

Now was not the time to argue that Jake Coulter had also created one of the best bronzes she'd ever seen. She was just thankful her father was taking this with apparent calm.

"I knew your mother was lying just the way I knew you were lying." He gazed at her with a bleak, level stare, still speaking in a relentless monotone. "You're exactly like her. Exactly. I'll tell you what's going to happen. A Coulter will ruin your life just the way a Coulter ruined hers."

"Now, Daddy—"

"Don't call me Daddy," he said, his voice low but lethally

serious. "You've made your choice. You're not my daughter. Get out of my life."

"Please, listen to me—"

"No! Get out!" he cried, showing the first real hint of emotion in his voice. "Get out of my office. Get out of my life."

Claire was halfway across the plaza, having left her father's office, when she spotted Lowell Hopkins. The older man looked as miserable as she felt. What had she expected? Her father was never going to accept Zach Coulter.

Perhaps they had nothing going except one night together. Zach hadn't said or done anything to make her think he wanted the kind of relationship she wanted. Maybe she was a complete fool for telling her father.

But she didn't think so. The problem was really with her father. He wasn't the only man on earth to lose his wife. Yet he hung on to his grief year after year despite living with a wonderful woman who adored him.

Claire truly loved her father, but he was beyond her help. She'd done what she'd believed was right. Her father's reaction hadn't changed her mind. Zach Coulter was getting his second chance.

"I guess you've heard the news," Lowell said as they met, his voice cracking.

Claire wasn't sure how to respond. The only news she knew of was Max's death, but surely, Lowell Hopkins wasn't broken up about that.

"Stacy has run off with Carleton Cole. After all I've done for her, spending every dime, she leaves me for the brainless hard body Angela brought to town."

Claire wasn't surprised, but didn't say so. She was too upset about her father to do much more than utter a few hollow-sounding condolences.

Angela was waiting for Claire at The Rising Sun Gallery.

She was gazing at the paintings of Paul's that she'd bought but not yet taken home.

"Oh, Claire," Angela cried when she walked in. "Paul's never going to paint again."

"Of course, he is. Paul just needs a little time, that's all." She was still reeling from her confrontation with her father. She did not need more bad news.

"No," Angela insisted. "We just had the most god-awful fight. Paul discovered the studio I built for him. He threw a fit. He says he doesn't want to be cooped up in a room painting. He wants to live."

Evidently, Paul hadn't told Angela about being "cooped up" in prison. Claire understood his desire to enjoy all he'd missed. "He just needs to get some stuff out of his system."

"I wish it were that simple," Angela said. "He packed his duffel and left. He said if I couldn't accept him the way he was, there wasn't any point in staying."

This sounded much more serious than she realized. Perhaps Paul Winfrey would never pick up a brush again. It would be an astounding waste of God-given talent, but considering the years he'd spent behind bars, Paul just might not want to spend hours with an easel and brush.

"Can you accept Paul the way he is? What if he's just an ordinary man, not a famous artist? Would you be interested in him then?"

Angela didn't hesitate. "Of course, I would. When he left this morning, I walked around the house, seeing the world through his eyes. He's so happy, so full of life. Things I take for granted, he sees as special."

"Have you fallen in love with him?"

"Yes," Angela admitted. "I never would have believed it could happen so quickly. I truly love him."

"Then tell him so. And dismantle the studio to prove it."

"Oh, Claire, this is going to be a disaster for you. Now you'll lose your best artist."

She shrugged. "What else can go wrong? My father just disowned me."

Angela listened as Claire explained how her father had reacted to the news she was seeing Zach.

"Don't make the mistake I made years ago," Angela advised. "Listen to your heart. I wanted to marry the tennis pro, but I let my father convince me that he was only after my money. Don't let your father say you're exactly like your mother or make you believe Zach is going to ruin your life. Give him a chance. Give love a chance."

Claire managed a smile as she sent Angela off to find Paul. Her "find of the century" was interested in living— not painting. Her father had disowned her over a man who might tire of her any minute. What else could go wrong?

It was late afternoon before Angela tracked down Paul. His pickup was parked in front of Zach Coulter's home, a lonely place at the edge of the national forest. She suspected he would be here. Zach was his only friend. Where else would Paul have gone unless he'd left town?

She had been terrified he had gone away. She'd found the one man who truly made her happy, and she'd lost him. What if he had driven out of Taos, out of her life?

Paul didn't answer her knock, so she peeked in. She didn't see anyone inside. Thinking she heard something, she went around back.

Behind the main house, under the shade of a stately cottonwood, was a small shed with a large glass window. She tiptoed up to the window, seeing it was dark inside. A soft *clink-clink* came from the room. Craning her neck, she saw Paul sitting in what was apparently a storeroom. He was tapping a bronze object with his fingernails, making a clinking sound.

She ventured into the dark room. "Paul, I need to talk to you."

Without turning, he responded. "You want talent?" He waved his hand at the table before him where statues of a bronze eagle and a bear were partially cloaked by a sheet to protect them from dust. "This is talent."

"Nice," she said as she pulled up a wobbly stool and sat beside him. "The studio's gone. Maria's brothers hauled everything down to the Indian School in Santa Fe. I'm sorry I broke my promise. I won't do it again, I swear."

He slowly turned toward her. She could never have explained the sense of dread that came with his steady gaze. He didn't believe her; he didn't trust her.

"I love you, Paul. I just want to be with you. I don't want an artist. I want you. Please come home."

He ran his hand over the surface of the bronze bear, lovingly touching the piece, studying it, not her. The words she'd just spoken seemed suspended in the air, then they drifted away, and the only noise was the chuff of the cottonwood branches against the roof of the small room.

"Please come home," she repeated, not knowing what else to say.

He turned to her, his gaze world-weary, and she was struck by how distant he seemed. Had they really been close, or had she imagined it?

"Where is home?" he asked.

Once, home had meant her father, money and security. She'd been on her own now for years. She had several homes, the one here being her favorite, but it wasn't her only "home." She hesitated a moment, the answer to his insightful question terrifying her. "Home is where the heart is. My heart belongs to you."

"Does it?" Sadness had extinguished the twinkle of delight she'd come to expect when she looked into his eyes.

"We haven't known each other long, but I feel I've been waiting for you my whole life." She took his hand and clutched it in both of hers. "I truly love you."

He rose, still holding her hand and led her outside the shed and up to the front porch of Zach's small home. They sat on the front steps, facing Taos Mountain as the sun slowly disappeared behind the bluffs, searing the drifting clouds with amber light. A breeze combed the meadow, parting the grass and ruffling the wildflowers. Paul's favorite time of day, she reflected as she recalled the other sunsets they'd enjoyed together.

But this time something wasn't right and her anxiety increased, leaving her feeling weak and helpless. She looked across the meadow, the clover shimmering in the golden light of the setting sun, but the peaceful scene did nothing to calm her.

"There's a lot about me you don't know." He turned to her, withdrawing his hand from hers in a way that chilled her even more. "Before you decide you love me, you'd better know everything."

She listened, never saying a word, to the story of his horse, Misty. Oh, my, God, he'd been in a fight and the other man had been killed. Paul's words barely registered. He was so gentle, it was impossible for her to imagine him causing anyone's death.

Yet there was earnestness in his words, and she knew he was being completely candid with her. Paul had spent years in prison. She listened, stunned, as he finished his story. The last, feeble rays of sunshine were nothing more than back lighting for the mountains. Somewhere the plaintive howl of a lonesome coyote lingered on the mountaintop, but Angela had no idea what to say.

"I paid for my crime." Paul waved his hand at the postcard perfect setting. "I lived in the Graybar Hilton. That's what they call prison. Nothing but gray walls. Twice a week—if you're lucky—they let you into the yard for exercise. Do you know what I'd do? I'd march around the yard, looking up at the blue sky, and promising myself that one day I'd be free. Then I'd spend time outdoors making up for all I'd missed."

Angela struggled to express herself, but it was hard. The last time she'd felt so strongly about a man, her father had convinced her to send him away. Now she loved Paul even more, but he was emotionally damaged. Could she give him the love he needed—enough love to make up for his years in prison?

Her whole life she'd been a taker, not a giver. She'd allowed her father to use money to isolate her from meaningful relationships. Paul had endured a life of hell, paying for his crime. He deserved to have someone love him with all her heart.

She scooted closer and looked directly into his eyes. "I love you. I can't make up for the past, but I want to be with you forever."

He pressed his lips to her forehead for a moment before saying, "Then there's something else you should know."

Angela stifled a groan. What else could there be?

"Those bronzes back there" he said. "That's an artist with immeasurable talent. There are at least a dozen of them. What did I do? Two lousy paintings."

"Fabulous—"

He silenced her with a finger on her lips. "Angela, everyone made a big deal about the cowboy and the woman. So mysterious, they said. Everyone had a different interpretation. I put my heart into that painting, but I had the woman turned away because I couldn't see what she looked like.

"The painting was me, offering flowers to a woman. I was so lonely and miserable in prison. The closer I came to getting out, the more I imagined meeting someone and having a life. The woman is you, Angela."

"Me?" Tears suddenly flooded her eyes as the impact

of what he said hit her full force. Art was—had been—her passion, her great love. His paintings were the most emotionally moving works she'd ever seen. How could they be her? "That woman is me? I don't understand."

"The woman is you, darling, believe me. I just hadn't met you yet, so I couldn't properly paint your face." He wiped away a tear on her cheek with his thumb, gently caressing her. "Now that I know you, I want to be with you. I love you. All I ask is that you love me—even if I'm never going to be a famous artist."

"I've been waiting for you my whole life," she confessed. "Your painting echoed my loneliness and search for love. Now I've found you and nothing else matters. Nothing on this earth will ever matter to me as much as you do. Nothing."

Paul sighed, pulling her into his arms. She eased her head down on his chest, the truth surging through her. At last she was home.

Twenty-seven

"I told you to wait out at my place," Zach said as she opened her front door that evening.

"Oh, sure. You expected me to stay there the whole day." She was unbelievably glad to see him, even if he looked dead on his feet and desperately in need of a shave. She had spent hours second-guessing herself, wondering if she'd done the right thing in telling her father. Just seeing Zach gave her the answer.

With a heart-stopping grin, he swung her into his arms, pulling her flush against his chest. "Good thing I know you as well as I do. I didn't bother to drive out to my place, expecting to find you there."

"Kiss me and we'll discuss my bad habits later."

Zach's eyes narrowed just slightly, and she knew her comment and light-hearted attitude had taken him by surprise, considering what had gone on between them last night. She wanted a relationship. But how did Zach feel?

One night together did not make a good basis for a relationship. It was too soon to tell where things were going, and it was most certainly too soon to tell Zach about her father. *Don't push it, Claire. Take your time,* cautioned an inner voice that was usually silent, causing her to blurt out her true feelings.

She put her arms around his neck, angling her mouth across his. She saw the startled expression in his eyes and knew he hadn't expected her to be so affectionate. His mouth was firm and warm against hers as her tongue teased his parted lips. He groaned, his entire body suddenly going taut and desire kindling in the depths of his eyes just before he closed them.

In a heartbeat, he took control in a sensual, possessive way. He seduced her with his tongue, curling it around hers and moving it back and forth suggestively. The muscles in the pit of her stomach contracted with a flush of warmth. Her spine arched backward from the pressure of his demanding body against hers, and she clung to him. He shuddered, a slight quiver that ran the length of his powerful body.

"Before *you* get too carried away, maybe I should use your shower," Zach murmured, his lips against hers. "I'm worse than roadkill."

Claire couldn't help smiling as she led him down the hall followed by Lucy and Lobo. Just inside the bathroom, Zach halted, eyeing the huge spa tub she'd filled minutes ago, intending to use a little aromatherapy to calm her nerves. Steeping in the water was an erotic blend of lily and hyacinth with a touch of cloves. The heady floral scent rose in vaporous waves from the tub accompanied by flickering candles giving off the powerful aroma of vanilla.

"Gimme a break! I don't want to smell like a French whore."

She unbuttoned his shirt, kissing his chest as she went, savoring the masculine scent and the crinkly hair on his torso. "I dare you to get in the tub," she whispered against his bare skin. "I double dare you."

"You're on," he said as she unbuckled his belt and popped the top button on his jeans. It took her a little longer to undo the rest, and he had to help her pull the jeans down. As they slid over his hips, his sex sprang free, hanging heavy against his powerful thighs. He was awesomely masculine.

Thank God, he wasn't aroused, she told herself, remembering the previous night. Even in this state, Zach was so uncompromisingly male . . . so magnificent that her throat constricted just looking at him. And the rest of her body—oh, well—she couldn't help herself, could she?

Totally unaware of how he affected her, Zach eased himself into the tub, wincing at the hot water she'd used to trigger the aromatherapic properties of the clove oil and dried blossoms. Lucy and Lobo stood at her side, watching. Zach slid below the water, dousing his hair thoroughly and raking his fingers through it. He emerged, pushing his hair back with his hands.

Claire was struck by how young and vulnerable he looked with his hair slicked back and rivulets of water dribbling down his face. Unexpectedly she remembered the summer day—so many years ago—when she'd met him at the mountain pool. He had been swimming; his hair had been wet and brushed back the way it was now.

Zach smiled up at her. "Okay. What next?"

Claire picked up the soap and sat on the edge of the tub. She lathered a loofah, then started with the back of his neck and shoulders. His body was the hardest thing she'd ever felt and the softest. There was a solidness to his bones and the muscles covering them, but the skin itself was supple and smooth beneath her fingers.

"Christ, that feels great. You're hired, Claire."

She put aside the loofah and used the heels of her palms to massage the tired muscles across the back of his shoulders. The dogs looked on as she rubbed, their heads cocked to the same side, studying Zach.

He grunted once, not a sound of passion, but a groan of pleasure at the relief she was giving his aching muscles. The intimacy of the situation, yet its naturalness felt so . . . right. She couldn't resist bending over and kissing the crook of his neck.

She inhaled the smell of the dried blossoms and a musky

male scent that was somehow much more provocative than the expensive aromatherapy. It was all she could do to keep herself from jumping into the tub with him. But she reminded herself that they needed to make a connection that wasn't purely physical.

"I'll understand if you can't talk about the Bassinger case," she said.

"What's to talk about? He was dead longer than Vanessa and Seth admit. Question is: Why are they lying?"

"Was anything missing?" she asked as she nudged Zach forward to scrub his lower back.

"Not that we could tell. The silver was there, his Piaget watch, a five-carat diamond pinkie ring. The safe is still locked."

Zach turned around to face her, and it took a little maneuvering. Even though the tub was large, Zach was a very big man. Who happened to look endearingly like a little boy—as long as you didn't look below his waist.

The candles flickered softly in the room, and the shimmering patterns of shadow and light were reflected in the beveled mirrors that lined the walls. Shards of light caught the rippling water around Zach's body. The floral scent was accompanied by a stronger aroma of vanilla. Perched on the edge of the tub, Claire took a deep breath, trying to keep her mind on the case.

"What possible reason could Seth and Vanessa have had to wait so long to call the police?" he asked.

Claire concentrated on the sensual curve of Zach's lips as he spoke, hardly caring about Max Bassinger. The man had always given her the willies. "So 'poor, poor Murray' could round up every journalist on the planet and make sure they covered the event."

"Maybe," he conceded as she washed his impressive chest with the loofah. "Yeager and I have a hunch something else went on out there. I damn sure hope we find something."

A note of discouragement underscored his words, and she knew that this case on top of Morrell's murder meant more trouble for him. She didn't mention Bam Stegner and the Hell's Angels that she'd seen earlier. Zach didn't need anything else to worry about.

She had turned on his small television this morning just in time to see the newscast. Zach had taken her breath away. No man on earth could wear clothes as well as Zachary Coulter. His jeans and chambray shirt had been nothing, monetarily speaking, compared to Seth's tailor-made suit.

But clothes did not make the man, and the camera knew it. Zach's posture had been relaxed, almost arrogantly so. What it communicated was an aura of assurance that you were either born with or would never possess. To millions of viewers, he'd come across as self-confident, not giving a damn that he'd contradicted the word of a famous actress because he believed in himself.

She prayed Zach was right. The camera most certainly loved him, but there were too many people in Taos waiting—hoping—for Zach to fail.

"I saw on the news the FBI is officially investigating Duncan's murder," she said, knowing some people, like Ollie Hammond, were using this to bolster their argument that Zach couldn't do his job.

"Yeah, it's official now," Zach said, not sounding the least bit resentful of the FBI intrusion into his case. "It's a team effort."

He took the bar of soap and reached under the water to lather his nether regions. Killjoy, she thought, then decided if she'd done it, she would have ended up in the tub with him. Just keep talking.

"I hope you haven't forgotten Duncan Morrell's murder?"

"No. Yeager and I were wondering." He put the soap

in the tray, then paused for a moment. "Do you think it's possible Nevada Murphy is gay or maybe a bisexual?"

Claire opened her mouth to say this was outrageous, then she stopped to think about the artist she'd discovered. Nevada Murphy was a phony through and through. He'd lied to her right up to the second he'd dumped her to go to Duncan Morrell.

"My gut instinct says no, but it's possible," she admitted. "Women love him. They're the ones who meet him, then buy his work. His career would be dead if they knew he was a homosexual. Why?"

Zach shrugged. "Just wondering. No one has a clue who Morrell was leaving his wife for. My hunch says that person is the key to cracking the case. Could it have been Nevada?"

"I always thought Duncan was straight. Like Nevada, he was a hit with women. That's how he managed to con people over and over, even women like Vanessa Trent. But I guess he could have been bisexual. That's rare, isn't it?"

Zach flashed her a devilish grin. "You'd be surprised."

She had the definite impression that he was keeping something from her.

"Claire." He reached up and brushed his damp hand through her hair in an uncharacteristically affectionate, tender gesture. "What's going on here? Is this invasion of the body snatchers? You're a different person tonight. You're being so . . . sweet. Why?"

She had a real fear of needing him as much as she was beginning to need him. She was tempted to tell Zach about her father now, but sensed it would be a mistake. He might feel she was pressuring him into more of a commitment than he was willing to give. Take things slowly, she warned herself.

"You think I'm being sweet?" she asked, striving to inject a light note into her voice. "I'm just being myself. Sometimes I'm angry, sometimes I'm sweet. You know, I have a lot of different moods."

His adorable smile made her want to hug him. "I like this mood."

"Well, earlier today, I wasn't in a good mood at all. Paul told Angela about himself, and she doesn't care about his prison record," she said. "And she doesn't mind that he has no intention of painting again."

"I know. Paul dropped by this morning when we were knee deep in the Bassinger stuff. He wanted to know if he could bunk at my place. Of course, I let him. Then he called later to say he'd patched things up with Angela." He smiled sympathetically. "I know you're disappointed to lose him, but you've got to understand his point of view."

"He came into the gallery to personally explain how he felt." Claire shrugged. "What could I say? Margaret Mitchell wrote *Gone with the Wind*. One book—a masterpiece. Paul assures me these two paintings are all he'll ever paint."

"Maybe he'll change his mind. It's a shame to waste his talent."

"I doubt it. Paul was very firm." She hesitated, reluctant to mention his father. "Speaking of talent, I saw that fabulous bronze owl on your coffee table."

He quickly reached for a towel, turning away from her, but she thought his expression reflected in the mirror was troubled. Or maybe it was a trick of the candles flickering in the dark room.

"What about the owl?" he asked, his face now concealed in shadows.

Claire hesitated again, wondering if their parents would always stand between them like an invisible wall. "Angela told me more of your father's bronzes are in your storeroom. If they're anything like the owl, they're fabulous. Your father was very talented."

His head angled to the right, his eyes narrowing for a second. "Yeah, he was a helluva guy."

"After your mother died, you left town. What did you do with all your things?"

"I didn't have much worth a damn. I left some stuff with Tohono."

She should have guessed, she thought, watching him let the water out of the tub. He'd turned to Tohono when everyone else in town refused to help him. Years later, it had been Tohono who had been instrumental in getting Zach his job as sheriff.

Without another word, Zach stepped out of the tub onto the marble floor beside the dogs. She watched him, amazed that such a large man could move with such athletic grace. His body was total perfection, she thought, discounting a few scars that said he'd been in more than his share of fights.

He took several swipes at his torso with a towel, then knotted it around his hips. She should volunteer to dry him more thoroughly, but she was suddenly overcome by the insane urge to throw her arms around him and cry. Not because she was sad. She was afraid, terrified that she had fallen in love with him.

She'd gone beyond the point of no return when she'd told her father. Her life was never going to be the same again. Knowing this, made her fearful. Yet with this fear came a contradictory sense of elation. In telling her father, she'd put the worst behind her. That sword was no longer hanging over her head.

"Are you hungry?" she asked as he followed her into the bedroom.

"Sure, babe."

She nudged him toward the bed, saying, "I'll be right back."

She hurried from the room, remembering the posole casserole in the oven. The rich hominy and pork stew laced with chiles was her own special variation of the traditional Southwestern dish. She'd made it when she'd come home, hoping Zach would drop by. After all, the way to a man's heart was through his stomach. Although she'd seen no evidence this would work with Zach, she wanted to give it a try. She took a bowl in to him.

His large body was sprawled across the bed, leaving no room for her. The tension was still there in his face, but she could see he was asleep. She set the steaming bowl of posole aside and undressed before easing her way into bed next to him. He was exhausted, she thought, noting how soundly he slept and remembering how little sleep he'd had since Duncan Morrell's murder.

She cradled his head against her bosom and lightly kissed his damp hair. There was an aching tenderness inside her, a longing to love and be loved. She recognized it, but had no idea if this man could actually fulfill her dreams.

Dreams? She again kissed his moist head, thinking about what she wanted from life. A successful gallery. Well, it seemed she was fated to have a gallery perpetually suspended on the tightrope between success and failure.

What else did she want? A home and a family. She knew that no matter how successful her gallery became, she would never be happy without a family to call her own. So, what was she doing here? Zach might not deserve her father's scathing condemnation, but was he father material?

He stirred in her arms, his body seeking hers, his leg capturing hers. There was a certain comfort to the feeling, a sense of being needed that made her forget the reservations she had about their relationship. She let her thoughts drift, determined not to think about her father.

* * *

Zach opened his eyes, trying to remember where he was. What was that noxiously sweet smell? It came back to him like a bolt of lightning. Aromatherapy. Had he really let Claire coax him into a tub full of stinky flowers?

Well, hell, why not? She'd been so sweet, so like the fantasy of her that he'd harbored all these years. He'd been powerless to deny her anything. What had changed her? He pulled her close, nuzzling her breast and realized she was still awake.

"Claire," he whispered, "have I been asleep long?"

"About four hours. You were exhausted."

The tone of her voice told him that she might actually care about him. It was a startling revelation and a sharp contrast to the way she'd behaved last night. A strange feeling surged through him. He wanted her to kiss him. He needed her to . . . to what? Hold him, he realized. Hold him and love him.

He'd experienced the same emotional upheaval the night he'd brought her home after inspecting the room at The Hideaway. He'd wanted her to take him into her arms and kiss him. Make love to him.

Of course, she hadn't. So what was he expecting after last night? He'd chased her across the meadow. She'd insisted on fighting him, needing him to almost force her to make love.

He listened to her breathing, his body touching hers at the hips and shoulders, his leg slung over hers. What was wrong with him? A flash of insight told him that he'd slept with too many women who hadn't meant a damn thing to him.

But one woman had always held the key to his heart.

There had been plenty of women who would have loved him—if he'd let them. But he didn't want just any woman. In the back of his mind hovered one special woman. Claire Holt.

He needed her to reach out to him, to make him feel

loved and wanted. He seemed to remember falling asleep and having Claire cradle his head against her breast, her hands gently caressing his head. Being sweet and tender.

Or had it been yet another dream?

He wasn't sure. He wanted her with a blind, ferocious need that stunned him, yet he longed for her to reach out to him. He stared up at the ceiling, trying to understand himself. Oooo-kay, he'd been alone since he could remember. His parents had been around, but they'd been absorbed in their own problems, never having time for him.

It was simple, he silently told the vigas traversing the ceiling. The wooden beams seemed to understand. As a kid, there hadn't been one chance in hell of finding the love and support every child needed. He'd been forced to grow up fast, a cocky kid with an attitude.

All along he'd wanted someone to genuinely care about him. Many women would have, he thought, but he'd never given them the chance. So, why Claire? Why let her get to him like this?

"Zach," she said, her voice pitched low. "I've been thinking."

"About what?"

"I was wondering . . ." her voice trailed off as her finger traced lazy circles across his stomach.

Uhh-ooh. "Wondering what?"

She angled her naked, sexy bod across his, and propped her chin up on his chest. She looked so adorable staring up at him, so different than she'd been last night. What had changed her?

"People in town are saying Max was in bed with Vanessa and Seth when he died."

She paused, obviously waiting for him to respond, but he merely shrugged. He couldn't discuss the evidence they'd gathered with Claire.

"I'm not asking you for details," she rushed to say. "I'm just wondering if threesome are more common than I thought. Suzi says all those adult movies they have in motel rooms show at least one scene with three people in bed together."

"Suzi? The kid who works for you? How in hell would she know?"

"She's twenty-three. Old enough, I guess." She kissed the whisk of hair just below her chin, sending goose bumps across his chest. "I was wondering . . ."

"What were you wondering?" He'd stopped wondering; he had definite ideas.

She kissed his chest again, but this time her hand roved lower. "Have you ever—"

"No, Claire," he responded, seeing where this was going. "I'm the kind of guy who likes having a woman to myself."

"Good. I thought so, but I was wondering if you have any fantasies."

He looked sideways at the candles flickering in the mirror. He had a fantasy all right, but he wasn't ready to share it with her yet. Saying he wanted her to come to him and love him made him feel vulnerable, dependent on her or something.

"Everyone has fantasies, I guess. Only a wild fantasy could make most people get into bed with Max Bassinger. What was that song Elvis sang about a burnin' burnin' hunka' love? That was good ole Max."

Claire giggled, then laughed harder at his dumb joke. He loved seeing her like this. He didn't want to fight with her ever again, but he knew there were issues that would come between them, including her damn father.

He trailed the pad of his thumb along the nape of her neck across her shoulder and down her bare arm. "What about your secret fantasies, Claire?"

He thought she'd hesitate, and he would have to drag it out of her the way he usually did, but she immediately responded.

"I want to make love to you." She raised her head off his chest and pointed to herself. "I want to be in charge. I want to be on top. Like last night when we were playing king of the mountain. Only this time I want to win."

"Is that what we were doing? Playing king of the mountain. That's your fantasy?" he teased. "Whoa! Let's not get too kinky here."

Her sharp intake of breath caught him by surprise. He could see she was holding back, getting up the courage to say something else. "Come on, Claire. Tell me what's the problem."

She stroked the soft skin beneath his bellybutton and searing heat shot through his body, centering in his groin. Suddenly, he was so hard that retaining a rational thought was nearly impossible.

"I guess I'm the old-fashioned, conservative type," she whispered. "There are some things I would never want to do—or have done to me."

"Really?" he responded, surprised that she was revealing so much about herself. She seemed so different tonight. He couldn't get over it. He didn't bother to point out the obvious contradiction; playing king of the mountain last night was hardly conservative or old-fashioned. "Where do you draw the line?"

She cocked her head to one side, turning away from him slightly as she answered. "I couldn't stand to be tied up even with silk scarves . . . or anything. I just couldn't stand it."

Like a knockout punch, it occurred to him that she shared the same fear of being tied up that he had. He did not want to talk about his fear of being helpless. But Claire was so different tonight. Things were changing between them. He could feel it, and he welcomed those changes.

"I'll never tie you up," he assured her.

He could see that she didn't *really* understand. She had a slightly stricken look on her face. It told him that she had confided something she considered embarrassing, and he'd let her down somehow. He didn't want to explain his fear of being tied up because it revealed too much about himself, things he'd never shared with anyone. But he didn't have any choice.

"Once when I was a kid, my mother left me to go to the Hog's Breath Saloon," he told her. "I'd gotten into trouble the last time she'd gone, so she tied me into the swing behind our trailer."

Claire gazed up at him with pity. Oh, Christ! He hated telling anyone—especially Claire—anything that would make them feel sorry for him. Against his better judgment, he continued, "It was summer, a blazing hot day. A diamondback slithered out of the bushes, clicking six big rattles. I remembered my dad saying to hold still when a rattlesnake was around, so you wouldn't get bitten. I froze, and stayed that way for hours until my dad came home and found me.

"He shot the snake, and untied me. I never cried, but I'd peed in my pants. I was so upset that I couldn't speak for almost a week. All I could think about was being tied up, unable to get away while death waited beside me." He touched her long hair where it brushed against his chest. "Nobody is ever going to tie me up again."

Her eyes were wide and glimmered with unshed tears. Aw, hell, just what he didn't want. If she cried, he might cry, too. A stunning thought. He clearly remembered the last time he cried. Snow had been falling as he'd shoveled dirt into his mother's grave.

He promised himself that he'd never cry again. And he'd promised himself a better life than the one he was living. When those tears had dried, he'd been transformed from a boy to a man. He refused to take a step backward and start bawling now.

"You want to be on top, right?" he said quickly to overcome the emotional moment. "So, go for it, just don't tie me up."

"Oh, Zach, I'm so sorry—"

"Forget it," he cut her off. "Going through hell has made me a stronger, better person. It was a long time ago. I'm over it."

A lie. He still had a secret dread of being tied up and helpless.

"Can you explain to me why you're afraid of being tied up?" he asked.

She hesitated a moment, looking a little disturbed. "I feel foolish telling you. It's nothing really."

He put his finger under her chin and lifted her head so he could look directly in her eyes. "If it's important to you, it means something. Please, tell me what you feel. Just be honest."

"I wish I could point to a bad experience that makes me feel this way," she began, her voice barely above a whisper. "But I haven't. Big men who can overpower me are intimidating. That's all."

He understood what she meant, and he had to admit he often used his superior height and strength to manipulate her. He'd done it unconsciously, hardly realizing what he was doing, but now that he thought about it, he remembered her reaction.

"Being tied up—even in fun—would be awful," she said. "I would feel so . . . so powerless. You understand. You've been through so much worse."

He put both arms around her, cradling her against his chest. "I do understand."

For the first time, Zach believed he was truly beginning to understand Claire Holt. But he wanted much, much more.

Twenty-eight

"Okay, Claire. You're king of the mountain." Zach grinned up at her. "I'm all yours."

"All mine, huh?"

Claire kissed Zach's bare chest, more than a little shaken by their discussion. His life had been hell, yet he had survived to become a stronger, better man. Was it any wonder he kept a certain distance between himself and others?

He didn't trust anyone. She had noticed the reluctance in his voice when he'd talked about being tied up. Pain had flickered briefly in his eyes as he had spoken, vanishing so quickly she almost missed it.

But he had gone ahead and told her, signaling a small, but significant milestone. It was a start toward a more meaningful relationship, she assured herself. There was a bond between them now, a physical and emotional link she intended to build on.

"All mine," she whispered, her lips moving against his skin.

She rested her head on his chest, absorbing his nearness and the steady beat of his heart. For several minutes she remained still, savoring the moment, an aching tenderness welling up inside her chest. She wanted to tell him how her feelings for him were changing. Take it easy, she silently cautioned herself. Too often, she blurted out her feelings, and found herself in trouble.

"I thought you were going to have your way with me."
Zach's voice was husky, a shade shy of a whisper.

She glanced up and was instantly undone by a look, as
deep and intimate as a kiss. He pulled her toward him
slowly, ever so slowly, until his lips met hers. It was a sweet,
almost tentative kiss filled with unexpected tenderness.

Longing hummed through her, a lonely sound like a soulful note from a blues singer, a sound only she could hear.
It was a searching, tortured cry, startling her because her
feelings for him were unexpectedly strong. She couldn't
believe what she was experiencing. Her throat was hot and
tight, clogged with words she wanted to say, but didn't dare.

She broke the kiss and returned her attention to the
masculine planes of his chest. She skimmed across his solid
torso, teasing lightly with her fingertips. A silent shudder
rumbled through him, and she felt him surrender to the
physical demands of his body.

Surrender to her.

Her heart jolted with a new rush of emotion that was
frightening in its intensity. She disguised the upwelling of
tenderness with sweet, lingering kisses as she moved lower
and lower. Her tongue danced across his smooth skin,
waltzing playfully over new territory until his body went
taut against her lips.

"You're good at this, babe. Real good."

"You haven't seen anything . . . yet." The throaty sound
of her own voice surprised her. She sounded as passionate
as she felt, fluid warmth suffusing every muscle in her body.

She moved lower yet, her hand roving across the skein
of curly hair to test the forbidden heat between his legs.
He arched upward off the bed and quivered at the intimacy of her touch. His reaction startled her and made her
bolder yet. She traced the diamond-hard line of his shaft
with her fingertip . . . a scant inch at a time.

He froze, his body rigid beneath her hand. A moan rumbled from deep within his throat, and she smiled, thrilled at her ability to arouse him.

He reached for her, but she cautioned, "Don't touch me. I'm in charge tonight."

"Quit stalling." The words came out from between clenched teeth.

She ignored his demand and took her sweet time to explore his erection, discovering the sensitive ridge along one side and the iron-hard contours of the other. She glanced at him, but his contorted features made it difficult to know if he was seized with pleasure or pain. She knew how she felt, though. Moisture continued to build between her thighs, a deepening sensual ache demanding release.

He reached out for her, but she swatted his hand away. "Don't rush me. Why don't you hold onto the pillow or something?"

His response was a sharp curse, half under his breath.

"Naughty, naughty," she teased as she tightened her grip on him, moving her hand back and forth slowly.

She clenched her thighs to control her own body as she lowered her head and finally took him into her mouth. She sampled every delicious inch, nibbling and flicking her tongue over the hard length of him. Her tongue caressed the velvet-smooth skin, throbbing beneath her lips.

Pulling away, she asked, "Am I doing this right? Do you want to give me some pointers?"

"You're doing fine." His voice was taut with need, the words almost garbled. "Just get on with it. You're driving me crazy."

"A short drive, I'm sure," she joked, or tried to as she explored him with her mouth. Actually, she had been dead serious about pointers. She'd never done this to a man, considering it too intimate. But she couldn't get enough of Zach. She wanted to know everything about him.

He arched upward even more, encouraging her to take him more deeply. She complied, sucking daintily and doing slow pirouettes with her tongue. She could feel him deep inside her throat, and the sensation was so fantastic it shocked her. She never imagined she would enjoy this, but she didn't want to stop.

He had yet to touch her, but she was aching with need. It occurred to her that she might climax like this, bending over him, making love with her mouth. The thought alone brought a fresh rush of passion, desire now at a flashpoint—almost out of control.

His breath was coming in long, deep shudders, lifting his powerful chest, then lowering it. Suddenly, his hands were on her hips, and he was pulling her upward.

"You're killing me, angel. You're killing me."

Before she could protest she was in charge, he'd positioned her so she could mount him. His hard erection nudged insistently between her thighs as he widened her legs and made room for himself. With an upward thrust, he was inside her, and she gave a sharp cry of pure pleasure.

Last night, they'd had difficulty the first time, but tonight she'd aroused herself tremendously by kissing him. He filled her completely, fitting easily, but the throbbing pressure was still there. She didn't move in that first awesome moment of utter pleasure. He'd burrowed so deeply inside her that she could barely breathe.

She was hardly aware of the dark room, lit only by the glow of the vanilla scented candles in the adjacent bathroom. The sweet smell of flowers hung in the air, but she didn't pay any attention to them. The mirror above the dresser captured the whole scene, but she just glanced at it.

Her entire being was focused on the man beneath her. His powerful body was hers now, hers to control. Or was it? True, she was on top—king of the mountain—tonight. But she doubted she was actually the one calling the shots. She didn't stop, couldn't have stopped, to analyze the situation.

"You're killing me." Flexing, he moved with her.

She rode him hard, increasing the pace quickly. He

stayed with her every inch of the way, his hands on her hips to hold her in place, his strokes swift and sure, reflecting the glorious power of his body. He bucked beneath her, surging upward with each thrust, delving deeper inside her than she'd ever believed possible.

This was like riding a wild mustang, she thought, gripping him with her thighs. It was the most thrilling, erotic experience of her life, and she didn't want it to end. But her muscles were contracting, pulsing with the need for release. Any second now and she would be over the edge.

She threw her head back, arching her spine, hearing herself moaning, but the sound was a distant echo dulled by the pounding of her blood in her temples. Release came in a blinding wave of unadulterated pleasure, penetrating her entire being, leaving her trembling. She closed her eyes for a moment, still bent backward, staying with Zach until he finished a few seconds later.

Her heart beat in uneven, jarring lurches, and she was suddenly so weak she could barely stay upright. She opened her eyes and caught her reflection in the mirror.

Her blond hair cascaded down her back, touching her naked buttocks. Her face was a study of carnal pleasure, clearly projecting the ecstasy still throbbing in every pore, every fiber of her being. Beneath her, the mirror revealed Zach, his eyes squeezed shut, his face contorted as if he were in immense pain.

She stared at the reflection . . . remembering . . . remembering. The memory brought a keening cry to her lips. The pain was so intense, so powerful that it obliterated every other emotion. She collapsed sideways onto the bed, sobbing.

Zach reached for Claire, stunned by the burst of tears. One minute she was moaning with pleasure, the next she was hysterical. "Honey, what's the matter?"

She turned away from him, burying her face in the pillow. Her muffled sobs brought the dogs in from the other room. Lucy licked Claire's bare foot, which hung over the side. At least the dog knew what to do. Zach was dumbfounded, never having experienced anything like this.

He didn't know how to deal with tears. Expressing his own emotions embarrassed him. Since his mother's death, he'd carefully avoided people with problems. But this wasn't just anyone; this was Claire.

He didn't know exactly what had changed between them, yet something had. Claire might not be ready to march down Bent Street with him at her side, but she was slowly coming to accept him as a person, not just a one-night-stand.

He took a bit of credit for her transformation. He'd known Claire wasn't the type of woman who could have a casual affair. Last night, he had made love to her over and over and over, believing that each encounter would bring them closer.

Zach put his hand on her bare shoulder, then ran it down the length of her back, a gentle, soothing caress. "Darling, tell me what's wrong."

She didn't answer him. Her face was still buried into the pillow. Her sobs had stopped, but he could tell she was still crying because her shoulders were shaking slightly.

"Please, go away. Leave me alone."

He rose and went into the bathroom where his things were scattered across the floor. The damn candles were still burning, and the room reeked of vanilla. He managed to find his clothes, but one sock was missing. He didn't bother to search for it, suspecting one of the dogs had dragged it off somewhere.

He shoved his bare feet into his boots, then walked back into the bedroom. Claire was still facedown on the bed.

"I can't help you if you don't talk to me," he told her.

"No one can help me. No one." Her voice was shaky, yet determined. "Just go away. Leave me alone."

Zach left without saying good-bye. He drove home through the dark, lonely night, more discouraged than he could remember. Why did he let Claire do this to him? When was he going to learn his lesson? Claire Holt was a crazy-maker. One second she was passionately making love to him, the next she had freaked out.

Weird. Too weird for him. Screw it.

But he was still thinking about her, remembering how she'd looked as she'd straddled him, her wild blond hair falling across her bare breasts, her eyes dilated, her lips parted. He'd had plenty of women over the years, but not one of them could compare to her.

The tune of an old song played in his head, expressing his feelings in a way he never could have. He couldn't recall the exact words. Something about being crazy for cryin' and crazy for lyin' and crazy for loving you. Yeah, that was him, all right. He was crazy about Claire, and there wasn't a damn thing he could do about it.

"Stay away from her. That's the answer."

He turned down the single-lane gravel road leading to his house and gunned the engine. He was so exhausted that he couldn't think clearly, which accounted for why he couldn't get his mind off Claire. With a little sleep, he could concentrate on Morrell's murder and the mysterious circumstances of Max Bassinger's death. He wouldn't have time to think about Claire Holt.

He pulled into his drive and the headlights picked up Yeager's car in front of his house, the way it had been last night. Great! What now? He took his time parking the car. The whole damn town wanted him to fail. The last thing he needed was another problem.

"What's going on?" he called as soon as he was out of the car.

Yeager came down the steps to meet him. He waved his hand in front of his nose. "Christ! What happened to you? Last time I smelled anything like you—"

"Can it. Are you here on business, or to talk about the way I smell?"

Yeager grinned, and Zach resisted the urge to slug him. "We've got a break in the Bassinger case."

"Yes!" Zach threw up his hand for a high five before he even knew what the news was. "Yes!"

Yeager slapped his hand, saying, "A maid working out at Casa del Sol told me that Bassinger often opened his safe with Seth Ramsey in the room. Wanna bet Ramsey knows the combination?"

Zach had never trusted the cocky little prick, and this confirmed his suspicions. It was all he could do not to throw his head back and let loose with a belly laugh. "You're damn straight Ramsey knows the combination. He and that bimbo took something out of the safe or altered a document or something."

"It was more than finding 'poor, poor Murray' that took up their time."

Zach gazed out at the meadow for a moment, barely noticing the summer breeze sloughing gently down from the mountains and ruffling the grass. "Bassinger was a major sleaze, fer sure, but I give him credit for being a good businessman. His office is in Dallas, and he has a legion of attorneys there. I'll bet one of them has the combination to the safe and a list of its contents."

"Great minds think alike," Yeager agreed. "We need to act fast before Ramsey or the Trent woman know what we're up to. You go to Dallas and see what you can find there. I'm flying out tonight with the body. I'm going to speed it through the system to get a better fix on the time and cause of death."

"I'm outta here just as soon as I pack a bag," Zach said.

"Not a word to anyone about where you're going," cautioned Yeager.

"No problem. No one gives a damn where I go, or what I do."

Twenty-nine

It was after eleven when Claire walked into her gallery. Suzi was already there, rearranging what inventory they had left. Claire barely managed to say good morning. She'd been trying to reach Zach, but he hadn't returned her calls. Could she blame him? Of course not. Last night, she'd lost it, falling apart in such an embarrassing way that heat rose to her face every time she thought about it.

What had happened to her? She'd spent the night analyzing her reactions. Everything about the way she had been dealing with Zachary Coulter had been . . . bizarre. And none of it was his fault; it was hers. She had a deep-seated psychological problem that had been brought to the forefront by seeing her reflection in the mirror.

The instant she'd seen her reflection, she had been thrown back in time to the day years ago when she'd unexpectedly discovered her mother making love to Jake Coulter. Her mother had been on top, her head flung back—exactly the image Claire had seen in the mirror right down to the expression on her own face.

And Zach's.

The sight had stunned her, siphoning every emotion from her body in an instant. All that was left was the pain she always associated with the image of the two of them making love. She had burst into tears, remembering how shocked she had been at the discovery and how she had run to her father.

The next thing she knew, the mother she adored was stretched out in a coffin, then she'd been cremated, reduced to ashes. Even now, Claire could feel the powdery ashes in her hand, all that had been left of her loving, vibrant mother. Then she tossed the gray dustlike flakes into the air and her mother vanished forever.

Ashes on the wind.

Years of guilt-driven pain followed until time blurred much of what had happened. But one image remained as sharp as the blade of a scalpel. Her mother making love to Jake Coulter.

Last night she and Zach had looked exactly the same, or so it appeared in the dim light of the candles. And she'd fallen apart in a heartbeat. She should have explained the situation to Zach, but words had failed her. Not only was she too overcome by emotion to speak, she had never mentioned to anyone how much she blamed herself for her mother's death.

Still Zach deserved some sort of an explanation about her behavior.

"Claire," Angela called, breezing into the gallery, cutting into her thoughts. "Let's go for coffee. I need to talk to you."

"I'll take care of the dogs and help customers," Suzi offered as Lobo and Lucy trotted toward the back of the gallery.

Down the street at the popular latte bar, Sacred Grounds, they found a table on the patio where flowers bloomed from small pots placed in vintage cowboy boots. Usually the smell of freshly ground coffee and croissants baking cheered Claire as much as aromatherapy. Not today.

"Claire," Angela said as she placed her double decaf latte on the table, "I came by to thank you. I took your advice and dismantled the studio that I had set up for

Paul. Then I went to see him and told him how important he was to me. It wasn't easy, but I convinced him that I don't care if he never paints another thing."

"Good for you." Claire thought she sounded appropriately enthusiastic, but inwardly she was groaning. What a waste of talent.

"I'm going away with Paul for a week or so. We're going to join an animal rights group that is inspecting farms where they are collecting urine from mares."

"Paul told you about his past," Claire said.

"Everything. I'm with him one hundred percent on this. It's time someone did something to stop these drug manufacturers from abusing mares."

"What about your art collection?" Claire asked before she could stop herself.

Angela shrugged as if it didn't matter. "I want to help Paul. This is important to both of us. I can get back to collecting later."

Claire sipped her latte, thinking Angela was doing the right thing. Art would always be there, but Paul had special needs. So did Zach. She desperately wanted to talk to him, to explain how she felt. Last night, he'd tried to talk to her, but she hadn't been in any shape to discuss the situation. Now, would he even want to talk to her?

Angela touched her arm, and Claire realized several minutes had passed. "What's bothering you? Do you want to talk about it?"

"You suggested telling my father that I'm seeing Zach Coulter, and I did."

"Your father was furious, right?"

"That's an understatement. He disowned me on the spot."

"It's the best thing you could have done."

Claire drank her latte, reluctant to discuss something so intensely personal as sex. Yet her relationship with Zach had her confused. She seemed unable to put it into the proper perspective. Over the years, she'd isolated herself, Claire realized. Angela Townsend was her closest friend, and a person who understood "father" problems.

"I'm terribly concerned about my relationship with Zach," she began, then stopped. How could she explain this?

Angela leaned closer, encouraging her with a smile. "What do you mean?"

"He brings out something in me . . . something I'm not sure I understand. When we make love, I want to play rough and I want to be on top." The words came out in a breathless rush, and Claire expected to feel embarrassed, but Angela didn't appear to be one bit surprised, making Claire relax. "I'm not like that . . . at least, I've never been this way with a man until now."

Angela nodded thoughtfully for a moment, then said, "Do you have any idea why you react this way?"

"I've questioned myself a thousand times. At first, I thought I did it to resist the urge to make love to him. You know, to keep history from repeating itself. A Coulter with a Holt woman—again."

"But now you think it goes deeper than that, don't you?"

Claire gazed across the small patio, momentarily distracted by noise from the gang of bikers that she'd seen with Bam Stegner yesterday, but he wasn't with them now. "I suspect there is more to it than not wanting everyone to think we're exactly like our parents. Emotions are complex, of course. Playing rough is exciting. That's part of it."

Angela nodded. "I was into kinky sex myself. And I thought I needed young studs. It was just a way of avoiding emotional attachment."

Claire thought about her friend's comment for a moment, then said, "I wonder if that's what I'm doing. Now that I think about it, I've avoided committing myself to

any man. When a man got too close, I talked myself out
of caring about him."

"Giving yourself to a man is scary. Believe me, I know."
Angela adjusted the silver cuff bracelet on her wrist.
"That's what happens when you stop fighting, isn't it?"

"Yes," Claire agreed. "That must be what I'm afraid of.
I'm terrified of giving myself to a man, then being hurt."

Late that afternoon, Claire was working at her desk in
the back of the gallery. She'd called the sheriff's station
several times, but Zach still hadn't returned her calls. Evidently, he was even more upset than she'd anticipated.
Tonight she'd go out to his place. He couldn't—

"Claire, some men are here to see you," Suzi said, interrupting her thoughts. From her assistant's concerned
expression, Claire knew something was wrong. "They have
a search warrant."

"What?" Claire vaulted out of her chair and stormed
around the partition into the gallery.

Chief of Police Ollie Hammond was standing beside
Zach's deputy, T-Bone Jones. The younger man sheepishly
handed her a sheet of paper.

"Where's the sheriff?"

T-Bone opened his mouth to answer, but Ollie spoke
first. "Coulter's out of town on personal business."

Thank God, he's not behind this, Claire thought as she
scanned the search warrant signed just that morning by
Judge Brodkey. The document gave permission to search
her home and her gallery for items that might link her to
the murder of Duncan Morrell.

"Go ahead and search," she said, trying to temper her
anger. "You won't find anything, because I didn't kill Duncan."

The deputy moved into the gallery, looking from side
to side, while Ollie guarded the door, his beefy arms

crossed at his chest. Something in his smug half-smile sent a frisson of alarm through Claire. Until this second, she assumed the warrant was some kind of mistake, but Ollie's smile and the deputy's deliberate movements frightened her.

Judge Brodkey was one of the most reputable men on the bench. He would never have signed a search warrant unless the authorities had convinced him they had good reason to believe they would discover evidence linking her to the crime. Suddenly, Claire felt shaky but she steeled herself, refusing to give Ollie Hammond the satisfaction of seeing her fall apart.

"If you tell me what it is you're looking for, maybe I could help." Amazingly, she sounded normal, but something in her tone must have alerted the dogs. Lucy and Lobo scooted out of the storeroom and came up to her side.

T-Bone turned red as he responded, "Where's the black and white pottery?"

"The collection from the Acoma Pueblo?" Claire looked at Suzi. "I don't know what pieces we have left."

"Just two," Suzi told her. "They were right by the front door, but I moved them to the back alcove."

T-Bone headed toward the rear of the gallery and Claire followed, the dogs at her heels. Ahead she saw two pieces of the distinctive black and white pottery on the alcove shelf. The deputy stood in front of the one with a lid and pulled a pair of latex gloves from his pocket. As soon as they were on, he removed the lid on the larger pot and reached inside.

"Is it there?" Ollie asked from across the room.

"Yeah, it's right here." The deputy pulled out something wrapped in white cloth.

A suffocating sensation gripped Claire's throat. *Beware the coyote.* Tohono's grim warning popped into her head along with something she'd learned in school. According to Greek mythology the trickster always led you into the woods. Oddly enough, Native Americans had thousands of myths about their own trickster—the coyote.

She'd been led—tricked—into the proverbial woods, believing that Seth had slipped the Roofie into her drink to try to get her into bed. Nothing more. She had stopped worrying about being framed for Duncan's murder. Obviously, she'd been duped. The deputy removed the white cloth from the gun and dropped the weapon into a plastic evidence bag.

"How'd you know to look in that pot?" she asked.

"An anonymous tip—"

"Shut up," Ollie cut off the deputy. "Read Ms. Holt her rights."

"You're under arrest for the murder of Duncan Morrell. You have the right to remain silent." The deputy mumbled the rest of the Miranda as Suzi watched, wide-eyed.

"Now wait a minute," Claire said. "That pot was by the front door for over a week. Anyone could have dropped that gun in there."

"Possibly, but no one else had a better reason to murder Duncan Morrell than you." Ollie sounded incredibly pleased with himself—suspiciously so.

The deputy pulled out a pair of handcuffs. "You're under arrest."

Lobo bared his fangs and the deputy took a step backward.

"Call off the dog, or I'll shoot him," Ollie warned, reaching for his holster.

"I'll put him in the storeroom," Claire offered, thankful for an excuse to think. She had to pull Lobo hard before he would come with her. Claire's first thought was to contact Zach, but he was away somewhere. Her father came to mind, but considering their argument, she decided against it. Angela would be her best bet.

"We're taking you to the police jail," Ollie explained

when she returned. "The sheriff's station doesn't have a separate facility for women. We do."

That explained Ollie's presence at what should have been a sheriff's office raid, but it failed to explain a frightening number of other things. Who would want to frame her? Why had they waited until now when Zach wasn't here to help?

"Call Angela Townsend," she told Suzi. "Tell her what happened, and please take care of the dogs."

"You're allowed to make one telephone call. That's it," a cocksure young policeman informed her as he led her into a small room.

He shut the door behind her, and Claire let her taut shoulders relax as she stood in front of a wall-mounted telephone. She had been in police custody for hours, undergoing the humiliating ritual of being searched, fingerprinted, and photographed. Finally, she'd been issued a Day-Glo orange jumpsuit with PRISONER stenciled across the shoulders in black and taken to a cell.

The wheels of justice being slower than a slug, the process had taken several hours. It was now pitch dark outside. There had been no word from Angela, so Claire assumed they had already left town.

What she needed was a top-notch criminal lawyer. Such a beast did not exist in Taos. Even if a lawyer augmented his practice with other types of lucrative litigation, crime was too rare here to support the type of criminal attorney she needed.

She stared at the chrome dial with no idea of who to call. Graffiti marred the gray wall beside the telephone. A tattered business card read: IN JAIL? NEED BAIL? CALL DALE—KING OF BAIL BONDS.

Money. It would take a lot of money to retain a good lawyer, money she didn't have. She was certain Angela would lend her the money, but it could be a week or more before she returned.

Her father.

He had the money to hire a lawyer, and he had friends in Santa Fe who could recommend someone. She hated calling him now, when she was in trouble, but she had no choice. If she didn't get her own attorney, they would turn her over to a public defender. Since Taos was too small for a public defender's office, cases were assigned *pro bono* to lawyers in town. With her luck, they'd give Seth Ramsey her case.

Fifteen minutes after she called her father, he appeared at the station. They brought her into the visiting room to see him, and left a guard at the door. She was so glad to see her father that tears sprang to her eyes. He'd always been there for her, and he was now. His love for her was mirrored in his eyes and in the deep grooves of worry etching his brow.

"Oh, Claire, honey." His voice was broken, and he started to reach across the table for her hand. The guard shook his head, and her father pulled back. "What happened?"

She explained how easily someone could have planted the gun. "It could have happened during the Art Festival when the gallery was so crowded, or someone could have come by when Suzi or I were in the back room and dropped the gun into the pot by just opening the front door. They didn't even have to come into the shop."

"Didn't Suzi notice the pot was heavier?"

"No. It's a small gun, and the pot is quite large. What makes it unusual is the lid. Most Acoma pots don't have them. The lid made it perfect for whoever planted the gun. No one would notice it until the police search."

Her father regarded her with undisguised worry. "They must have more evidence than just the gun. I hear the DA is rushing this case. They'll arraign you tomorrow."

The speed with which this was happening staggered her. It was almost as if someone had plotted to get Zach out of town, then zeroed in on her. You're overreacting, she told herself. She had no idea where Zach had gone or why. Even if he were here, he represented the law. What could he do to help her?

"I know a lawyer in Santa Fe with a young gun in his firm who specializes in criminal law. Fremont Simmons got off that man who killed his wife and baby, remember?"

She did—with sickening clarity. Fremont Simmons was perfect for a role as a lawyer in a movie. Slick. Arrogant. A man who twisted the law to service the interests of criminals rich enough to afford him.

"Great," she said with much more enthusiasm than she felt. What was happening to her? She felt as if she were being swept downstream into dangerous rapids without a moment to think or catch her breath.

"We'll fight them at the arraignment," her father said. "If they don't have enough evidence, they'll be forced to dismiss the charges against you."

They did have enough evidence to persuade the judge to indict her, she realized, feeling the hangman's noose around her neck, tightening with each passing second. Now was the time to tell her father the whole story.

"Dad," she said gently, "about that night at The Hideaway."

"Seth put one of those damn Roofies in your drink. That's what started all this."

"True, but I knew better than to go to The Hideaway." She inhaled a calming breath, praying her father would understand. "After Seth left me, I don't know who I was with . . . or what happened exactly. But when I woke up the next morning, I didn't have the panties I'd been wearing, and my wallet had fallen out of my purse. I'm sure all of this is in the sheriff's report."

"Coulter tried to frame you," her father said flatly.

Sheesh! Would this ever end? Her father hated Zach
with an obsession. None of this was Zach's fault, yet her
father *lived* to blame him.

"Zach didn't have to frame me. I went to The Hideaway
and got myself in trouble. I blame no one except myself.
What would really help is having an alibi."

"I'll bet the good-for-nothing sheriff didn't even look
for the man."

For a moment, she wondered if he'd forgotten their
conversation yesterday. Of course, he hadn't. Her father
was pulling one of his usual stunts by ignoring something
he didn't like.

"This is Zach's case. When he returns—"

"Do you think Coulter will try to help you?"

"Yes, Father. Zach will do his best to help me."

Her father sat back in his wheelchair and pulled himself
up to full height. His expression changed from one of
compassion to his banker's analytical stare. He spoke in
the same calm, emotionless voice he'd begun with yesterday.

"Be reasonable, Claire. Coulter has a job to protect. If
he can hang this murder on you, he will. Don't you know
how stupid he's looked challenging Seth and Vanessa
Trent about Max Bassinger's death?"

"The special agent from the FBI agreed with him."

Her father continued to assess her from beneath level
brows. "I'm positive Zach Coulter is trying to get back at
me through you. I—"

"You're wrong. He wouldn't—"

"It's my fault. In my life, I've done few things I'm
ashamed of. The way I treated Zach after the accident is
one of them." Her father gazed down as he ran his palms
over the tops of his knees. "Zach looked so much like his
father, and you'd been seeing him. All I wanted to do was
run him out of town, so I could forget. I saw to it that he
was fired from every job he got."

On one level this confession surprised her, yet on another she had always known her father had a vindictive streak. She hadn't wanted to believe this about him, so she'd ignored the signs. Now, she had to admit her father had a serious character flaw. What kind of man would pick on a young boy?

"You wouldn't lend him the money to bury his mother either," Claire reminded him—bitterness underscoring every word. The image of Zach walking down the street returned with startling clarity. Snow swirling around his thin windbreaker. Hopeless. Alone.

"I was wrong," her father conceded. "He was just a kid." His words were so sincere that she couldn't bring herself to criticize him even though he'd slipped considerably in her estimation.

"Coulter's never forgotten what I did," her father insisted. "He's going to destroy you, the way his father destroyed your mother."

That's absurd, she thought, but didn't voice her opinion out loud. Obviously, her father needed professional counseling. When she got out of here, she was going to see he received the help he needed.

"Claire, I'll do anything," her father said, a note of desperation in his voice, "spend any amount of money to help you." Two full beats of ominous silence. "All you have to do is promise me that you'll never see Zach Coulter again."

She saw the love in his eyes and knew he would move heaven and earth to help her out of this mess. Whatever his faults, her father had always been there for her. Common sense said to accept his offer.

What did she have going with Zach, anyway? They'd never discussed the future. Yet, she'd been profoundly moved by her experiences with him. And the time she'd spent with Zach had given her insight into his character. She wanted to give their relationship a chance.

"I can't give him up," she said, praying Zach would not make her regret this decision. "I just can't."

Her father wheeled back from the table. "That's *exactly* what your mother said when I gave her the choice between giving up Jake Coulter or staying with you and me. So, now I'm going to tell you *exactly* what I told her. You deserve what you're going to get."

Thirty

It took Judge Rameriz less than ten minutes to hear the state's case and decide Claire should be tried for the murder of Duncan Morrell. The *pro bono* attorney assigned to her usually practiced probate law, but that wasn't the problem. At this point, all the state had to show was enough evidence to warrant a trial. They had the murder weapon as well as her wallet and panties that had been found in the room next door to the victim.

"No bail?" Claire clutched her attorney's arm as the judge refused to set bail for her. "Can he do that?"

The elderly lawyer sighed. "Yes. Very few first-degree murder suspects get bail."

She lowered her head, ignoring the crowded courtroom. What did it matter? She had no hope of raising bail. She owned little of value to put up as a bond. Angela might be persuaded to help, but Suzi hadn't been able to locate her. Zach hadn't appeared either. Not having him here at such a crucial time frightened her.

Two deputies led her out of the court's back door. Tohono was waiting in the hall, his weathered face troubled. She'd been conscious of his presence in court, the only friendly face among the crowd.

"Claire," he said, and the deputies, being part pueblo Indian, halted out of respect for their leader. "Are they treating you well?"

She tried for a joke. "Sure. No wonder they call jail the Gray Bar Hilton."

Tohono's eyes narrowed, and she could see he understood how upset she was. How frightened.

"Remember Popé. His spirit is with you," he said quietly.

"Popé?" It took a second to make sense. Centuries ago, Franciscan friars had whipped Popé for practicing his native religion. The Taos pueblo, known for their peaceful Indians, staged a bloody uprising and drove the Spanish back into Texas. "Don't talk in riddles, Tohono. Not now."

"Popé had right on his side and won against tremendous odds. Right is on your side, Claire. Be strong and your enemies will suffer."

Sometimes she wanted to throttle Tohono for talking in riddles. Couldn't he see she was in terrible trouble? "Last time you said to beware of coyote. That's closer to the truth."

"Ah, Claire, you did not understand. I warned you that coyote was waiting—hiding. Your enemy is out in the open now where you can defeat him if you have the courage."

Tohono walked away and the deputies returned her to the lonely cell. Despite his cryptic words, Tohono's message made sense. She'd been framed for a reason. If she knew what it was, she could defend herself. Someone had called the police about the gun. Who? Why had they waited so long?

Thinking about the evidence the state had against her made Claire shudder. Most of it was circumstantial. These things alone did not prove her guilt, but when added to the fact that she had no alibi for the night of the murder, it was not difficult to imagine a jury convicting her.

She was pondering the frightening turn of events when the guard announced she had a visitor. She hurried into the visiting room, hoping Zach had returned. Bam Stegner was waiting for her, wearing a black and white cowhide vest and deadly-looking stiletto spurs.

She stopped near the door, thankful for the guard. "What do you want?"

Bam chuckled, his Budda-like gut jiggling over his belt. "Don't be a bitch. I'm here to help you."

She bit back a scathing remark, wondering if Bam could possibly help her. Right now, she was desperate enough to try anything.

Her hesitation brought a smile. "Do you know why they call me Bam?" He didn't pause for her response. "It's short for 'Wham, Bam, Thank you, Ma'am.' Women just love me." He put his knuckles on the visitor's table and leaned toward her. "You and me could be right friendly."

"In your dreams." She turned to leave.

"I could help you," he said quickly. "I hear your pa kissed you off. I'll pay for one of those hot-shot LA lawyers to defend you."

She looked over her shoulder at him. "Why would you do that?"

He studied her for a moment before saying, "It would be a fair trade. You tell me where to find my bear, and I'll get you a lawyer."

The bear meant that much to him. Unbelievable.

"Even if I knew where Khadafi was, which I don't, I wouldn't turn him over to the likes of you. No way. No way in hell."

A sound erupted from his throat that might have been a laugh. He stomped his boots and the vicious spurs clinked. "Just remember, bitch, I gave you a chance."

Brad Yeager was waiting for Zach as he walked off the plane from Dallas. "We were right," Yeager told him with a smile. "Bassinger was dead at least two hours longer than Vanessa Trent and that sleazeball attorney claimed."

Zach shifted his bag to his other shoulder so he could

give Yeager a high five. "Damn! We're good. Any chance they killed him?"

"Nah. He had a preexisting heart condition. Death was due to a massive coronary." Yeager walked beside him as they crossed the terminal. "What did you find out?"

"It took some persuading, but one of Max Bassinger's attorneys gave me a complete list of everything in the safe and the combination. It seems Bassinger was real anal about things like that."

Yeager led him out of the building, saying, "Anything in there worth taking?"

"Copies of contracts. Lists of investments." Zach couldn't keep himself from smiling. "And five million dollars in bearer bonds."

Yeager stopped dead in his tracks. "No shit! Wanna bet when we open Bassinger's safe, those bonds won't be there?"

"What does that prove? They'll claim Bassinger gave them to him before he died. Since those bonds don't need to be signed or anything, it'll be their word against ours."

They began walking again, and Yeager said, "True, but there may be another angle on this. Let's keep the time of death secret while we check the safe and then take a look at Seth and Vanessa's bank records."

Zach agreed even though he didn't like people not knowing the truth. Most everyone in town believed Seth Ramsey and the dumb actress. He wanted to be right about this case, then solve Duncan Morrell's murder.

Yeager unlocked his car, and Zach tossed his bag into the back seat. He was climbing in when Yeager said, "You've got problems with Ollie Hammond. While you were away, he took over the Morrell case. Claire Holt's been arrested for his murder."

For one gut-cramping minute the world froze. "Arrested?" The word was a hollow echo like a voice in a crypt.

* * *

Just after dinner, the guard escorted Claire into an interrogation room. Zach was waiting for her inside, and the guard left them alone. Just the sight of him brought the hot sting of tears to her eyes. She hated admitting she was so weak, but she'd felt so alone. Inhaling a deep breath, she managed to smile.

"Claire . . . I'm so sorry." He looked confused and upset.

In that moment, he seemed more vulnerable than she ever could have imagined. His strength had always fascinated her, but the ruthless loner seemed to have vanished, leaving this man. His obvious concern for her touched her in an unexpected way. Why, he honestly cared about her.

His hand curled gently around her shoulder and she moved into his arms and hugged him tight. Closing her eyes, she willed herself to enjoy the moment and surrender to the comfort and security his embrace offered. No matter what happened, knowing Zach cared made her stronger, more able to face the ordeal ahead.

"Where have you been?" she asked.

"Away on business." He pulled back studying her face, his arms still around her. "We only have a few minutes before the night duty officer rousts Hammond from home. I had to do some fast talking to get to see you alone."

"I'm so glad you're here. Someone found out I spent the night at The Hideaway. They planted—"

"I know all about it. Don't worry. I'll get you out of here." The fierce determination in his voice should have reassured her, but there was something troubling about his expression. "I want to know if you can hang on for another day or two."

"Hang on?" she asked. "Do I have a choice?"

His eyes reflected pain and a tremendous strength of will. "Yes. I can get you out tonight, but if you can wait just a day or two, I'll be able to do better. We'll trap the real killer."

"Who is it?"

"I can't tell you right now. I need you to trust me."

She stopped herself from arguing that she was the one in jail, the one who had a right to know. Maybe this wasn't just about giving her a name. It could be for her own protection. Or, even more likely, this was about them.

About her trusting him.

The whole town could doubt him, but she believed in him. More important, she wanted him to know she had faith in him. Too clearly, she remembered the young Zach Coulter coming to her father's bank, humbling himself to try to get money to bury his mother. She had wanted to help him, but her father had stopped her. Now she had to show him that she trusted him.

"I can take this place. Don't worry about me." She sounded a lot more upbeat than she felt. "It's thinking they'll convict me that had me terrified. But if you're sure I'll be cleared, then waiting isn't a problem. I trust you."

"Good," he said quietly.

She had hoped her response would encourage him to tell her more. Instead he kissed her, a light almost tentative kiss. Permitting herself to revel in the warmth of his powerful body, she savored the bittersweet ache radiating outward from her heart. So much had gone on between them, yet so little had ever been discussed. She broke off the kiss, searching for the words to express how she felt.

"Zach, about the other night—"

"Hush," he said, brushing a wisp of hair back from her temple. "It doesn't matter."

"Yes, it matters to me—to us. I want to tell you what happened. I began to cry because I looked in the mirror and saw our reflection. Do you know what it reminded me of? Our parents."

He pulled away, frowning, "Can't we get beyond them?"

"That's what I'm trying to do, get over the past. I'm living my own life, doing what I want to do. But I couldn't help being upset because I looked in the mirror and saw my mother on top of your father, her head flung back. That's the way I discovered they were having an affair. The image is seared into my brain like a brand. I remember the shock, then running straight to my father's bank."

Zach nodded, sympathy in his eyes. "You told him what you'd seen."

She thought she could explain, she honestly did. Of course, she'd anticipated problems. The riveting memory never failed to evoke powerful emotions, but this confession was much more difficult than she'd expected.

"I killed them, Zach. If only I'd kept my mouth shut, they both would have lived. But I was so stunned. I didn't stop to think." She blinked back the tears burning in her eyes. "It's my fault—"

"Have you blamed yourself all these years?"

"Yes. I should have kept my mouth shut and waited to talk to you."

He put his arms around her again, pulling her close. "I wish you had. You don't know how much I wish you had."

The quiet anguish in his tone added to her feeling of guilt. "I knew you would blame me. I understand. I hate myself for what I—"

He cupped her face with his hands and gazed into her eyes. "No, Claire. I don't blame you. If anything, I blame myself. I should have told you about the affair. I knew all about it."

She had always suspected that he had known. "Why didn't you tell me?"

He shook his head. "You were so damn innocent, and I was the bad boy from the trailer park. I was crazy about you. I didn't want to ruin your illusions about the perfect family by saying our parents had been carrying on for years."

Years. The word staggered her. She gazed into Zach's earnest face and saw how much he cared about her. Oh my God. He was telling the truth. What she'd thought of as a short fling had been much . . . more.

"They'd always loved each other, and your father knew it. When you confronted him, he was forced to do something. They chose to leave town. You can't blame yourself for the automobile accident. Those things just happen."

"All these years, my father's acted as if—"

The door swung open. "Sorry, Sheriff, but the chief is on his way. He says the prisoner had better be in her cell, or he'll fire me."

Thirty-one

Time passed in a monotonous blur, days melding into nights, distinguishable only by the change in the guards' shifts. Prison, Claire learned, meant the lights were never off, the guards' radios never stopped playing. There was never one second of the day when she was assured of privacy. Going to the bathroom, showering—every intimate moment became public.

She wasn't being treated differently than any other prisoner would have been, she realized. Accused of a crime, you automatically lost your rights. Claire was the only person in the jail, making the guards even more vigilant, more watchful.

Despite the hovering guards, she felt alone, isolated from the rest of the world. She had always had someone— her father. But he wasn't with her now. He'd deserted her when she'd needed him the most.

Had her father twisted the events surrounding her mother's death to suit himself? Once, she would never have believed that her mother had indulged in a long-term affair with Zach's father. She had clung to her idyllic view of her family life. Her parents adored her and were deeply in love. The perfect, happy family.

Had she been wrong? Had there been problems in the marriage? Why hadn't Claire been able to detect any trouble?

Back then, her father had been good-looking, successful, a community leader. Jake Coulter had been a handsome devil like his son, but hardly competition for her father. Perhaps her mother had been attracted to Jake because he was a gifted artist, she thought, remembering the magnificent bronze of the owl. That must have been how they'd met.

She could understand it. Fatal attraction. She reacted to Zach's virile appeal the same way, unable to resist him despite her better judgment. But she was free to do as she liked; her mother had been married and had a child. Hadn't her marriage vows meant anything to her mother?

"You're wanted in the visitor's room."

The guard interrupted her thoughts, and Claire jumped up, hoping it was Zach. He had made it sound as if he would quickly see to her release, yet days had passed and she hadn't heard from him.

When Claire arrived in the visitor's room, Angela was waiting, her expression tight. "Are you okay?" she asked the second Claire sat down.

"I'm fine. Tired, that's all."

"We just returned," Angela explained. "We heard you had been arrested. Paul couldn't believe it. We know you could never have killed anyone."

Hot, salty tears rose in her eyes at her friend's words. It was great to have people with faith in her. Claire batted her eyes quickly to banish the tears, saying, "Thanks. This is all a big mistake. I—"

"Claire, your father. Why hasn't he hired a good defense attorney?"

"My father was willing to help—if I promised to never see Zach."

Angela nodded, her expression troubled. "Why am I not surprised? My father would have pulled the same stunt." She leaned across the table, coming so close to

Claire that the guard stepped forward. "Don't worry. I'll find you the best attorney available."

Claire almost opened her mouth to say Zach had the situation covered, but something in her, a lingering doubt, kept her quiet. Where was Zach? Why hadn't she heard from him since the other evening? He'd asked her to give him time, and on faith, she had, asking no questions. Days had passed, and she was beginning to regret her decision.

Zach rocked back in his chair in the Federal Marshal's office in Santa Fe, watching Vanessa Trent play the falsely accused woman. The interrogation had dragged on for much longer than he'd expected. With each movement of the wall clock, he imagined Claire sitting in a lonely cell wondering what had happened to him.

Not since he was a kid and his mother had tied him into the swing and the snake had slithered out of the brush had Zach felt so helpless. Vanessa had a hot-shot attorney at her side. Zach doubted if God himself could get her to admit anything more than she already had.

"Like I told you, Seth opened dear, dear Max's safe." Vanessa batted false eyelashes at Marshal Greer. Not that it did any good. The elderly federal marshal stroked his beard and stared at her. "He said Max wanted me to have that bearer bond to finance my film."

"How many times is she going to say the same thing?" Brad whispered to Zach.

"Until time runs out and we have to either release her or charge her," Zach answered as he flipped through the file. He was convinced they were missing something. What was it?

He spotted a small detail, something probably not worth checking, but he needed to get out of the interrogation room for awhile. He told Brad he was taking a break and

left the agent with the marshal to continue questioning
the actress.

It was dark by the time Zach returned. He rushed into
the federal building and down the hall to the Federal Marshal's office. Vanessa and the arrogant attorney she'd hired
were just leaving.

"Unless you have any further questions, Sheriff Coulter,
the marshal is releasing my client," the lawyer said more
smugly than necessary.

Zach was too proud of himself to give a damn about the
lawyer's attitude. "I have a question." He blocked Vanessa's exit, catching Brad Yeager's eye over her shoulder.
"For the record, tell the marshal where you were on the
night Duncan Morrell was murdered."

"I missed my flight." She quickly looked to the attorney,
obviously sensing she was in trouble. "I was in Los Angeles."

"My client doesn't have another thing to say."

Zach walked over to the marshal's desk and put his
folder in front of the older man. "Ms. Trent missed her
flight, but she found a private plane to bring her to Albuquerque. Then she rented a car and drove up to Taos."

He turned to face Vanessa, so he could have the satisfaction of seeing her face. He gave her credit for staring
at him as if he'd just arrived from another planet.

"When she didn't find Duncan at home, she remembered that he was going out to the club to hear Flash and
the Rusty Roots. She drove there and found Morrell's car
parked next door at The Hideaway."

"That's ridiculous," the attorney said, but he didn't
sound convincing.

"Works for me." Yeager played along. "Witnesses reported a rental car in the lot."

Zach met Vanessa's glare with a cool smile. "I have statements from the private pilot and the rental car agent, saying you were here on the night of the murder."

Vanessa moved closer to her attorney, but her head was still set at a defiant angle. "It's true. I was able to get here that night. But I did not kill Duncan. I drove up to The Hideaway, saw the ambulance, and police cars and left. I didn't want to be involved with anything that went on out at that disgusting club. It was only later that I learned someone had killed Duncan."

Zach almost smiled. "There wasn't any ambulance—or police cars. I was the only one on the scene for over an hour. Then a van from Hemphill's mortuary removed the body."

"Don't say another word," cautioned Vanessa's attorney.

Zach knew she had killed Morrell, but the evidence was circumstantial. Worse, the murder weapon had been found in Claire's possession. She could easily be found guilty of the crime. He had believed the lies Seth and Vanessa had told about Bassinger's death would lead to solving Morrell's murder.

He'd been wrong. He needed Vanessa to confess to the killing. That was the only way he knew to free Claire. He decided to roll the dice and bluff. His career in law enforcement would be over as soon as the whole truth was known about the events at The Hideaway on the night of the murder.

What did he have to lose?

"You might as well confess," Zach told the actress while everyone else stared at them. "Stacy Hopkins can put you at the scene of the murder. She saw you open the door and find her in bed with Duncan."

"No, she didn't," Vanessa replied, shaking off her attorney's hand as he tried to keep her from speaking. "If she had, Stacy would have come forward before now. Anyway, there wasn't anything to see. I never got out of the car."

"Yes, you did." Zach hoped his voice sounded as if he

were telling the truth. "I just spoke with Stacy by telephone. She's left her husband and is in Los Angeles with Carleton Cole. He's taken her to a drug treatment center. She's in counseling and she told him all about sleeping with Duncan."

It was difficult to tell if Vanessa was buying this. Everyone else was hanging on every word, even Yeager, so Zach thought he sounded as if he were telling the God's honest truth. He had to sound convincing. Claire's life was at stake.

"Stacy didn't give a damn about Duncan. She only slept with him to try to get money back that Carleton had invested in Morrell's bogus prints. Stacy didn't come forward earlier because she didn't want Carleton to find out what she'd done. But she has her head on straight now. She's willing to testify."

"Claire Holt shot him," Vanessa insisted, but Zach detected a hint of desperation in her voice. "The murder weapon was found in her shop."

"The gun could have been planted," Yeager put in.

Zach played his trump card, "It was planted because Claire Holt has an alibi for the time of the murder."

It took a little more badgering, but the bluff worked. Vanessa Trent confessed to the killing. Zach was positive her attorney would cut some type of deal, but he didn't care. It was the only way he knew to solve the crime and get Claire out of jail.

"Nice work," Yeager told him as he walked Zach to his car. "Did you really speak to Stacy Hopkins?"

"Hell, no. I have no idea where she is. Hopefully, she is getting treatment."

Yeager's brows drew together. "As sheriff—"

"I'm turning in my badge," Zach said. "I've abused my authority."

"This is tough. You're one of the best," Yeager said. "You pushed the envelope, but you solved the case, providing some smartass attorney doesn't try to pin it on Claire."

"No way. I was bluffing about Stacy Hopkins, but Claire does have an alibi."

It was midnight when he drove home from Santa Fe and pulled up to the jail. Two hours later Claire was released.

"Zach," she said, as she came toward him, her clothes rumpled from days in a holding bag, her eyes glazed from lack of sleep. "I thought you'd forgotten me."

"No way." He pulled her to him, wondering if he could ever bring himself to tell her the whole story. "It took longer than I expected. I'm sorry if you were upset."

"I knew you were coming," she assured him, but something in her tone told him that she had questioned him. "Let's get out of here."

In the parking lot she asked, "They said the charges against me were dropped. Did you find the real killer?"

He opened the Bronco's door for her, not wanting to brag, saying, "The federal marshal is handling the case now from his Santa Fe office. It's not just murder. It's an international print fraud ring that the FBI has been tracking for over a year."

"Who killed Duncan?" she asked as he helped her inside.

"Can't you guess?" He closed her door and went around to the driver's side.

"This isn't fair," she complained as he started the engine. "I've been racking my brain for days, asking myself how the killer knew I had spent the night at The Hideaway and didn't have an alibi. Only you or someone in your office knew."

"Max Bassinger saw you the next morning when you were hitching a ride home. He saw you getting into the van outside The Hideaway." He drove out of the lot and down the dark street toward Claire's house. "Remember, I said Duncan's mystery woman was the key to this case. I was right. He was divorcing his wife to marry Vanessa Trent."

Claire gasped, then shook her head. "That's hard to believe. Duncan was attractive, but someone like Vanessa had her pick of men."

"You overrate her. Vanessa's career is stalled. She was desperate for money to produce a film starring herself, of course. Duncan's little print scam was much more extensive—and more lucrative—than anyone realized."

Zach pulled into her drive and shut off the engine, explaining how Vanessa secretly flew into the state, then drove to Taos and discovered the man she loved sleeping with Stacy Hopkins. During the explanation, he didn't tell Claire about his bluff, a risky gamble that had led to the confession.

"I thought Duncan loved Vanessa," Claire said as they got out of the car.

He opened the front gate, and the dogs were waiting for them. He ruffled Lobo's ears saying, "He probably did love Vanessa, but Stacy Hopkins was just too tempting."

Claire unlocked the door and flicked on the lights. They went into the living room and collapsed on the sofa. He put his arm around her, wishing he didn't have to tell her this story. He'd much rather curl up, holding her, but she deserved to know the whole truth.

"Vanessa killed him in a fit of jealousy," Claire said.

"You're right. Jealousy and greed. Morrell sold her a lot of phony prints that she'd been hoping to use to finance her film."

"I thought Vanessa had an alibi."

Zach shrugged, still amazed at Vanessa Trent's arrogance and toughness. She almost got away with murder. "She lied and expected us to believe her. Know what? We almost fell for it. Then I checked and discovered she wasn't on the early morning flight."

"But how did she know Duncan was at The Hideaway?"

Zach gave Claire a little squeeze, again wishing all of this was behind them. "Duncan told her that he was going to the club when she called to say she'd missed her flight. When she arrived here and Duncan wasn't home, she drove out to the club, then walked in on them. She flipped and went out and got the gun Duncan kept in his car and a small pillow she'd taken from the airplane to use as a silencer."

Her green eyes narrowed speculatively. "I can't believe it! I saw Vanessa the morning after Duncan's death when she came into my shop. She seemed genuinely grief-stricken, crushed by his death. In a million years, I never would have suspected that she'd killed him."

"It was probably her best acting ever. She brazened her way through the entire situation."

"What made you suspicious?"

"Motive," he explained, still downplaying his role in solving the case. "Eliminating as many suspects with motives as possible is the foundation of police work. Yeager hadn't gotten around to checking Vanessa's alibi when Max Bassinger died. We knew they were lying about the time of death. It made us wonder what else they might be lying about."

"You were able to prove Max died earlier?" she asked, snuggling closer.

"Yes. He died between midnight and one in the morning. Seth couldn't resist crowing to Vanessa that he knew the combination to Bassinger's safe. There was a fortune in bearer bonds inside."

"They stole them?"

"Vanessa persuaded Seth to take them, or so he claims. Knowing the bonds were missing, we obtained a search warrant for both their homes and a court order to check their financial records. We squeezed Seth hard, and he confessed."

Claire shuddered, her body trembling in his arms. "Circumstantial evidence can be incriminating. I was headed for the gas chamber. Thank you so much for all you did. I truly appreciate it."

He listened to her, his eyes on her lips. He longed to kiss her, and make love to her all night, but he needed to tell her the rest of the story. He knew she was going to be angry, and she had every right to be. Things were changing between them. He felt more and more comfortable with Claire each time he saw her. The last thing he wanted to do was ruin his chances with her.

He could wait and keep this night for himself, but what good would delaying do? The entire story would be in the morning papers and blasted across every television screen in America.

He had to tell Claire himself.

"You were never in danger of going to prison," he began quietly. "You had an alibi."

Claire pulled away from him, a frown etching her smooth brow. "You found the stranger? Why didn't you tell me?"

"Remember the morning I came into your shop and asked if you'd lost your panties? How do you think I got them?" He watched her slowly shake her head. "I put them in my pocket when I left you in bed that morning . . . in The Hideaway."

She gazed at him a moment, then his words registered. "You? You were the man I spent all night with?"

"Yes. I was the man with you at The Hideaway."

"It couldn't have been you," she cried, utterly astonished. "The man had a full bushy beard."

"I was wearing a fake beard."

"You creep!" She scooted away from him, anger under-scoring every word. "How could you take advantage of me like that?"

"I knew nothing about the Roofie." He vaulted to his feet and shoved his fists into his pockets to keep from grabbing her and kissing until she forgave him. "How was

I supposed to know you were in some altered state and wouldn't remember anything about me come morning?"

"Didn't you notice I was acting strange?"

"Not really. You hadn't bothered to even say hello to me since you moved back to Taos, so I had no idea how you normally behaved. You seemed a little tipsy, but I honestly didn't think you were drunk. Claire, I told you who I was and you willingly made love to me."

She pondered the information, then said, "You should have told me that morning in the shop instead of letting me think I was a suspect."

"I should have," he conceded. "I walked into your shop expecting you to remember our night together. You acted weird, and it wasn't until later that I realized you didn't remember a damn thing. I thought you'd reverted to being snooty."

"Why didn't you tell me later? It wasn't as if you didn't have the chance."

"I didn't want to give you a reason to hate me any more than you already did. I thought I could protect you . . . and myself."

"Protect yourself from what?" Her voice was toneless now, and he could see Claire was beyond anger. She had trusted him enough to remain behind bars while he solved two crimes. Would he ever be able to get her to trust him again?

"I didn't want anyone asking questions about what I was doing there."

"Everyone would assume you were looking for drug dealers or something. No one would care."

"Bam Stegner will care. When he hears this story, he'll know exactly what I was doing there."

Claire looked at him blankly, then a small gasp escaped her lips as she finally realized exactly why he had gone to Stegner's club. "You stole Bam's bear. You freed Khadafi! I never dreamed it was you!"

"When you represent the law, you don't break the law. I didn't want a soul to know I was there, or I would have lost my job. My car was hidden in the woods. I was going back to it when I saw you." He pulled his fists out of his pockets and turned his palms up, shrugging. "What can I say? I've always been crazy about you. I slipped into the room and called your name."

"I thought Seth was calling me."

"How was I supposed to know that? You walked in and let me kiss you. It wasn't until later when I researched the effects of Roofies that I realized you were mentally disconnected from what was happening and would never remember our night together."

She studied him, her expression cold and closed. "Do you know how many nights I was awake worrying about not having an alibi? I just spent days in hell because of it."

"If I'd been in town, you never would have been arrested." It was a lame excuse and he knew it. "I should have told you when I returned, but I was afraid to tip off Vanessa by getting you released. She might have destroyed incriminating evidence."

"You asked me to trust you, and I did, but you didn't trust me one little bit. Did you?"

"No," he admitted. "I didn't. Be honest with yourself, Claire. Why should I trust you? You're not even willing to be seen in public with me."

She turned away from him, but not before he saw the hurt expression. Man, oh, man. He was not explaining his way out of this the way he had hoped. He was just making things worse.

"What else have you lied about?" She sounded tired and disgusted.

"Nothing." He bit out the word, barely resisting the urge to haul her into his arms and kiss her until she admitted they were meant for each other.

"I don't believe you." She turned on him, anger spiking

every word. "I'll bet my mother wasn't involved with your father for years. He was a talented sculptor and he used his talent as a way of getting close to my mother. You made up the long-term affair to get back at my father."

"Oh, for God's sake, Claire," he began, but he could see he was wasting his time. "It always comes down to the same thing, doesn't it?"

"I should have listened to my father—"

Zach headed for the door, shutting out her words. He'd been wrong, and he was more than willing to admit it. But he didn't want their parents dragged into the middle of every argument. Weren't they beyond this?

He snapped his fingers, calling, "Lobo! We're outta' here."

Lobo bounded up to the door, and Zach walked out without looking back. He drove home, disgusted with himself and angry with her. He'd been kidding himself if he thought this relationship was going anywhere.

At home he dropped onto the bed without taking off his clothes or boots. For once luck was with him. He was so damn exhausted he didn't toss and turn, thinking about Claire.

Hours later, he awakened, the gray light of early dawn filling the room. Lobo was beside him, his hackles raised, growling, low and fierce. There was another noise, too, but his groggy brain couldn't immediately identify the low rumble. The noise became an ominous roar. He jumped to his feet and rushed to the window.

In his driveway were a dozen Hell's Angels, revving their Harleys. Bam Stegner was leading them, his silver spurs gleaming in the early morning light.

Thirty-two

The morning sun was warm against her back, and the scent of dew-wet sage hung in the summer air. From the top branch of the cottonwood a blue jay scolded Claire as she knocked on her father's door.

After Zach had left last night, she had forced herself to go to bed, but she'd barely slept, awakened by disturbing dreams. She'd been stunned to learn Zach had been the mysterious stranger. Her memories of that night had been elusive, true, but she had never suspected Zach had been the man.

The mystery man had seemed so gentle . . . so sensitive. Those were the last words she would ever use to describe Zach.

Maybe her brain had played a trick on her. She'd done a little reading about Rohypnol. It was a powerful drug that induced memory loss. The impressions she had were vague at best. Still, it seemed to have been a pleasurable experience unlike the traumatic incidents reported by many other women who had been secretly given Roofies.

Zach had not been responsible for giving her the drug, but she still couldn't help being upset with him. He had let her worry herself sick because she didn't have an alibi. Then she'd sat in jail, terrified circumstantial evidence would convict her. Anger burned hot and raw inside her.

If possible, she was even more furious with Zach now than she had been last night.

Her father's front door swung open, and Maude said, "Claire, thank heavens you're out of jail. Imagine, Vanessa Trent charged with murder."

Claire stepped into the entry hall. "She had plenty of motive."

Maude lowered her voice. "Did you hear the CNN report on how the police broke the case?"

Claire shook her head. She had been too preoccupied to turn on the television.

"They're saying Zachary Coulter tricked the actress into confessing. It was a brilliant move. A little shady, I guess. It looks as if he'll be forced to resign."

"Zach?" Claire said, astonished. "Resign as sheriff."

"Yes. The FBI agent and the Federal Marshal Greer give the sheriff full credit for bringing her to justice. But the reporters say he did it in an underhanded way. Some people are howling for his badge. Others are calling him a hero."

Zach had never given himself credit for doing anything more than checking Vanessa's alibi. She was angry with him, true, but if he had gone out on a limb to help her, she hadn't properly thanked him. She'd breezed out of jail, never thinking her freedom might cost Zach his job.

Suddenly, it became more urgent than ever to talk with her father. Zach had been wrong not to tell her about the night in The Hideaway, but he had done so much to help her when no one else could.

"I need to see my father."

Maude adjusted the apron covering her denim dress. "Claire . . . he hasn't changed his mind about Zachary Coulter."

"I just want to ask him one quick question."

Maude reluctantly led her down the hall into the breakfast room overlooking the courtyard. Her father was seated at the table, the morning paper beside his plate, the television on CNN.

Claire sat down beside him, saying, "There's something I need to ask you."

He refused to answer or even look at her.

"Don't you think you're behaving childishly?" she asked. "I want to talk to you."

He slowly turned to face her. "What do you want to know?"

"Promise you'll be totally honest with me," she said, and he nodded. "Was Mother involved with Jake Coulter for a long time, or was it just a short fling?"

Claire heard Maude's startled intake of breath, but her father's gaze remained steady, emotionless. He let the question hang in the vacuum of silence as if it were beneath him to answer it.

"Look, I've just spent time in jail. I had plenty of opportunity to think about my life. I need to know the truth about Mother, so I can—"

"Justify your relationship with Zach Coulter."

The animosity in his voice shouldn't have surprised her, yet it did. Even though he had been the one to be so cruel to Zach her father still harbored an unhealthy amount of anger. She refused to give him any more ammunition against Zach by telling what Zach had done. Their relationship was over—not that it had ever really gotten going.

"If it weren't for Zach, I would still be in prison," she informed her father. "This has nothing to do with him. I need to know the truth about my mother."

Several uncomfortable seconds ticked by as her father watched her with an unwavering stare. Finally, he said, "Amy became involved with Jake Coulter shortly after you were born."

She couldn't stifle her gasp. Zach had been telling the truth; her image of her family had been nothing more than an illusion. Finally, she managed to whisper, "That long ago?"

"Yes, that long ago." His voice broke, and he averted his head self-consciously.

"Why didn't you divorce her?" she asked, struggling to understand how he could have put up with the affair for almost fifteen years.

Maude rushed from the room as if she couldn't bear to listen to his answer, Claire realized the older woman had never been told about this. Claire waited, unable to imagine a man with her father's pride ignoring his wife's affair.

"Maybe it's time you did know the whole truth," he said finally, his voice leaden with stark pain.

"It's more than time," Claire told him. "I *have* to know."

"Your mother would have divorced me in a second except she knew I had the money and connections to prevent her from taking you with her. She loved you so much that she stayed . . . She stayed for you."

Oh, my, God. Claire tried to imagine how torn her mother must have been. Yet she had carried on, living what had seemed to be a happy life. All the while, she had secretly loved another man. "You used me to keep her."

"Yes," he admitted without a hint of remorse. "Sometimes you can love a woman too much."

Dangerously close to screaming at him, Claire rose, asking herself what kind of a man used a child as a pawn. All these years she'd condemned her mother, never once suspecting her mother had sacrificed her own happiness because she loved Claire.

And in the end, the child Amy Holt had loved so much, had been the one to cause her death.

The ache in Claire's chest grew more intense with each heartbeat. If she had been less of a "little princess" and more worldly like Zach, Claire would never have run to her father after discovering her mother with Jake Coulter.

She had embarrassed her father, forcing him to take action.

"I just had one more year with Amy," her father said. "I knew the day you went off to college, she would leave me for Jake Coulter."

An overwhelming feeling of pity engulfed her and she saw her father for what he was—a pathetic man. He had emotionally blackmailed her mother into staying with him. Her death had only intensified his obsession.

"Why can't you stop living in the past, pining for a woman who never loved you? Take a close look at Maude, and you'll see all the love you'll ever need." She put her hand on his shoulder. "Get a life, Father. Let me find a counselor who can help you."

"Help me?" Her father turned a mottled red and shoved her hand away. "I don't need help. There's nothing wrong with me."

How could she make him see his obsession was unhealthy? Maybe she couldn't. After all, he had clung to this for years. "Let's get counseling together."

"Claire, there isn't a damn thing wrong with me. You're the one who loves a Coulter. You're the one who needs help."

Heartsick, Claire drove directly from her father's home to the gallery. So, Zach had been telling the truth. For years, her father had let her believe a lie. He had also encouraged her to think Jake Coulter was a man who hopped from bed to bed. She didn't have to ask to know this was yet another lie. Jake had loved her mother; she had no doubt he'd been faithful to her even though he was married to another woman.

I've always been crazy about you.

Zach's words echoed through her head, a bittersweet refrain. Had he always loved her? At this point, she had to admit anything was possible. She just didn't know what to believe any longer. She'd assumed he was a tom cat just like his father, but maybe, it wasn't true. She'd hadn't actually seen him out with a woman. But he was so handsome that it was impossible to imagine there were no women in his life.

I've always been crazy about you.

She remembered the night of the Art Festival. She'd asked him how he interpreted Paul's painting. Zach had said the cowboy loved the woman, but didn't know if she would accept him the way he was. Had Zach been trying to tell her something?

Suddenly, she was no longer as angry with him as she had been. Sure, she was still upset, but she understood. Trust did not come easy to Zach Coulter. At what point in their relationship had she really given him reason to trust her?

If she had told him about going to her father, things might have been different. At first she had hesitated, not wanting to push him into committing himself. Last night she could have told him, but she had been too angry to admit she had chosen him over her father.

Knowing Zach had risked his career to help her made Claire feel even more ashamed of the childish way she had behaved. He had been wrong; she'd been wrong.

They both had to learn to trust each other.

She parked in the lot behind The Rising Sun, then let Lucy out. As Lucy's paws hit the ground, Claire heard a whimpering sound from beneath the old cottonwood. Lucy dashed over to the figure huddled in the shadows.

"Lobo?" Claire cried, coming closer.

Blood oozed from a gash on the dog's side, matting the dense fur. One of his ears had been partially severed and hung limp against his head, coated with dark-red blood. A peculiar looking puncture had narrowly missed putting out his eye; the lid was drooping at half mast.

He lurched to his feet, staggered two steps, then collapsed with a heart-wrenching yelp. Lucy lovingly licked the wound on his side as Lobo whimpered, seeming to plead with Claire to save him.

"Where's Zach?" Claire cried, frantic. She glanced around, half-expecting to see Zach. Instead, she noticed the trail of blood across the parking lot. Had Lobo come here seeking help?

"Zach must be at the station or something," she said out loud, knowing Lobo had lost so much blood that she didn't have time to locate Zach.

She had no idea how she found the strength to lift a dog so heavy, but she managed to boost him into the Jeep. Foot to the floor, she sped the few short blocks to the veterinarian.

"Lobo's been in a fight," she breathlessly explained to Dr. Walker once she was inside. "A mountain lion or something got him."

The vet peered at Lobo over half-moon glasses, shaking his head. "An animal couldn't do this. A knife or another weapon caused these wounds."

"Can you save Lobo?"

"Don't get your hopes up," the veterinarian warned. "He's in critical condition."

Claire put her hand on Lobo's noble head, and he opened his eyes just a crack. "Come on, big guy. Hang in there."

Lucy whimpered from Claire's side as if she understood and was encouraging Lobo to fight for his life. Lobo's one good eye was glazed over, but he trained it on Lucy. Claire wondered if Lobo had come to get her, or had the dog sensed he was going to die and come to say good-bye to Lucy?

Claire ran her hand over his muzzle. "You're a wonderful dog. You saved me from the rattlesnake. Hang on and let Dr. Walker help you."

Lobo's eye snapped shut, and his body went limp. Lucy barked twice, but Lobo didn't move. Claire petted Lucy, and the two of them stood watching helplessly as the doctor and his assistant carried Lobo away.

A knife. What had happened? Claire wondered. A chill of apprehension invaded her bones, making her tremble. She was shaking even harder a few minutes later when no one answered at Zach's home. A call to the station confirmed Zach wasn't there either. No one knew where he was.

She called Paul Winfrey and arranged for him to meet her out at Zach's place. On her way there, she swung by the chapter house, betting Tohono would be there as usual consulting with the tribal council. When she explained what had happened, he came with her, his expression grim.

Paul and Angela were waiting for them at Zach's. They had discovered Zach's Bronco was in the garage and the house had been left unlocked, but he was nowhere around. There were bloodstains on the path leading up to the front door.

"Lobo must have come all the way into town to get me," Claire cried.

"We'd better call the authorities," Angela said.

Claire could just imagine how much help Ollie Hammond would be. After all, he'd sided with Vanessa Trent, insisting her version of the time of death was correct. When the actress had turned out to be the killer, Ollie had been humiliated enough to announce his retirement, but he hadn't left yet.

While they were discussing what to do, Tohono walked down the lane that led up to Zach's house, checking the ground as he went. He returned to the porch, saying, "I will call the pueblo trackers to examine the marks in the dirt. They appear to be single tire marks—"

"Bikers on Harleys," Claire interrupted. "They've been

in town for several days. I think they're friends of Bam Stegner."

Tohono's grizzled brow contracted as he nodded his head. "Stegner. The bear. I see what this is about."

Instantly Claire knew who had helped Zach liberate the bear, but now wasn't the time to thank the older man for rescuing an abused animal. God help her, she had been the one to get Zach into this mess. Undoubtedly, Stegner had heard about Claire's alibi. Putting two and two together, Bam Stegner knew Zach had been instrumental in freeing the bear.

With startling clarity she recalled Bam exploding into her gallery the morning after his bear had been taken. She had never expected him to confront her in public, yet he had. Then he'd put the deadly rattlesnake into her mailbox. She had escaped injury—thanks to Zach. And he'd taken on Bam Stegner to protect her from any further harm.

But what had he done to protect himself? Nothing. She knew that without giving it a second thought. His whole life Zach had stood alone. He hadn't expected anyone to help him.

Bam Stegner's visit to the jail had seemed odd to her at the time, and she had wondered why the bear was so important to him. Now, the reason was clear. Bam had an ego the size of the *Hindenburg*, yet he was a coward. After Zach had roughed him up, extracting a promise not to hurt her, Bam Stegner had bided his time. He'd called in his markers, rounding up bikers from God only knew where.

They'd caught Zach alone—and off guard.

"They could have killed Zach right here," Paul said, his voice pitched low yet charged with emotion. "But they didn't. They took him somewhere."

"You are right, my son," Tohono agreed. "The trackers from the pueblo will help us."

"I hope it's not too late," Angela told Tohono. "Do you have any idea when this happened?"

"I am not an expert in reading the signs, but the blood is no longer red. It is now almost black, but still wet. I would say the men rode up just after dawn."

Claire hung her head, remembering the crimson glow of the sun as it rose above Taos Mountain, clear and bright and warm, flooding her room with the first rays of light. She'd been worried about herself, cursing Zach for not telling her that he had been the man at The Hideaway.

Could she possibly have been so self-centered?

You bet. From the day Zach had walked into her gallery, she had thought only of herself. She had looked at the world from her point of view, rarely considering his. If only she hadn't been so upset last night after learning Zach had been the man with her in The Hideaway, she would have made Zach spend the night. They would have talked and she would have told him about Bam's visit.

The group went inside and Tohono immediately telephoned the trackers and called in the Mounted Patrol to assist them. Then Paul contacted Brad Yeager and asked for help.

Claire sat on the sofa, gazing at the magnificent bronze owl. She'd never been so helpless in her entire life. Bam was a coward, but a sneaky one. It wasn't going to be easy to find Zach. When they did, it might be too late.

Thirty-three

It seemed as if days passed before the trackers arrived, but Angela informed Claire that it had been less than an hour. The pueblo men were examining the tracks in front of Zach's home when Brad Yeager drove up. He stood transfixed as they explained what had happened.

Tohono joined them. "The trackers tell me that eight or nine motorcycles drove down this road. There was a fight. Five perhaps six men were involved and a dog."

Claire squeezed her eyes shut for a moment, imagining Zach fighting, outnumbered, battling to save his life. With no one to help him but his dog.

"There are odd marks like spurs but sharper—"

"Bam has new stiletto spurs," Claire cried.

"Ah, yes," Tohono said. "Spurs filed sharp like knives. Bloody spurs."

"Oh, my God." Claire gripped the sofa's arm for support. "Lobo went after Bam. He kicked him with those deadly spurs and almost put Lobo's eye out. The vet doesn't know if he's going to live."

A hush fell over the room, and Claire knew everyone was imagining Zach on the ground being pummeled by the lethal spurs.

"Arrest Stegner," Angela said. "Make him tell you where Zach is."

"He'll stonewall," Claire said. "He's sneaky. He'll cover his tracks."

"You're right," Brad agreed. "Arresting Stegner will get us nowhere. Not letting him know we suspect, and following him, might help us find Zach."

"They took Zach away on a motorcycle," Tohono said. "My men followed the tracks up the gravel road to where the asphalt begins."

"They can't pick up anything on the pavement," Yeager said. "Where would they take him?"

"They have him in a place where only motorcycles can go or they would not have come for him on these motorcycles. Does this not make sense? That is why I called the Mounted Patrol. On their horses, they can check the forest service trails," Tohono said.

"You're right," Paul said. "Those trails are all dirt. If the bikers are on them, there will be signs."

"Oh, Christ!" Brad Yeager dropped into a chair. "There must be thousands of those trails."

We'll never find him alive. The unsaid words hung in the air like a vision of hell.

"I've spent a lot of time recently riding those trails." Paul broke the anguished silence. "I can tell you many of them aren't in good enough condition to ride a motorcycle on. Harley owners take great pride in those hogs. They're not going to bust them up. Let's get a Forest Service map and red-line the trails that are usable. Have the Mounted Patrol and the trackers check those first."

"Good idea," Angela said, jumping up. "I'm going to call the Kit Carson Ranger Station and have them bring out detailed maps immediately."

Brad Yeager studied the bronze owl perched high over the table. "Why did they take him? Why not beat him up here?"

Or kill him here. Again the unspoken words hung in the

air even more chilling because they hadn't been said out loud.

"Bam's going to torture Zach until he tells where the bear is," Claire said before her throat locked up. She was more frightened now than she'd been in jail when she believed circumstantial evidence would send her to prison. She had known how important the bear was to Bam, yet she had failed to warn Zach.

"Zach will never tell," Tohono informed them.

Claire agreed; Zach was too stubborn, too tough. He'd die before he would tell. But how much would he suffer before he died?

"Every man has a breaking point," Paul said.

"True, so true," Brad added. "At some point even the toughest men give up."

"Zach cannot tell," Tohono insisted. "He and I stole the bear, but I am the one who drove Khadafi away. Only I know where the bear is now."

The Forest Service maps arrived, and Paul marked off the most usable trails. Tohono and Claire divided the Mounted Patrol into teams and assigned a tracker to each. Yeager left for town without saying what he was doing. Angela manned the telephone and marked off Forest Service trails as the trackers called in eliminating trails they'd checked.

By late afternoon, most of the accessible trails had been inspected. No Harley tracks had been found on any of them. Brad Yeager returned to report that Bam Stegner wasn't around. The bartender at Hogs and Heifers claimed his boss was in Santa Fe on business.

"I acted as if my questions had to do with the Morrell case," Yeager told them. They were all gathered in Zach's living room where a map had been taped to the bronze owl. "I don't want Stegner to think we're after him . . . yet."

"I don't see what difference it makes," Claire said, her tone bitter, desperate. "Zach has been missing almost half a day. If he's still alive, how much longer can he hold out?"

"I say we get Stegner, take him on the reservation beyond anyone's jurisdiction and beat the crap out of him until he tells," Paul said.

"I'm going to pretend I didn't hear what you said," Brad told them. "If a felony is committed on the reservation, the FBI gets the case. That's me."

"Careful, Paul," warned Angela. "You could go to jail again."

Paul shrugged. "Zach helped me when I needed it. I can't turn my back on him."

Tohono held up his hand. "Violence only begets violence. Why speak of it? Agent Yeager tells us Bam Stegner is not around. We are wasting valuable time discussing violence."

"I don't believe the bartender. Bam's around somewhere." Frustrated, Claire jumped to her feet. Her knee hit the coffee table and the bronze lurched to one side before she could grab it. With a *thunk,* it landed on the floor. "Oh, my God, did I break it?"

Paul retrieved the bronze and pulled off the map. "The only weak spot is where the owl's feet curl around the branch. It's okay."

Claire sat down again, her hand on her throbbing knee. "I'd never forgive myself if I were the one to ruin the bronze Zach's father left him."

Angela and Paul exchanged an odd look. Tohono and Brad seemed perplexed as well. All of them were now looking at her strangely.

"Zach's father didn't sculpt the owl," Paul said. "Zach did; he has a dozen more out back in his studio. He's tremendously talented."

"Yes," Tohono agreed. "Even as a child, he would whittle kachinas out of cottonwood and paint them. Most were better than those done by his elders."

"This was his first bronze," Brad put in. "That's why he didn't sign it. He didn't think it was his best work, but it was his favorite because it was his first."

"Zach," she said, the word barely audible.

Zach an artist? An exceptionally talented artist. This contradicted everything she'd thought about him. He seemed rough, ruthless, hardly the sort of man to observe every minute detail of a rare owl, then painstakingly reproduce the creature. The piece must have taken months of study and many more months to execute.

It would take an extremely high level of sensitivity and patience. Words she did not associate with Zach. Wait, Claire mentally stopped herself. Was she being like her father, stubbornly clinging to her personal version of reality?

Sensitive. Gentle. Tender.

Words *she* did not link with the name Zach Coulter. Because she had preconceived ideas about the man. She looked around her, silently observing his friends. All of them knew he was a gifted sculptor, yet she did not. Worse, she hadn't even suspected he was an artist.

And she'd never even considered that he might have been the man in The Hideaway. Sensitive. Caring. Those were the impressions she'd been left with after that night. But those impressions hadn't fit the image she'd had of Zach, an image she'd stubbornly harbored all this time.

It reminded her of the years she'd spent believing her mother's affair with Jake Coulter had been nothing but a short fling. If she'd listened to her heart, it would have told her how loyal and loving her mother had been. For her to have broken her wedding vows, Jake Coulter must have been the love of her life.

"Claire?" Angela gently touched her arm. "Tohono was

telling us that the Mounted Patrol will have to quit soon. It's getting dark. The trackers won't be able to see either."

Before she could respond, the telephone rang. The call was for Brad Yeager. He listened, nodding, then hung up.

"I put out a Comfax when I went into town," he told them.

Earlier the special agent had told them about the Law Enforcement Comfax linked to the FBI computers in their regional offices. Bulletins were downloaded three times a day. Law enforcement incidents, even minor ones, throughout the state were recorded, then transmitted to local authorities. That way other agencies like the highway patrol and sheriffs in different counties would be aware of problems.

"A motorcycle gang was stopped for speeding and noise violations near the Arizona border. The Highway Patrol didn't have enough to hold them, but the officer did ascertain that the group had spent the night here. He checked IDs. Stegner wasn't with them . . . neither was Zach."

"Stegner just used those men to corner Zach." Paul's voice was bitter. "Then they hightailed it out of town."

"Bam has Zach around here somewhere," Claire added. "Where?"

"Let's be logical and methodical," Brad said. "Get the Mounted Patrol off their horses and into cars. Have them go door to door in the less-populated area outside of town. Someone must have seen something."

Tohono stood. "I will have the Tribal Police check with those who do not live at the pueblo. Many live on the reservation in hogans far from each other where their sheep have room to graze."

"We'll check around town, asking at cafes and bars," Angela said.

Claire was so heartsick, she could hardly speak. They were just grasping at straws in the wind. The more time

passed, the less likely they were to find Zach alive. Bam
Stegner had been committing crimes for so long, and getting away with it, he wasn't likely to be caught easily.

"Claire," Yeager said. "I want you to stay here. I'll have
people phone in their information. You write down where
everyone has been. That way we won't miss anything, or
check the same area twice."

"I'll take care of it," Claire agreed, anxious to have
something useful to do. She stopped the agent before he
walked out the door. "I understand Zach was responsible
for getting Vanessa Trent to confess."

"Yes, he exceeded his authority to do it, but his bluff
worked." The agent's voice was full of admiration.

"He saved me," she said, her voice low and charged
with emotion. "I could have been convicted on circumstantial evidence, but he gave me an alibi. That's what this
is all about, you know. Stegner had no idea who stole his
bear until Zach admitted he had been at The Hideaway
on the night of the murder."

The agent studied her a moment, then asked, "You really care about Zach, don't you?"

Even though Brad Yeager was little more than a stranger,
she had no trouble admitting, "I love Zach. If anything
happens to him, it'll be my fault. I should have warned
him."

"He knows you love him," Brad assured her. "That'll
give him courage."

She watched the agent walk away, heartsick because
Zach did *not* know how much she loved him. For all he
knew, he had no friends. No one to care.

But people were concerned about him, she thought, encouraged by the number of people who had come out to
his home, offering help. If only Zach knew, she thought,
but he probably thought no one had even missed him yet.

We're here. Don't give up hope, darling.

In a matter of minutes, Claire was left alone with Lucy.

The dog gazed at her mournfully, and Claire remembered Lobo. She quickly called the vet to see how the dog was doing. She spoke with the doctor, then sat on the floor beside Lucy.

"Good news, sweetie." She stroked Lucy's golden fur. "Lobo is going to make it. He's one tough dog." Lucy licked her cheek as if she understood. "He won't be the handsome devil he once was because they had to sew his ear on, but at least he's alive."

At least he's alive. The thought echoed in her brain as she clutched the portable telephone and wandered out to the wooden shed. She had thought it was a storeroom, but Paul had called it Zach's studio. With Lucy at her side, Claire uncovered a number of bronze statues, each more beautiful than the next.

"Here's the artist I've been looking for," she told her dog. "Incredibly talented. But why didn't he ever mention his interest in art?"

She found another piece sitting on a shelf covered with a towel. A bust of a woman, she decided, seeing the back of the head with long, wavy hair. The work was so fine, so lovingly done that each strand of hair was visible, which was unusual in a bronze. She turned it and found herself nose to nose with her mother.

Claire took a quick step back, bumping into Lucy. She put her hand down to pet the retriever. "It's not mother. It's me."

She inspected the bronze closely and found it was an astonishing likeness. He'd even caught the way her nose canted to one side—just slightly. And her lips were a bit fuller than she liked them. But it was the expression he'd used, that truly captivated her. She looked happy, yet alluring in a provocatively sexy way.

"Is that how Zach sees me?" she asked Lucy.

He'd signed this piece she noticed, checking the base. She took a second look at the date. Why, he'd done this bronze while he'd been living in San Francisco. He hadn't forgotten about her, the way she had assumed, then become interested again when he'd returned home.

I've always been crazy about you.

How could she have misjudged him so badly? All right, he should have told her about the night in The Hideaway . . . at some point. When? When had she given him reason to trust her enough to confide in her?

He might have told her had she explained that she'd gone to her father. But she hadn't wanted to put any pressure on him. Later, when she was in jail, she didn't tell Zach that her father had again refused to help her because she was seeing him.

She had attempted to close the bridge between them by telling her father, but Zach never knew it. Now, she wondered if he ever would.

"Hello! Hello!" called someone.

Claire dashed out of the studio, Lucy at her heels. Maude Pfister was standing in Zach's yard.

"I came to see if you needed help," the older woman said.

"Where's my father?"

Maude shrugged, her expression solemn. "I heard what you told him. I thought about it all day. I, for one, am taking your advice. I'm getting a life. I've been your father's nurse for almost ten years. In truth, our relationship went way beyond that. But does he want to marry me? No. I gave notice after you left. The agency has sent a new nurse."

"Where are you going?"

Maude's forced smile brought a rush of affection to Claire. Maude was a wonderful person. She was truly going to miss her, but she deserved a better life than loving a man who was obsessed by a dead woman who had never loved him.

"I want to help you find Zach. Then I'm going to cruise

the Greek Isles and maybe travel to China. Afterward, I've saved enough money to retire in Florida. I just may take up golf."

Claire held out her arms, and Maude willingly came into them. They hugged each other, saddened by what might have been.

"Be happy, Maude. You deserve it. And keep in touch. Promise?"

Maude swiped at her eyes with the back of her cuff. "Promise. Now what can I do?"

Claire explained the arrangements, then said, "I can't just wait here. I'm going crazy. I have to try to find Zach. Please take over the information center."

Thirty-four

"Running Water Draw must be where Bam took Zach," Claire told Lucy as they drove into the countryside.

The dry riverbed on the outskirts of town had a lean-to shack on the south facing bank. Teenagers often came to the isolated area to drink. Heaven only knew what else went on at such a lonely spot. The gathering dusk cast deep purple shadows over the stone-lined creek and the dilapidated shack, but no one was in sight.

She hopped out of the car, and Lucy followed her. As they walked closer to the bungalow, Claire saw no one was inside. The whole gulch was deserted and silent except the screech of a vulture overhead. Brushstroke clouds against the dusk sky warned her that night would soon fall.

Claire asked herself where Bam could have taken Zach as she climbed into the car again. A man bordering two hundred pounds. A motorcycle was a powerful machine but not capable of transporting an unwilling man terribly far. The bikers certainly wouldn't have spent much time on the highway where they would have been seen by passing motorists.

Zach was still in the area. She could feel it in her bones. But where was he? Think, she told herself, think. Bam Stegner is not a genius. You can outguess him.

Where was Zachary Coulter?

Hogs and Heifers, Bam's nightclub was too obvious. But

what about The Hideaway next door to the infamous club? Perfect, Claire decided as she put the car into gear. She backed up so fast that rooster tails of dust kicked outward from beneath the tires, clouding her rearview mirror.

By the time she'd reached the club, it was just dark, so there were few cars parked in the lot. There were no motorcycles in sight, not even Bam's crimson Harley with the spit-shined chrome. She hadn't expected to see any of the bikers. The highway patrol report was probably correct. The gang had left the area.

She turned off the engine and sat in the dark, inspecting The Hideaway. The only light was on in number five. She got out and hurried across the parking lot, Lucy following her.

She had to peer through a crack in the blackout drapes to see what was going on in number five. Two women were entwined on the bed, a whipcord thin man watching them, grinning.

"Disgusting!" she said under her breath.

The other deserted bungalows provided no more clues to Zach Coulter's whereabouts. She kneeled down to pet Lucy, thinking.

The last place you'd ever look.

Those were Zach's words when they'd discussed the placement of the laser printers used to duplicate original art in Duncan Morrell's scheme. The words echoed through Claire's brain like a mantra. *The last place you'd ever look. The last place you'd ever look. The last place you'd ever look.*

"The last place I would ever look is that horrible, rat-infested shed where Bam kept the bear," Claire whispered to Lucy. "Or Bam's own house."

She glanced toward the thicket of pine trees behind the club and could just barely make out the weathered gray shed with the sagging roof. She hurried to her car for the small flashlight she kept in the glove compartment. Then she veered into the dark shadows, stepping as carefully as possible to avoid broken bottles that had been tossed out the back door of the club.

The jukebox kicked on, blaring sound suddenly filling the warm night air. The noise startled her and she flinched, brushing against a jack pine. Lucy cowered beside her.

From what she could tell, no one had been down the weed-choked path to the shed lately. The only other time she'd been here was when she'd sneaked out to take pictures of the bear. This was probably a complete waste of valuable time, but next to Bam's house itself, the shed was the last place she'd expect to find Zach.

The club was only a mile or so down the road from the turn off for Zach's house. The bikers could have easily driven along the highway just this far, then veered off to leave Zach without being spotted.

"Phew! Do you smell that Lucy?"

The light breeze riffling the pines was blowing in their direction. She would never forget that smell. The poor bear had been chained in the small shed. No one ever bothered to change the straw or shovel out the poop. Even though the bear was gone, the smell remained. The roof had leaked and the summer showers had kept the straw and dung moist, intensifying the horrid smell.

Tires squealed and blaring headlights hit her. She dropped to all fours beside Lucy as a carload of noisy men drove into the parking lot. From the sound of the group, they were already half drunk. They climbed out of the car and stumbled into the club without looking in her direction.

Once they were inside the club, she ventured forward, Lucy at her heels. The shed door was held shut by a wood lever. She eased it back and pulled on the door. The rusted hinges creaked loudly enough to be heard over the chorus of crickets tuning up in the bushes. She looked over her shoulder to make certain no one had come out of the club.

Inching the door open, she peered into the dank darkness. Yuck! The smell was even worse inside the windowless shed. She clicked on the flashlight, and a faint glow barely illuminated her feet. Great! The battery was going fast.

She stepped inside and her shoe hit something squishy. "Watch out for bear poop, Lucy," she whispered.

The amber glow deepened the shadows in the small area that had once been divided into two rooms. All that remained was a half wall, which was off to one side, and a larger area where the bear had been chained. There was moldy straw and bear poop everywhere, but no sign of Zach.

The light went off, leaving her in foul-smelling darkness. Lucy whined and licked her hand. Claire shook the flashlight. It came on again, but wasn't much more than a warm glow like a single match.

She carefully stepped to one side to take a look at what was behind the low wall. A mountainous heap of straw and dung was piled up against the far wall. It was probably remnants of an attempt to clean the bear's pen.

"So much for my idea," she told Lucy. "I guess I'll have to check out Bam's place."

The dog wasn't paying attention to Claire, the retriever was looking at the straw pile, her tail wagging.

Claire tiptoed around bear dung toward the heap of straw, mindful of rats, Lucy lived to maraud through the fields striking terror into the hearts of rabbits and squirrels. There could easily be some field animal hiding in the heap, attracting Lucy's attention.

As they approached, Lucy wagged her tail furiously. Claire stopped beside the enormous heap of moldering straw and dung. She pulled back her skirt and prodded the mound with the toe of her shoe and detected something . . . solid. She reached one hand into the straw and felt— warmth.

"Zach? Is that you?"

Holding the flashlight between her teeth, she used both hands to pull away the clumps of straw. Lucy helped, digging into the heap with her front paws. At last they uncovered enough to see Zach curled into the fetal position, his wrists bound by a length of heavy chain that hung down to his knees.

"Damn Stegner! Damn him all the way to hell. It's a miracle Zach didn't suffocate."

She could just imagine how miserable Zach had been. He hated being tied up. And helpless.

His eyes were closed, and a huge purple bruise marred his cheek. Dried blood was caked on his upper lip just above the duct tape that would have kept him from speaking—had he been conscious. Miracle of miracles! He was still breathing.

Too clearly, she imagined his gut-wrenching pain as the bikers ganged up on him beating him mercilessly. Then she felt the hopelessness and frustration of being shackled with heavy chain and buried under a mountain of debris.

"Thank you, God, for keeping him alive."

Claire hooked the flashlight, now emitting wobbling light, in Lucy's collar. Then she clicked her fingers, giving the dog the command to sit so what light there was would shine on Zach.

She dropped to her knees beside him. "Darling, can you hear me?"

He groaned, slowly opening one bloodshot eye, then the other, but she could tell nothing he saw was in focus. She ripped off the duct tape and tossed it over her shoulder. Zach's head lolled to one side, and he spit into the straw. Out came a stream of saliva and blood. Then part of a tooth.

"Oh, my God. What have they done to you?"

He said something, but his words were so garbled by pain that they sounded like "tight wire." He must mean the chain binding his wrists, she thought. His hands were cinched together, palm to palm as if he were praying. Chain with links as thick as her thumb shackled his hands together, secured by a padlock. At least his legs were free, but one seemed to be bent at an odd angle as if it were broken.

Common sense said to get out of here and find help. There was a payphone at the back of the club near the rest room, she remembered.

Zach shoved at her with his hands, mumbling something that definitely sounded like "wire." His eyes had a glazed, frantic look and his chest was hunched forward as if it hurt to draw even the smallest amount of air into his lungs.

"Don't try to talk, darling. I'm going to get help."

Zach shook his head and heaved himself into a sitting position, his eyes narrowing with pain. "St-stegner . . . wire—"

She leaned over and gently kissed his cheek, taking great care not to hurt him anymore. "Hush, now. I love you. I'll get help."

"N-o-o-o . . ." he moaned. "Stegner. Stegner."

"He's trying to say I put a trip wire on the shed. So'z I'd know when you'd come, bitch!"

Claire froze, instantly recognizing the voice behind her as Bam Stegner's. The hard muzzle of a gun prodded the back of her head. Lucy growled low in her throat and reared up on her haunches. The flashlight dropped from her collar and rolled into the straw.

Zach stared past Claire for a second, then he moaned, doubling up and clutching his gut. He collapsed to one side, eyes closed, his face a mask of pain.

"Zach," she cried, reaching for him.

Stegner shoved the gun between her shoulder blades. "Touch him and you're dead."

She slowly turned her head and gazed up at Bam. His naked belly, peppered with coarse black hair, was close to her nose. As usual he was wearing a vest; this one was black suede studded with silver conchos. Like the barrel of the gun in his hand, the silver conchos gleamed even in the dim light.

"If I don't get Zach to a hospital, he's going to die."

The grin that spread across his thin lips to jowls like saddlebags would have made the devil proud. "That's the idea. Let the fucker die."

"I can get your bear back. I know where he is," she said, making it up as she went. "It's a fair trade. Zach for the bear."

"I don't give a shit about that bear. Smell this place. Look at all this crap" He kicked aside a lump of brown straw.

"I don't understand why—"

"The asshole sheriff beat the shit out of me and left me on the res for the injuns to haul into some half-assed clinic. Nobody does that to Bam Stegner and gets away with it. I knew Coulter had the hots for you. I tried to horn in on his action by offering to help when you were in jail. 'Course, you're a stuck-up bitch. It didn't work. So now I've got you both."

Claire told herself to remain calm. Panicking would get her nowhere. "You won't get away with this. Special Agent Yeager is smart as a whip. He'll—"

"Have to find a body. Make that two bodies." Bam chuckled, a sound straight from hell that jiggled his belly, sending it quivering across his skull and crossbones belt buckle. "Vanessa Trent has big tits, but no brain. She left clues all over the place. I got me a four-wheel drive. I'm takin' you so far back into Kit's land that no one will ever find your bodies."

Kit's land. Kit Carson the famous Indian fighter and scout had loved Taos, settling here and marrying a local woman. The dense national forest had been named for him, and many parts of it had never been completely mapped. Even if it had been, it was a protected area where few people went.

"You're sick," she said before she could stop herself.

Bam grinned as if he'd just received a supreme compliment. Then he grabbed a fistful of her hair and twisted her head around.

Lucy growled, baring her fangs, then snarling so viciously it was impossible for Claire to believe this was the same dog who could be cowed by a strutting tomcat. It must be the gun. The man who had abused Lucy had used a similar weapon. The dog associated handguns with the kind of pain that had left her with only three good legs.

Bam let go of Claire and cocked the gun. "Get that mutt away from me, or she's dead meat."

"Lucy, sit," she said, struggling not to sound as hysterical as she felt.

The dog sat, but her eyes never left Bam. He nudged Zach's head with the silver-capped tip of his boot. Zach didn't move; she wasn't positive he was still breathing. Bam swung back his leg, getting ready to kick him squarely in the liver.

Claire launched herself against Bam as his leg shot forward. She yelled, "Lu-cy! Help me!"

Bam lurched sideways, grabbing the air with one hand, attempting to aim his gun with the other. Lucy sprang, snarling like a pit bull, and Bam lunged sideways away from them. He tottered on one leg, then toppled into a heap of straw and bear dung with a meaty *blunk* like a fallen rhino.

Lucy pounced, sinking fangs into his arm as Claire grabbed for the gun. It had already been cocked, so it went off with an ear-splitting *boom*. Lucy yelped with fright and leaped aside. The gun flew into the air and landed out of reach, but closer to Bam than Claire.

On all fours, Bam scrambled after the weapon. Claire jumped on his back, thankful for his bare skin as she clawed him. She sank her teeth into the nape of his neck, kicking him with all her might while she dug in her nails. Lucy charged again, drawing blood this time.

"Motherfuckers!" Bam howled and rolled across the floor taking Claire with him. A second later, he had her facedown in the straw, his knee in her back. Lucy attacked, snarling and biting with unimaginable viciousness.

With a string of curses, Bam let go, kicking at Lucy. Claire vaulted to her feet and ran flat out for all she was worth toward the door. She heard him behind her, then his fists slammed into her back. He shoved her forward off her feet. Her hands hit the earthen floor first, next came her knees. The air whooshed from her lungs as she belly-flopped.

Stunned, she battled mind-numbing panic. What would happen to Zach if she didn't get help? She couldn't let him down. Not now. Not after all he'd done.

"Fuckin' dog!"

Her head cleared just enough to realize Bam was fighting off Lucy. Claire rolled over and sank her teeth into his bare belly with a death grip while she slammed her knee into his crotch.

"Ayiiih!" he screeched. Clutching himself, he scrambled sideways, mincing along like a fat crab.

Too late, Claire saw he'd found the gun. Breathing like an asmatic, he heaved himself across it. A tendril of fear formed in her chest unfurling upward, ending in a silent scream of desperation. Even if she could get out of here and find help, Zach would be dead by the time she returned.

Lucy trotted over to her just as Bam recovered from the blow to his crotch. He eased up to a sitting position, the gun in one hand, the other across his fly. He leveled it at her, taking aim . . . cocking . . . laughing.

Suddenly, the flashlight went out, leaving them in total darkness. Claire rolled to one side, taking Lucy with her, then quickly moved backward. If he fired the gun, they would not be where he'd last seen them. He shot and with the deadly bullet came a blinding flash of light. Claire surged to her feet and jumped the short wall dividing this smaller space from the main part of the shed.

Zing! Zing! Two more shots split the rank air. She was

on her tummy now, sliding through straw and dung, heading for the door. "I'm over here," she screamed, desperate to draw him away from Zach. It worked, Bam fired the gun, spraying the shed with bullets.

Click! Click! The heavenly sound of an empty bullet chamber. Unexpectedly, the flashlight came on. Claire jumped up, set to run for help. She saw Zach was standing, his hands raised high above his head, the heavy chain dangling.

Bam turned. "What the fu—"

Clink-clink! Whack! Whack! Zach whammed the chain into Bam's head once . . . twice. The force of the blows split Bam's skull, and blood spurted from the wound.

"A-a-a-h-h . . ." Bam keeled over, his eyeballs rolling backward, and slammed face first into bear dung.

Claire charged across the shed. "Zach, are you all right?"

"Remind me never to cross you." He managed a lopsided smile. "You fought like a hell cat. Both of you." He leaned down, his hands still bound together, and gave Lucy a pat.

Claire threw her arms around him. "I couldn't let him kill you. I love you with all my heart." She gently kissed his cheek, afraid she might hurt him. "It's a good thing you regained consciousness when you did. No telling what Bam might have done next."

The blue eyes she loved so much had a spark of amusement despite his obvious pain. "I wasn't unconscious. I was faking it. I didn't know what else to do. I was desperate. I hoped you'd distract him enough for me to use the chain. When he got the gun again, I turned off the flashlight. Then I just waited until he was out of bullets."

"You're clever, so clever. I thought you—"

The sounds of shouting and people running toward the shed distracted them. In seconds, the shed was filled with people drawn from the bar by the gunfire. Minutes later the wail of an ambulance could be heard as well as a siren.

Bam was still unconscious, but one of the men found the key to the lock on the chain in Bam's pocket and freed

Zach. Claire never let go of Zach. Even when they loaded him onto a gurney and carried him out to the ambulance, she went along, holding his hand.

At the hospital, she had to let him go for the doctor to examine him. She waited outside with Lucy, and was joined by Brad Yeager, then Paul and Angela. Tohono came in a few minutes later. They were all there when the doctor came out.

"The sheriff is one tough guy," said the doctor. "Broken ribs, deep tissue bruises seems to be the worst of it except for a ruptured spleen. We're going to have to operate immediately."

Claire barely heard the doctor explain the surgery wasn't serious and Zach could lead a normal life without his spleen. Why did he have to suffer even more? she wondered.

"He wants to see you," the doctor told her.

She found him in a room and he was already prepped for surgery.

"Have you seen Lobo?" he asked as she walked in.

"He's at the vet's recovering. He's one smart dog." She walked up to the bed and took Zach's hand, noticing the ugly red welts at his wrists where the chain had been as she told him about Lobo coming all the way into the gallery to get her. "That's how I knew to go for help. You have Lobo to thank."

"No, you took on Bam." Zach's voice was husky. "The minute he tied me up with that chain, I thought I was a dead man. You saved me."

"I didn't do anything special," Claire told him, fighting tears. "I love you. I want you to know that after the first night we made love, I told my father I was seeing you. I was never ashamed of you. I wanted to walk down the street with you at my side."

He tried to smile; obviously it hurt to move. "Really? Why didn't you tell me?"

"I didn't want to put pressure on you to make any kind

of commitment before you were ready. When I was in jail, I called my father for help. He said he would . . . if I never saw you again. I refused." She leaned over and kissed his forehead. "I'd rather rot in jail than give you up."

"Really? I'll be damned." He shook his head, then winced. "I love you. Don't you know that? I'm sorry I didn't tell you before. I should have."

"Let's put the past behind us," she said. "What counts is we love each other."

Two orderlies interrupted them to take Zach into surgery.

"I'll be right here when you come out," she told him.

"Aromatherapy," he said with a half-smile. "Try it while I'm under the knife. You're beginning to remind me of a bear."

She laughed at his joke, but she wasn't laughing when she walked into the rest room. Her hair looked as wild as a West Texas tumbleweed. Her cheek was smeared with dirt and blood.

She went home and quickly showered, shampooing her hair twice. She was waiting for Zach when they wheeled him in from the recovery room.

"I love you so," she told him even though he couldn't hear her. She sat in the chair beside him, holding his hand.

Slanting bars of sunlight through the shades woke her the following morning. Claire quickly sat up, looking around, disoriented for a moment. Zach was awake, his head propped up by two pillows, studying her.

"This is how I want to wake up every morning," he told her. "With you. Will you marry me?"

"Of course, do you even have to ask?"

"I love you," the both said, the words overlapping just slightly.

They shared a smile as sweet and tender as a kiss. At last they were together. This time—forever.

Epilogue

Claire stood near the entrance to The Rising Sun Gallery, pride and happiness making her smile as guests arrived to view her husband's work, The Zachary P. Coulter Collection. She didn't bother to check to see how many sold stickers had been placed on the pieces. She already knew Zach was one of the most talented artists in the country.

And he loved her.

She gazed across the gallery and caught his eye. Zach winked as he showed Tohono the new pieces he had made for this showing. The older man was carefully inspecting the bronze of Lobo guarding Lucy, who was nursing four young pups.

"Life imitates art," said Brad Yeager.

The agent had been standing nearby talking with the new chief of police when Claire had last seen him. He'd moved up beside her and had followed her gaze across the room. Claire smiled at Brad, happy that he hadn't returned to Washington after the Morrell case had been solved. Instead, he'd taken over the FBI field office in Santa Fe, and he spent many weekends with them.

"When am I going to be able to take home my puppy?" Brad asked.

"You're positive you want a part shepherd, part timber

wolf, part golden retriever—bundle of trouble?" she joked, saddened by the thought of giving up the puppies who had been born that spring.

"Sure," he said. "They're a bit funny looking, but smarter than hell. Without them, Bam Stegner wouldn't be in prison."

"True," she said, yet the thought of Bam and Vanessa behind bars did little to comfort her. Something seized up in her chest every time she thought of how close she'd come to having Zach die.

As if he telepathically picked up her distress, Zach looked at her. Are you okay? his eyes asked. She smiled to reassure him, but he quickly shouldered his way through the crowd and came up to her. He slid his arm around her shoulders as he greeted his friend.

"Something wrong?" he whispered when Brad walked over to the bar.

"No. Everything is just fine." She smiled up at the blue eyes she loved so much and wondered how she ever could have doubted that this was the only man for her.

"Then why are you standing by the door?"

"I'm waiting for a friend."

He cocked his head toward the corner where Paul and Angela were standing near a bronze of a bald eagle that already had a red sticker on it. They had fallen in love with the piece even before Zach had completed it. "The Winfreys are over there."

"I know," she said, still thrilled that Angela and Paul had married at Christmas and permanently settled in Taos. "I didn't mean them."

Zach pulled her closer and kissed her despite the crowd around them. She returned the kiss, still not quite able to adjust to Zach's affectionate side. He was never shy about letting her know how much he cared about her. She wouldn't have suspected he would be that type of man, but she loved it.

Zach's brows drew together. "Honey, you're not hoping your father will show, are you? I don't want you to be disappointed."

"I'm not upset," she responded with total honesty. Her father had chosen to ignore their marriage; he went about his business at the bank, acting as if they did not exist. She had learned to accept it. "I'm expecting a friend."

"Really? Why so mysterious?"

"I'm surprising a friend." She turned her head and saw the person she'd been waiting for. "Maude, I'm so glad you flew in."

"Sheriff, how are you?" Maude greeted Zach and smiled to Claire.

"We're fine," Zach replied. "Tell us how you've been. Postcards now and then aren't enough."

"I'm doing a little traveling, playing a little golf at my place in Florida. I'm very happy." Maude looked down and spotted Claire's surprise. "Oh, my! You're—you're going to have a baby!"

"Three months to go," Claire said. "The baby won't have a grandmother. We'd like it very much if you would do us the honor."

"Me?" Tears filled Maude's eyes. "I'd love it."

Suzi signaled to Claire, and she left Zach with Maude to see what the clerk needed. By the time she finished helping with the transaction, Zach had drifted across the gallery to talk to Brad, and Maude was standing with Paul and Angela. Claire glanced around the room, not surprised to find red dots on every piece.

Claire ambled into the back room, her hand on the small of her aching back. Having Zach's baby was going to be much more fun than being pregnant, she decided. Already she was waddling like a hippo in cowboy boots.

She dropped into the chair beside her desk. *Wild Horse* the bronze her mother had left her was on the desk. Since she began to represent Zach, she no longer had the bronze up front, but she kept it on her desk to remind herself of how much her mother had loved her.

She placed one hand on her mounded tummy and was rewarded with a hearty kick. Rising to her feet, the baby kicked again, harder this time. From inside the gallery came the deep, masculine sound of Zach's laugh.

"Your world will be filled with love and laughter," she whispered to her baby.

She opened the back door, feeling happiness welling up inside her the way it did so often these days. For the first time in years, the aching sense of loss wasn't her primary emotion. Her world was a happy place now, full of promise and discovery.

The cool breeze washed over her face, bringing with it the scent of chiles roasting in the plaza. High above stood the noble silhouette of Taos Mountain surrounded by stars like chips of diamonds. One star twinkled at her, and Claire smiled. When she'd been younger, she pretended winking stars were her mother, watching after her.

"I found him, Mama, just the way you did. The love of a lifetime."

Please turn the page for
an exciting sneak peek of
Meryl Sawyer's
newest contemporary romance,
Tempting Fate,
coming from Zebra Books in May 1998!

One

Kelly dropped her evening bag onto her desk, then rifled through her messages, thinking she should go home. But deeply ingrained habits were hard to break. For as long as she could remember, she had slept until almost noon, then worked all night.

Her usual schedule did not allow for time with Pop. And time had become all too precious.

"Go home now," she told herself. "Set your alarm for sunrise so you can have breakfast with Pop."

A sharp, insistent knock interrupted her thoughts, echoing through the deserted building. A warning bell sounded in the back of her brain. Who would come to the newspaper office at this hour? The second knock caused the skin on the back of her neck to tighten.

She walked out of her small office into the semi-dark day room where two reporters shared a desk near the receptionist's bay. Sedona was a safe town, a haven for artists and writers who believed the majestic red rock formations inspired them. Along with the artists came the wealthy, drawn, too, by the awesome landscape and the ambiance of the cultured community.

She paused, her hand on the doorknob. What was wrong with her? She wasn't the type who had premonitions. So why now?

"Sheesh! Your imagination is in overdrive," she whispered to herself.

The rustle of sound beyond the door unnerved her, and she hesitated a second before she turned the knob. In the shadowy darkness stood a tall, handsome man with dark hair.

"Matt," she cried, stunned. "What are you doing here?"

He pulled her into his arms and hugged her, a powerful squeeze that filled her with bittersweet sadness for the time when they'd been inseparable.

B.D., she thought. Before Daniel.

"Hey, Ace," Matthew Jensen said. "Why didn't you dress like this when we were working together?"

Kelly glanced down at the silk slip dress she'd chosen because the splashy violet print emphasized her blond hair and brought out the amber lights in her brown eyes. The dress nipped in at the waist, then draped softly over her hips and thighs. It had been perfect for the dance, dressy yet casual, but it looked ridiculously out of place in an office reeking of newsprint and ink.

"It's a long way from New York City to Arizona," she reminded him. "I just came from the Sedona Arts Center Ball. It's a must for anyone in business here."

She laughed and he chuckled along with her, his flint brown eyes reflecting the sense of humor Matt always used to his advantage. Still, it felt great to share a laugh. How long had it been since she'd genuinely laughed?

Since Daniel Taylor had died.

"Come in, Matt." She tugged on his arm and he walked into the semi-dark reception area. "What are you doing here?"

"I was in the neighborhood," he answered as they walked back to her office.

"Yeah, right," she said, puzzled about what could possibly have brought him out West. As certainly as her career had eclipsed, Matt's star had risen. He was now publisher of the New York based news magazine *Exposé*, a major achievement for a man not yet thirty-five.

"Actually, I came to see you, Kelly."

"Really?" She didn't venture a sideways glance at him. The last thing she wanted Matthew Jensen to see was her cubbyhole of an office. Her official title was editor-in-chief, but in reality she did whatever it took to get the bi-weekly on the stands from selling ad space to writing copy to billing. It was a long, long way from the city desk she'd once shared with Matt.

"Not only did I come all this way just to see you, I've been driving around until you showed up." Matt sank into the chair opposite her desk, sprawling in a loose-limbed way that was endearingly familiar. "You don't belong here. I want you back in New York working with me."

His words brought an ache of gratitude, and she managed to smile as she gazed into his dark eyes and saw he was serious. Of all the people to continue to have faith in her—despite her terrible mistake—it would be Matt.

"Thanks for your support," she said, justifiably proud of her calm tone. "My grandfather is very ill. I can't just walk out on him. Pop needs me to run the paper. Besides . . ." She let the word hang there. They both knew she'd disgraced herself; Matt might want her, but the owner of the magazine would be outraged.

"I have your ticket back to the show, Ace," he told her with a smile.

The show. New York. The big time. Last year she'd been there, poised at the pinnacle of success. An ace reporter. It had been a long, hard fall, a descent into oblivion.

"Remember the disappearance of the boy Senator Stanfield adopted?"

"Sure, it happened right here over twenty-five years ago, but parents still warn their children about it," she told him, wondering what this old news had to do with a break-

ing story. "Every May on the anniversary of Logan Stanfield's disappearance, the paper recaps the story."

"I'll bet that issue sells more papers than any other."

"It's one of the best sellers," she conceded. "People are
still fascinated. A little boy—just five—goes out for a pony
ride and falls into a ravine. His older brother and sister
go for help, but when they return, the child has vanished."

"I read the UPI clips on it. Senator Stanfield financed
quite a search. Bloodhounds, the Mounted Patrol, heli-
copters, an Indian shaman, then private investigators
scoured the country."

"I guess," she replied, even more confused about Matt's
interest in the case. "It happened a few years before my
parents were killed and I came here to live with my grandfather."

"Two weeks ago Logan Stanfield turned up."

"You must be kidding!" she cried. "How did they ID
him after all this time? Why doesn't anyone around here
know about it? The Stanfields' estate is just outside of town.
They're big news around here."

Matt leaned back in the chair and swung his legs up to
her desk, resting his Ferragamo loafers on the scarred
wood. "They IDed by matching the man's prints with the
missing person fingerprints of the boy."

"Back then, it was unusual to fingerprint a child. If he
hadn't been adopted, I doubt his prints would have been
on file."

"The FBI is using a sophisticated computer with digi-
tized fingerprint analysis, and they added a lot of old files
to the system. They were running a top-secret check for
the Secret Service when they discovered Logan is working
for the U.S. government in Argentina, using the name
Logan McCord."

She slid off the edge of the desk and paced across the
small office. "How did he get there? Where's he been?"

"That's the mysterious part, the interesting angle on the

story. It's why I need your skills as an investigative reporter. Logan McCord didn't officially exist until his eighteenth birthday when he walked into a Marine recruiting office in Northern California and enlisted. The records don't tell us anything about his life before then."

"Wait a minute! He had to produce a hospital birth certificate to enlist."

"Not if you were delivered by a midwife. Then all you need is a form signed by a registered midwife."

The quiver of excitement built in her chest, the way it always did when she was onto a great story. "He must have had a social security number. Parents have to—"

"What if your parents were hippie types who wandered from town to town and never bothered to pay taxes? Logan McCord filed for his own social security card when he was accepted into the Marine Corps."

"It still sounds fishy to me." She tucked a strand of hair behind one ear. "You know, my grandfather was right. He thought some weirdos had been at the *Yei-Yei* vortex, which was near where the boy disappeared. Someone discovered the child and took off with him."

"Two weeks ago Senator Stanfield was notified his son had been found. Logan McCord took a leave from his security position at the embassy and flew here. I wouldn't know a thing about this except a top secret source in the CIA tells me Logan McCords' security clearance is on hold until the legal questions about his name are resolved." Matt smiled, unable to conceal his own interest. "I'm wondering why the Stanfields have kept this so quiet."

Kelly dropped into her chair, the excitement she'd experienced just moments ago had evaporated. "It's not strange. They're a rich, powerful dynasty. Believe me, they are waiting to steal headlines nationwide. Senator Stanfield is retiring and his son, Tyler is going to run for the senate seat. This news will get media attention no other candidate can compete with."

"Maybe that's why they've kept quiet." Matt braced his elbows on the desk and studied her. For a moment it was like old times; they were sitting together, working on a story. "But what if I told you that Logan McCord doesn't want to be associated with the Stanfields?"

"I'd say he's smart," she replied before she could stop herself. "It's hard to believe, though, coming from a guy whose job it is to guard the embassy. The Stanfields are one of the richest families in this country. Their name alone opens doors that are forever closed to someone like him."

"Sorry if I gave you the impression the man was just a grunt stationed in front of the embassy with a rifle. He's part of the Cobra Force. They're responsible for anti-terrorist activities abroad." He rolled his eyes and smiled at her. "God-only-knows what else they do. Cobra Force activities are classified top-secret."

The beat of silence following the statement warned her that he was withholding information. "Okay, Matt. What aren't you telling me?"

"One of my sources gave me the CIA report on McCord. It's out in the car I rented. Why don't you read it?" He checked his watch. "I've got to get back to the airport. I have a jet standing by to fly me to Washington for a meeting."

"Save me some time. Tell me what the top secret report says."

He turned his head slightly and gave her the half-smile she remembered so well. She couldn't help wondering what would have happened between them if Daniel hadn't come into her life. Then died so tragically.

"Kelly, I suspect Logan is nothing more than a trained killer with a psychological disorder. I'm not going to be surprised if the Stanfields want to distance themselves from him. The senator may be retiring, but he's still on everyone's short list to run for president. With Tyler Stanfield running for his father's seat, I don't think they want anyone looking into Logan's work with the Cobra Force."

"You're saying he was involved in one of those controversial government projects or something?"

"Absolutely." Without warning his hand closed over her right shoulder. "The military always breeds certain men—like Logan McCord—who are nothing more than trained killers."